For: Tay

HAPPY READING!

STRANGE
EDEN

For: Taylor ♥ 2023

HAPPY READING!

GINA GIORDANO

STRANGE EDEN

A NOVEL

ISBN Paperback: 979-8-9869834-0-0
ISBN Ebook 979-8-9869834-1-7

Design and publishing assistance by The Happy Self-Publisher
Cover design by Coverkitchen Pte. Ltd.
Author headshot by William Thomas

KÄFERHAUS
PRESS

Für meine Oma.

In Loving Memory…

"Ich bin bei dir, du seist auch noch so ferne, Du bist mir nah! Die Sonne sinkt, bald leuchten mir die Sterne. O wärst du da!"

"I am with you, however far away you may be, you are next to me! The sun is setting, soon the stars will shine upon me. If only you were here!"

- Goethe

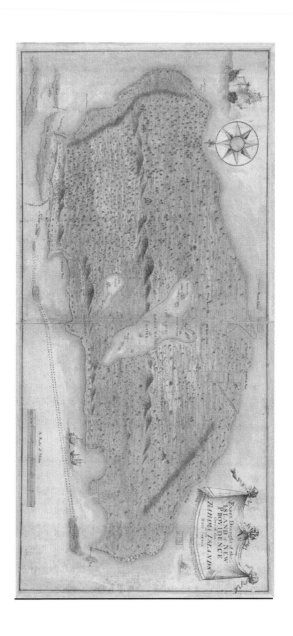

Exact Draught of the
ISLAND of NEW
PROVIDENCE
one of the
BAHAMA ISLANDS

CHAPTER I.

- Somerset, England, 1791 -

E liza Hastings was almost oblivious to the burgeoning crowd of suitors gathered for her hand that warm afternoon. Their dusty wigs and ivory satin waistcoats intermingled with one another on the great expanse of lawn over drinks and aristocratic conversations about roebuck hunting and the lucrative profits of Cornish ore. She had no care for such discussions, and she blithely ran through them.

Most of the gentlemen did not even appear to notice her presence or realize that she was their intended prize. Her mother had instructed her to make a grand entrance at exactly half past seven and to alight the steps so the guests could see her. Eliza should have been in her dressing room, allowing Beth to complete her hairstyle. But something startlingly different, first observed through the wavy glass window from the third floor where she had impatiently failed to sit still, had arrested her interest. A large dark form, its coloring like a biscuit with stripes, had nestled against a southerly wall interspersed with clumps of ivy across the way. Towards its bottom, two dark spheres that contained circles of white and yellow stared at her like a pair of peculiar eyes. It had seemed big enough to be a bird, yet the flatness of the creature suggested otherwise.

Eliza could only conclude that it had to be some sort of moth, but she had never seen such a strange and massive creature like it before.

She crunched across the lawn in her flat, grass-stained shoes, keeping her face down lest someone should recognize her. Her raspberry-colored silk dress was laced tightly closed, but the rest of her appearance was highly improper. Her dark curls were not arranged gracefully around her face, and her skin was bare of fine jewelry. Beth's shrill voice had tried to stop her when she slipped away from her pudgy hands and the silver comb, but Eliza ignored her and continued running to the hall, down the servants' cramped staircase, through the kitchen, and out the door into the early summer sunlight. Eliza paused behind a large blooming rhododendron bush for a few moments until her surroundings grew quiet again. Her footsteps were far too quick for Beth's lumbering gait.

Then she saw the creature for the second time. The moth had stirred and moved closer to the ground. It was easily the most beautiful insect she had ever seen, and she was desperate to study it. Its brown fur-covered frame sat frozen on a large waxy leaf. Then it took pulsating flight and ascended once more.

Eliza pursued it, wanting to gaze at it longer. The moth flew near the line of trees at the forest's edge and vanished. She stayed in the area for a few moments, expecting to see it again. When it did not reappear, she begrudgingly retreated to the small iron bench towards the house with a sigh. It was situated around a large corner, with more rhododendron bushes crowding its rear, and offered some privacy from the gathering.

As she sat, she contemplated how her life could change that day. A husband. The thought seemed overwhelming to her. Her delay of marriage wasn't for want of looks. She knew very well that her abundant opinions and sharp tongue were detrimental to such a cause. Besides, she had never excelled in the art of housekeeping. She had shirked her feminine duties in favor of more time in the library. While her sisters, Grace and Laura, had fawned over dresses and fabrics in their youth, she had savored reading books alongside her father and debating philosophy and politics. She could more easily discuss the founding of the Roman Empire than determine which shade of blue was most appropriate for a London ball.

Eliza was the eldest daughter of the family, but she now found herself the last Hasting girl to find a husband, and she had proudly accomplished this feat by no easy means. Her lack of a spouse resulted from years of finely crafted obstinacy and downright refusal. Echoes of her mother's grave and continual disappointment lingered in her mind. But it had never stopped Eliza. It was a small price to pay for an even greater reward: her freedom.

Her very life could dramatically alter in a matter of a few hours. The more she pondered the idea of marriage, the more anxious she felt. All she knew and felt familiar with could be violently uprooted for a life with a stranger in an oversized house riddled with the coldness of marble and the echoes of unfamiliar servants. Instead of answering to a loving and doting father, the one person who seemed to entirely understand her complexities, she would have to follow the guidance of someone unknown and foreign. She would need to share her life and her bed with this person, and she would be expected to give him children. The thought of childbearing seemed particularly offensive, and she shuddered at its implications. The entire idea seemed a conclusive and sullen chapter marking the rest of her life—one that promised misery and unbearable restriction.

"*A most difficult child!*" her mother's scolding voice sounded in her mind.

Eliza had never quite attained the ability to rein in her thoughts. She could recall many a dinner party stifled by awkward interruptions because she had voiced a curious question or an untimely observation. Society expected a delicate balance concerning the statements a woman could make: she should possess a limited amount of knowledge without retaining too serious an understanding of any one subject. The briefest intellect and the dullest wit appeared to be valued more highly than any woman in possession of both mind and appearance. From her observations, such an arrangement nearly always worked to the benefit of the gentleman in question, and because of this realization, it was an unspoken rule she frequently ignored.

Eliza studied her hands and the hem of the silk dress she had soiled from trampling through the yard. She yearned to be treated as someone other than a troublesome girl. Moreover, she knew she was no longer a girl but a young woman. But if being considered a child afforded her an inch more independence, the prospering woman inside her would have to wait. She already refused to conform to wearing tighter stays. She shunned rouge and perfume like a pestilence. But there were some feminine matters she could not avoid.

Beth had commented on her growing figure in the past months, and Eliza took every precaution to hide her silhouette. She sighed again, easing herself into the cold iron back of the bench, and closed her eyes in the sun. The warmth on her face was soothing, and the birdsong beckoned her into a temporary state of peacefulness. She began to envision herself in a faraway place—a place without a name, a place that was most decidedly not there.

"*Antheraea polyphemus*, I do believe. Curious to see that creature on this side of the Atlantic," a smooth and distinct voice said.

Eliza looked up, startled by the intrusion. A tall man wearing a khaki frock with a dark-green waistcoat stood before her. He possessed an athletic frame that seemed to amplify the somber color he wore, and on the whole, the display presented quite a commanding effect. But his choice of outfit seemed incompatible with the social event that day. He appeared to have come from a hunting party. He was much younger than most guests there but still several years older than her. Perhaps he had attended the wrong gathering.

She inwardly cursed at her foolishness at having thought her evasion of all the guests to be successful. Moreover, she was not dressed properly. Most scandalous of all these troubling thoughts was the fact they were entirely alone. She had never spoken to a man without the watchful eye of a chaperone. But then her thoughts turned to the advantages of her unfinished appearance. He most likely had no inkling of who she really was.

"May I?" he asked, motioning towards the bench.

She acquiesced and shifted to the side.

His light-brown hair was pulled back from his face with a black ribbon, and his wary green eyes focused on the estate lands before them.

"I did not think moths of that size were found here," she said, her voice timid.

She was amused at her predicament as if it was a game. Despite this, she still felt her nerves making her voice quieter than she intended.

"No, most certainly not. But we are close to the coast here. It may have traveled."

Eliza was used to having gentlemen presented to her. Courtship was generally an obnoxious spectacle of undignified staring, only made virtuous by requesting permission to be formally introduced. And by that point, she had judged the potential suitor before he made his eventual way to her, escorted by a third person for decency's sake. She had been afforded no fortuitous opportunity in this stranger's case.

"How do you know about insects?" she asked, looking at him.

His eyes were a pretty shade of green, much like the leaves dappled with sunlight around them. She wondered if he realized how distracting his gaze was. At a second glance, his eyes seemed intelligent but guarded. And there was an intensity present within them that she could not quite place. Eliza decided to look away.

"From my travels, I suppose. And my inquisitive nature. It would appear you have one as well."

"My nature? Yes, my temperament is not what my family would take pride in. They would like me to be more like my sisters. But that is not who I am."

"Is one of your sisters making her debut today? There seems to be great excitement over there," he remarked with a flat tone.

Eliza hesitated to answer. Her heart began to sink as she was reminded of her bleak situation. She looked to where the noise of chattering and clinking glasses emanated from.

"No, I am afraid it is mine. Although it is not a true debut."

"I did not see you amongst the London society last winter, although I recall seeing your sisters," he said stiffly.

"Yes, I was…ill in January," she replied, annoyed that she had to reveal herself.

It bored her terribly to tell an old lie again. She had bungled a proposal so miserably that her mother had felt it best for her to remain home. She did not regret her past conduct. The suitor in question had been older than her father.

The strange man seemed to detect an edge to her voice.

"I apologize, but this sort of thing is not very enjoyable for me. I confess I am not fond of socializing. A business partner of mine invited me to join him today. But I must say, it is peculiar to find you here, away from the others as well."

He was gazing down at the grass, then looked up abruptly at her.

"I do not care for such things. I find it absolutely intolerable. I am in no hurry to find a husband. There are other things I'd rather pursue first," she said.

"I, myself, have no inclination to marry. But it begs curiosity…What would a lady like yourself have a mind to pursue?"

She blushed, confused by his sudden interest in her. Perhaps he found her lack of ostentation amusing.

"I'd like to study more. And read. As well as travel."

"To the Continent?"

"The world."

"If you are being presented tonight, surely you must have completed your education."

"It is my belief that one is never truly complete with their education."

He scoffed. "If it is your intention to never find a suitor, you would be well equipped in that endeavor."

Eliza remained silent for a while. She couldn't decide if she should pretend to be offended or allow herself to be flattered.

"Perhaps that is the basis of my stratagem," she said pertly.

He smiled. "You have a quick wit about you."

Beth's piercing voice suddenly rose above the crowd. Eliza would have to head in another direction to sneak back to her room.

"I must go. I wish you a pleasant afternoon." She stood up and curtsied, hurrying back down the lawn to the safety of the rhododendron bushes.

Later that evening, she joined her mother as they retired for the night. It had been a dreadfully long and horrible event. She descended the sandstone steps leading to the great lawn at precisely half past seven, as instructed, flanked by wavering glass lanterns, with a string quartet awaiting her at the bottom. She abhorred making such a scene, but she followed her mother's wishes.

It had been a torturous opening, but then the real misery had begun as the introductions started. Eliza had succeeded in ostracizing every suitor equipped with impeccable and well-mannered conversations. A certain gentleman from Sussex had come dangerously close to enjoying her rude remarks until she artfully spilled her wine on his shoe. Overall, she felt content with her performance today. It had required every measure of self-resolve to not retreat inside the house with another imagined illness.

Mother and daughter climbed the carpeted stairs arm in arm.

"I regret that no suitors approached father for my hand this evening. Perhaps next season we will be more fortunate," Eliza said with feigned disappointment.

This had no immediate effect on her mother. Eliza clasped her hand.

"Good evening, dearest Mother," she said as she turned to make her way toward her wing of the house.

"Perhaps the evening shall not end as early as you desire, dear child," her mother said.

Eliza paused expectantly.

"Are there other festivities planned? Surely not. I saw the quartet leaving earlier. Besides, I am feeling a bit weary," she replied. "I'd like to retire to my room."

She turned and began to step away. Her mother suppressed a giggle with a gloved hand.

"So...you do not wish to see your suitor?"

Eliza stopped in her tracks.

"Suitor? Of whom do you speak, Mother?"

"I always knew this day would come. I did worry for quite some time as you seemed more taken with books than gentlemen, but it now appears that our lucky day has arrived!" her mother said, beaming with joy.

"Mother, surely there is some mistake. I have spoken to no one at length. I would even go so far as to say I failed quite miserably in presenting myself to any possible suitor. Perhaps Grace can advise me on what I'm doing wrong."

"I know that is how you would wish the course of events to have run, but fortunately, one suitor was quite taken with you. He is in the study with your father this very moment, arranging your marriage."

Eliza felt her face pale.

"He is a dragoon in His Majesty's Army. And he is a planter with property in the West Indies," her mother continued, her eyes huge. "A sugar fortune, to be sure. With a newly inherited title! I could never dream of such a match for you, dear Eliza!"

Eliza released an agitated sigh.

"I spoke to no officer tonight, Mother. I can assure you that. Indeed, I was not even introduced to any military men. I am not like my sisters; I do not chase after uniforms. Regimentals do not make my heart quiver."

"He said you were introduced by way of a certain…Mr. Antheria, I do believe. That is what he told us. Eliza, the man will not cease singing your praises! I cannot fathom what you spoke about, but he seems enraptured with you."

Eliza started to rush towards the opposite side of the hall. Her mother chased after her like a clucking hen.

"What on earth do you mean to do? Eliza!"

"I am going to put a stop to this. What utter nonsense. How can I marry someone I did not speak to or see?"

Her mother caught up with her and blocked the door to the study. Muffled, deep voices issued through the crack in the door.

"Eliza, you will do no such thing. This is your duty!" she said sternly.

Eliza felt decidedly lightheaded, even though she had barely touched the wine tonight.

"This is some device to punish me. I didn't behave as I should have tonight. Surely…" she said, laughing nervously, "Will you not even afford me the courtesy of meeting the man I am to be wed to?"

Her mother did not smile.

"Please…this must be artifice, Mother—"

"Have a look for yourself then. You ungrateful, foolish girl," she said, no longer amused. Her mother opened the door, folding her arms in indignation. "After all we have done for you, I can scarcely believe it!"

In the chair opposite her father sat the man Eliza had talked to on the bench, the very one she complained to regarding tonight's event and who had seemingly shared

11

her discontent. He looked up at Eliza with surprise at the interruption.

Eliza felt a sudden rush of heat to her head and the uncanny sensation of losing control over her body. She saw the gilded ceiling next, swallowed by patches of black, and then nothing at all.

She came to her senses with the sensation of two burning pokers in her sinuses, a terrible sting, and her pulse racing as she felt her eyes open wide. A faint waft of lemon oil pervaded her nose. Her mother, father, and Beth huddled around the chaise, watching her with suspended horror.

Eliza placed a hand on her forehead and groaned.

"You are cruel…" she said slowly.

"Come, come. You never listen! How many times have I told you to carry your own hartshorn? You never listen, child!" her mother retorted immediately.

"The remedy is worse than the fainting. I have *told* you…"

"Hush, your suitor is waiting patiently, Eliza. Come now, attend to your hair—it has all fallen out!" her mother said, digging her cold fingers into Eliza's scalp.

Eliza's dark eyes widened further.

"I am not marrying. I will not marry!" she said, raising her voice as she rushed to get off the chaise.

Despite her short stature, her mother posed a dominant force, and now she stood in her way.

"Quiet your tongue. The man is within earshot!" she whispered violently to her.

Eliza's father joined in, anxious to quell the looming argument.

"You are burdened with emotion, Eliza. You must balance yourself!" he said, the frame of his powdered wig trembling as he spoke.

"I will not marry. Send him away!" Eliza said defiantly.

Lord Hastings looked to his daughter and then nervously behind him. Lady Hastings narrowed her eyes with a temper that would frighten a rabid dog.

"He is a West Indian planter. Think of how you will live! You'll be decked in diamonds like a queen! You'll want for nothing, you fool!"

"No! You are insufferable, Mother!"

"I must say, Eliza, do be practical. This is a solid match if I've ever seen one," her father said in a low tone.

Her mother sighed and looked away with impatience.

"A match this beneficial would have really suited Laura's temperament so much better, but we are still grateful, are we not, George? We'll just have to accept the cards as they fall. The man is absolutely love-stricken with you, child!"

Only Eliza's stubbornness could equal her mother's temper.

"He will no longer be charmed after tonight," she retorted.

"Nonsense. Perhaps another sniff of hartshorn..."

"No! If you come towards me with that vile bottle, I will dash it to the ground. Where is he? I will tell him myself!" Eliza said, looking past them to the man pacing on the other side of the room.

He appeared to be doing his best to ignore the disarray on their side of the parlor, but from the tightness of his jaw she knew he was merely acting polite.

"You will have to stop this childish nonsense after tonight. It simply will not do. A woman your age should be more refined, Eliza!" her mother barked.

Eliza moved past her parents, and her proposed suitor looked completely startled to see her racing toward him. Beth grabbed hold of her arm. In one deft movement, Eliza shrugged her away.

"I will not marry him…I will not marry any man in all of England!" she said furiously as she brushed past the servant.

Within a few steps, she was face to face with him. Looking at the surprise in his eyes, she tried to rein in her fury, searching for the right words before speaking.

"If this is how she feels, then so be it. And be done with the matter! You know Dr. Engelson warned me about my heart. I do not need such controversy under my roof!" Lord Hastings erupted.

"George! You said you wouldn't do this! You agreed with me nigh on an hour ago!" her mother blathered.

Eliza turned, allured by her father's display of sympathy. She had known it all along. This was entirely her mother's doing. An unexpected grasp of her hand returned her attention to the man before her.

"Excuse my intrusion, Miss Hastings, but I do feel that I must clarify my situation in one regard. I have no home in England. I have been traveling wherever His

Majesty has seen fit to send me for the past fifteen years. However, I do intend to settle my roots now in my father's house on Providence Island," the man spoke, focusing solely on her.

"Confound it!" her father shouted.

"He wasn't supposed to mention that yet. He'll completely scare her off. She'll think him no better than a Hessian mercenary!" Lady Hastings cried.

"Hush now, Harriet. You do forget my cousin Francis and his service to the Crown. Hush, hush!" Lord Hastings muttered under his breath, his hand flying in the air with exasperation.

"Providence Island?" Eliza asked, stammering.

"Yes, yes. A small colony in the Bahamas."

"Across the Atlantic?"

The man nodded. Eliza slipped away from him and moved to a darkened window.

"I know you may find this displeasing, Miss Hastings. It is indeed a daunting proposition. You want for nothing here at Bleinhill Manor. I do understand the reluctance you have shown," he said, stepping behind her.

"Fools, fools! The both of them! I have never seen a match so poorly handled—" her mother hissed.

"Harriet! Silence!" Lord Hastings ordered.

Eliza and her would-be suitor ignored the hysterics of her family.

"And when would we leave?" she asked him.

Her mother's tirade continued. "I have been cursed with a harebrained daughter! She will live alone with a pile of moldy books, and by the grace of God, some benefactor will let her a room somewhere! Perhaps Grace's husband…he is a sympathetic man. He nursed that pigeon back to health once!"

Eliza wheeled around, glaring at her mother.

"Unfortunately, we will have to leave in haste. I am sorely needed to tend to the affairs of my family's estate, and some other urgent business in the colony."

"I asked when, my lord?" she repeated, trying her best to ignore the other side of the room. They could barely hear each other over the din.

"Three days' time," the man finally answered.

Eliza heard him say it, and she knew her answer. She felt it drop like a stone in her stomach. Despite her wild hesitations and feelings about marriage, she knew she had been turned. Her dreaded problem appeared to be the very solution to all of her concerns. The realization was startling.

"If you need time to reflect on your decision, I will grant it. You can tell me of your intentions by Tuesday," the man said as he turned towards the door.

He seemed anxious to leave the scene before her parents grew even louder.

"Yes," she said quietly.

His attention suddenly shifted back to her.

"Beg pardon?"

"Yes...I will marry you."

He looked as if he had seen a ghost and dropped to his knee, stooping to kiss her hand.

Eliza colored and looked away; she did not even know his name. This was entirely too much of a spectacle. The whole affair was embarrassing from start to finish. She heard the words she had shouted time immemorial, again and again, with every fiber of her headstrong will, now all reduced to ash by her capitulation.

The bickering between her parents lasted for half a second more until they realized what had occurred, and then her mother wailed like a banshee who had just won a windfall in a game of Pharaoh.

"I've done it! I can scarcely believe...By God, I have done it! George, break out the vintage from '35! We must toast. We must—not another word, George, lest she alters her decision. Come now! Let's celebrate!" Lady Hastings shrieked with glee.

Unsure of what to do next, Eliza curtsied and promptly left the room. This was all too much attention for her. She hoped her hurried footsteps would carry her away from any looming misgivings or regret. At any rate, it helped her leave the pandemonium of the room and her mother's incessant tongue.

CHAPTER II.

The clock struck half past three in the morning. Eliza sat in bed, holding the stiff sheet tightly against her body. The wedding had been a quick, rushed affair; it was a blur of smiling faces and hasty words in her mind. She had walked down the aisle to meet the stranger she was to be wed to. Lord Charles Sharpe.

The name was new and unfamiliar to her lips, much like the man who carried it. A baron and lieutenant colonel of the British Legion, she had been told he had recently served in the American War and, in more recent years, at posts in New Brunswick and Gibraltar. An arc of dusty light had filtered in from the church window behind him, lightening his pale-brown hair and making his hawkish green eyes appear to glow. He had barely looked at her during the ceremony, and she was grateful. His gaze focused instead on the altar in front of them. They both retained a serious disposition, and she was pleased to not have to feign a sense of happiness.

Her mother had been overjoyed. Lord Sharpe had shown up for the occasion in full military regalia, the sight of his tightly fitted scarlet coat only adding to Eliza's intimidation. Her sister Laura, however, seemed green with envy, despite her love match to a captain two years earlier. Grace, her other sister, remained tight-lipped since the announcement. Eliza had the discerning feeling that they were distractedly counting the profits of his purse. Everyone knew the planter class was rapidly becoming the *nouveau riche* of society. But this did not catch Eliza's fancy. Her mind was consumed with thoughts of her new home. The Bahama Islands.

When she had looked at him, standing so very tall in the pale church light, she mused that his proud bearing almost made him look like a statue. Indeed, it was easy for her to forget that he was a living, breathing man. Her mind was focused on adventure. She wondered what the island looked like. What the people looked like. What plants grew there. The reverend droned on the sanctity of matrimony, but her mind was consumed with thoughts of flora and fauna. She needed something to distract her from the less entertaining aspects of her future.

They had departed from town with haste, with two coaches carrying the new couple and their belongings to Portsmouth, where they would stay the night before boarding *The Albany* the following day. The innkeeper had prepared a small dinner for them in their room. It was a handsomely appointed chamber but a small space nonetheless. Charles had barely spoken in the coach. He retained his stony silence except for a small apology for any awkwardness on his end. She had brushed his comment aside, maintaining the perfect portrait of meekness and diplomacy that her mother had trained her to perform.

But her mind was burning with questions. She wanted to know who he was. It was incredibly complicated to pry this sort of information out of someone who was mostly silent. At some point halfway, her mind finally connected the dots concerning the mystery of Mr. Antheria. She recalled that he had described the moth as *Antheraea polyphemus*. It had been nothing but a play on Latin words, and her father had been none the wiser.

One side of her found this revelation disconcerting. Had this strange man before her no other viable connections to present that fateful night? Another part of her found the idea charming. It proved that the man had a droll side to him, although it was a dry sense of humor at best. Besides this small observation, she could barely detect any measure of levity. He seemed at all times to be serious and focused on something. His demeanor was nearly always one of brooding. It was as if the very workings of the world perturbed him. After dinner, he had excused himself to bade farewell to some companions. She had politely acquiesced, choosing to use her privacy to read a book. But that had been five hours ago, and he had not returned.

She heard shouting and a raucous chorus of drunken songs and wondered what he was doing. A part of her was desperately curious to see what happened this late in taverns, but she knew she was required to stay up there. Now, a series of booming footsteps sounded on the stairs, echoing from the wall behind the bed's headboard. So, she sat, covering herself with the sheet, half in dread and anticipation.

Her sisters had given her a brief description of marital duties, but she knew better than to trust them amidst their frenzy of giggling. They had not given her a complete education, and she knew they intended her to be completely shocked when the moment finally came. She had sense enough to know it occurred at night and in bed, so she readied herself as her current situation appeared to be an opportune environment.

Perhaps he would leave her alone because of the late hour. As with all activities of life, there were always rules of decency and decorum. Eliza was not sure if Charles had been the source of the footsteps by the stairs, but as they approached the door, and it flung open, she immediately regretted the revelation.

He was entirely drunk. His agile body bore the drink well, considering the late hour and the heavy amount he must have consumed. This idea she could only ascertain by considering the length of time that had passed since she had last seen him. The untidiness of his hair and the lack of sharpness in his eyes seemed to give away his insobriety. He looked briefly at her in the bed, mumbling something with surprise in his tone. When she did not answer, he spoke again.

"Oh, I suppose ladies do not keep late hours. My apologies for disturbing you," he said dryly.

His hands were clasped behind his back as he returned to a more formal stance.

"Good evening," she said, unsure what to say or do next. "I do read into the night sometimes."

Charles sat down on a wooden chair, the frame creaking as he shifted his weight. His eyes flicked up to her as he studied her momentarily.

Eliza had felt prepared for this moment the entire day, but his physical presence staring directly at her made her blush. She looked away and then hesitantly at the clock face.

Despite her nervousness, she could tell that something was not quite right. They seemed to share in a moment of reluctance, although the reason for any on his part was unclear. She began to worry if she was committing some error by remaining in bed.

"My father died," he said bluntly.

Once it was spoken, he sighed and readjusted himself in the chair.

The shock of what he had said silenced her for a moment, and she searched for the proper response.

"Oh, I am sorry to hear…When did you find out?" she said as she rose to a stand and approached him.

He looked alarmed as she timidly put a hand on his arm. She withdrew it and awkwardly stood next to him, only too aware of the sheerness of her shift.

"If you would like to speak about it, I am here. And if you perhaps need more time, if it is too delicate a matter, I understand. If we need to postpone our voyage, then it must be done. We must—"

"There is no need. I have known for about a month," he interrupted, his gaze steely. "He is with my brother now."

Confusion flooded her face as she tried to comprehend the stranger who faced her. Was he angry with her? Had she already committed an offense? Was this the reason for his stony silence and preferment of drink instead of her on their wedding night? She wracked her mind trying to remember if her mother had ever mentioned anything about this, if she had possibly been remiss in offering her condolences so late.

"I have only discussed this matter with you," he said. "Presently."

"And is this the reason for our trip? Will there be a funeral when we arrive?"

He scoffed at her question.

"No, he is long buried in the churchyard. The heat is a scourge there. Bodies rot at a much faster rate. There was no service."

"We can have one for him when we arrive if you wish. I am so terribly sorry. And your mother, will she be waiting for us?"

Charles rushed to a stand, pacing until he focused on the table laden with fruit and wine. He reached for the decanter.

"I am sure your father informed you. I am the master of Pleasant Hall now. I will be managing the daily affairs of the estate, as well as offering my services to the governor. I am to train the regiment stationed there. We will be starting our own family now."

He poured himself a drink. Eliza took his last sentence as a cue and climbed back inside the bed, her hands folded tightly against her chest. The room was not drafty, and the fire was more than comfortable. But she could not sit so exposed in front of a stranger.

"What book could have possibly kept you awake this long?" he mumbled as he struggled to remove his jacket.

She wondered if he aimed to distract her. Were her shaking nerves so clearly noticeable?

"I was reading Rousseau at first, and then I switched to *The Sylph* when it became too tedious," she said shyly.

"Ah, a venerable French thinker. What a constructive contribution to society. He can clearly point out all the ills of our current government but offers no effective remedies for the problems he outlines. France did not want him for a reason," Charles jeered as he planted himself in the armchair again.

"I am only in the middle of it, but he seems to offer a valid argument. If man is naturally and inherently good, why shouldn't we have a sort of social contract to help ensure that there is only good governance? To ensure full equality for all men? It seems intriguing at best—"

"My dear, anyone who spends their time reading his dross is a worthless fool," he snapped, seemingly unaware of the objectionable book lying near her leg.

Eliza took a deep breath, attempting to dodge his rude comment. But she was still intrigued by the conversation they had begun.

"Well, then educate me on your point."

"Where to begin? The man first naively states that mankind is naturally good—"

"If we were all saved by God's grace, are we not? We—"

"Which is incomprehensibly stupid. Man is not good. Man is weak. And as a consequence, he can be evil."

"I wouldn't go that far. I think—"

"Meet me on a battlefield and tell me if your innocent view falters."

There was an uncomfortable silence between them. She was not ready for the intensity of his comments. His pessimistic attitude only doubled with drink. Her expectations were quickly dwindling. At any rate, the moment her sisters had terrified her over seemed to dissipate. This much was plain to her. He could sense he had perhaps spoken too strongly, so he continued with a softer tone.

"You have not seen the world as I have, Eliza. These matters are unknown to you."

"But he speaks of the dangers of an authoritarian monarch and slavery. Surely these institutions are not healthy," she replied.

"He speaks of liberty whilst speaking of the need to be a collective. Tell me, where is the liberty in that?"

"But the social contract is there to ensure that there is liberty. In a social contract, all members would lose some rights and thus be made equal to each other. And then a preferred type of governance could be chosen by the people."

Charles laughed.

"Thank God this man only rules the quill and paper he writes with and not an actual society. Although I would beg to say that he doesn't even master that arena. His arguments are nonsensical and weak. The man is a lunatic. Hume understood this only too late."

"You haven't responded to my answer. And I do believe the man died quite a while ago."

"I speak of his words, Eliza. The danger lies in the words he recorded and the books still sold in shops. They have been and will be immortalized for as long as these texts are distributed, and people read them. The social contract, as glorified by Rousseau, is an abject failure. There cannot be true freedom if that freedom only exists on the whim of the mob. Governance by the '*general will*'...tyranny by the majority is still tyranny, make no mistake. It is playing with fire to assume that the job of any government is to improve the men who live under its domain."

The darkness outside the window was slowly giving way to light. Charles stood up and rushed to the bed, taking the book in his hands. She quickly grabbed it, making him pause.

"You should not read this," he said, annoyance rising.

"I think it is even more unwise to suggest certain books are not to be read," she countered.

"If the book only spews nonsense, it weakens your mind," he retorted.

"You are stronger in an argument if you know what your enemy believes."

She easily kept pace with every comment. Charles sighed and released his grip on the book.

"It is only a waste of time to debate someone with such a contradiction in their beliefs. I would not tolerate their company," he said.

"And you will be stronger still if you actually understand your enemy. You would have more success in pointing out the errors of their thinking. Then, surely, they have a better chance of agreeing with your point."

"Ah, so you seek conversion in disagreements. Not me. I do not suffer fools," he snapped.

"I did not intend to dismay you. It is our wedding night, after all," she said quietly, her eyes focused on the dwindling hours revealed by the clock.

"Yes, it is, isn't it?" He looked at the time. "We need to be on the dock in an hour. They intend to disembark sharply at six."

Her stomach dropped. They would not be getting any rest before their trip.

"I did not sleep at all."

She regretted her decision to stay awake.

"It is not necessary. There is time aplenty for that once on board," he said.

She didn't know what else to say or what to expect next. Thankfully she did not have to.

"I will go downstairs and request breakfast be served at once. Then you may have time to eat. I wish to stretch my legs on level ground once more before we go on the ship."

Eliza nodded, and he left the room once more.

She proceeded to tidy the bed and pack her books away. The food arrived momentarily, but Charles still did not return. When the time to leave almost approached, she began to dress but needed the servant to come and close her gown. She started to pace, wondering why Charles had not returned. Her stomach was queasy with excitement and anticipation. But the longer she was left in the empty room, the more she began to worry. Everything had been so perfectly arranged, yet she was no closer to understanding the man she was wed to. And now she would be leaving for a faraway island colony with only him to keep her company. She had lost track of time, gazing out the window, when he finally entered the room again.

"Are you ready? I will tell the boy downstairs to get your belongings. The rest is already being loaded onto the ship as we speak."

He checked the room, tossing some personal items into a leather case. Eliza's ears burned when she realized she still needed help dressing. He intended to leave now, and she could no longer wait for the forgetful girl.

"Come, let's go to the coach," he said, finally glancing at her.

"I asked the servant to return to the room to assist me, but it seems she's forgotten. I don't think she quite understood me. Could you...I need my dress..." she started to say. "It's a French style."

Charles stopped what he was doing and turned her so her back was facing him. She felt his rough grip fastening the tiny hooks shut and his breath on her neck.

"Another French inspiration that's completely lost all sense of utility. Tastes of fashion generally escape me, even more so when a woman can no longer dress herself."

"My mother had it made for me. She said it was quite the ton in court," she mumbled, feeling her cheeks flush.

"Yes, they certainly do not have their priorities in order, do they? It never ceases to amaze me that the world of style only seems to spin on the tastes of the French."

He turned her by the shoulder so he could observe his handiwork. She looked downwards at the wooden floorboards peeking from underneath the oriental rug. He was staring at her body, and she waited for some flattering comment to come from him.

"I suppose it accomplishes the task," he said.

Now she was thoroughly embarrassed. Part of her wanted to impress this man standing before her, but another wanted nothing to do with him. It seemed as if nothing she did could please him. She met his green eyes with a determined glare. She refused to let him see her vulnerability.

Eliza sighed as she tried to quell her impatience. It had not even been twenty-four hours since their wedding. She reminded herself that misunderstandings were to be expected between two unacquainted people. She swallowed her pride and left the room as he directed.

An hour later, they transferred the remainder of their belongings to the ship and waited for *The Albany* to sail.

"Something troubles you," he said, as he climbed the stairs to join her on the forecastle deck.

The ship was ablaze with activity as the sailors rushed to prepare for departure. Gulls wheeled and squawked around them, and the breeze from the sea was far too damp to be considered pleasant.

"At our first encounter, you said you had no inclination to marry. You can confirm my shock when I saw that it was you vying for my hand later that night."

"Yes, it is true that I had no inclination to marry, but I failed to mention that there was indeed a *necessity* to marry," he replied dryly, leaning against the railing as he looked out to the horizon.

Eliza bit her lip, surprised at the sudden onslaught of emotions rising within her.

"It is all so overwhelming. Forgive me. You must think me a child."

He turned and concentrated his gaze on her.

"I've always wanted this for as long as I can recall. I have always wanted to leave everything behind and embark on a new adventure, to abruptly change my daily life and travel into the unknown. Only now that it is finally in front of me, it is all so terribly daunting. Even the sea itself, it is so very wide," she said, her voice quiet.

He took her hand in his and pressed his lips to it.

"Be reassured, my dear. I am your protector in this world."

But something more pressing concerned her.

"I also fear that perhaps you have made a mistake."

"What is your meaning?"

"We only spoke on the bench that day. I feel so unsettled. What if I displease you in some way? We are but strangers. I worry that…"

He grinned. "That, in time, I may come to regret my decision?"

She nodded, her ears burning with embarrassment. She wanted to keep her emotions guarded in front of him, to preserve some part of her inner self away from his sharpened judgment. But she could not pretend that these fears did not exist.

"No, Eliza. We did not exchange many words. But I observed you the entire evening from the edge of the crowd. And I have seen women enough to know precisely what I do not want in a wife. Once I've made a decision, I find that I never waver in my choice."

"That is an admirable trait to be sure. And my age does not concern you?"

"Ah, I believe that is your doing, though, is it not? I have heard that you turned down many suitors. But you said yes to me. It is curious."

The pale hue of the morning made his eyes appear lighter. Whenever he smiled, faint lines appeared at the corner of his eyes, reminding her of their difference in age. He was thirty-five, nearly eleven years older than her. He had seen more of the world than she had. What had he already experienced in life? Could she ever catch up to him? His remarks suggested that perhaps her fears of his decision were only a reflection of the fact that she was still unsure of hers. It had been days since the wedding, and she was still yet to be reassured. The nagging persistence of her worries had yet to be quelled. She mused whether it was a natural feature of new marriages.

"It seemed a union of desires. I can finally please my parents. And they can finally stop presenting me to society," she replied.

"And your desires?"

She colored under his direct question.

"I can finally travel to unseen lands. To the places my fingers have only brushed across on my father's globe," she said, looking out across the water.

He laughed.

"With such idealism, I can only hope that you are not disappointed. Reality often has that effect."

Eliza said nothing, wondering if she should have answered differently.

"I read something once in a gentleman's magazine. I can't recall the verse exactly. But it spoke of women your age who waited to marry like you. The age of supreme loveliness," he said as he took a step behind her. "Beauty and elegance in full bloom."

She felt his lips press against the side of her neck. She stiffened up but inwardly felt a rush of heat that surprised her. Eliza turned, only to see he had already stridden off and was engaged in a conversation with another gentleman down the steps.

Eliza stared ahead at the tiny glass panes covering this level of the aft. During the day, it must have afforded the captain's cabin a luxurious amount of light. Now, at night, it only served to further disorient her. She saw the innumerable reflections of candle flames rocking and swaying against a deep blue wall of sea and sky.

The line of her drink tilted back and forth. The red wine threatened to escape the rim of the crystal glass with every large wave they crossed. She took another sip, not knowing where to look. She was not used to dining only with gentlemen present. There had always been another woman nearby, even if it was only a servant bringing hot plates of food. That role had been delegated to a boorish man who fulfilled the roles of valet, footman, and parlor maid in one person. She had caught Mr. Jones gawking at her on more than one occasion, and between the captain's fabricated interest in their new marriage and Charles' taciturn habits, she felt stifled beyond relief. Her voyage across the Atlantic was already altering her perspective on matters. It seemed as if most ships were not created with women in mind.

"So, tell me, Charles. Is Lord Dunmore the only man who can coax you onto a ship?" the captain asked with a chuckle.

This new line of conversation, which did not involve wind speeds, available fare, or business partners, caught her attention. She demurely smiled as she pretended to be more involved with their talk than she actually was.

"Indeed," Charles said. "Only a night of heavy drinking and debauchery could convince me to step foot on board. Meaning no insult to your captaincy, I assure you. I know you are a capable man on the sea, Captain Pascale. And nearly everything is more tolerable than the Bay of Biscay."

"Right you are about that," the captain rejoined with a laugh.

Eliza looked down at her plate and blushed. Insecurity began to flood her mind; he had not taken part in any debauchery with her. He surely could not have counted their debate on philosophy as any form of indulgence. Unless he had satisfied himself somewhere else that night with some other woman. She had naively believed him to be drinking downstairs the entire evening.

She looked at him again. He did not seem to be one of those kinds of men. He was entirely too serious and principled. It must have been a necessary bluff, convenient to the conversations of the other sex.

The rest of the discussion faded in her ears, and she idly stabbed a piece of fish, having decidedly lost her appetite. They had been at sea for over a month, and she still did not know the man to her left. Perhaps they needed privacy. There had to be somewhere they could discuss things alone, some secluded corner of this massive ship where they could finally talk as husband and wife. She downed her wine and motioned for her glass to be refilled. She would resolve this issue once and for all tonight.

Charles guided her down the hallway when they had finished, as the ship always seemed to be the most treacherous after the last meal of the day. The alcohol she consumed was most likely to blame for this, although Eliza did not know how to pass the time at night. She had trouble making structure of her days, and could only read books for so long. She liked the drowsy, heady feeling the wine gave her, which made falling asleep much easier. The drink, combined with the boat rocking, made her feel giddy, and it was a much more enjoyable sensation than feeling tense and bored. Whenever she walked too fast while the ship was moving, it gave her the impression of flying upward, and so she did this often, much to the chagrin of her new husband.

Now, she rushed headlong through the ship, grabbing purchase of anything she could reach to keep her balance. She found it amusing that he seemed distressed whenever she walked ahead. She could hear him click his tongue behind her.

The nights were long and silent. And her husband did not make matters any more diverting. She sighed as they stepped over a door frame and into their section of the ship.

"I do not wish to retire so early. Is there someplace we can talk awhile?"

"I do not think so. No," he said.

He kept his eyes on the sailors as they came and went about their business but hardly on her.

She stopped by a set of stairs, leaning on the railing. When moving about the cabin, the feeling of waves was an enduring impression, but whenever she stopped and stood motionless, the reality of how ceaseless the careening of the ship truly was made her lightheaded. It was not only a back-and-forth movement in a perpendicular sense, but when the waves were large, it seemed to carry her body upwards and downwards in dizzying circles as well, on an endless repetition that only seemed to slightly regulate when the sun returned. Or perhaps the blue sky and light of day helped her adjust her senses. She did enjoy her time above deck when the weather permitted. However, as was most often the case, she could not frequent that area nearly as much as she would have liked.

Disorientation was the standard. Below deck, the cramped quarters of the ship were dark and stuffy. The ceilings were low, and she frequently needed to bow her head to walk any distance. It was easy to injure oneself, and a step too quickly in the wrong direction, at the wrong angle, could result in a bruise or two. All this to deal with while feeling the very floor undulate beneath her feet made movement a challenge. It was something she had never experienced before.

With his domineering height, Charles did not appear to find the novelty of life on the ship as exhilarating or entertaining as she did. He barely had space to stand at his full stature unless he was at dinner or above deck. Now he appeared disturbed to pause on their walk.

"I wish to have a moment of privacy, Charles..." she said slowly.

She avidly watched for a reaction but was once again disappointed. His face was emotionless. She knew there was more to marriage, but what it entailed or how one went about it was still unknown to her. He had kissed her neck once, that first day on the forecastle. In the church, he had kissed her mouth, but it had been with closed lips. A chaste kiss by any moniker. He had not shown her affection in the inn the night before they boarded the ship, and then they had withdrawn to separate chambers once the voyage had begun. Charles had said it was best they each possessed ample room while living in such strained quarters, and he had made sure to place their valuable items in his cabin, where he alone could guard them.

The entire situation was foreign to her, and he had more knowledge in these matters than she, so Eliza did not question it. She appreciated having a little corner of the ship for her own use but found herself strolling about the open deck more often than not, much to the dismay of the sailors. She had her books for company, and she also had the sea during the day. Her world consisted of spars and bowsprits, of the pitching and rolling of the waves, but even in the excitement of a new day, her hours grew tedious. She observed the sailors and how they did their work. She admired how they tied knots so gracefully with such thick, heavy ropes and how the captain and his crew seemed to operate with their own language and set of unfamiliar rules. Of course, such an activity was impossible in the evenings, and she consequently found the nights long and dire.

"There is hardly any such place to be found on a ship, my dear," he replied, stepping back from her.

He wished a good evening to a passing officer and then directed her further down the hallway. They would part amicably without another word, and their routine would start again at dawn. They stood outside the door to her cabin within moments, the feeling of a full stomach and copious amounts of wine only adding to her increasing awareness that she had failed once again in her objective. The sheer idleness felt suffocating to her.

"Would you like me to read to you tonight? I can come to your cabin," Eliza suggested at the height of her desperation.

Charles looked long and hard at her and then sighed.

"I do not require that, my dear," he said, his voice low. "I thank you."

He took her hand and kissed it.

"I wish you a good evening."

Charles bowed and then walked further down to his cabin. She had yet to step foot in this seemingly forbidden room. Eliza intrinsically knew it most likely resembled hers, but the absence of his invitation made his small room seem overwhelmingly appealing to her. She closed herself inside her cabin, listening to the receding thump of his footsteps. Then, she opened her door and rushed back towards the other side of the ship.

The one thing she enjoyed about being at sea was how infinitely small the ocean made her feel. On land, everything seemed so tame, so utterly ordinary. There was a certain equilibrium on solid ground. Such a thing was not found at sea. There were up swings and down swings; the floor could rock left to right and right to left, and it did not always follow a precise pattern. On the ship, she felt like a leaf, bobbing and swaying to an unseen hand that propelled her and everyone on board forward. It was a constant rhythm, and the rhythm was always changing.

And there was the slightest feeling of danger, a perception that rushed through her nerves. There was no guarantee they would ever make landfall on the other side of the Atlantic, despite how diligently and hard the crew worked hour after hour. But yet, these men had done this before. Countless times. Some had even survived shipwrecks. And yet they had returned to life at sea. She felt like she could understand the attraction of their vocation. It was a grueling, merciless job, to be sure, but it also offered an experience unlike any other. It was an exploit and an adventure to them and a marvel and a wonder to her.

Eliza crossed back through the swinging hammocks. Confident that sailors kept late hours, she assumed that most would be empty. Towards the end of the row, she spotted one large man snoring alone, so she hurried past and into the officers' quarters. She did not know what she was looking for, but this seemed to be the point of acting spontaneously.

"May I help you, my lady?"

A commissioned officer startled her. He was young and wiry, his thin frame easily absorbing the shock of the waves. His white waistcoat retained a golden hue from the soft lighting. She stood in amazement that even after four weeks, there were still faces she did not recognize on the ship.

"I am Second Lieutenant Braddock. Forgive me. I did not mean to startle you."

Embarrassment flooded her face as she realized she did not know what she was doing. Or if she was even allowed here. He seemed to be checking the candles that illuminated the hallway.

"Have you traveled by ship before?"

"No, no, I have not. It is all very foreign to me," she said quietly.

"My day is almost done, but not before inspecting a few matters. Sentries must be at their posts. No tobacco between decks. No enclosed candles. Would you like me to guide you back to your cabin?"

"I, I…had trouble sleeping, and so I thought I could come and borrow a book from Captain Pascale," she stammered.

The young man smiled, looking down and then back at her.

"Perhaps some company would be more diverting than a story," he said slyly.

Eliza suspected his superiors would not be pleased with his newfound distraction, yet she did not excuse herself.

"I don't always read novels. I find real life more entertaining at times, don't you?" she replied, extending her hands against the narrow, white-paneled hallway.

"The captain is occupied, I believe. But I can escort you if you wish. I was just about to retire myself."

Despite the incessant rocking, he moved easily, stood back, and opened the door to the captain's quarters. She thanked him and entered the room. She would have preferred to be alone in the cabin, so she could have the liberty of examining the maps and books around the room unobserved. Now, she pretended to know which book she was looking for. The selection was shockingly drab and unintelligible. She could feel his eyes on her. She heard the officer step closer, disregarding the small space between them.

"You are traveling alone, miss…"

"Lady Sharpe. No, alongside my husband."

"Ah! I think I have seen him moving about the deck. Have you been married long, my lady?"

"For over a month, I believe," she replied, trying to keep her eyes on the leather spines of the books. Every tome concerned nautical science. She assumed the captain would have possessed some books on geography or history, but they did not appear to be stored in this section. She stood upright again and attempted to move to the other side of the cabin.

"Perhaps I can be of some assistance, Lady Sharpe. What precisely are you looking for?"

Eliza paused. She did not like the tone of his voice or the stance he held.

"I do have a small set of books in my cabin. Perhaps you'd like to take a look there—" he continued.

"Good evening, sir," she said abruptly as she headed towards the door.

Eliza ran to her room, stumbling with every swell of the sea until she was safely back in her cabin. She pressed her back against the wall, thrilled by the peril she had just narrowly avoided. Eliza ensured her door was thoroughly locked and then threw herself on her bed, laughing.

There was a primitive and unchecked force of energy surrounding a set of strangers confined to close quarters for an extended time. The ship seemed to operate in its own sphere, beckoning her to behave much differently than she would have otherwise. Besides alleviating monotony, she had gained some degree of satisfaction from her encounter. If she could not attract Charles' interest, then perhaps a stranger's interest would inspire his attention.

The guts of the ship creaked and groaned with a monstrous ferocity. The next evening had started and ended like every other, only the seas were too rough for Eliza to wander about. The wine had soothed her into sleep, but her slumber had proved restless before long. She started to have vivid hallucinations of the dark wooden walls moving and pressing forward as if they could touch her. Eliza would wake up in terror, only to feel alertness settle over her as she watched the walls return to the ordinary boundaries of her small space. Then, as she tried to force herself to sleep, she could not help but hear the creaking and groaning of the ship, as if it was not an inanimate object but a haunted one. The more she listened, the more she swore she could hear water filling the wooden beams around her and the harsh contours of a man's solitary breath near her ear.

Tonight, the boat tilted so slowly, in an endless back and forth sawing, that she feared it would tilt and fall in perpetuity. The constant unseen slow dripping of water that usually served as background noise, an afterthought, now seemed unbearably loud. Each drop, every noise, heightened her dread. The longer she lay awake, shifting from her back to her right side, the louder her thoughts rang in her mind.

In the senseless veil between dreams and sleep, Eliza felt an acute pang of guilt. She had not taken the time to choose one of life's singularly most important decisions. She had not properly attended to the matter of her marriage. Instead, she had rushed headlong, like a child, to sign up for a journey abroad. She had been reckless with her future. As she lay there, floating and rocking, a mere speck in a bottomless and vast sea, she did not see any surety that she could continue on such a path.

And now, whenever the ship reached the port, if the seas would spare *The Albany*, then and only then would she truly have to deal with the consequences of her rash decision. Only then would she see if Lord Sharpe was a wise choice and if he was indeed the right man. She realized a part of her did not want the ship to stop. Once it did lay berth, her actions would finally catch up with her. And there was no return, no sense of easement. From that moment, everything she knew would change, and she would be alone with a strange man to endure life's trials in a strange land.

Now a maddened banging sounded at her door, and she immediately let Charles inside at the revelation of his voice.

His eyes looked panicked, his white shirt damp. Her heart fluttered as she wondered if the moment that had eluded their marriage thus far was finally upon her.

"Whatever is the matter? Did something happen to your side of the ship?" she asked.

"The storm," he answered, his eyes huge.

As soon as he spoke, she knew disappointment was imminent. He was such a grave man. The only subjects that goaded him into conversation were politics or bleak, unavoidable topics.

"Yes, it sounds terrible, doesn't it? Those brave men on the top deck must be having a dreadful time."

She sighed and opened a chest, stacking a few books in piles on the bed.

"It could tear the ship in two," he said, watching her with confusion.

"This situation must be quite a common occurrence when crossing the Atlantic, though, surely?"

"What are you doing?"

"I realize I can't prevent the water from coming in, so I am moving my books to keep them dry. My garments can be stored elsewhere."

"Then your clothes will be ruined. Silk and satin cannot withstand salt water, I assure you."

"That is not my intention. I simply want to ensure that the books do not face damage."

Charles watched her place the newly organized books on the shelf above her bed.

"Eliza, can you swim?"

She looked up at him, pausing momentarily.

"No, I was never afforded the opportunity," she replied, her voice wistful.

"And yet, you are not troubled by the current state of affairs on this ship?" he asked, sounding perturbed.

"No, I daresay it hasn't crossed my mind."

"Then, you are fearless."

"Well, why should I—" she began to say.

A thunderous groan sounded throughout the hull. A rogue wave hammered into the port side, careening the boat at a sharp angle. They tumbled headlong to the floor, knocking the candle out with a sizzle. Despite her bravado, she let out a small scream from the surprise. Her hands struggled to find purchase as his hands clamped down on her arms. He was shaking.

"That is unfortunate!" she shouted above the melee.

He said nothing but muttered a prayer under his breath, repeating it endlessly. The total darkness and rocking of the ship were disorientating. Eliza worried about the other books in the chest. She found her way to the door and out the hall to find another light. She returned, slowly swaying with the boat, to find Charles pressed up against the wall of the cabin, looking forlornly at the ceiling.

"What is the protocol?" Eliza asked him as she replaced the candle.

"Beg pardon?"

"The protocol for disembarking if the ship…if, if the need arises?"

"If the need arises, then we are dead," he replied flatly.

"I hardly see the need for dramatics. Perhaps it would be best to make our way to the captain's quarters to hear what we should do. We are insensible remaining here."

More water began to seep into the cramped space. Charles' face paled as he watched her step through the creeping puddle. A foul odor was starting to take hold of the air as seawater flooded the bilge below them.

"How many articles are we allowed on our person when we board the cutter?" she asked, reconsidering which books she preferred.

"There is no use for a book out on the open seas in the height of a storm," he said, glaring at her.

"You fought in the American War…with the cavalry, I believe?"

When he nodded, she continued.

"No wonder it was not with His Majesty's Navy."

He failed to see the humor in her statement.

"No man is a match for the wrath of God."

Watching his vulnerability on full display was a peculiar sight. It nearly bordered on the side of comedy. She strained to keep her lips in a straight, humorless line.

"You believe the source of this maelstrom to be divine? Curious," she managed to say.

Eliza sat on the bed, lightly tapping the inch of water with her shoe. She sighed and pulled her feet up to lie down. They remained in silence as the ship tossed back and forth. Muted shouting could be heard from the crew around them.

"We might as well get some rest until we ride the storm out," she suggested.

He stood pressed against the wall as if steadying himself for an inevitable blow.

"You may join me in bed, husband," she said, unsure what to say. "You need not stand to attention all night."

His darkened eyes flicked over to her.

"You may rest. But I'm afraid this is no time for sleep. One must be ready at a moment's notice."

She sighed. It felt strange to lie on her back while he remained leaning against the side of her cabin. Then she thought of a new topic for conversation.

"I believe you are right. I should be prepared for action myself. Which book should I keep on my person if we must leave the ship? Plato? Or *Clarissa*? I wager Plato can be easily replaced with any merchant…"

His loud whispers of prayer drowned out her conversation, and despite the violent movements of the ship, she finally managed to drift off to sleep.

The next afternoon was fair, the ocean surprisingly smooth and calm.

A rush of sailors moved from one side of the ship to the other, and as she gingerly climbed up the wooden steps, she could feel the clamor above deck. Eliza had slept later than she usually did, but the evening had not afforded the opportunity to seek real rest. She fully expected to observe damage from the storm last night but could not spot a single part of the ship that appeared awry. The men had clearly been busy that morning.

Clutching a sketchbook and a stick of graphite, she began walking to her coveted spot when she saw the tall masts of a neighboring ship to her right. She stopped and leaned against the railing. It was a smaller ship—a schooner, to be exact. Only a handful of men stood topside. They moved at a slower pace than the ship she was on. In the schooner's wake, she could make out dark shapes in the trembling water trailing behind the boat. She stood transfixed until the wind shifted its course and a hideous odor, foul and putrid, came to her notice. At first, it resembled raw sewage, yet there was a metallic sharpness to the stench she had only ever encountered when passing a slaughterhouse. The smell was so strong it seemed to assault her nose, and before she could move to breathe, she felt herself gagging.

She heard leather boots march up behind her, and she felt a hand lightly press her arm. It was Second Lieutenant Braddock. He extended a white handkerchief; she took it immediately and covered her nose and mouth.

"Lieutenant Braddock, is there sickness aboard that ship?" she asked, watching the creeping boat.

Only five sailors appeared above deck, and they were not actively moving about the ship like the crew of *The Albany*. Instead, they languished in their exertions as if they could not summon the strength to move.

"That would be *The Charming Betty*, Lady Sharpe. We encounter her here and there. You are most observant. Disease is rampant aboard that ship."

She coughed, still struggling to quit the smell from her nose.

"Do they require assistance? Do they not have a surgeon on board?" she asked, watching the dark shapes in the water around the schooner.

Two creatures seemed to collide, and a series of sharp-angled fins and white water thrashed through the surface. Sharks were following the ship, and the more she looked around the boat, the more she could count.

"No, no, my lady. They are Guineamen. They need no assistance from us."

"Guineamen? I do not understand."

"Slavers. There are most likely four hundred slaves on there, I wager. If they've had a good haul this run," he said, leaning forward on the railing, taking a solid breath.

The smell did not seem to bother him at all. She assumed he had grown used to it on previous trips. She considered whether she was overreacting to the smell, so she loosened the handkerchief. A gust of wind hit them, bringing a fresh batch of the rancid odor, and she had to turn to breathe. It took her a moment to process what he had said. Then she scoffed.

"Four hundred? I see five men topside and what appears to be a rotten, foul, and abandoned ship, Lieutenant. I think you are mistaken. She's less than half the size of our ship."

Eliza felt very shrewd with her assessment.

"No, my lady. No mistaking a ship like her. They most likely started out with four hundred slaves when they left Africa. They would have lost a few dozen here and there, so the number may now be less. But they'll be satisfied if they reach port with more than three hundred. I've heard merchants say they lose the most right when they're leaving the coast. That's when they put up a fight. They prefer to cram them below deck right away—makes the business that much smoother."

He made a menacing laugh.

"But I do not see any slaves. Where can they possibly store them? Their hold is not very large."

"Oh, they've managed to figure that out, Lady Sharpe. You can fit an infinitesimal number of bodies in a hold when you lay them flat. It's simply a matter of organization. They are likely headed to Charleston. At their speed, they'll make port in nine days if the winds hold true."

Eliza was silent, observing the stinking ship a few yards from them. She was calculating what he said, comparing the interior of their vessel to what appeared to be a much more confined space across the way. And she could barely fathom what he found so amusing about the enterprise. She could not imagine what he had proposed.

"Do you mean to tell me they lie on their backs the entire way? Without ever moving? For months on end?"

"Yes. And that's the smell. They lie in their own filth. It is a gamble. They lose a lot of cargo that way. But the quicker they bring more bodies from one coast to the other, the more profit there is to be gained."

He took a deep inhalation and sighed, gazing out into the distance.

"I will tell you who has a miserable lot, though. You couldn't pay me to be a surgeon on one of those boats. I wouldn't have the stomach for it. If the odor is so offensive at this distance, can you imagine what's crawling about in the hold? It's a wonder the crew survives at all. I hear they regularly get the flux, even with all the precautions they take. Those are some desperate men to work on a ship like that, Lady Sharpe."

"Are there many such ships on this side of the Atlantic?"

"As many as there are merchant ships. It has taken off quite nicely. My father was in the navy, and his father was before him. There were never as many ships like this in the water in their days. It's a thriving trade, to be sure."

Eliza watched on, feeling a tightening in her abdomen. She placed a quivering hand on her stays.

"And the sharks…"

"Ah, yes, you've noticed. They're smart beasts. They know a meal is ready for them. It's only a matter of waiting. I wager they can smell them coming, miles off. The closer to the coast we get, Lady Sharpe, the more creatures you'll likely be spotting."

Eliza nodded, her eyes locked on the dark bodies in the water. An emotion was taking hold of her. One she did not know whether to attribute to her ignorance of how the world operated or whether there was something deeper brewing in the pit of her stomach. Perhaps it was a symptom of womanhood that a thing not belonging to the realm of beauty or grace was so utterly offensive to all of her sensibilities. The schooner finally lagged behind their ship until it was a distant object bobbing in the waves.

Eliza was aware that the officer was watching her. She had found him pleasant enough, but there was a shallow quality to how he viewed things. He possessed an indifferent and detached way of observing his environment that Eliza vowed she would never suffer. She did not know why such a realization bothered her quite so strongly. For two people to have divergent perspectives on the same object was hardly a novel concept. But for all of his redeeming mannerisms, his well-fitted uniform, and his desire to please her, he could no longer smell that awful stench. And that, in her eyes, rendered him an unfeeling man.

"Eliza! Why are you here?"

A loud voice made them both turn.

Charles strode over to them, the sight of him above deck during the day an unusual feature. Now, thoughts about who she had joined in matrimony consumed her. Was Charles exactly like him? Were all men so dreadfully cold?

She said nothing, still clutching the handkerchief to her face. Charles put an arm through hers and began directing her back to the stairs.

"You cannot be up here. There is a miasma in the air! You should not breathe that putrid air in," he started to say.

She turned back to Second Lieutenant Braddock, who folded his arms behind him and began walking in the opposite direction. A wry smile crossed his face, accompanied by a slight shake of his head.

"That was rather rude. You hardly said a word to the man," she said as they reached the second deck.

Eliza actually cared little about what she had just said. She was more annoyed that her absent husband should reappear only to drag her below deck on his whim.

"Who? Braddock? He's a fool. And from my observation, you have clearly already been acquainted," he snapped.

"He was explaining the ship abreast of us."

Charles looked to the side and took a deep breath. He was bracing himself and seemed troubled; sweat beaded on his forehead.

"It is pleasant to have someone to converse with. I hardly see you during the day, and then at night only…" she blurted, her tone revealing. "You hardly look at me or touch me!"

This caught his full notice and changed the tenor of the conversation.

"And the fault is mine. Entirely mine," he said abruptly.

A team of sailors descended the stairs, and he took her off to the side.

"Do not think you are to blame for my disappearances," he began, his hands on her arms. "Life at sea does not bode well for someone of my…constitution. I understand my timing could not be executed more poorly. And I am incredibly anxious to know you, my dear. Believe me, I think of nothing else."

Relief and realization settled over her. She found his words pleasing.

"You mean to say the sea makes you feel ill?"

He urged her to lower her voice and nodded. An older officer acknowledged them as he walked down the passage.

"That is hardly anything to feel shame over. Besides, you are entirely too tall to ever be a captain. You are much better suited to the army," she said reassuringly. "It would be cruel to make a man like you subsist on maggoty bread."

To add emphasis to her words, she reached for his shoulders playfully. He leaned towards her and pressed his lips to her forehead.

"I thank you for your patience and understanding, Eliza. And you will be *fully* acquainted with your husband once we make landfall."

He squeezed her hand and smiled. Eliza began to excitedly picture their life outside of the ship. It was dark and smoky below deck, but she felt such a light around her now. Her worries and apprehensions had been dashed to the ground, and she was weightless in his hands. The warm appearance of a friendlier side of him rendered his rugged features infinitely more handsome in her eyes. She inwardly promised to make it a point to please Charles in all matters, if only to see this part of him more often.

CHAPTER III.

E liza slowly brushed her finger against the damp wooden railing, marveling at the grains of salt on her skin. The sea air had deposited droplets on the upper deck, leaving small saltwater stains on everything uncovered. She also knew the residue lightly covered her skin, and realized she would miss some part of living on board a ship, despite its innumerable disadvantages. *The Albany* had carried her from one port to another and from one stage of life to the next. She was grateful for it.

The air had already changed around her. Despite the ever-present sea breeze, she could feel the heat buzzing against her skin. Eliza closed her eyes in the bright sun, wondering how insufferable the warmth would be without the constant wind. Countless birds shrieked out and cried above her. Water sloshed against the ship as smaller pilot boats appeared from the mainland to unload supplies and cargo. The crew had cast anchor as close to the town as possible, and she strained to catch the first glimpse of her new home.

Her attention was enraptured with the waters around her, and she found it difficult to focus on the distant shoreline. As they had crept closer and closer to their destination, Eliza had marveled at how the water changed with nearly every mile. She had never seen so many shades of blue or such an immaculately clear ocean. In the West Indies, the sea was not a mystery. She could lean over the sticky salt-covered railing, peer down and see the blurred images of coral rocks and moving masses of fish and sea turtles beneath her.

The mystery and terror of the ocean that man held in his heart was partly due to the unknowable, impenetrable nature of miles and miles of dark, unpredictable water. Such an ocean revealed nothing and threatened to take everything. But here, in a veritable paradise, in a place where no such darkness was detectable, where the sea opened up and welcomed her with a flurry of vivid colors and dancing reflections, she could only harbor an instinctive love for it. They had left the deep, desolate indigo swells of that passage behind forever, and her heart brimmed with intense anticipation. Her future had arrived. It was detectable, like the salt-laced air that blew through her hair.

Charles appeared topside, giving a farewell to certain officers. They hadn't spoken more than the occasional airy conversation about the weather or the waves during the last few nights. She had still expected him to knock on her door every evening after dinner, but he always retired to his own cabin. She knew she was foolish, but she found comfort with the knowledge she now carried. There was a reason for his lack of presence. Once the rolling waves that had made him so unwell were eliminated, so too would this awkward stage of their marriage likewise evaporate.

When it was finally their turn to disembark, she moved with a burning optimism. Eliza stepped off the small pilot boat and onto the weathered dock, the merciless midday sun radiating off its bleached beams. Charles had extended his hand towards her in assistance, but now that she was finally on land again, her steps propelled her forward with unabashed curiosity. Her leg muscles felt strange and untethered, wobbly from weeks of endless rocking back and forth on the slow and sometimes comfortless voyage. She did not look back at the ship that had served as her home for the last several weeks.

There was only one direction to head into town, so she walked on without hesitation. There was a flurry of activity, loading and unloading, hawking wares, and displaying goods, a mixture of French, Spanish, and English tongues punctuated by the stranger-sounding voices of African languages. There were, in fact, more dark faces that looked back at her than Englishmen. The natural disarray of the market invigorated her, and she fell into the crowd, examining the goods around her.

A few minutes later, Charles caught up with her, taking her by the arm and leading her through the crowd. Once they stepped away from the main dock, a waterside arcade offered a pathway with patchy shade from the beating sunshine along a row of merchant stalls. Rows of roughly hewn logs carved from palm trees, their wood stained lighter by the heat and nearly unrecognizable, whistled and creaked in the breeze as she walked underneath them. Overall, it was a crude construction, but the respite it provided from the relentless sun was a mercy.

One seller displayed more pineapples than she had ever seen. The next booth offered seashells as large as her head, another a cascading pile of sea sponges. Salted meats and the earthy smells of cut wood pervaded her senses. Strangely shaped fish, glowing with bursts of color in the light, stared back at her with lifeless eyes. Casks of lime juice and bright pyramids of fresh oranges appeared. Fruits in baskets of all shapes and textures, which she could not recognize by name, lined the ground. Black women carried produce, balancing the containers on their heads. Their necks were straight and their backs erect, as if the load of fruit weighed nothing at all and was not in danger of tilting or spilling over. Even the sea itself was not immune to the overflowing expanses of the market. Green sea turtles and hawksbill turtles dotted the shallow water in clumps within the confines of hastily constructed sea pens.

They continued walking as the town's first houses came into view on either side of them. Her distant observations proved correct from the ship. As *The Albany* had swung around Hog Island, the small barrier strip of land that buffeted Nassau harbor, the town's features had surprised her. Now, as it appeared before her, she could confirm what she had seen from a distance. Not a chimney top was to be found. A single limestone church spire with a cross towered above the otherwise low-rising buildings. The ever-dominating presence of the governor's house on the hill loomed further back in the town, its land enclosed by a wall and a series of cannons flanking bursts of violet flowers in a tropical garden.

The architecture of Nassau was simple to the eye yet charming; row upon row of wooden structures, some double-boarded, some with free-standing second-level balconies, dotted the hill. Most homes displayed the naked beams of the wood that covered their frames, bleached gray by the sun; some were painted white and paired with complementary green and red shutters. A few windows were paned with glass. Bay Street was the only regular straight street, and while most of the dwellings were wooden, some limestone-built facilities like the garrison, a market space, and one or two businesses figured among the structures.

Charles released his hold on her to purchase something from a recognized merchant. She stepped forward to look at the Bourse, an open-air market that offered a permanent roof for respite from the sun and a meeting place for other salesmen. Eliza recognized the building at once from Charles' description on the boat. The architecture she had seen so far had been uncomplicated, but the Bourse boasted a set of Corinthian columns. It was the starting place where customers began their journey down the harbor, and where domestics would meet and waste a few minutes with idle gossip while they ran their errands. Behind it stood a forest of wooden masts, with many ropes crisscrossing each other.

Red-billed tropicbirds swooped and darted between the ships, but she ignored their cries. She could smell that curiously horrifying smell she had encountered only a week before. So far, everything about her first moments marked Nassau as any other English trading port. Except one key distinction made this island vastly different from the ports she had experienced at home. In this bustling town, human flesh was for sale, and what she saw made her incredulous with disbelief.

Crowding in their own stink and misery were rows upon rows of dark faces, limbs covered in heavy iron chains, some with their hands outstretched towards the passersby. Further down the path, a man dragged a slave out to a crowd, displaying the man's muscular body like he was nothing but a fine specimen of meat. Indeed, he was an object for sale. The merchant handled the man no differently than the other merchants had hawked their ripened fruit or freshly caught fish.

Her first encounter with the slave trade had offered the convenience of not seeing a single enslaved body, and now that the spectacle was in front of her, it made her speechless. Its obvious brutality could no longer be masked. She stood transfixed by the sight until Charles was at her side again.

"You must try this pineapple, my dear," he said, chewing on a piece, "I know you surely have tasted its sweetness before, but this will be your first fresh morsel."

She barely heard him, and he noticed her distraction.

"This is why you must not wander by yourself, Eliza. In time you will come to avoid certain less desirable parts of town. For now, you should only walk alongside me."

"Is it necessary to cage them? Like they are…are livestock? Are they not men and women, like you and me? Surely…"

Charles seemed puzzled by her reaction.

"Some sellers choose to create displays such as this, but we only purchase from within the Bourse itself. Wells

& Gibbons never parade their Negroes around. They are bought and sold in a more appropriate manner. You need not concern yourself with affairs of the trade."

He offered her the fruit again, and she meekly took it from him, chewing it with reluctance. The fruit burst in her mouth with an unexpectedly delectable juiciness. It instantly satisfied her parched lips. Before continuing their walk, she took one last look at the merchant and the fruit to remember the type. She wanted to appear interested in what Charles showed her, but she could not shake her distraction. She simply could not remove the image of the chained man's face from her mind. She tried to focus, but she had never seen so many men and women of African descent in one place before. The more they walked, the more she realized that they clearly outnumbered the English faces she saw. She couldn't remain silent.

"It does puzzle me that the trade prospers in a place like this. I have never seen so many people like them before. Are they not distressed to see their fellow countrymen confined in such a manner? Are they—"

Charles stopped, stepping in front of her.

"I'd have you know that the Africans started the slave trade. We merely adopted the idea, my dear. It does not cause any consternation for them. I can assure you. They are living better lives in this hemisphere. You only need to see the abysmal conditions of where they came from to be persuaded. Even the state of their village here, New-Guinea, some call it, can attest to that. You'll never see a place filled with more content mulattoes and free Negroes as you will on this island."

They moved to the side, allowing a donkey to pull a cart of rope through.

"But are not the English the least bit distraught to see their numbers figure so low compared to the Africans? What is to stop them from revolting? And our proximity to the Americas…"

"Show me any society where this is not the case. The planters are naturally few in number because they are at the top of the pyramid, my dear. That is the way of the world. Besides, even though we are far from home, we are still on English soil with English laws. Law and order is enforced by His Majesty's finest. These are the workings of an empire."

His green eyes were penetrating and direct.

"I am perplexed to see it all in front of me so clearly. It is much different than reading about it in a book. It seems to me that we are on the edge of a frontier, a new world."

"After nearly a hundred or so years, I can attest that there is nothing novel about arrangements in the Bahamas. This is the case naturally all over this side of the Atlantic."

"Are many of these people freed? I must admit I found the sights of the Bourse disturbing. But there is a village of freed slaves on this island? There is such room for possibilities, I can hardly…"

He put his hands on her shoulders.

"Eliza, mark me, you will need to rein in your comments. We are to head to Lord Dunmore's house next, and believe me when I tell you that such questions will simply not be tolerated. There are many refugees here, and there is a sensitivity to these matters that you can scarcely comprehend. There was much fighting between the established landowners and the recent arrivals. And it continues to this day."

They resumed their walk, the curved shade of palm trees offering some coolness from the heat. The back of her neck and hairline were damp with sweat.

"So, have many refugees come lately from African shores?" she asked.

Charles laughed.

"No, my dear. Many disabused refugees from the Americas have recently learned that the fledgling nation offers no surety of freedom. Some planters from the southern colonies have had no recourse but to come here. They have paid a heavy price for their loyalty to the Crown, and many are in town solely to rebuild their lives and regain their lost profits from the war."

"What a terribly interesting mix of people and cultures," she remarked, observing the town and citizens around them.

It seemed evident to her that he did not want to discuss the subject further. She tried to remain quiet and watched the sights around them. The slightest breeze stirred the brilliant orange petals of the royal poinciana trees bordering each house. She paused to look at the trees' curious fern-like leaves, marveling at their beauty. Nearly every dwelling appeared to have lush, blooming gardens and large trees dotting each yard. Tiny lizards basked themselves in the baking sun on the bleached walls. They fled every approach of her curious finger with an agility she had never seen before. She was fixated on her new tropical surroundings, and Charles' attention was directed solely on her wonderment.

"When we are at home later this evening, we can discuss all this and more, but for now, we are presently expected at the governor's," he said. "Ah! Julius and Josiah are here with our horses."

Charles engaged in polite conversation with the short black man who stood next to a team of sweating horses. Three young boys crowded in nervously towards Julius, their wide eyes staring up at Charles. The taller man named Josiah greeted her with a charming smile from the back. A large dark bay stood at the front of the horses, snorting with exertion. Julius was attempting to convince Charles that this horse was the ideal choice for him, while Charles appeared concerned that the stallion was too dark to tolerate heavy use in the sun.

Josiah came over and directed Eliza to mount her mare. She was a much leaner chestnut bay. She had a calmer temperament and had been reserved for Eliza's use. A few moments later, the party had mounted their horses, their belongings appropriately secured, and they headed south to the governor's mansion. The horses' hooves rang out with metallic clarity against the hard limestone road.

Inside the estate, a groom assisted Eliza with dismounting from her horse. The white wooden mansion was two levels high, with a veranda porch wrapped completely around the house on the second floor. Doric columns stood between every glass-encased window on this level and completely flanked the railing, making the property appear quite grand against its humble surroundings. A series of columns was also below the balcony on the ground level. It seemed extraordinarily quiet and peaceful on top of the hill compared to the noise of the waterfront below. And the prospect it commanded of Nassau and its turquoise waters studded with ship masts was impressive to behold.

They followed a second servant into the vast house. Inside, it was much cooler, but the full effect of the heat finally bore down on her now that she had stopped moving. As her eyes adjusted to the dimmer light, Eliza looked at her surroundings. Dark-mahogany floors complemented wooden paneling and yellow damask wallpaper. The shutters, window cases, and dentil-style molding below the ceiling were all similarly carved of the same wood. Large mahogany overdoor pediments flanked every single archway, each crested with a carved flourish, some crowned with the shape of pineapples.

She walked straight through an open hallway to another grand door on the opposite side of the house and saw a lush private garden. The rich contrasts of vivid blues and greens made her head spin. Everything was bright and filled with a heavy swathe of heat. Her eyes fixated on this second door; it seemed like a portal revealing a world of gently swaying green leaves.

The sun dominated the western portion of the great mansion, so Lord Dunmore's guests were directed to the back of the house. The servant led them through the hallway, up the curved walnut stairs, and into a parlor room, where she beckoned them to sit on a golden bronze sofa. The fabric covering it matched the damask patterns on the walls. A tall black coromandel lacquer screen with ten panels was placed near the entry. It featured delicate oriental designs of pagodas, landscapes, and domestic scenes with gregarious dragons hovering on the bottom of each panel. Their large, scaled bodies coiled around each other, with mother-of-pearl inlaid teeth and eyes, as they appeared and disappeared through swirling clouds.

Eliza's fingers traced the curved back of one of the dragons. She had always been intrigued by Eastern art and had never encountered a screen quite so large and commanding. Chinese calligraphy was inscribed beneath each dragon, and she wondered what the strange characters meant. She could look at it for an hour, lost in its intricate and mystical design, but she knew Charles was watching her.

She turned to sit on the sofa with him, her head suffering a sharp rush. A nearby table presented a silver bowl filled to the brim with strange fruits. The fruits, however, were covered in black flies, making the presentation wholly unappealing.

A second servant came around with a shining tray offering a pink drink. Eliza accepted eagerly, taking a quick sip, assuming it was juice. The burn at the back of her throat told her it was decidedly not. She coughed bitterly.

"There, there, my dear. That is our lordship's famous punch. I know men who have dogged him for years, desperate to figure out the exact recipe. It's light on the tongue, but the rum offers quite the kick," Charles said to her, leaning forward on the sofa.

A bustle of activity near a side door erupted just as a boisterous voice entered the room, followed by a retinue of people. A garishly dressed black footman announced the governor's arrival in a flat voice.

"His Excellency, the Earl of Dunmore, Governor of the Bahama Islands..."

An unimpressive corpulent man with red hair stepped forward, possessing ruddy flushed cheeks. Beads of sweat decked his furrowed brow. As he surveyed his new guests, his hooded eyes were decidedly calculating, and they fixated directly on Eliza. Introductions were hastily made. Many of the names were forgotten almost as soon as her ears heard them. The party recommenced sitting around the small table.

"I would like to extend my sincerest gratitude for this post, my lord. It is an honor to—" Charles started to say.

"Nonsense. It's a backwater colony, Lord Sharpe, nothing more. Now...I'm sure you are itching for news after your voyage. Have you heard of the troubles in France yet?" Lord Dunmore began, his face red from his limited walk.

Charles shook his head.

"No, I have not, my lord."

"Allow me to inform you then. I just received the most riveting letter," Lord Dunmore replied. "We obtained word a few days ago that the King and Queen of France had effected their escape to the Austrian border. But they were apprehended! This will produce some considerable consequences, no doubt. I, at first, thought that if they got off safely, a war would surely start, but now that they have been retaken, it seems war is inevitable. Monarchical government is nearly completely suspended in France now. A travesty."

"A consequence of their liberal philosophers, no doubt…" Charles said tersely, shaking his head.

"To treat the monarchy with such blatant disrespect…it's reprehensible. I fear what this world is coming to, I do. What will the next century bring? I can hardly fathom it."

He paused to sip his drink, and Charles followed suit.

"Ah, I'm glad you've finally arrived, Lord Sharpe. I remember Lord Cornwallis singing your praises in the Carolina campaigns. I hope to utilize that resourcefulness and efficiency for our island. We could use a lieutenant colonel around here," he said with a short-winded rush. He paused for a breath and then continued. "You are to command the garrison at Fort Nassau as well as oversee the construction of the new fort, Fort Charlotte."

That name rang a bell in Eliza's mind, and she quickly recovered the name of the woman to the governor's right. Charlotte fanned frantically in his direction until the governor shooed her away. She looked perturbed for a moment, then flashed a genteel smile at Eliza.

"Yes, my lord," Charles replied solemnly. "And the present conditions?"

"Well, we've lost nearly a hundred men in the last two months," Lord Dunmore said as his drink disappeared. "You know how the nature of these matters precedes. It could take four days or four months to obtain any sensible military goal. It never follows a predestined course."

The governor motioned for the servant to bring another beverage. It was brought forth instantly and disappeared as quickly as its predecessor.

"I'm surprised to hear this, my lord. Has there been much activity?" Charles asked, sitting on the edge of his seat.

Eliza detected a slight sliver of excitement in his voice. Lord Dunmore scoffed, turning red with exertion.

"Malignant fever. Battle casualties are few and far between. We have the occasional outlaws roaming the outer cays, but piracy, for the most part, is dead now."

The governor turned towards Charlotte, growling in a low tone.

"Share with me, my darling. Come now," he said as he leaned into her neck.

His tone was entirely unfamiliar to Eliza, so she immediately looked away, blushing slightly, desperate to retain her composure.

"John Murray wants more punch..." the governor said again to the woman as his splotchy hand reached for her glass.

Charlotte looked away in disgust and held her drink aloft in the air.

"Ah, yes, tropical disease. A silent killer amongst our men," Charles said.

Lord Dunmore hacked a wet, phlegmy cough, withdrawing his handkerchief at one point when his exertions overcame him.

"Two-thirds of the garrison were sick. May was a terrible month. I am hoping it will abate and not carry on through November. One year, we lost nearly six hundred men."

He motioned towards Eliza but stared at her as if surveying a map.

"I would watch this one—she is new to this climate."

She looked down, bothered by the way he looked at her. The man disgusted her. He seemed vulgar and in disregard of polite conventions. Moreover, she could already feel a heated rush descend the back of her head from the seemingly potent rum. This social call was nearing the end of her tolerance. She was impatient to see her new home.

"And congratulations are in order! To newly wedded bliss," Lord Dunmore quickly added to shorten the silent pause.

The group toasted. The young woman to his left smiled at her like a cat, but then her eyes fixated on Charles.

"Take advantage of this time as much as you can. I assure you the novelty wears off rather quickly. At least she has been able to journey alongside you. My dear Charlotte is staying in Italy for the time being," Lord Dunmore continued.

Eliza looked up, confused. Surely, the woman she was introduced to had said her name was Charlotte. As Eliza studied her face and frame a little more closely, she noted that the woman was rather young. Perhaps this was his daughter, named after her mother.

She was still questioning their association when Lord Dunmore leaned alongside the woman's body again. She had never observed such a feeling father. Eliza ignored it and began to muse about all the questions that nagged her mind. She began to fade, the warmth of the rum buzzing through her, the solid ground and cushions setting her body at ease. Charles' hand grasped hers, breaking her reverie.

"I could not handle politics, my lord. I am flattered but possess no interest in such affairs. I could not be civil to my enemies. I'd much rather meet them on the field," Charles replied to some inconvenient question.

She wondered if the sweet alcohol was affecting Charles at all. He seemed incapable of being anything other than grave in front of his superior. On the other hand, Lord Dunmore clearly preferred to get business out of the way first, then move on to more entertaining topics. Indeed, he hardly seemed to possess any sober demeanor at all.

"Ah, yes, the infamous sabers of the dragoons. Striking terror into the heart of every American. We best not discuss such matters in front of Lady Sharpe, or you'll strike fear into her as well," Lord Dunmore said, making a comical face.

He turned to the woman named Charlotte a third time, using a singularly loud and embarrassing growl to express his wishes. She seemed absolutely mortified. Then she turned her attention to Eliza.

"Lady Sharpe, would you like the use of one of my Venetian fans? I ordered duplicates by mistake, but now I see that you could benefit," she said.

Eliza thanked her, and Charlotte rose from her chair and left the room. Lord Dunmore cocked his head, watching her as she went through the door.

"I know we only occasionally spoke years ago, but you can see I am not a stupid man. If I'm sent away to some godforsaken mosquito-infested island, I clearly intend to make the best of it. I've made extensive renovations to the house, particularly to my bedroom, if you garner my meaning. Spectacular investment. Costs a pretty penny. I daresay I've never seen someone so badly gifted with economics. She'll order three dresses from Paris only because she can't choose which shade is more flattering. Once decided, she'll never touch the other two gowns since the silhouette has already been debuted. There they sit in the box, unmolested. But I make a considerate return if you catch my meaning. Oh, I wouldn't want to embarrass the young Lady Sharpe."

Lord Dunmore smiled, revealing stained teeth. Eliza was unsure how to react. She overwhelmingly felt as if she alone was the cause for hastily ended conversations. Now that Charlotte had left, Eliza remained the only woman in the room. All the men clearly followed a code of unspoken propriety, but she greatly disliked the condescension. Perhaps she was overthinking.

"My lord, I hope you do not find me speaking an interruption of your affairs, but I would like to ask a question. If you do not mind," she said as all the men turned to look at her.

If Charles had found any good humor within himself, he quickly returned to a somber pose. He seemed uncannily nervous, like that night on the ship during the storm.

"You mentioned pirates before. What is the history of them on this island? I am greatly intrigued by it."

She felt satisfaction at finally speaking her mind.

"Pirates? You have nothing to worry about at all, my dear," Lord Dunmore answered brusquely.

The conversation started to pick up anew, and the men focused on trade. But she yearned to interject.

"I am not worried, my lord. I simply mean to learn about the subject. Many years ago, legendary names roamed these waters, but I am not certain of current events. Has it been an issue for the island? What remedy have you employed?"

Lord Dunmore looked at her impatiently and coughed again as if answering her was too much of a hassle. She decided then that she had never encountered a fellow person who resembled a hog more than him at that moment.

"I am fully aware you do not know. The island has never been safer, and as you adjust to your new home, you'll become preoccupied with other matters. There is nothing to fret about, my lady. Set your mind at ease."

"Yes, my dear, there is certainly more danger from the place we have just left. They finally caught the deranged lunatic, the so-called *Monster*, my lord. He was just about to go on trial when we disembarked. Responsible for nearly fifty attacks on innocent women on the streets. London was abuzz over it. Madness, truly," Charles spoke.

Eliza was still determined to speak.

"Is this the residence governors of this colony have always inhabited? Did Woodes Rogers live here? My, I do wonder what these walls have borne witness to. I've read much about him and Selkirk, that poor castaway he found. I found it all very fascinating."

"Today, the West Indies is a much different place, my dear. There are no starving men marooned on these islands. There is no pirate nation, and there are certainly no men clad in goatskin awaiting salvation on some abandoned cay. It was a work of nonsense, that is all."

He sniveled and then called for more drink.

"I think you're mistaken, my lord. I was solely discussing Rogers. Selkirk may have inspired Defoe's *Robinson Crusoe*, but reality and plot vastly differ. Crusoe was said to have been stranded in this region, but Selkirk was found in the Pacific. Defoe's book doesn't hold my interest very well. I always find the source of his inspiration to be more valuable," she replied.

He cleared his throat, and his face reddened as if he was having trouble breathing.

"I am in the business of governance, my lady, not whimsical fantasy. There is nothing of note to recount in this island's history. It is not made of the stuff where we come from. We are sitting on the very edge of empire, not within civilization itself. We can only do our best to make our lives comfortable here on this rocky outcrop, and I assure you, it can be arranged very comfortably indeed. Would you care for more refreshment?"

He had made her an offer, but there was little hospitality in it. All the men were staring at her, and although it made her uncomfortable, she was still desperate for conversation.

"In my experience, a gentleman only says that to a lady when he means to end the discussion on a topic. Very well. What about the local fauna? Is there anything of interest that I should keep an eye out for?"

Charles' eyes widened at her boldness.

"There are no lions or tigers on this island, my lady," Lord Dunmore said, causing the rest of the men to laugh. "Just an occasional troupe of lizards. A few marvelous insects. Colorful birds. Nothing to snatch you away in the night."

"I am fascinated by nature. I mean to study and explore the island as soon as I can. I'd like to—"

"This island is quite the paradise, isn't it, my lordship?" Charles interjected, clearly wanting her to remain quiet.

"Yes, a veritable Eden," another gentleman concurred.

"A strange Eden, indeed," Lord Dunmore said, looking at her with a different glance.

His refusal to discuss anything with Eliza was frustrating. She was growing bored; Charlotte never returned to the room. Eliza sighed. She was finally here on foreign soil, yet confined to a stuffy, hot parlor room away from the blazing sun. She knew that wondrous discoveries awaited her outside the walls of this room. She excused herself and walked outside through the French doors as the men began to talk loudly.

"I know women are capable of possessing minds, but for my part I am not entirely sure if it's worth the trouble!" she heard one man say as the group broke into laughter.

"Charles, have you robbed the schoolroom a pupil? I daresay even an encyclopedia could not satisfy her."

"That is why gentlemen are best suited for the library and women the bedroom. You best hide your books when you arrive, Lord Sharpe, or she may be entirely distracted from her matrimonial duties yet."

She froze, feeling eyes on her back. Her ears turned red, and she hesitated to keep walking. Drink made the men's voices louder than they intended. The heat was searing, but the jasmine and honeysuckle flowers dotted between the green fringes of palm beckoned her further onto the porch until she could no longer hear the gentlemen.

Eliza stood against the railing. The wood was scorching hot, but the wispy island breeze made her linger. The flowers secreted an intoxicatingly sweet perfume. A black butterfly whose wings were edged with flashes of blue and red settled on a flower and flew to another plant. She felt Charles approach her a few moments later.

"I am sorry if I have done something wrong. This is all so different and new, and I am terribly excited to be off the ship."

Eliza kept her gaze downward.

"Nonsense, my dear. I know the journey was long, but I hope you will grow to love your new home," he said sweetly, placing a hand on hers.

She took a step away from him, unaccustomed to a man touching her. She felt shy but terribly exhilarated. She wanted to explore every inch of this new world.

"I've never felt such heat on my skin before," she remarked, turning an arm in the dappled sunlight. "I confess I feel incredibly lightheaded. I think it's some effect from the ship."

"Even I must reacquaint myself with the tropics, despite having been raised here. But do not fear. You will find more regulated temperatures when you remain inside. There is constant light to aid in needlework and other activities of your sex. I will have to battle the heat, I'm afraid."

Charles smiled for a moment and looked outward towards the garden, worry darkening his features.

"Would you like to visit your father's grave on the way?" she asked quietly.

His mood did not alter.

"No, it is not necessary. There is time enough for that."

Satisfied that she had done her duty as far as that topic was concerned, she returned to their original subject.

"I am sure if your house is on the coast, it must possess some breeze. I will find a way to cope. Otherwise, I will become a recluse. And I believe there is much to see."

"Life is quite simple here. There will be social events for every season, but these will mostly occur in the evenings when it is cooler. You will be kept comfortable inside the rest of the time," he replied.

"I'm afraid you misinterpret my meaning. I do not mind this heat. And the shore must be delightful. From what I've seen so far, I can only imagine what species reside here. I mean to explore every mile of this island. This beauty...it is unimaginable," Eliza said, toying with a jasmine flower.

"Perhaps you will reconsider when we continue our journey. It is a paradise, to be sure, but a dangerous one. I daresay I'd go so far as to describe it as deadly. Aha! Our drinks are ready!" Charles said, stepping back into the room.

Eliza sighed. She wondered what could be so threatening on a barely inhabited island. From the maps she had studied, these islands were no more than dots on the parchment. It couldn't take that long to explore. The intrigue of what could make Charles possess that kind of attitude to a place he had grown up in fascinated her. He appeared a robust and thriving man, and she saw nothing but beauty and flowers around her.

Eliza took a few steps down the balcony, studying her stark outline against the sturdy boards of the deck. A slave dressed in what appeared to be livery stood towards the end of the row. As she looked closer, it became apparent that he was a free man. The clothes he wore were too fine for a lower member of society. He was thin but poised and brimming with confidence. The man was short in height, but his stature lost no effect due to the extravagant silk hat with a yellow band he wore upon his head. It was tall and cylindrical, crafted in a modern French style. It was an unusual fashion, but his boldness made him appear charming.

Eliza nodded and curtsied as he approached her. He smiled, his lively eyes contrasting starkly with the lines of age that graced his face. She slowly moved to return to the room.

"I know about you, but you don't know about me," the gentleman said.

She stopped. His accent was exotic. She wondered if he was a native of this island or if he had come directly from Africa.

"My apologies. What do you mean? My name is Eliza. I have just arrived from England—" she began.

"I *know* about you, but *you* do not know about me," he repeated, revealing an infectious smile.

He stood erect, balancing his thin figure with a silver cane. His pearl-white teeth glowed against his skin. Eliza was unsure how to react. She tensed up, awkwardness making her feel uncomfortable.

"I open the gate," he said, blithely unaware of her reaction. "And I hold the key."

He flourished his cane in front of him, returning to his former pose, and stamped the cane on the deck. He kept his look down with a serious manner on his face, which he quickly replaced with another grin.

"One will strike from the sky, his mother...the sea."

Eliza heard Charles' measured steps approaching. She wasn't sure what was happening, but she couldn't help but return a smile. A breeze wafted past them, and a giddiness rose up in her.

"Oh, is it a riddle? I'm afraid I'm not very good with them," she began.

"Here we are, my dear. Another glass of punch made with fruit right from that garden."

She turned to take the glass from Charles.

"This gentleman was just sharing a delightful riddle. Or maybe it's a fortune. I'm not very skilled with parlor tricks. Maybe you can have a crack at it—"

She stopped because of Charles' bewildered glance. She looked behind her. The man was gone.

"There is no one out here, Eliza."

"No, he was. I saw him. Perhaps he returned inside," she replied, looking around them.

Her heart sank. That man, in particular, had seemed the most intriguing of all the people she had been introduced to. Charles began to steer her inside, a hand brazenly guiding her waist. She let him, the heat of embarrassment assaulting her more strongly than any Bahamian sun. The disappearance of the mysterious man was one matter, but her perpetual hesitation concerning any attempts of public affection when they were properly married was a deeper issue. She had grown too accustomed to his frequent disappearances while sailing on *The Albany*. Perhaps time would resolve it. After all, this was all so new to her.

"Maybe you've had too much punch, my dear. I would hate for it to be the cause of any ruined merriment. Perhaps you could imbibe it more slowly," Charles said as they sat in the parlor. "And please, only speak to the governor when spoken to. We need to make our best impression today."

Three hours and many glasses of punch later, they finally left Lord Dunmore's house and made their way to Pleasant Hall. Eliza had passed through several stages of delirium, which she attributed to the all-pervasive heat and rum, until she finally attained a level of clear-headedness, accompanied by a headache and a penchant for water. Either way, she was much happier to be out of the governor's mansion and on the move, exploring the rest of the island.

As they made their way inland, there were less pastureland and hills to be seen, and the vegetation increased in density and size. East Indian fig trees looked down on the riding party, with their unusual roots hanging down like ropes that reached earthbound to the bottom of the tree. She understood that the planters mainly lived outside of town, but so far, she had only seen what appeared to be abandoned properties.

Flies covered her poor horse, distracting her from her observations. The constant swatting of them had made her paranoid and itchy. Frustrated with scratching, Eliza hoisted her skirts to find the source of irritation. A moving mass of black mosquitoes crowded her ankles, biting her mercilessly. Disgusted, she hit them away and kept an eye on her legs. The sun was much lower in the sky, but its heat still bore down on their faces, coloring the riding party in golden apricot tones.

The small black boy leading her horse was barely keeping the rope, his hold on the animal slack at best. He seemed more preoccupied with running ahead of the company and grabbing flowers to give her. The first occurrence was charming, but the boy kept doing it and even stalled her horse from continuing with the group. Besides, she quickly learned that the huge hibiscus flowers and violet bougainvillea attracted more bugs. She amassed quite a collection in the horse's withers, but then, when he wasn't looking, she tossed them to the side.

They moved past chickens and goats, the faraway sound of a baby crying in the shade of a distant house, and alongside limestone walls crawling with clumps of weeds. The landscape changed from the torrid and open beginnings of society in town to a steady patch of vine-covered trees, humidity, and insect-flooded air. Most of these trees, besides the regular pines, she did not recognize. Some seemed to grow into others, their different barks and foliage blending under the same curving vines, with bursts of striped leaves and flowers intermingling. At times, the woods were quite dense, and this is when the mosquitoes were at their worst, and they bounced successively off her neck and arms.

Julius, the leading groom of the party, would periodically look behind him, making sure she was keeping up. He would rise to a stand on his stirrups, hacking and slashing itinerant vines and branches out of the way with a rusty machete. A faint scent of body odor mingling with the moist breeze wafted past her. She trotted past the yellow edges of palm leaves, fences, manicured properties, and dense bush, followed by more palms and mahogany forests. Massive green leaves covered nearly everything that stood tall. A few open fields were scattered here and there, and the ocean's roar was never far away from her ears.

A fouler and more putrid stench arrived next, and Julius was quick to point out a swathe of rotting seaweed alongside the trail. At times, they rode on the beaches between rough limestone rocks, the sand the purest white she had ever seen. Her horse's steps were unsteady on the pebbles and bits of broken coral, but she savored its slow, cautious movements. It allowed her to fully observe her surroundings. She desperately wanted to drive the horse to the water but remained restrained, quietly following the other men.

Charles was a restless rider. He would lead his horse into a bursting gallop, then circle back around with the group, testing the abilities of his new steed. It was an alluring sight to watch him charge headlong through the damp sand, his horse darting along the glassy reflection of the setting skies. He would even release the reins for a few moments, extending his arms outwards, his hands outstretched in the air, the horse an extension of himself. Eliza watched from a distance each time he passed, mindful not to stare. Now that their journey on the ship had ended, Charles seemed to be reinvigorated. He had clearly returned to his element, and she felt as if she was watching a different man. Something like anxiety burned in her gut as she watched him charge the shoreline alongside the riding party again and again.

The sun was beginning to sink into the horizon, framing the palm trees in dark shadows as the sky illuminated hues of yellow, orange, and purple. This was when she felt the tolls of the heat and the pace of their day finally catching up with her. Her horse was an easygoing mare, marching in step with the other horses. She barely needed to guide her, and the rhythmic swaying of its haunches was beginning to tire her.

Without realizing it, she relaxed her posture and suddenly felt herself swing downwards. Hands were immediately at her back, pushing her into balance once more; her horse snorted at the immediate intrusion of Charles' stallion flanking it. Charles clicked his tongue at her horse and patted it.

"You're leaning left. Ride straight with the horse," Charles said, his green eyes fixed on her. "Right shoulder back. There."

She sat stiffly in her sidesaddle position, her right leg squeezed against the horse's left side harder than before.

"I am an accomplished rider, I assure you," she replied, looking ahead, her ears flushed with embarrassment. "I am happy to see you've regained your health."

Now she really wanted to ride off into the water. She didn't like criticism and certainly didn't appreciate it from someone like him.

"Yes, now I am quite restored. You cut a striking figure on horseback. You can ride. I can easily tell that. In England, I am sure. Temperate climate, even terrain. You're growing weary. It's the heat."

"I occasionally join the hunts on our land, and I can jump a fence if I need to."

He laughed.

"I do not doubt it, Eliza. Most ladies in this town will only ride by carriage. Sidesaddle requires the same amount of horsemanship as riding astride, make no mistake," he said. "I personally feel that riding astride offers the most control. I like to ride with the animal between my legs."

"I have just as much control with my two legs on one side and this crop on the other," she replied, keeping her face stiffly locked forward.

"I was a part of the Legion during the war. Did you know we were among the few cavalry regiments to fight in the colonies?"

"You must be very proud of your service to the Crown," she said, demurely covering her annoyance.

"My aim is not to boast, but horses are one of my few passions. With me as a teacher, I could help you learn to ride like me. I could have your thighs wrapped around a horse quicker than you know."

She looked at him, and they locked eyes for a moment. She knew she was supposed to reply but couldn't find the words. Eliza turned her face to the other side lest he see her excitement. In fact, she would like that. She had done it once when she thought no one could see her. It had been exhilarating.

He squeezed his stallion into a run, leaning forward as he maneuvered through the other horses.

"We'll be home soon, my dear," he called out.

She sighed, batting away flies. The path along the beach expanded again, followed by a border of tall trees on either side. They entered a short stone fence. Silk cotton trees, with mammoth roots visible above ground, offered a dusky shade; a dark green canopy covered the sky. The leading groom sheathed his machete and motioned for a boy to run ahead of the group. Her horse quickened its pace.

An elegant white house came into view on the horizon. A bell tolled as they passed through a second stone wall bordering the house's property. There was a flurry of activity as servants lined up in front of the porch in the still, gray light.

She knew she should have been looking at her new home, but she could only see the ocean. The air was quiet, punctuated only by the gentle crashing of the waves. The shoreline lay less than a hundred yards away from the property, its limitless sand offering an unobstructed vista. The sun had turned the water into a rippling expanse of molten gold.

"Welcome to your new home, Pleasant Hall, my dear," Charles said, as he dismounted.

He came around to help her descend from her mare. She didn't even flinch from his proximity, continuing to look at the shore.

"It's the most beautiful thing I have ever laid eyes on," she said quietly, stepping towards the ocean.

"Yes, my father built this house himself. It's not as opulent as Lord Dunmore's residence, but I do believe it is a rather attractive property for what it's worth."

"Yes, but the water…" Eliza replied, stepping into the warm sand.

"I assure you I've never seen the water come close to the house itself, even in the worst of storms. And my father was a very clever man. He made sure to utilize crosswinds to fully aerate the house. There is always a gentle breeze, as you can tell."

The beach stretched as far as the eye could see, back towards town, and curved around a bend on the other side of the property.

"You own all of this land?" Eliza asked, increasingly mesmerized by what she saw.

She felt like a small child, astonished by every inch of her surroundings.

"Yes, Eliza. I'm afraid it is smaller than what you are used to, but you will acclimate yourself in no time. I know this may not be the kind of life you had envisioned, but this is where we will start our family."

Tearing her eyes from the beach, she followed Charles towards the front of the house where the domestics had lined up. A chicken fled on their approach. Eliza was extremely aware of how she was carrying herself, and all eyes were on her. She hoped this was the final set of introductions for the day. She was growing weary. Whenever she stopped moving, she felt a constant swaying in her limbs despite the flat steadiness of the ground. She wondered when the sensation would stop.

"If you need anything, anything at all, you can call on these servants," Charles began as he paced in front of the assembly. "Cleo, here, is the main house domestic."

A stout middle-aged black woman wearing a headwrap watched her with deep eyes and smiled wryly.

"And this is Celia. She is a wedding gift." Charles clasped his hands behind his back and smiled, seemingly content with himself.

Celia would not look up at her. She appeared close to Eliza's age.

"Oh," Eliza responded, thoroughly confused. "From whom?"

"From me to you, my dear. She will be your personal attendant," he answered.

A strange bird trilled in the distance.

"Oh," Eliza replied. "You mean to say that the cost of her services is a gift. Thank you, you are very kind."

"I am more than that, I'm afraid," he said, a slight edge to his voice.

Eliza tried to smile and acknowledge Celia, but the task was made infinitely more difficult by Celia's refusal to even meet her eyes. Charles seemed displeased. He took Celia's face by the chin, forcing her to look at his new bride. The look she finally gave Eliza seared into her; Celia's strange honey-colored eyes narrowed with sharpened disgust.

"She is young. She is healthy. She has yet to bear children, I am told. But when the time comes, or should you wish it sooner, her offspring will also be your property. Soon you will have more servants than you know what to do with, I wager."

Eliza looked at him dumbfounded. He waited for her to say something, eager to be rewarded for his marital thoughtfulness.

"That is hardly necessary. That is…" she began to say.

Celia was almost the same age as Eliza, but the difference between them was almost too vast for comprehension. At that moment, standing in front of her new home in a new land, taken so many miles across the sea, the thought of all the ways her life had suddenly changed and would continue to change was utterly incomprehensible.

"Is there something the matter, my love?" Charles asked, his patience appearing to wear thin.

This additional title from him made her head throb.

"I am not quite ready for this," she managed to say.

She turned on her heel, the weight of the slaves' silent eyes boring down on her unbearable. She could hear him chastising the servants for their inability to prevent the chickens from entering the front yard. His desire to please her felt suffocating. The unavoidable conflict of her new reality constricted her even further.

One by one, his words slowly resounded through her mind. She thought of the sickening smell she had encountered that day on the sea and the sight of the human bodies sold on the wharf like sheep. She had stupidly voiced her opinion to this man, a near stranger, despite the weeks spent together on the ship. And more foolishly, she had expected him to understand her concerns. But he was a planter. And not just any planter. His father had been a well-known, established planter on this island. Jeremiah Sharpe had been one of the original landowners in the colony after the Crown had regained control of the unruly pirate kingdom.

She knew families like this existed. But she had always pictured them as another group of English subjects. They had seemed far away, even inconsequential at times. But now she had married one. Despite his educated philosophical debates, perfectly styled regimentals, and precise and careful manner in every regard, he was wealthy enough to own other people. And he would provide their living from such a trade.

Eliza at once understood all those years ago when some fashionable ladies banned sugar in their tea. She had thought it nothing but a superficial, short-lived phase. After all, what impact could boycotting sugar in one or two parlors really have on the trade? But now she knew she stood squarely on the other side of the line. A line she had known existed but had never really given much thought to. Despite her intelligence, curiosity, and sharpened wit, she was powerless. At least the girls she had once judged as foolish could do something. From their positions, belonging to some of the most powerful families in England, they could threaten an end to commerce. From her position in the heart of the Atlantic, she knew more and had seen more than they ever could, yet she could do even less. And now she was culpable. The idea of owning another person as a wedding gift horrified her.

"What are you doing?" Charles asked, interrupting the torrent of her thoughts. He grabbed her arm with an unexpected force.

Eliza froze, the ability to speak stricken from her mouth. The sun had disappeared, and the yard was swiftly swathed in shadows.

The features of his face softened.

"You are tired and weary and in need of food. Come inside. I can show you the rest of the property tomorrow, my dear."

The heaviness from the wine was settling over her body as she felt herself relax into the wooden chair. She had been determined to avoid drink after Lord Dunmore's mansion, but that had been in the heat of the day. Her first sunset in her new home had taken her breath away. The coconut trees around the house had darkened into black silhouettes as lavender clouds surrounded the setting orb. As it sank lower and lower, the clouds had grown more violet then peach-hued in their density until even the still water of the sea had reflected a nearly perfect mirror alignment of the sky above.

A chorus of birds and the metallic clicks of unseen insects followed it and crowded the air. The beauty of her surroundings lulled her into a state of repose; even the incessant whine of the mosquitoes no longer roused her ire. Since evening had fallen, she had been able to bathe and change her dress. Now that she had been afforded time to refresh herself, the notion of wine had seemed agreeable again. What a long and exceedingly eventful day it had been. She knew she would fall asleep quickly tonight.

The night was surprisingly cool, and the fire roared in front of them, highlighting the sharp angles of Charles' face. He had given her an enthusiastic tour of the house, pointing out the verdigris hue of paint in the foyer and parlor and that all beds and chairs in the house would generally be dressed for summer due to the perpetually warm climate. Charles had shown her every room on both floors, including her bedroom, where her trunks had been stored. He commented there would be no need for such formalities between them. He had emphasized her comfort in all matters and wanted her to feel at ease in Pleasant Hall.

Her eyes could focus on nothing but the colorful flowers draping around the eaves of the porch and the crystalline water beyond. Afterward, during dinner, she learned that mostly pineapples, yams, lemons, oranges, and limes were grown on this soil, as well as maize, in limited quantities. The Bahama Islands did not belong to the coveted chain of 'sugar islands' as her mother had mistakenly assumed. Yet, the fruit she had sampled so far seemed to beckon the promise of cultivation on this island. Then she had been briefed on the various difficulties this particular terrain presented.

Agricultural talk soon bored her, but he was happy to discuss the ocean and its creatures instead. Eliza could scarcely believe it. He hung on to every word she said and appeared interested in every question she asked. Most men grew tired of talking about insects and creatures. He seemed fascinated. He answered all of her queries and even asked her questions in return. He shared his observations of the wild and promised to take her to the Black Reef in the upcoming days. They had a pleasant meal together and conversed for nearly two hours. She felt at peace; she could grow used to this.

It was so pleasant to encounter someone who understood her and what intrigued her. She hoped that this was truly the case and that, in time, they could move past any misunderstandings. She reminded herself that they were still strangers after all. And now they were residing in a strange, new land. There were many adjustments to be made.

As she swirled the remaining drop of wine in her glass, she thought of when they had first met on the bench at Bleinhill Manor. All those men and those suitors in their gaudy waistcoats had vied for her hand. He had never been a part of that crowd. She smiled. Nearly all her worries and troubles had dissipated within one day on land. He had acted strangely after their wedding because he dreaded the journey by ship. Now that the traveling was behind them, he was a changed man. As a multitude of night creatures blared in the background, Eliza looked toward the future with even greater anticipation.

Charles watched her sip the last of her wine as he sat across from her.

"I think I'd like to retire now. This was a wonderful evening," Eliza said, placing her glass on the table.

Every time she had looked up tonight, she had found him observing her carefully. He seemed so eager to please her in every way. Now his eyes lit up. They both stood and made their way to the hall.

"Goodnight…husband," she said, with giddiness in her voice.

This is what it must feel like to be married, she thought. *I've found such a suitable companion.*

She extended her hand for him to kiss. He did so, but it seemed that he wanted to say something more. Eliza smiled and made for the stairs. He grabbed her arm sharply and kissed her deeply, pulling her off the bottom step. She immediately stiffened up, confusion flooding her face. His countenance darkened with an expression she had never seen from him before. A few moments later, she found herself in his bedroom, his lips on hers again. Her neck began to strain as he leaned on her body with all his weight.

Fear started to make her heart race. She didn't know what she was supposed to do. She thought this would have happened weeks ago, but that time had never come. She had anticipated something like this that night in the inn over a month ago, but she was entirely caught off guard tonight. And she was so utterly exhausted from the day. What had made tonight any different? Until now, she hadn't even been reassured that he had found her attractive.

She awkwardly put her hands on his arms. She couldn't help but feel that she was pushing him away from her. Charles started to unfasten her dress, roughly pulling it down from her chest and unlaced her stays. She heard something rip, and he sneered as he accomplished his aim. A cool breeze collided with her quivering ribs. Charles seemed to know exactly what he was doing. He did not say a word. She felt his warm hands roam over parts of her body that no one had ever touched. Perhaps she was supposed to help him remove his clothes? Her face was seared with heat from being so crudely exposed.

She looked down at her feet, her arms instinctively covering her breasts. The opportunity for her to help him undress was lost as she looked back up at him. She had never seen a naked man before and quickly determined that she didn't want to. Not now. She tried to say something. She wanted *him* to say something. Was it supposed to be so terribly silent? The stillness was broken when he led her by the hips, moving her to the edge of the bed. It started to creak. It seemed too loud. She rested on her back uncomfortably, trying to shield her nakedness.

"I don't know how to…"

Charles was poised over her, putting her arms by her sides.

"I am well aware," he said, his voice blunt.

"Will it hurt?"

"Sometimes you must endure a little pain to have satisfaction, my dear."

His mouth covered hers as he kissed her over and over again. When he started to moan, her hands flew to his chest, and she weakly tried to push him away.

"I beg of you to wait a moment. I am not ready. I don't know how to…What, what if the servants hear?"

Charles moved down from her face, holding one of her legs up as he slowly pressed his lips to her calf. She looked away in distress. He parted her legs and leaned over her. The uncanny feeling of air in strange places unsettled her even more.

"Then they'll know I'm making love to my wife," he said, his hot breath in her ear.

He moved her further up the bed, kissing her lips and neck.

"No, perhaps we could wait for—"

"I have waited to have you long enough, and I am not a patient man."

And then she felt it. A sudden strike of heat and pain. Eliza lay there, still unsure of what she was supposed to do. Her hands awkwardly clutched him as he rocked her back and forth. She winced from the pain. She didn't know where to look. She felt ridged lines along his shoulders and moved her hands to the small of his back, where his skin felt smoother. He was staring at her face. It was too intense for her. The silence was deafening, broken only by his excited breaths.

"Wrap your legs around me, Eliza," he said, pulling on her thigh. She did as he requested, then regretted it instantly. He moaned again, and she could feel the throbbing pain even deeper. She tried to breathe to calm herself and turned to look at anything besides his face hovering above hers. Her eyes focused on the lines of the wall.

His hand brought her head back to his so he could kiss her. She could taste the wine they had just been drinking. Their bodies repeated the same movements for what seemed like an eternity. Her panic increased as she realized she did not know how long such an affair was meant to last, and she could not bear another moment with him on top of her. She felt as though she could not breathe. His body was now wet with sweat from exertion. She wanted him to stop; it was too painful. He pushed into her even harder, crying out. And then he was done.

He said nothing as he pulled out. Charles moved to the other side of the bed. Eliza wished the mattress was larger than it was. Then heat flooded her face as she realized he had never been interested in her conversation. He had just wanted her body. She had always known it was wise to hide her figure and understood that men coveted a woman's curves. But until this moment, she had never truly understood why. She felt nauseous and incredibly stupid. Her mind flashed back to the night the officer on board the ship had coyly suggested she look for books inside his cabin. Now she understood his true intent. And that of her husband.

He was asleep and completely oblivious to her horror. He was just like every other man. He was simply better at hiding his intentions. He had eagerly listened to every word she uttered tonight with one intention only. New pain flooded her thighs as soreness began to take hold. Charles started to snore as he fell into a deeper sleep. She felt terribly alone and scared, with only the flickering candles in the branch present with her. Her pulse throbbed in her ears, her vision was blurred, and she could not stop her body from shaking.

She rose slowly, watching the door with the unsettling fear that it could open at any moment. She desperately wanted to cover herself. She had a fresh shift in her trunk in the other room, but it seemed so far away. And she couldn't return to the dress she had worn before. Looking at it crumpled on the floor in a sad heap, she could see he had torn it when he had taken it off.

And then she felt a cascading warmth seep down her thighs. She panicked, shoving her shift between her legs to stop the flow while she desperately looked for a chamber pot. She tried to squat next to the bed, her back turned to him. He remained fast asleep. When she was done, she dropped the soiled fabric in disgust. Horrified that she had lost the one security she possibly had left, Eliza covered herself with her hands and slipped under the sheet as far away from his warm body as possible.

She watched the silhouettes of unfamiliar furniture moving in the wavering light. The room seemed to be spinning, and the air appeared smoky in the darkness. The fact that he had fallen asleep on top of the sheets brought her a slight amount of comfort. She knew it was irrational, but the fabric seemed to be a barrier between him and her. He had not even bothered to cover himself. His naked body was a painful reminder of what had just transpired, and she instead focused her gaze on a stain on the bedside table.

A pale blue glow ebbed from underneath the closed shutters into the room. Morning was soon approaching. Strange birds began to sing to one another. Eliza lay there, hardly moving. She was as still as the bed itself. Her eyes gazed at the ceiling, growing watery as tears spilled down her face. They were sore and overtired from the tumult of thoughts that had passed through her weary mind, her raw emotions seemingly worse than any physical discomfort. A damp spot had stayed between her legs all night, its refusal to dry made worse by the pressing humidity.

She tried to shift her body to stretch. The heavy weight of shame sat on her chest. Her breath came out sharply once, stirring her husband. Without turning to look at him, she could tell he was awake. She felt his hand brush the tears off her face, then rest upon hers. She jerked her arm away.

"I know you must miss home, but those feelings will subside," he said in a soft voice, "eventually."

Eliza didn't want to answer but knew she should say something in return. The quiet between them was awkward. The urge to act as she assumed a wife should gnawed at her.

"I am sorry if I did something wrong last night…"

She halted her speech. That was not something she was trying to draw attention to.

Charles sat up and suddenly leaned over her. His long tawny hair spilled over his shoulders; he effortlessly joined her under the sheet. The heat of his body next to her again made her stiffen up.

"Wrong?" he asked, his voice sounding alarmed. His green eyes roamed over her face as he looked at her without truly seeing her. "My dear, you are exquisite."

She was about to flee from the bed when she felt him come back into her, stronger than the last time. He scooped her up by the waist and repositioned her. The bed frame began its awful creaking rhythm. She was horribly aware of how she must have appeared—much like the dead fish sold at the market in town. She refused to look into his eyes, preferring to study the cracks in the wall next to her instead.

She could only think to cry again, but the pain between her legs caused a sobering effect. Eliza wondered if this would be satisfactory. Did a husband prefer his lust to be met with passion, or was merely satisfying that lust enough? Either way, her tears were horribly misinterpreted. They were clearly of no use with him. Her feelings were cast down from a place of genuine sorrow to the mere follies and weakness naturally ascribed to women.

Charles said no other words. It was as if he was not thoroughly awake and was driven only by his bodily sensations. He seemed content with the way things were. The polished gentleman and all decency seemed to have walked out the door when they had gone upstairs last night. Her thrilling journey over the Atlantic felt like nothing compared to the rude awakening of what exactly the gold band on her finger signified.

A few rough jabs later and he was finished. He rolled off her and squeezed her hand. She drew the sheet back over her body, the starched fabric feeling hard and stiff against her bare skin. She was disgusted by the fresh wetness gathering below her hips. She moved her hand away from his.

A few moments later, Charles was out of bed, getting dressed and prepared for the day. She shifted her body in discomfort, wondering if it was appropriate for her to run back to her room. She received her opportunity a little later when he left, and she bolted back to the room where the servants had placed her trunks. She sat down on her bed, her inner thighs aching from the strain. In the morning sunlight, Pleasant Hall seemed a more forgiving place. But she could not forget what had occurred, no matter how hard she tried.

Now she began to cry in earnest, wondering if this was how her life would be every day as a wife. She felt incredibly foolish. She wondered if the tumult of emotions she felt would ever subside. Had she made a mistake? Had she really had any choice in the matter? She was never supposed to be transplanted here, thousands of miles away from England. But here she was. Alone, confused, and scared of her future. But she wasn't alone for long.

Cleo burst into the room with a wide basket at her hips, humming a tune.

"Lady Sharpe! What are you doing here at this hour? Why are you not staying in Lord Sharpe's room? That room is bigger and brighter. That is where I would be."

The woman had a foreign accent with a cadence that added a soothing rhythm to every word that passed from her lips.

"Because this room is the one thing that's mine," Eliza replied, wiping away a tear.

"Why have you been crying? You can tell me now. I will listen."

Cleo looked at the way she was sitting on the bed.

"Oh, Miss Ellie…it will be all right," Cleo said softly as she sat down next to her. "Dear, it will be all right. It is just the first time. It will get better. It is just the first time."

"I can't do that every day. I cannot."

"It will hurt in the beginning. If you want, I can make something for you. Some strong herbs that can help you there. I can make any kind of tea you need. It never hurts to drink a little fevergrass tea."

Eliza's stony face remained the same.

"Or are you worried about something else, miss? Come now, Miss Ellie. I am going to call you that because I will treat you like no one else treats you. You can tell me."

"I do not love him," she said, her voice cracking.

"There, there, it is going to be fine. Lots of wives do not love their husbands. Same goes for husbands and their wives. Sometimes two people grow in love. Other times they do not. What matters is that they take care of you, buy you the things you need, and keep a roof over your head. That is what counts. And you did a fine job of that, marrying Lord Sharpe, Miss Ellie."

CHAPTER IV.

I t was only her second day on the island, and her
mind was rapidly trying to keep track of all the
changes happening around her. She left the
darkness of the cool house, heavy with the smell of damp
wood and neglected furniture, and stepped out into the
blinding white sands of the beach, mesmerized by the
strange tropic beauty around her.

She passed an old rubber tree on her way to the shore,
its massive trunk intertwined with the sprawling limbs of a
neighboring seagrape tree and its colorful round green
leaves. A clump of ivy and violet bougainvillea flowed
from the entangled timber. Next to it stood a thin but
sprightly magnolia tree with enormous finger-like foliage
and white saucer blossoms. She recalled that it had been
gifted by distant relations in the Carolinas when the
Sharpes had first arrived in the Bahamas. Charles had
mentioned his surprise that the tree tolerated the island's
climate, as specimens like it did not naturally occur here.
She wondered what properties enabled the tree to flourish.
Behind her, she faintly heard a male voice and the sounds

of a machete hacking back growth from around another tree.

She continued walking until she saw iguanas gathered further down shore to her left, congregating near a sea almond tree whose limbs were curved like the weaves in a basket. The reptiles stood motionless, like dark prehistoric statues with serrated ridges on their spines and pink-flushed necks, watching her walk with only the slits of their eyes open. One iguana was in the tree, struggling with sluggish limbs to reach appealing leaves. She wanted to explore the property and examine every plant and animal, but it would have to wait. She needed to quiet the pathos of her mind, and for that purpose, she continued walking until she reached the water.

Yesterday she had seen exceptional, wondrous beauty; today she could not help but feel a lingering sadness that seemed to permeate the land around her. The island was beautiful because it was wild, but there were forces at play that sought to tame it and conquer it, and she could not soothe this heavy impression away from her mind.

It was startling to behold the warm water's vivid hue in the sharp morning light. It lapped gently at her feet as Eliza stood there, gazing northward at the horizon, deep in thought. Her limbs were covered in welts from insect bites, and her body ached with a horrible tension that ran from her thighs to below her ribcage, wrapping around her back. But if she stayed very still, the gnawing pain almost seemed to disappear.

A larger wave came into shore, and the water rose above her calves, wetting her skirt. It was surprising and uninvited but not altogether unpleasant, and with her skirt already wet, she proceeded to step further into the sea. The soft pulsating movement of the water enveloped her legs and beckoned her mind into a soothing quiet.

Her thoughts had been consumed with creating lists of information to mollify the questions that endlessly piled up in her mind. She wanted to know when the tides came and went on this part of the island and what types of fish could be found in the water. Eliza observed the lack of current on this beach and wondered what accounted for its seemingly glassy appearance. She had already witnessed three distinct changes to the sea as the sun had risen, and she wondered what new hues could be discerned in the afternoon. She desperately wanted a set of watercolor paints to capture the intensity of the endlessly shifting shades of blue before her.

But threatening to smother all her mindless distractions were the emotions she was trying to evade. There was a tightness in her chest that owed nothing to her physical pain, and if she fixated on it for even a minute, she knew it would consume her already fragile self-composure. What weighed most heavily on her mind was last night and what had occurred. What *he* had done.

She had tried not to think about it. But she had also failed a dozen times. Now in the water, where it was so serene and still, the events of last night rang loudest in her mind. The more she thought about it, the biting edge of a cold, unfortunate reality interrupted any other reflections. There was no one to blame except herself. She had said yes to this stranger. She had accepted his offer. And finally, she had trusted him.

In her heart, she couldn't ignore her foolishness. She had dodged all the other men and their superficial demonstrations for years. She had so clearly and keenly seen them for what they truly were. But she had been captivated by Charles and his offer of a much different life. In truth, it had been this island and the voyage here, and not the man, that she had been bewitched by. She would have been drawn to live in any other place as long as that journey allowed her to take leave of her home. A land's allure subsisted on its foreign mystery and its seductive peculiarity. She had yearned to experience movement, to understand what it felt like to travel to a different place, to leave behind everything she knew.

Eliza craved freedom and a distinct break from her childhood. The latter had certainly been crudely accomplished last night. But now it seemed the changes she had so desperately sought only curbed her freedoms further still. Above all, her appetite for adventure was decidedly not satisfied. Seeing what she had the last few weeks only whetted her hunger to explore even more parts of the world. It now seemed to her like she had been duped. She would not continue to travel onwards; she would not even visit other nearby colonies. She was planted here and would remain here with a man she did not love until she breathed her last breath.

She questioned if it was all worth it. Eliza would most likely never see her family again. Everything familiar, despite its tired monotony, had been ripped away from her. And she knew the cruel deed had been done by her own hands. She had accepted Charles' offer of marriage. She had stepped onto the ship in the Portsmouth dockyard. She had thought of nothing but her new beginnings as she looked outwards to the sea every day thereafter and eagerly stepped onto the dock in Nassau harbor. Eliza had accepted drink after drink, despite never consuming so much liquor in all her life. She had known better. She had known that giddy excitement, impatience, and alcohol did not portend a wise starting point. What else should she have expected from her first night here? What other reception should she have expected from a stranger?

And most of all, she had been weak. She could have spoken to him more strongly. The voice in her mind that now rang out with piercing warnings had been silent when it had happened. She could have moved away from him sooner. She could have pushed away his advances. She had willingly followed him up the stairs and into his room. She could have told him her thoughts more clearly.

Eliza could debate the worthiness of Rousseau at any time, but she could not speak the concerns of her own mind. She could not fight for herself when the need arose. And this fact alone made her feel like an abject failure. She did not understand the workings of her own body or what exactly made her a woman and him a man. Knowing that the knowledge she prided herself on towards nearly every other subject actually held an egregious hole when it came to more instinctual matters made her feel ashamed.

Eliza had never realized that the simple vows she had uttered in the church that day would be so bitterly painful to uphold.

"Wilt thou obey him, serve him, love, honor and keep him in sickness and in health, and forsaking all others, keep thee only unto him, so long as ye both shall live?"

She had stupidly said yes, a mere girl, wholly ignorant of any implications. But after what had transpired last night, she knew she could not summon the will to maintain a single one of those precepts. Indeed, she refused to. And yet what troubled her even more was the dreadful idea that there simply could not be a solution. Her hardship would be permanent. She had eagerly charged forward, blinded to any risks, yearning to seize the future, and had instead struck against an immovable wall.

What information she could retrieve concerning the female anatomy was inconsequential. That innocence had already been lost and could never be recovered. She had tried to express her concerns, but they had mattered little to him. He had quickly assumed her tears and sadness this morning belonged to another variety and brusquely pushed them aside. It appeared that something was lacking in their communications, but she did not know how to resolve it.

What frightened her the most was that she had little to no understanding of the man she called her husband. She had observed him for weeks, arriving at a base conception of how he operated, only to have it all turned on its head the minute they were finally in seclusion. Seclusion. Isolation. How else could their arrangement be described? She was marooned here, thousands of miles away from any family or acquaintance, and the prospects of cultivating new friendships appeared bleak. She was not used to a house that was so unsettlingly quiet. Bleinhill Manor possessed a massive sandstone form, but it was nearly impossible to find any corner of privacy. She had known this all too well as she had grown older. Here, she almost felt that if she drowned or the ocean suddenly swept her off her feet and carried her away, no one would notice. It was just her and the sea.

And it was beautiful, devastatingly beautiful. She swirled a hand in the sparkling crystalline water, a tear streaming down her face. How could one feel so much pain in a paradise like this? Tiny silvery fish darted between her feet. She nearly jumped from their unexpected closeness, but she was also intrigued. What else lay under the surface of the waves? She could not swim, but the natural buoyancy she already felt the further she crept into the expanse of blue only reassured her. Eliza had never wanted to go into the oceans of England, but this sea before her was an entirely different matter. The white powdery sand she stepped across felt like the finest of silks. A rush of warmth from the current came and went, reminding her of water from a bathing tub. The seas she was used to were dark and dingy; their water was cold and bracing, and their shores were lined with discarded seaweed and pebbles. It seemed nothing but a home for fish. But this ocean was a different world.

The water was now up to her waist, a creeping warmth that ebbed and flowed around her body. She turned to look back at the house, satisfied that the scene remained much the same. No one was looking, and no one was watching her every move. With intrepidity and perhaps a sliver of morbid curiosity, she stepped further until she felt her feet slide off a sandbank and into much deeper water.

Eliza instantly panicked and reached her arms outward, only to find that the water was holding her and that she was floating. She had an impulse to kick her legs and felt herself rise further. Marveling at her discovery, she laughed and turned again to look at the house. She assumed Charles would not like her swimming like this, but her profound distaste for him was only growing. Her satisfaction with her newfound activity increased with the realization that it was outside the bounds of decency. But perhaps decency was only a factor in the presence of others, and she was certainly alone.

A wave came, and she felt her body curl inward until she was on her back, watching her outstretched legs as she nimbly glided over the crest. Fascinated by how her body felt suspended in the water, she moved around and turned to her stomach. A dark shadow approached ahead of her, and she watched it cautiously, swimming back to more shallow water. Then she realized it was nothing but a mass of coral. The gentle resistance of the water around her caressed every inch of her body and seemed to slow her mind.

Now she focused solely on the sea and how it made her feel. Eliza floated on her stomach, stretching her limbs out and reveling in how she could expand her body. Her skirt felt airy and hovered around her skin. The tightness and pain she had felt only moments ago had vanished. She felt the water flow around her, and as she moved, every part of herself seemed to melt into a soft stretch. She had been weighed down by the burdens of all her troubles on the shore, but here in the shimmering waters, she was utterly weightless. There was silence surrounding her, yet the waves held their own timeless internal rhythm. A slow and steady beat from the earth's core rocked and carried her. She understood from her books that the moon was responsible for the movement of the ocean's tides, but she had never felt more grounded and more present with her environment.

She lay there floating, wholly ignorant of the time, save for the slow pacing of the sun as it descended. Slightly bigger fish swam by in lines around her, appearing wary of her if she stirred. She marveled at the tiny outlines of rainbows that danced on the sand floor beneath her and how they instantly disappeared if the sun went behind a cloud. Her favorite moment was when the sun returned, and the ocean shimmered with an intensity that defied reality. She had never seen a sea quite like this. As the ship had approached land, she had watched with anticipation as the water grew more transparent and intense in its glowing hue. But her new home surely held the world's most beautiful waters. Rising from the dim light of the deck below, she had to shield her eyes the first time she had seen it. From her understanding, the startling electric blue grew brighter and expanded the further south one traveled.

She thought it an abject shame that swimming for ladies was frowned upon by society, but as with most things society dictated, she didn't give a damn. She understood some of the concerns. The locals stayed clear of the water unless they were wracking or diving for sponges. There were dangers to be found in this sea, but with a feeling she could not explain, she felt nothing but comfort and serenity. She bobbed there, musing about sharks and other nefarious creatures, yet felt they were barred from entering her secret cove. She felt safe in the water and realized with slight apprehension that the same was not true on land.

The dismay came from the realization that she would need to leave the water at some point and return to the house as evening steadily approached. And most concerning was that he would arrive home soon. She closed her eyes to the world, letting the waves rock her uneasiness away.

The sun was setting, casting a blazing fire across the rippling surface. She basked in its warmth as the waves rocked her. Then she felt a whoosh of a cold current beneath her. A series of different fish spurted by. The clarity of this sea astounded her. It was as if the surface of the water was glass. She could clearly see their eyes and beautiful yellow and black markings. And then she saw what they were hurrying away from. A dark-gray fish with lifeless yellow eyes glided slowly by her, its body like a thick snake. Its menacing mouth was slightly open, revealing sharp teeth; it was easily one of the biggest fish she had seen. She froze in the water as she watched it disappear feet away from her. When she lost sight of it, she became afraid and dashed back to shore, swimming and then running and tripping in her skirt.

Once she was in the shallows, she bowed her head and laughed. A group of iguanas had watched the spectacle and darted away into the undergrowth. She sighed. From this vantage point, the sea still held its seductive tranquility. She would do well to remember that the bigger fish came out at night. She was still a newcomer to this territory, and the saltwater world before her was not her own, despite how quickly she felt herself acclimatize to it. She had seen a small library in the house and decided to look for a naturalist guide. Maybe one of the servants would know what fish she had seen.

Eliza wrung out her skirt, her calves caked in the fine sand. On dry land, it became an awkwardly heavy and ill-fitting piece of fabric, so she tied it into a knot against the side of her legs. She began walking up the sand dune that ascended to the house when she saw two horses tied to the post. The men they belonged to were further ahead, standing on the porch. One turned to look at her, but she couldn't see them very well from the sun's reflection. Eliza knew she shouldn't be seen in her stays and skirt the way she was, so she looked down and rushed towards the back of the house. Once she was in privacy again, she walked more slowly, enjoying how soft and relaxed her body felt.

Cleo was on the back porch sweeping alongside the servant girl with strange eyes. She looked up and smiled at her, but Celia kept her glance downward, her brush strokes more agitated as Eliza approached.

"Don't think you can come up here and track that damn sand all over this house," Celia muttered under her breath as she passed her.

Eliza stopped, unsure if she had heard her correctly. She looked down and saw immediate confirmation of swirls of sand upon the porch beams.

"I'm sorry. Maybe if you could arrange some kind of washing bowl out here so I can clean my feet before stepping into the house, I think—"

"Oh, that won't be necessary, Miss Ellie. Not necessary at all," Cleo said, butting into the conversation.

"I can see it is rather difficult to get off," Eliza said, examining her calf. "It sticks to one's skin. I don't want to make your chores more tedious. I think the bowl would be the best solution."

Cleo nodded.

"If that is what you would like, Miss Ellie, I can arrange for a pail to be set out here in the back. This is your home now. If you need anything, anything at all, let me know," Cleo replied with a smile.

Eliza looked towards Celia, who continued her impassioned cleaning. She thanked them and went inside, but their voices were still audible.

"It would not hurt to show a little kindness, Celia. This is all new to her, and knowing how Lord Sharpe is, she's probably hungry for a friendly face. Poor girl is nearly the same age as you," Cleo said to Celia.

"Don't think I haven't noticed."

There was a boom on the deck as her broom slammed down, and a series of footsteps rushed down the porch stairs.

Freshened up, Eliza sat down with some awkwardness due to the pain in her thighs and waited patiently for Charles to join her at the table. She hadn't felt its intensity for some hours, but now her muscle tension began to return as the evening cooled slightly. The stiff hardness of the chair frame did not help matters. Heavy boots clacked down the stairs, and she rose from her seat. The brass buttons on his scarlet jacket gleamed in the candlelight as he swept into the room. He paused briefly to kiss her hand, and they sat down.

"Pleasant Hall is treating you well, Eliza. You have a certain glow about you," Charles said, observing her.

Lucy, the serving girl, placed a steaming bowl in front of her, and Eliza thanked her.

"My pleasure," she replied.

She then placed a bowl in front of Charles. He said nothing.

"My pleasure," Lucy said again.

"Yes, I was in the water today, and it was delightful," Eliza remarked.

"Yes, it can be refreshing," he said as he plunged a spoon into his pepperpot stew. "Only do not make it a habit."

"May I have more water, please?" Eliza asked.

She gazed at the glass candle holder placed directly in front of her plate while she waited.

"Yes, my pleasure," Lucy said brightly. "Do you like the candle holders, Lady Sharpe? Brutus recovered them from a wreck a few weeks ago, and he was keen on selling them, only I said no, we should use them in the house for your enjoyment, Lady Sharpe. I figured it would be better than the ordinary silver ones we used to use now that there's a lady in the house again."

She prattled on as she filled the glass, nearly spilling it over. Eliza smiled and nodded, sensing that the young girl was anxious about their new presence.

"My pleasure."

"To heavens, Lucy, must you say that no matter what you do at the table? And do not speak unless spoken to!" Charles snapped.

Lucy stopped, slowly lowering the pitcher. Her mouth hung open, sensing she had erred.

"She is simply nervous. She has likely never served guests here. Am I correct in that assumption, Lucy?"

Eliza smiled, confident that she had smoothed over any tension. But Charles was glaring at her once more.

"Do not speak to her. One should act like she is simply not there."

His acerbity caused Eliza to drop her spoon. It clattered to the floor. Lucy bent down to grab it and rushed back with a replacement.

"Forgive me. Thank you," Eliza said to Lucy, ignoring Charles' sour mood.

"My pleasure, my pleasure, Lady Sharpe."

"Goddammit, Lucy!" Charles' fist slammed down on the table. "Go! Go to the kitchen. See if you are required there. Leave us."

Lucy nodded, her eyes wide in fear. She dashed out of the room, her small steps pattering down the empty hallway.

Charles shook his head, clutching his temples with a hand.

"Forgive my temper. I have had a trying day at the fort."

Eliza said nothing and stared down at her soup. She hesitatingly swirled the fresh spoon around the vegetables in her bowl, uncertain about what she was eating. The food in this colony was vastly different from what she was used to. There seemed to be little poultry and beef, and far too much seafood for her taste. She feared she would lose weight rapidly. She was also unsure if this was the first or the only course.

She reached for the bread. She remembered how delicious it had tasted in her exhaustion yesterday. Chewing on it for a second time, she confirmed her observations. The crude stone oven it was prepared in must have accounted for the taste. She savored it, briefly looking in Charles' direction. Silence surrounded them for several minutes, and then he looked up at her abruptly.

"You say you went into the sea? Today? I didn't realize you could swim."

"Yes, that is what I said. It was so unexpectedly soothing," she replied quietly.

"I do not think it is a good idea to go in these waters."

"But surely, the reef farther out acts like a barrier to any dangerous fish?"

"It is not seemly for a woman to swim, my dear. Especially for a refined woman. It is just not done."

He continued to eat ravenously, requesting a second portion. He called out Lucy's name, mumbling at her lengthy disappearance. He tore apart some bread while he waited.

"Ladies of our class take to the waters at Bath—" Eliza countered.

"That is for health purposes and not the open water."

"And at Brighton, or so I've heard. That is the ocean…" she continued.

"Those women are there because their doctors advised them so. What health concerns do you have? You are a bright and vivacious creature. I can testify to that."

He placed a hand on her arm, which she promptly withdrew.

"It is stunningly beautiful. I have never seen waters like these."

"Yes, stunningly beautiful and deadly. We have currents that could carry you straight to Cuba. Make no mistake, my dear," he said between bites.

"I felt no current when I swam. Nothing but gentle waves."

Her reply went unanswered as he continued to scoff down food. She awkwardly swirled her wine, wondering if most of their meals would be ensconced with silence.

"Tell me, how did you occupy your day, Eliza? Have you let the servants unpack your belongings? Have you used the sewing table in the parlor? I've been told this lighting is magnificent for needlework. Perhaps you started some embroidery…"

"I walked around the grounds for a bit. And then I was in the water, as I've told you."

She dared to look at him; his sharp green eyes were fixated on her.

"All day?" he ridiculed. "Surely not."

"For some hours, I wager," she replied, looking off to the side.

"You must equip yourself with some measure of industry. You cannot swim all day. Soon you will have a routine and command over the household duties. You can review the task list and supervise the servants' work. I have not been here in years, so they have mostly been left to their own devices. They are not used to having a proper lady of the house, as you can plainly witness tonight."

"Oh, I see…but your father surely ran the household while he was alive?"

Charles looked at her with scrutiny.

"Towards the end, he was…er, ill. Quite ill. Cleo has been tasked with the management of Pleasant Hall. The place hasn't burned down yet, but I am sure with a lady's presence, slight adjustments to detail will surely be made."

"I see no room for such adjustments. I find she manages it perfectly. The house is immaculate," Eliza said reassuringly.

"My dear," he said, taking her hand. "Surely, you misunderstand. It is not Cleo's job to manage this house. It is *yours*. Only you have the requisite standards and bearing to understand what makes a house a great estate. Cleo is not without fault. You will need to chastise her when she makes certain errors to ensure the plantation runs smoothly. That is your occupation now. Indeed, you should have corrected Lucy earlier. She needs to be more discerning, especially if we are to entertain guests. I cannot be present all day, so you will command the house when I am away. Besides, what other diversions would a lady of your standing choose to fill their time with? You surely cannot fill your days with swimming."

Eliza presented a forced smile and dutifully nodded, deciding then that she would *only* fill her days with swimming. He hadn't forbidden her to do so. She was grateful Cleo managed the house so well; a man like Charles could hardly be bothered to tell the difference between her oversight and that of Cleo's. Eliza knew of many estates where the principal servants truly ran the households, with the great lords and ladies residing inside hardly knowing where the true balance of power stood.

Reassured with her plan, Eliza rested easier against the chair as he began to drone on about his regiment and his day at the fort. His complaints about the weaknesses of the recruits, their inability to follow simple commands, and his subsequent frustration were now affecting her patience. It was then that she understood the value of silence.

The old bell rang in the front yard, signaling that Lieutenant Colonel Sharpe had returned. Swallowing her dread, Eliza made her way down the stairs. She had watched Lucy help him undress every evening last week, and he had remarked that he wished for her to do the same now since they were married. She had acquiesced, though she regretted being agreeable to anything he wanted. Charles entered in a flurry, barely looking at her. The sheath of his saber clacked as he walked to the end of the hallway where the sideboard filled with household silver stood. She was grateful for his indifference. The less interaction she had with him, the more peaceful her evening would be.

Eliza curtsied and held out her hands as he handed his tight jacket to her. The wool was damp with sweat. She found the hook she had seen it hung on before. Next, he sat in a chair, removed his saber, and gave it to her, but the weight of it surprised her, and she dropped it. It clattered loudly on the polished hardwood floor.

As she reached down to retrieve it, Charles grabbed her and sat her on his lap. She stopped trying to retrieve the sword, wholly unsure of what to do. Then he began to move her hips in small, slow circles, rubbing her against his legs. He grunted; she could feel his breath on her neck.

"I could think of nothing but you all…day…long…" he said in her ear.

He toyed with a loose curl on the side of her face. She didn't know how to respond to him, so she said nothing. The innocence that had been robbed from her since her arrival and her newfound knowledge did not ease matters. This man only made her feel small. She tensed up and closed her eyes. Time crept uncomfortably on, and then he released her, and she sprang up. He smiled and finished removing his other articles, including his holster and pistol. She was distressed that his attention was fixed solely on her now, and she had the uncanny sensation that he was taunting her.

She realized he was staring at her, but when she looked up at him, his gaze did not flinch. It was constant and predatory. Her mind was racing with thoughts of escape as her feet rushed to retreat. She tried to move out of his way, but he blocked her and then took two slow steps toward her, driving her back to the wall. Charles took her by the chin and kissed her deeply.

"I would have you kiss me," he said as he pulled away, his eyes searching hers. The light-green shade she usually saw had turned darker, and the blackness of his pupils was enlarged. She had once thought his eyes beautiful, but now she knew she could not trust them. His eyes seemed to shift and alter according to his mood, and now they seemed to threaten danger.

Eliza looked to the side for a moment, bracing herself, and reached for him and kissed him, but she felt him part her lips with his tongue. She instinctively withdrew from him, but he would not move away. He shifted her whole body as he kissed her. She gasped to take in the air. Charles hoisted her skirts up and to the side and undid his breeches in one rapid move. He roughly parted her legs with a knee and struggled to achieve his aim. She felt him drive himself deep inside her, letting out a muffled moan. She grimaced in pain, her body tensing up.

The friction of their bodies seemed to increase his pleasure. He was breathing loudly in sharp and broken fragments. Heat flooded her face with embarrassment. They were out in the open, in the hallway. She felt stupid for assuming that her marital duties could be confined to one room, but surely this was not proper. She closed her eyes as he thrust harder. Each move felt like a blade; her eyes drifted to the golden saber lying passively off to the side. She gripped the top of the sideboard, her knuckles turning white.

Charles leaned over her right shoulder and continued to drive into her with short, jagged movements. He clenched her upper arms to steady her at one point. Her body was wracked with pain as she endured another assault. The buttons from his buckskin breeches dug into her thighs. Eliza opened her eyes to see a servant walk past the opening that led to the southern part of the house. The woman did not realize what was happening at first, but then her eyes grew wide, and she hurried away. Eliza fixed her gaze on the ceiling above them in shame.

The clock seemed to tick slower and slower. Each beat marched in time with his exertions. She watched one clock hand torturously arc upwards, but its slow pace made her feel more panicked. Time dragged on slowly and without mercy. Eliza did not think her face could get any hotter. Her ears burned, and she knew she was red in her cheeks. She had never felt hatred towards another person, but now she could think of no other name for the fire burning inside her. His breathing grew louder. Each noise he made stiffened her frame up, and she waited in apprehension for someone else to walk in on them. After what seemed like a longer time than all the others, he finished and dropped his heavy head down on her breasts.

She tried to hide her expression. Her eyes were watery with the realization of what she had just gone through. Of what he had committed. Again. He was breathing heavily on her, tired from his endeavors. She strained her neck away from him.

"I could not restrain myself nor wait for a bed," Charles said with a laugh. "Such is your beauty, my dear. I have told you once before I think of little else."

Eliza swallowed and looked down at her scratched chest.

"Go upstairs and have Celia dress you. We are expected at the governor's tonight," he said as he sniffed and rubbed his nose.

Charles marched away from her, adjusting his breeches, his boots reverberating down the hall. Eliza remained there, her legs fixed in an awkward position, her lower body racked with pain. The abhorrent dribble was making its way down her leg once again, but this time she was prepared for its arrival. It had lasted nearly an entire day the time before, but a well-placed rag had seemed to remedy the worst of it.

The effects of that first night came vividly back into her mind. The pain, the embarrassment, the strange warmth, the smell, the incessant dripping. It was a nauseating business. She had understood marriage would upend certain liberties, but she had never anticipated how much misery it could cause. How repulsive she would find his touch. It was a natural enterprise, but to complete such acts with him only felt unnatural. She had always prided herself on knowledge, but it had never seemed more apparent that she knew little of her own biology. It only increased her humiliation.

Eliza had never known that one man could make her feel so worthless and devoid of hope. She could not understand the matter entirely but was certain of one thought: he had grievously wronged her, and she hated him for it.

The fading noise from his steps signaled it was safe to move, and she slowly made her way up the stairs. Each step reminded her of her new reality. She tried to force her tears to stop. She had to show a brave face to Celia. She knew she would judge her and show no compassion. It seemed as if her miserable encounters knew no end. She longed to be back on the ship, away from him, feeling the calm, steady peace that only traveling along the water's surface could bring.

Time passed around Eliza. Her clothes came off with Celia's nimble fingers. A damp cloth pressed against her skin in swirling motions up and down her body. When she was dry, Eliza stepped into a new skirt, keeping her arms lifted as Celia tightly laced her stays. Every move was like a silent dance, the routine of being female long and tedious. She carefully sat down in a chair, wincing. She briefly looked in the mirror, watching Celia gather the tools to finish her look. Her checkered headwrap seemed more tightly wound than usual. She didn't seem to be in a pleasant mood, but that did not mean much. Eliza had never witnessed any other emotion on her face.

Celia grabbed more hair and brushed it forcefully. Eliza sat quietly at first, and then a fresh wave of emotion overcame her. It was too much to bear. She felt the warmth of tears breaking over her cheeks and knew she could not hold back any longer. Her reflection in the mirror became distorted and grew wavy.

"You ain't got nothing to cry about," Celia said, her voice dismissive.

She lowered a pearl pendant around Eliza's neck, closing the necklace.

A few torturous minutes passed without remarks. Celia dabbed perfume on Eliza's chest, lined with tiny cuts from his fingernails.

"I don't think you understand, Celia."

Celia stopped and glared at her. She picked up the brush and went to style her hair once more. She pulled and twisted her dark curls.

"That hurts," Eliza said, turning. "That hurts!"

Celia slammed the brush down.

"You ain't got nothing to cry about!" she said louder.

This time there was no masking her malice. Eliza stood up, strength returning to her voice.

"Have I offended you in some way?"

Celia crossed her arms.

"No, my lady. You're the mistress of the house," she replied. "Which is why you ain't got a damn thing to cry about. Not now, not ever, unless—"

"I have had enough of your vitriol! I am requesting a new servant. One who knows their place! The audacity of you to speak to me in such a manner…"

"You ain't got the fire to do nothing about none of your problems. I seen you when you first got here. You ain't nothing but a lost girl in a woman's clothes."

"Leave!" Eliza said, raising her voice.

Celia barked out a laugh.

"You a fool," she said, folding up Eliza's worn clothes. She stopped, looking at the faint blood stains on the inner skirt. "Just a girl. Can't even get a man to fit inside you."

Eliza rushed at her, her face hot with shame and fury.

"Tell me what I need to do to make you go away," she said.

Celia lost her smile, a look of deviousness replacing her dark mirth.

"I have nothing but the clothes on my back and a long way to go to get where I need to be."

"Money? Money? Is this about money?" Eliza asked. "Here! My peace is worth more than this trinket." She removed the necklace and handed it to her.

Celia looked at her incredulously.

"I ain't allowed to take this," she said, her huge yellow-colored eyes darting from Eliza to the necklace, then back again.

"You have my permission. You are free to leave. Take that. Sell it. Leave tonight!"

Celia dropped the necklace down her top and rushed out of the room with the soiled skirt.

After an exceptionally long and tiring meal filled with even fewer entertaining conversations, Eliza followed Charlotte into a smaller room, where a gilded birdcage hung in the corner between two open windows. Two small birds sat on a red-painted swing. The rustling of the palm trees outside nearly sounded like rain, but by now, Eliza knew better. It was simply the wind rattling the dried leaves. Eliza sat in the seat Charlotte offered her and arranged her skirts meticulously, more out of awkwardness than concern for her appearance.

"Oh, thank you, Lady Dunmore," Eliza started, aware that such a private conversation signaled favor in Charlotte's eyes.

"Charlotte will do," she replied with a frosted smile.

An uncomfortable moment of silence lingered between them, and Eliza felt pressed to speak.

"And how long have you been married to his lordship?" Eliza inquired.

Charlotte laughed suddenly, nearly spluttering the ratafia liqueur from her rouged lips. "How very charming," she said slowly, her cheeks flushed.

Charlotte focused her gaze on one of the windows.

"My apologies. I did not mean to cause offense," Eliza said solemnly.

Charlotte turned her head to observe her, a scrutinizing look in her eye.

"None taken, my dear. I have been with him for three years now."

Once again, the conversation withered between the two women. Raucous laughter and shouts sounded from the gentlemen in the main room.

"May I ask a question?" Eliza said.

Charlotte nodded.

"You must know since you have only recently been in such a situation yourself…must the marital duties be so very frequent?"

The moment she asked it, the vulnerability of her situation seemed almost too heavy a weight to bear. She felt her ears grow hot as she waited for almost certain ridicule.

"Well, you are indeed recently wed. It is to be expected. You must secure him an heir."

Now Eliza looked away to the window, attempting to mask her reaction. What if she was already carrying his child? She felt a cold, bony hand press hers. It did little to relieve her terror.

"But here is the lesson, my child," Charlotte said with a wicked look. "Men are rulers of the bedchamber in name only. We possess what they crave; *we* have what they want."

Eliza could see in this light that Charlotte appeared only a decade older than her and found her patronizing tone unpleasant.

"I fear I do not understand."

Charlotte sipped her liqueur.

"You must make the situation work for you. I can see you are unschooled in the ways of men. They enjoy the hunt. You must make them chase you. You cannot simply lie there and have them dictate all the terms. That will not do. Otherwise, they can go to any woman to satisfy their urges. And this they *will* do. I assure you. It is simply inevitable."

A particularly loud jeer echoed throughout the house; Charles' deep voice was immediately recognizable.

"My lord, you cannot be serious!" he said.

"Mark me, I did not make poor decisions. It was simply set up that way! I do not feel shame!" Lord Dunmore's obnoxious voice boomed.

Charlotte and Eliza exchanged a smile and took a sip of their drinks.

"Are you suggesting there is a way to retain control in intimate friendships?" Eliza asked, moving closer to her so they could keep their words hushed.

"Naturally, my dear. That is how the world turns! You must never give any part of yourself for free. It is a trade. You are a merchant, and you must make your husband realize this. You are not any woman, and you will refuse to be treated as such. Whether it is for more control in the household, a new dress from Paris, or a bracelet perhaps," she said, gently shaking the dazzling diamonds on her wrist.

Eliza sighed.

"I am afraid none of that interests me. What if what I desire is more natural? More simple in nature?"

"Perhaps you should examine your desires more carefully. Lord Sharpe is no farmer, my child. And whilst he is from an established Conch family on this island, I can see he does not spurn all the revelry of our age, as that ilk generally tends to do. Most Conches are an entirely disagreeable lot. Besides, from what I've been told, he has quite the fortune backed behind his name. Take a dangerous bet on Pharaoh. Order all the styles when the dressmaker comes to your house. Do as you like! Let him worry about the consequences."

"I like...freedom," Eliza said wistfully.

"Oh. I see," Charlotte said, pressing a finger to her lips. "Well, there are many ways to curb your husband's appetite."

Eliza watched as a particularly large black mosquito landed on Charlotte's thin, pale arm, and she crushed it.

"Please tell me!" she whispered harshly.

Charlotte made a look of surprise at her desperate tone.

"He must learn to be patient. Have you really no idea how this works? Have you no sisters or cousins? My, my," Charlotte leaned forward, a gleam in her eye, as she brushed her fingers down Eliza's neck. "'Charles, I truly regret this, but I am simply exhausted from the day.'"

Her voice was slow and sensuous, and Eliza flinched from their proximity. But Charlotte continued with her masquerade.

"'I've decided to dedicate my evening to reading, dear husband. Tomorrow night I shall visit your bed...I have taken ill...for the week. But I trust I shall be ready for you very soon,'" she said and then whispered in Eliza's ear. "'I am aching with anticipation, my love.'"

She returned to her former position on the couch, looking quite pleased with her performance and seemingly entertained by Eliza's embarrassment. She sipped on her drink demurely.

"And saying something like that would work? Would he not see that I am healthy despite my protests and such lies?"

"You are not feigning the pox, you silly girl. I mean the affairs only a woman must deal with, my child. You know of what I speak. Men understand that most precipitously. It horrifies them. I daresay he'd leave you in peace for two weeks if he had cause to do so."

The more Eliza thought the idea over, the more relieved she began to feel. Something like a breath of hope filtered over her for the first time in two weeks.

"I see," Eliza replied, smiling to herself. "It was just so very distressing to me. But I thank you for your advice."

"Distressing? My God, child. Is Charles unskilled in that way?" Charlotte turned to face the other room, bobbing her head side to side to catch sight of him.

Eliza blushed wildly. She did not appreciate Charlotte calling him by his first name as if they were on familiar terms. She refused to answer her. Perhaps she was being too sensitive.

"He possesses quite the athletic build, and he is rather young for a man of fortune. I would have expected more of him," Charlotte said, eyeing his back as he stood up from his chair. "And a handsome frame if ever I saw one. Quite tall…and rather muscular…"

Eliza watched her inspect Charles and sat frozen, fearing any crosswind would carry the words within earshot of the party in the next room. Charlotte turned to face Eliza again.

"Oh, heavens! I've made you a mute. I am quite a forward woman, Eliza. Make no mistake about it. I simply meant to suggest that it is very surprising to hear this. But of course, if you do not find Lord Sharpe's lovemaking satisfactory, then there is only one possible solution to such a problem."

For a moment, Eliza considered that Charlotte's appraisal of her husband might prove detrimental, but then she inwardly recoiled. Any such worries only suggested envy on her part, and she refused to acknowledge any sentimentality towards him, even if another woman rushed into his arms. In fact, such a vision would make her happy if it meant securing some measure of peace.

"There is?"

"Yes! Of course! The only reasonable course is for you to take a lover!" Charlotte said.

Once again, such an utterance was much too loud for Eliza's security.

"No, no, you misunderstand me entirely," she said, mortified.

"Oh, do not let one sour apple ruin the basket. Surely, there is a man who can suit your fancy."

"Well, it is too late for that now. I am wed, and unfortunately so." Eliza looked down, her mind flooding with regret.

"Nonsense! This is precisely the time for it! You are freer now than you ever were as a single woman. No need for chaperones to monitor your every move. You have already been taken and are matched with a husband. You cannot possibly be debauched. Restrictions are loosened regarding the late hours a married woman may keep. Your last name speaks for you now, Lady *Sharpe*," Charlotte replied brightly as if she was discussing a needlework technique and not amorous affairs.

"My morals couldn't possibly allow it. I have taken solemn vows. I could never…" Eliza said firmly.

"Oh, that's the drivel of youth. Do you know not a single fashionable couple in London takes dinner together? This is simply the way of the world! You must open your eyes, my dear! Men think they hold power because they can command other men on the battlefield, but a single woman can turn the tide of war. Make no mistake! Look at Ellen of Troy!"

Eliza's first impulse was to laugh, but she feared insulting her.

"Forgive me, but do you mean to refer to Helen of Troy? That story did not end well for the woman or her lover."

"No difference. You overthink, my dear. This may indeed be the source of your discontent."

"And history, especially, has not been kind to Helen. Do you not realize how terribly she was hated?" Eliza said with dismay.

"Ah, yes, because with great beauty comes great resentment. I would know. The gossips will always wag their tongues, Eliza. You might as well do as you please in life, for it is so very short. Especially here on this island. There simply isn't the same selection of lovers that London boasts. Ah, what an awfully depraved city it can be, but one would hesitate to ever call it dull."

Eliza said nothing, emptying her ratafia. A servant came and refilled their drinks. The dainty glasses they used were much too small, and her tolerance of the conversation was rapidly drying up. She judged she would need another within a matter of minutes.

"Is there no one you can think of that might be interested?" Charlotte asked her, continuing the topic despite Eliza's unwillingness. "Perhaps it isn't due to his performance but to your seeming quite prudish. How can one enjoy themselves in the bedchamber if your only concern is propriety? '*What will society think?*' I can tell you now, there is simply no society on this island, child."

"He is a poor lover, and I scarcely believe he can satisfy anyone other than a whore, whose trade is to lie by profession," Eliza snapped.

Charlotte gasped at Eliza's sudden burst of invective.

"I would never have known! Remarkable! But there must be someone else that is more to your satisfaction. Has any other man approached you? You do appear quite the vision at times, with your dark hair and that waist. The ladies and I were talking after we left Christ Church last week. How do you maintain such a shape?"

Charlotte put her hands on Eliza's waist, padding at her sides.

"Heavens, your stays are barely tight! Ah, the favors of youth."

Eliza moved away from her, brushing her dress back into place. She didn't know whether to be thrilled to be the subject of such gossip or disappointed. She hadn't spent much time dwelling on what the other residents thought of her. And it was a small town. She was foolish to believe that her newly arrived presence had gone unnoticed. She had always pictured life on an island colony as a bustling one with a constant stream of new faces, but the reality was that once one stepped away from the port of Nassau, the stillness and isolation of those who lived on the island only compounded by the hour. Such idleness naturally produced spurious tongues.

"Now think, Eliza. Have any particular gentlemen frequented Pleasant Hall? Perhaps a clerk that comes twice a week instead of the one day he should? A friendly courier? Does Charles have any male companions? From the regiment, perhaps?"

"No, we hardly receive visitors except those on business ventures."

"Has any gentleman taken more than one opportunity to converse with you? Lingered a little too long in your company? Requested a word in private? Any friendly glances or small favors?" Charlotte continued.

"Well, there is Mr. Wells, the bookseller. The last time I saw him we had a delightful conversation about

Gibbon's books on the Roman Empire. And he even gave me a small book as a token of friendship," Eliza said, her eyes widening at her delayed realization.

"John Wells? The owner of the *Gazette*? The American Loyalist from Georgia? That Mr. Wells?"

"I believe he is from Charleston originally but had to relocate to east Florida before coming here. Yes, that Mr. Wells."

"The man is near approaching forty, is he not? He's older than Charles and not a pound richer. That simply will not do."

"But he owns so many beautiful books. And he is capable of getting the latest titles despite the difficulty in trade. And he writes the newspaper. He always has the latest information from around the world. He's rather informed."

"From what John divulges to him," Charlotte mocked, referencing Lord Dunmore.

"He told me he has his own sources. I didn't realize it at the time, but surely it is not common for a merchant to gift his goods to mere strangers," Eliza pondered aloud.

"And what book did he give you?" Charlotte asked, her intrigue rekindled.

"*Some Historical Account of Guinea…*"

Charlotte's disappointment was palatable.

"My dear, perhaps he was just clearing shelves."

"I must be mistaken then," Eliza said. "It's a fascinating book, and I am quite taken with it, but it is critical of what my husband does. I thought perhaps we shared an intimate displeasure of the slave trade."

"I absolutely abhor politics. That's all I hear from that one all day long," Charlotte whined, gesturing towards the governor.

"I suppose he had difficulty selling it on an island like this. It was a foolish idea to think it meant anything more," Eliza said.

Charlotte sighed and seemed to share in her discontent.

"I would have thought better of Lord Sharpe. His physique seemed…promising. Ah, well. To each their own. Shall we rejoin the men?" she asked, rising from the couch.

CHAPTER V.

E liza lay on the bed, the daytime noises around her slowly swirling into a soft monotone buzz of activity. She could faintly hear a slave outside singing something incomprehensible, his deep masculine voice rising in the sultry air.

Sleep descended over her in invisible sheets of warmth. The sensation was much more soothing than the constant assault of suppressing heat she would encounter were she to get up and start moving again. Some days the heat was so intense even the water did not cool her down. On an afternoon like this, she could only lie there and pretend the heat did not brush her skin with its blistering weight. Remaining perfectly still, she could begin to tolerate the searing temperature and even detect a light breeze off the water.

Falling deeper into a dream, she began to see a boy.

He is no older than seven, and he runs around the yard with a laugh. He has not a care in the world and does not understand the meaning of pain written on the dark faces of those who care for him. They watch over him, caring with a concern borne out of the desire to safeguard his childish innocence. A room appears, much like any other on this upstairs level, where the boy, a man, and a slave stand.

"He broke the china," the man says. "He must learn of his failing."

A voice, stern and cruel, emanates from the man. He grabs the boy and pushes him to the bed. The slave hesitates, holding a horsewhip, wanting to leave the scene but knowing he must obey.

"Five," the older man says.

He nods. A second command. If repeated once more, the punishment will be turned against him. The slave takes a step back and raises his arm, but the scene fades, and she sees the yard again.

The sun is lower now. The boy is older and closer to becoming a ma, but is halfway on the journey. He must be the son of an overseer. He moves with familiarity among the slaves and lacks the condescension of a higher class. The older man storms out onto the porch, his face grizzled with drink and age. He is the outsider. The disruptor. He stumbles to the dirt, wiping his mouth with a dirty sleeve.

"Tie him," he says, motioning towards the post in front of the almond tree.

The boy's face does not change. He understands the process. But a woman watching cannot bear the thought. She breaks rank, the other servants watching.

"Please," she pleads.

She must be connected to the boy in some way. Only she stands in front of the man no one dares to cross. He ignores her as if she is not even there. Two men remove the boy's shirt and tie him to the post.

"Thirty," the man says.

No one moves. One man drops the whip. He is silent, but his action is tremendously loud. It resounds across the yard. He is going against the order. But it will happen, even if the drunken old man must accomplish it himself.

He stumbles over, grabs the horsewhip, and strikes the back of the young man. Once, twice, the line of red grows darker and darker. The women look away; the men stare into nothingness. They have seen this many times before. The boy cries out, unable to remain stoic. Ten. His skin hangs down in strips, shredded, mutilated. Fifteen. He bows his knees, only the rope around his wrists supporting him. Twenty. All the women look away except the one who stood up to the old man. She watches him with fury in her eyes. The whip cracks again. She will not forget.

Eliza came to with a gasp. She felt an uneasiness in her stomach. Cold sweat dampened her pillow. Life at Pleasant Hall was beginning to make an impression on her mind, and it frightened her. It disturbed her to her core, to the point of feeling sick. She had read about trade on this side of the world, about slavery, but nothing described what it was really like.

She immediately thought she understood the meaning of the dream. The brother Charles hesitated to speak of. She struggled to remember how he had died, so little was he ever mentioned. But she knew one thing: he had not been content with life here. He had returned to England as an adult. And the woman that had looked at the scene so troubled by what she witnessed had looked like Cleo would have in her younger years. But she had never mentioned the brother either. Perhaps it was too painful. Eliza's mind was hazy with sleep and confusion. Then she realized she was not alone.

A servant stood by the foot of her bed, boldly watching her. Eliza had never seen her before. She was unfamiliar. She was probably one of the many faces she had glanced at when Charles had given her a tour of the property. She was young and attractive but appeared cunning. She reminded her of Celia, and she wondered if they were sisters.

"I am resting. I do not need anything," Eliza said, annoyance creeping into her tone.

It was incredibly rude to be there now. She had clearly sought privacy, yet it was so brazenly invaded. The servant stood there, not moving. Eliza wondered how long she had been there. She studied her red garment, noticing how dated it appeared. She was not dressed like the others; even her headwrap was crafted in such a unique way that it seemed to be derivative of her homeland. Small pewter hoop earrings hung from her ears. None of the other slaves wore jewelry. The style suited her, but Eliza's unease grew. Perhaps she didn't come into the house because she could not be properly presented. Her dress did not match the rest of the domestic staff. The woman did not speak, and her dark eyes did not flinch.

"You can leave, please," Eliza told her. "If I need something, I will call."

She shifted onto her side in the bed. But she still did not hear the woman leave. The stillness of the room was misleading. It could have appeared she was alone, but Eliza could still *feel* her there. Something was amiss. What else could she do? Her commands clearly fell on deaf ears.

She looked at the mirror, its dusty reflection revealing the front of the bedroom to the window. No one stood at the bed now. Eliza turned back, her frustration mounting. Yet, the servant was still standing there, watching her. And now she had stepped closer. The situation was growing awkward. The air hummed with a metallic ring, the silence between them seeming to protest against the noiseless space. Perhaps the woman was deaf. Or perhaps she could not properly speak English. But even the Creole slaves understood basic commands. What was she doing?

Then a darker thought crossed her mind. What if she was dressed differently because she had run away from another plantation and was there to steal from the house? It was the middle of the afternoon, and from the stillness around them, Eliza could tell that the rest of the house was empty. Perhaps this woman wanted her to feel fear. Maybe she had been sent as part of a larger group and tasked with watching Eliza. If Eliza did not protest, there was a chance that she could come away unscathed. Not knowing where to look, Eliza turned to the wall. She was growing more uncomfortable by the minute.

The mirror next to the bed loomed large and bright. It was impossible to not see its contents. She gazed into it again, leaning forward, and saw only herself in the room. She twisted back towards the door. The woman standing there, a few feet from her bed. Only now, she had shifted slightly, and a new feature had emerged in the slow curve of her neck. The side of her face was missing, a once round head sharply flattened off. Dark red blood mottled her amber skin.

Eliza's stomach sank. At first, there was emptiness, a frozen, unfeeling void where all time stopped for just a moment. And then her reaction sped up. She felt violated. She understood that she was awake, but the sight before her was too incredible to believe. This was not a dream. It was too tangible.

She felt jolted to a place of childhood fears, a return to the horror of seemingly impossible things, a time when terrifying creations of imagination lay just behind her shoulder or underneath her bed frame. When the adults would not believe the fantastic things she saw or heard in the great old house. But now, as a grown woman herself, she was terrified.

She should be alone in the room. And she was not. The servant before her would not answer because she could not answer. She was not truly there. The woman occupied space without truly filling it. Indeed, she was so apparent, so consisting of flesh and blood, that the first sight of her did not immediately raise alarm. Eliza had spoken to her and fully expected a response.

A chill descended her back. A combination of empiricism and a mirror's reflection had been the only things that revealed the woman's ruse. Then Eliza heard a noise, the shift of wood against wood and air being released. A door in the hallway opened, and with dread, she knew this sound was likewise unexplainable. A second noise issued from the abandoned hallway: an abrupt slam caused by the force of an unseen hand.

Eliza was familiar with the noise and now understood who was responsible for it. She had heard it often as she fell asleep or just before she woke. As was often the case concerning the tiniest details of dreams, the seemingly innocuous sound was often forgotten the more consciousness consumed her and the more the light ascended in the morning. But it had occurred now while she sat there tense and alarmingly awake. It astounded her that such a simple noise could be so very unsettling. Like the presence of this unnatural woman before her.

Trembling, Eliza tried to move, to flee, but she stayed, transfixed. As more and more matters fell away to the realm of the extraordinary, settling in the land of impossibility, her heart raged inside her. She felt betrayed by reason. She was desperate to escape but could not move. If she ran, she was only acknowledging the present danger. If she ran, she was decidedly not a woman but a being transported back to childhood, frightened by a harmless dream. But a dream this was not.

A strong breeze swept through the room, billowing the faded white curtains, and the woman was suddenly gone. The room felt lighter, brighter—a normal bedroom restored. Eliza's face turned pale, and she began to shake. She had taken a short nap, but her world had utterly changed in that brief span of time.

Now she fled, her feet barely touching the ground until she was safely outside in the sun, surrounded by other living people. The white wooden house appeared so different before her now, as if it yearned to moan and change its weight. The darkness she felt within its walls did not stem solely from the rough hands of her husband. It emanated from its very foundation. It was alive.

Eliza had been living in the new house for three weeks, but she could still feel the effects of her former cramped space on the ship. The strange dreams had come less frequently, to be sure, but they were no less unsettling. Perhaps what truly disturbed her was that the journey was over. She was no longer traveling over a vast ocean to a new adventure, approaching an expansive unknown with every gust of wind. Instead, the mystery and allure had sharply ended; her bright prospects and hope had unraveled, and she was left here in Pleasant Hall. Eliza was not truly alone, but she had never felt more abandoned. She looked out to the ocean beyond her window, its dazzling water her sole consolation. And then a peculiar sound stole her attention.

She heard the noise again, a sharp crack. A pop that braced against the still morning air. Already, the heat was settling down on the ground, and the air that blew through the window was no longer cool. A second crack and a third. There was something swift, something devastating about the noise. She got up, looking out the window.

Slaves passed by the seagrape trees at the front of the house, carrying tools and baskets of produce. The rhythms of plantation life were regular and constant, and they always began early in the day. A woman came by with soiled sheets. The shore was still and tranquil. No one that passed seemed to notice the noise. She heard it again. It was coming from the front of the house. Eliza crept to the hallway, and on confirming she was alone on the second floor, she moved to a west-facing room. This room stored furniture. Yellowed cloth draped over forgotten chairs and trunks; musty wooden cabinets and side tables stood neglected in the heat and dust. She moved between them, anxious to see the view this window afforded. It was even louder on this side. As she drew closer, she cowered from the noise.

Charles stood beside his horse, shirtless, holding a whip. At first, he had the horse on a long lead, and then his arm moved to snap the whip toward the ground. The sound was loud, not unlike a firearm. The horse's head bobbed, its tail flicking with anxiety. After the noise issued, he reeled the horse closer to him. He repeated the motion. The horse flinched but remained obedient. He focused on the right side of the horse and then the left. She watched in confusion as he rubbed the whip on the horse's legs and then on his back, only to crack the whip downwards again, stirring the otherwise motionless dirt.

Charles turned the horse, making him face the direction he had thrashed. He pulled the horse to the spot where the whip had touched. Eliza continued to watch, mesmerized by such a peculiar scene. She felt distressed over whether Charles would start to abuse the animal. The stallion sputtered in frustration but did not try to run. The noise echoed around the yard as Charles snapped it faster and faster. The other horses in the stable began to neigh, and Charles patted Alastor. In one swift move, he mounted him, and keeping him still, he introduced the whip off his back. He flicked the whip side to side, but the horse did not rear up or bolt.

Eliza sighed; the training did not seem to be finishing soon. She washed and dressed and then headed downstairs. Lucy brought her breakfast, explaining again that she could bring it to her room—she was a married woman and did not need to leave her bedchamber to be served. Eliza politely refused, unable to withstand being confined to her tiny haven any longer.

And then a gunshot exploded. Eliza dropped her roll, rushing to the window. Her heart trembled as she strained to look outside. She feared she would see the horse lying down, killed on the spot. Perhaps it had not obeyed his command.

But Alastor stood in the same place. The chickens that had pecked the dry dirt reconvened on the edges of the yard, jerking their heads with caution. Charles pressed his head against the horse's muzzle and caressed Alastor. Then he stopped, stood back, shortened the reins, and fired again, his flintlock pistol pointing downward. The horse flinched. Charles spoke to him and reloaded. He gently marched him to the spot where he had discharged his firearm. He did not force the horse into movement but encouraged him gently. In the next interval between shots, he rubbed the horse's neck. And like the previous time, he mounted Alastor. She watched him perform motions she had never seen before. The sweat glistened on Charles' back, and now in the daylight, she could see the scars she had felt when he had hovered over her. She shuddered when his gun discharged.

From the few mornings she had observed him, he seemed preoccupied with fitness and physical training. She chalked it up to his profession. He was used to constant movement; he relished challenging his body, and sitting still at his writing desk did not suit him. She wondered when he had found the time to read his philosophy books and political texts. Eliza could tell he was well-versed. His intelligence was nearly as sharp as hers, although it seemed he possessed knowledge in areas entirely foreign to her.

He seemed listless since they had arrived on the island. His every move beckoned his impatience, and every step he took appeared apprehensive. He had presented himself with the same restlessness in England, a kind of irritability a man displayed right before undertaking a long journey. But now that they had arrived in Nassau, she was not sure why his temperament had not yet shifted. It seemed as if Charles could not find comfort anywhere other than that which he felt on the back of a horse. As if the perpetual jolt of the ride made him feel weightless, and he craved his surroundings veiled in flashes of movement.

These effects served as a balm to a troubled man, haunted by unseen ghosts of the past, desperate to escape his wheeling thoughts, ever anxious to reach his next destination. But it only occurred to Eliza now that perhaps Charles, for all his years and experience, was utterly unsure of his future. It seemed as if his return to the island had not been without regret, and she still did not understand why.

Charles took a break from his training and goaded Alastor to canter, urging him into a full gallop through the lane of silk cotton trees that lined the entrance of Pleasant Hall. They disappeared in a trail of slow-settling dust.

Julius, the groom and slave who was entrusted with the care of the horses, ambled into view and leaned against the fence, fixated on Charles in the distance.

Charles returned now, and just as he entered the gateway, he stood up in his stirrups and withdrew his saber, striking at the nearest branch above his head. It was a dizzying display of confidence and skill. He circled the yard, pulling Alastor to an abrupt stop. Just as Eliza had thought the commotion in the yard had abated, he whipped out his pistol and fired it into the air. She flinched from her viewing spot behind the window, but Alastor did not move. This final time he had not started at the sound of Charles' pistol, and his rider seemed pleased.

Julius walked over to him, offering Charles a wet rag as he dismounted. Through the glass, she could discern their muffled conversation.

"He was a good purchase. Well done," Charles said, smiling as he patted Alastor's flank.

"They all said he couldn't be broken, sir, but I knew if no one couldn't, then Lord Sharpe could."

The men laughed, and then Julius ventured to remove the branch lying on the lane. Charles wiped his brow and squinted into the sun. Eliza decided she had never seen a more intimidating figure. But the way he held her intrigue was what truly frightened her. She wanted to look away, but in truth, she could not. She could not always remain hidden inside, confined to the walls of the dark, cool house. He was no stranger that would eventually leave. She had agreed to become his. And she was no closer to figuring out who Charles truly was than on the first day she had met him.

The sinking feeling in her stomach raged on as she watched him shoot at various-sized glass bottles lined up on the fence. Julius had strategically placed the targets in such a way as to present varying levels of difficulty, but Charles effortlessly struck them down one by one. Her sense of foreboding was overpowering. Nothing this man did put her heart at ease. She only felt a reassuring stillness when she was alone.

He was looking up at the house now, scrutinizing in her direction. She remained motionless at the window.

"Eliza? Eliza, is that you? Come outside!" he called.

She hesitated. She wanted to hide but knew she would appear ridiculous. She joined him in the courtyard with a sigh and a knot in her gut. The chickens scattered with her approach. The horse seemed relieved at the reprieve.

Charles was smiling again, dabbing at his forehead with the rag.

"Come, the morning is still young. I want to teach you to ride astride," he said, caressing the horse's thick neck. "Good boy."

"Thank you, husband. Only I do not feel up to the challenge."

"It's as good a day as ever. One must start somewhere."

He was pushy and domineering. She refused to come closer.

"Come, come!" he beckoned.

With grudging steps, she walked around the horse and joined him. The stallion snorted and seemed perturbed by her presence.

"Really, I do not feel well this morning. I've hardly slept. Another day would be more suitable."

"You'll feel brighter on horseback."

"No, really, I must refuse."

She had once been excited at such a prospect, but now the idea had entirely lost its appeal. Weeks ago, his offer had seemed out of place, but after her first night with him, she knew better than to surmise that any proposal came from random kindness.

She remembered the pain she had felt before. It was not unlike that of riding astride. She had the irrational fear he intended to break her body to suit his needs and that he was willing to go about it as methodically as he had stood there training Alastor that morning. His naked chest further affronted her. His every breath made his tense muscles undulate, and she found it difficult to look anywhere but the ground. Charles seemed to remember her earlier enthusiasm, and he now eyed her with scorn. She was desperate to shift his attention away from her.

"Why are you doing that?" she asked, pointing to the now coiled whip.

"A horse that is not gun broken is a useless animal. I intend to train him not to start at the sound of gunfire. And when I'm through, he will be used as the lead for training other mounts. He'll show others how it's all done."

The way he spoke about the animal revealed a fascination and deep respect towards horses that surprised her. Focusing her gaze on Alastor was a more soothing alternative than her prior position. She had never met another person who could make her feel as trapped and cornered by their presence as Charles could with her. They stood in the open yard, a gentle breeze traveling through the dry palms, but she felt as enclosed as she would have in a closet.

"Does the cavalry frequently engage the enemy with pistols? I always thought the infantry used firearms more."

She petted Alastor gently, feeling the heat searing off his panting body.

"Indeed. Sabers first, then pistols as a final resort. Moreover, I need the horse to charge forward into fire, no matter how loud and terrifying his surroundings are. Dragoons cut through the noise of the field, and then, when we've instilled terror in the face of our enemies, we take aim."

There was a misplaced mirth in his features as he spoke about war that was disconcerting to her. Instead, she chose to focus on the horse.

"How do you know it will work? That you can train the animal to be used to fire?"

"All horses can be trained. No matter their temperament."

"I confess that I found Alastor startling when we first arrived, but now he appears a different horse to me."

"Yes, he is a good study. This is his second day. I started with the sounds of a flag in the beginning. I confess he's made incredible progress today. One must keep him moving into whatever is frightening him until he is no longer scared by the successive shots. The rider must be gentle with the horse, above all."

Charles was watching her observe Alastor. She looked into the stallion's big black eyes, reassessing her attitude toward what she had witnessed when she felt herself rise into the air. Charles had taken her by the waist and lifted her onto the saddle. The horse started, but he snapped the reins tightly.

"Please put me down! I…"

She was horrified that in such a brief movement he had the ability to displace her entirely.

"There you are. Lift your other leg to that other side. There."

"I am not dressed properly. This is—"

"Oh, nonsense. You're not going on a hunt. Now, control the horse by squeezing your legs. Here," he said, a hand finding the presence of her thigh underneath her skirt.

She wanted to jerk away from his touch but could not move. She looked down, the height from his steed dizzying. The saddle was foreign to her. She was nervous and feared the horse would sense her anxiety. She had pity for Alastor moments before, but now she realized how foolish the sentiment was. He was a strong and powerful animal, and now she was at his mercy. The hard ground was a long way from where she sat. If Alastor reared up, she did not know if she could endure it. Charles fiddled with the stirrups, adjusting them to her height, and slipped her shoes into them.

"There we are. And now to introduce movement."

"I am not comfortable."

"I daresay you won't find much comfort in stretching your legs so very wide just yet, but in time you will grow used to it."

His words seemed to confirm her darkest fear.

"It is not decent."

Charles laughed.

"There are no witnesses that I can see. And it is highly improbable that you could be indecent in front of me, my love."

Her cheeks colored as he led her in a slow circle. An array of mortifications passed through her in various degrees. She wanted to yell out.

"Now, to introduce speed."

He slapped the horse, and Alastor immediately set into canter. Eliza screamed. The horse passed under a tree, and she grabbed onto a low-lying branch.

"You must find your balance in the seat. You are simply unaccustomed to the exercise, but we can change that," he said, running over to them.

"Take me down. Now."

Charles sighed, taking the reins from her shaking hands, and watched as she awkwardly shifted her legs and skirt back to the same side of the saddle. He secured the lead to a post and then lifted her down. He seemed to delight in their closeness and her uneasiness. She was repelled by his damp chest and the half embrace he held her in.

"That was highly irregular," she said, her breath shaky.

"You surprise me. I believed you had an interest in it. Are you this fickle in all matters?"

Still holding her closely, he looked down, his face animated. He seemed to enjoy toying with her. He would have used her smaller mare to start if these lessons were halfway innocent of intention. But he had not. Instead, he had forced her to do it on a horse much too large and unruly to be considered safe.

"I regret to say I no longer do," she said quietly, backing away from him and the horse.

"Stay, keep me company."

His voice was authoritative, and she questioned whether he was actually intent on training her as well as the animal. She kept her eyes down on the ground once again. Eliza always told herself she would be more confident around him and would not allow him to make her feel this way. But every time she stood before him, her resolve weakened into nothing.

"You slept late today. Is that your usual habit?" he asked as he fed the horse some oats from his pocket.

Eliza looked at the height of the sun in the sky. She wondered why he was there. It was not a Sunday. He should have been at the fort.

"It is a wonder to find you here still, I must admit," she said.

He looked up, his green eyes surveying her.

"My presence was not necessary at Fort Charlotte today. Besides, I am behind with Alastor, and he is in sore need of training," he replied, whispering words of encouragement to the horse. "There are quite a few matters I can occupy my time with here."

Eliza tried to swallow away the uneasiness welling inside her. She had to show him she was engaged in something. She needed to be occupied herself.

"Besides, I can now begin target shooting off of Alastor. It is no easy feat to fire a pistol from the back of a horse," he said.

"I saw in the mail that there's a new market opening today in town and—" she said.

"You read through the post?"

"I was looking to see if my mother or father have replied."

"Please don't read my mail," he said bluntly.

Charles brushed the horse with intensity.

"Yes, of course. I would never. I was simply looking for letters addressed to me."

"You don't receive mail here. When and if you do, I will alert you."

His remarks were a bitter reminder of her situation.

"The market sounds lovely. Shall we go?"

"I don't see a need for that, do you?"

"It sounds diverting. Maybe there is a merchant with books, or perhaps—"

"There are many things to do here."

She assumed this would be his response, but she feared to see his meaning actualized. He was watching her closely.

"No, no. I am so awfully tired of the house. I am here almost every day, as you know. Perhaps I could go into town with Lucy, and then—"

"I won't allow it."

His answer was short and irritated. They seemed to be on the brink of a disagreement as if he was desperately trying to communicate something. His mood fluctuated like the sky above them. The waves off to the side seemed to graze the sand even louder.

"Beg pardon?" she asked nervously.

"I won't allow it. You leaving here. I won't allow it."

Eliza was unsure of what to say. Her mind raced for a way to escape his presence. She should have stayed inside the house.

"You're right. There are many books here I have not perused yet. I did mean to organize them on a rainy day, but today is just as good a day as any, I suppose. I will take my leave," she said quickly.

"Fear not, Eliza. I will have you riding Alastor one way or another. I find you capable enough," he said as he began to untie his horse.

Julius reappeared at just the right moment. She smiled briefly and then curtsied before heading back into the house. She sighed, releasing the strain she had held in. The clock in the hallway gonged for the hour. Yet when she faced the dusty bookshelf, she wanted nothing more than to be outside again. She wanted to swim in the water but did not want him to see her.

Eliza glanced out the window. Charles and the horse had disappeared. She could swim further down the beach, away from the direct view of the house. She quickly moved some books around on the shelf and purposely left one on the side table to make it appear as if she had earnestly begun the task. And then she headed through the study and out the side door, running before anyone noticed her leave.

Eliza could easily lose track of time when she was in the water. Once she was swimming, her cares beyond the wet sand seemed to dissipate, and nothing mattered any longer. The water began to turn golden, and she knew it was nearly time to return to the house. She had tried her luck swimming today with Charles home, but barely anyone had seen her. From her vantage point behind a series of dark limestone rocks, she had watched two slaves place laundry on the lines. The task generally took a good deal of time, but they had already finished the job. Wide sheets swung in the breeze, the whiteness of the cloth startling in the searing sun.

Eliza waded her way out of the water, legs weak and foundering on the shifting sand. She squeezed out the side braid she had wound her hair into and then moved to do the same with her skirt. Cleo had devised a plan to create a pair of loose breeches she could wear while in the water. She had come up with the idea to solve the acute problem of modesty, but Eliza had only agreed to it for the ease of movement such pants would allow her. She hoped Cleo would finish them soon; squeezing out her skirt was tedious, although the heat ensured the cloth dried rather quickly.

As she moved back toward the house, she spotted a pair of boots dashing past the edge of the swaying linens. With a passing breeze, she saw Charles, his face cast downwards, walking with intent in her direction. He rushed between the row of drying clothes. He had not seen her at that moment, but had he watched her swimming? She could not think of any other reason for his presence on this side of the house.

Eliza scrambled to the opposite side of the laundry lines, desperately hoping the sheets would shield her from his view. She wanted to return to the house unnoticed. She stepped past a series of bed sheets that were large enough to cover her entire form, but a gap in the line followed it, and she hesitated to continue moving. Eliza could no longer hear the sand shifting underneath his steps. All she could discern was the wind and the water slowly coming up to lap the shore.

A combination of dread and lengthening awkwardness urged her to retract her steps, and she walked back to the first sheet. In her imagination, she could see him moving closer toward her as she moved away, but she could no longer see him. She only knew that he had never come to the end of the laundry line. He must have stopped where he was. With horror, she realized that the sun's position behind her likely made her silhouette abundantly clear to him. She turned to the side, unwilling to look at the sheet face on. She didn't understand why he remained unannounced for this long. He was silent, and he was waiting for something.

For the second time that day, she felt that he was taunting her. Charles wanted to catch her off guard. And she could think of only one purpose for such a ruse. He was stalking her like a hunter, and she felt increasingly trapped. The sun was much lower now, casting a fiery glow across the waves and the sand. The wind barreled across the beach, causing the white laundry to blow up in the air. And then she saw the front of his black boots.

Eliza took off running towards the house, the sand ensuring her flight was soundless. The idea of appearing visible was no longer as daunting as the idea of him catching hold of her so far away from the others. She liked to think he retained some air of self-control in view of the slaves, but they were alone on this side of the beach. She inherently did not trust him. And she did not want to find out why he was there. It could not possibly end well for her.

She ducked behind a palm tree, able to view his position clearly from a distance. He was still fixated on the sheet where she had lingered the longest, but now she could see why. The low-swaying palm tree cast a shadow on almost the same spot where she had stood. She often times mistook the shifting shapes of the palms for people. It never ceased to amaze her how the smaller palms and the fronds closest to the ground seemed to take on a life of their own. Sometimes from the corner of her eye or from the distorted gaze of a reflection, she swore it was a slave approaching or going about their work. But in every instance, the ruse would be revealed. Now the mirage had worked to her advantage. She understood how she had slipped away with success.

He lifted his hands to the sheet, grasping the fabric with a jerk. When his hands made no purchase, he wildly shifted the linen to the side, dumbfounded by the sight of the water. She could hear him curse, and as he made his way back to the house, she slipped around the front and ran up the stairs. She would have to face him at dinner in an hour. She dreaded the event like most nights and planned to eat as quickly as possible. The sooner she could retire with some concocted excuse, the better.

Charles was leaning against the railing on the back porch, impatiently waiting for her to return. Eliza saw him from a distance and changed her path through the seagrape trees. She avoided him for the better part of a week and was not confident of a pleasant outcome. Moreover, her hair was damp from swimming, and her clothes were thoroughly soaked. He had repeatedly asked her not to go into the sea, but his request had fallen on deaf ears. Now noticing her hasty retreat, he rushed from the porch with an agile step to join her on the ground.

"I cannot help but wonder at the difference in your temperament since our arrival, my dear," he began with contrived cordiality.

"I see no such thing."

"I do wonder…if something has occurred between us," he said slowly, the sunlight making his eyes appear translucent like green glass.

He backed her toward the rough bark of a coconut tree. The ground in this spot was a mess of dark, tangled roots, and there was a mound where two of the trees collided that was too massive for the sand to shroud. She stepped back uneasily, mindful of her footing.

"I have been carried through several powerful transformations. I will need time to adjust, that is all," she said resolutely.

"Yes, indeed. But I fear that is not entirely true," he countered with a smug smile.

Eliza looked at him with impatience to leave. She no longer concerned herself with efforts to mask her hatred towards him.

"I fear, if I may speak plainly, that the intimacies of our marriage are not as they once were," Charles said.

His gaze was direct and intense. She gave no response, the distant roar of the waves crashing audible to her ears. Charles leaned in and gently kissed her on the lips.

"I can be tender, Eliza…" he said softly as he held her chin.

Despite showing a more vulnerable side to his grave demeanor, Eliza still found his attention agonizing. She stiffened up and refused to meet his eyes.

"…if you would allow me to show you my sincerest devotion," he continued earnestly.

He pressed his face to hers again, his lips salty from touching hers, and then made a slow, wet trail to her neck. His fingers tossed her damp braid to the side. Eliza said nothing, her fury growing because he did not seem to be at all affected by her stony silence. She was nothing but a cornered captive to him, and he seemed barely interested in what she desired. Charles began to proceed further with his affection.

"It is too little, too late. It is of no consequence to me," she finally said, breaking her face away from his.

He did not seem to hear her and pushed himself against her, touching her sunburnt chest. Eliza winced in pain and shifted away from their strained proximity. He finally stopped his advances.

"You are cold. Surely, this cannot be. I have never met so unfeeling a woman," he said, his voice wavering.

"Nor I a man."

He sighed, looking toward the beach.

"You should remain indoors. It is unsightly to have your skin in such a condition," Charles said, his hardened demeanor restored.

"While you are away, I am at liberty to do as I please, and while you are home, as best as I can manage."

"A woman of breeding should not have her skin as red as a laborer toiling away in a field. It does you no justice."

"Perhaps this accounts for the lack of intimacies in our marriage, husband."

"And your manner of dress…to heavens woman! You are wearing breeches! You reveal yourself! I will not have my wife looking thus!" he said angrily.

He came toward her again, pulling at her neckline in horror. "You have damaged your beauty!"

Eliza moved away from him in disgust.

"Sometimes the sun is too strong, and it burns before you realize it," she said with venom. "It is only temporary; the outside will heal. Eventually."

Her true meaning did not go unnoticed.

"Are you speaking of the sun, or is this a poor attempt to weakly disguise your contempt for me?" he spat.

"I am trying to explain a natural phenomenon to someone who appears incapable of understanding matters beyond his grasp."

He turned with a jeering laugh.

"Let me explain this. I am your husband. I forbid you to keep hours outside. You are to remain inside and work on your embroidery or read or practice your music like any other lady of your station. I forbid you to dress yourself in this manner. It is an utter disgrace."

"I will not make a promise I do not intend to keep."

"Then let me remind you, Lady Sharpe, that you did make a promise, several of them, if only a month ago. Vows to obey. Me."

She met his glaring face.

"Yes. We do find ourselves in a marriage, Lord Sharpe. Notwithstanding, I will only express and participate in what I find mutual. If you feel strongly that something is lacking in this regard, perhaps you should turn inward."

"Damn you, woman. Damn your insolence and damn your tongue. I…" he began to shout.

She looked at him with satisfaction.

"Ah, it's precisely what I thought. Tenderness is nothing but a thin pretext for what I've only recently discovered truly resides in your heart."

His face was red with frustration, but he seemed panicked by her last words.

"Eliza, please…we can talk through this. I beg of you…" he clumsily began.

She sauntered off toward the house, ignoring him entirely.

"I could not begin to fathom why a desirable lady such as yourself could remain the only unwed sister at such a late age," he suddenly said in a much-altered tone.

She paused before reaching the steps to the house.

"I at first thought it a cruel fate that someone like you could be undesired even at the age of twenty-four," he said, his words cutting. "But I am beginning to understand why no man would vouch for your hand."

Eliza bit her lip and marched back toward him.

"I only remained unwed because I refused every single suitor who ever approached me," she replied.

"Yet you did not refuse me."

She tensed up, ashamed to be reminded of her poor decision.

"No, I did not. Take small counsel by it. It only serves as a reminder that everyone, even the most discerning of us, can commit the gravest of errors."

With that, Eliza made her way up the stairs and entered the house, slamming the door behind her.

She refused to come down to dinner later. Lucy informed Lord Sharpe of her intentions that evening.

He dropped his napkin with disgust on hearing the news.

"Why ever not?" he asked.

Lucy stood before him, wringing her hands.

"She said she'd prefer to dine in her chamber tonight," she answered nervously.

"She will do no such thing. If she cannot join me at the table, she simply will not eat!"

"Yes, sir," she replied, backing away. "My pleasure."

"I forbid you to bring her any food!" he shouted, with his eye on the stairs.

He knew full well that Eliza could hear him.

Lucy nodded again and rushed outside to the kitchen to inform the cook. Cleo, polishing the silver near the sideboard, had overheard the discussion. She visited Eliza's room later in the evening, surreptitiously carrying a slice of bread and some fruit in her apron. Eliza thanked her but showed no interest.

"You need to eat, Miss Ellie. You are not shapely enough as it is," Cleo said, preparing her bed for the evening.

Eliza remained silent, gazing out at the darkened skies.

"And if it is your intention to make Lord Sharpe lose interest in you by losing your hips, that will not work. I have seen how that man looks at you. He will not leave you in peace any time soon."

"How dreadfully unfortunate," she said in a detached voice.

Cleo eyed her suspiciously. Eliza turned with a wry smile.

"For him."

Cleo pursed her lips.

"You are going to get yourself in trouble, Miss Ellie. And I will not always be here to clean it up. That fruit better be gone when I come back in the morning."

An inescapable silence lay over the dining room, occasionally punctuated by the clinking of silverware and glasses. Even the objects around them held a presence of subtle discomfort as if they themselves had not agreed to be present. They, too, had languished, forgotten in the heat and dust of this house before Eliza's arrival. She glanced ceaselessly at a map of the world on the wall and the gleaming straightness of a sword taken from a battle in Scotland. She passed the time lost in thoughts of yellow elder flowers, a stingray she had observed in the shallows, and the sight of a ship in the distance framed by this evening's orange sunset and the darkening pine and palm trees.

Eliza was searching for something to say to Charles when the front door burst open, and chaos sounded. Angus

Bailey, the longtime overseer, rushed into the room, sweat flooding his brow as he breathed heavily. They dropped their forks in surprise. At Angus' side, he carried Celia, but the sight of her was shocking. Her plain white garment was ripped. A blue mass covered one eye, and the other was devoid of its usual fiery intensity. A look of fear replaced it now. A crude rope leash had been placed over her neck and constrained her wrists. Angus pulled on it, dragging her forward.

Charles shot up from his chair. "What is the meaning of this?" he asked his temper rising.

"My lord, apologies fer disturbin' ye, but I caught her tryin' tae flee. I received word from the tax collector tha' he saw her. Aye, the same shape of her and look in her eye tha' he seen many times before, attemptin' tae board a boat at the harbor in town. I went down there, I did, as is my duty, and there she was! She had stolen money on her person! A crafty chancer, if ever I saw one."

Charles sighed. "Was it entirely necessary to bring her inside? She is filthy."

Eliza swallowed, and her ears felt as if they were on fire. She wondered if physical words of her guilt were plastered across her face. Celia would not look at her.

"Aye, my lord, I know this must not please ye, but whit will ye have me dae? She's not any slave; she serves the Lady Sharpe. Her punishment must meet her crime." Angus nodded to Eliza as he said this.

"What have you done to her face?" Eliza asked, now rising to a stand as well.

"My dear," Charles said, extending an arm to keep Eliza at bay, "this is a matter to be handled by someone with a stronger constitution."

Angus gripped the rope tighter.

"Proceed the customary way. I do not care, but leave us to our dinner, which has been so rudely interrupted," Charles replied as he lowered himself back down to his chair.

Angus seemed perturbed that his intentions had conflicted with his master's wishes. He nodded and then dragged Celia back outside and down from the porch. She seemed to resist every step.

Eliza timidly joined Charles back at the table, searching his face to see if she could detect any explosive emotion. Her involvement had yet to be revealed. He had his hands intertwined, studying the wall across the way. He sighed.

"I apologize, my dear. Bailey is a Scot; you know how they can be. I will speak to him in private. He'll frighten you half to death with a presentation like that. You did not need to witness it," he finally said.

She felt a small amount of relief. He suspected nothing. They continued to eat. Then she heard the first scream. It was a noise unlike anything she had ever heard: a desperate wail of anguish that hit such a note that it seemed to pierce the night air. It was Celia. Lucy, who had stood behind them throughout the entire ordeal, instinctively tensed up. A sharp crack followed, and Celia screamed again. Eliza dropped her fork a second time.

"What is he doing to her?" she asked, outraged.

"When a slave is disobedient, they need to be meted out with the appropriate punishment. She would receive much worse if she tended to the fields. Perhaps she should after this incident," he replied coolly.

Her hand reached for the utensil again, but she could not think of eating. More screams rang out from the yard. Eliza felt her eyes well up as she desperately tried to remain emotionless. Still, Lucy would not look up. Eliza could not stomach the thought of food and felt even more nauseated that Charles seemed to be able to.

"This claret has kept intact; it is a wonder that such a simple cellar can store it well past its years. Even in this humidity," Charles said as he swirled the remaining wine in his glass.

He seemed to notice the pain in her face and placed a hand on hers. Charles' gesture was strange and unwelcome, but she remained still. The room grew blurry around her as her tears fell.

"Eliza, this should have never occurred. You should have never seen that. I know it is an unpleasant reality of keeping this great house, but that is why I am its master. One must keep a cool, detached distance. It is a business transaction, after all. Nothing more."

"You must stop it, Charles," she said.

She knew she shouldn't react, but she could not stand it. She knew she was treading closer to a dangerous revelation.

"Ah, that fool has ruined your appetite with his intrusion," he said, shaking his head.

She shot up and made for the door. His tall form blocked her pathway in an instant.

"If you will not end this, I will," she said. "Please."

Charles put his hands on her shoulders.

"Go back to the table and have some more wine. It will soothe you," he said.

He called for more claret. Lucy obliged, her hands shaking as she poured the wine. She clinked the crystal decanter against the lip of the glass. Celia's screams grew more broken and raw. Eliza pushed him and tried to move past his side.

"It is not Christian! This is not just! To treat a woman…" she started.

"It is not Christian for a mere slave to turn her back on us after all we have provided her, my dear. This is the way you must perceive matters. We provided her with shelter, food, the very clothes on her back. I daresay these slaves are happier compared to the miserable Irish! Celia was even raised to a more esteemed position and asked to work in the house. You, of all people, should be angry with what she has done. Do you not see it so?"

"Please make him stop. It is my fault! The blame lies with me," Eliza finally said.

He was reactionless with the confusion of not comprehending her words. "I do not understand."

She realized she still had an opportunity to evade the truth, but she could no longer bear to keep the secret.

"I asked her to leave and gave her a trinket of value. She did not run away! She only did what I asked her to do. I am sure she can find gainful employment in another house. Our temperaments do not complement one another. She does not like me. She—"

His temper was quickly ignited like a burst of gunpowder brought too close to a flame. Charles rushed toward her as she hurried backward.

"I *own* her, you fool!" he seethed.

Eliza tripped on her skirts and fell to the floor.

"I thought her service was a gift. I thought you said she was mine."

"She is not merely a servant. She is a slave, and I own her! My late father owned her mother, and I will own her children. You would rob your own house!"

He bent down and pulled Eliza up to her feet, shaking her.

"I have a Judas for a wife! You have not been here for a month, and yet you aim to ruin me!" he shouted.

Lucy screamed and fled from the room.

"I did not know!" Eliza screamed, crying.

"I deal with an intolerable excuse for His Majesty's army day in and out, ungrateful conniving slaves who mean to destroy me, and a wife that is my chief adversary! This is not matrimony! This is Abaddon! I vowed to remain a single man if it were not for the promise of progeny you have yet to bear me!"

Eliza's tears ceased with the mention of producing him an heir. A combination of steely resolve and dread consumed her.

"Do not speak to me of our union. I will never bear you children for fear they would even in the slightest resemble a part of you. The world does not need more men of your character."

Eliza glared at him and then turned on her heel toward the darkened hallway. One of the servants was gawking at her but quickly lowered her gaze once more. Lucy had retreated to the far end of the hall, a hand covering her mouth. As Eliza passed through the doorway, Charles grabbed her arm.

"You will bear me children. Whether it pleases you or not—that is not my intent. I would carry it out in the hallway this very moment for all to see just to reduce the height of your pride," he said, pressing her to the wall. "You have no reason for your bold conceit. Your blood and background have done nothing in the way of improving you into a decent wife."

"You will not lie with me, and even if you attempt it by force, I will never carry your child, mark me," she replied with malice.

"You would threaten me? That is not a wise decision," he said, his eyes searching hers with disgust. "Your insolence knows no bounds. It will be your downfall."

She did not answer and would not look at him.

"I cannot stand the sight of you!" Charles shouted as he stormed off to the study. He slammed the doors shut, leaving the frightened women motionless in his wake.

CHAPTER VI.

W hen Eliza decided to find Cleo, she had never walked that far into the estate. She understood Cleo was not scheduled to work in the house at the time but needed to speak with her. She was the only person who seemed to understand her, and recognize the pain she was enduring.

She walked past the kitchen and the outbuildings, past the curving rows of guinea corn and banana trees, until a line of modest dwellings appeared. She peered into shadow-filled dirt-floor homes, trepid eyes looking warily back at her. And then she stopped. Two women stood outside one dwelling. It was not unlike any of the other huts, but the presence of the women begged to differ. They looked up at her in surprise and parted, giving her a chance to look inside. As she ducked down to enter through the doorway, the sweet and salty aroma of thatched palms dried out by the sun's heat assaulted her nose.

Cleo was in there, consulting with another woman.

"He did this even after it happened?"

"Yes, how did you know?"

"I see it on him. He carries a long shadow. Take his signature, wrap it up in four ways, sprinkle this dirt over it and then place it in the jar, just like I told you. Shake it up and swirl it. Do so after every full moon. He'll leave you alone then."

"I cannot thank you enough."

"It was bad, but it will be better. This will help."

Eliza walked closer, intruding on the scene. It was cool inside and dark, with a tinge of smoke lingering in the air. The scent of wood burning and another unfamiliar smell hovered around them. The other woman looked up, then nervously gathered her belongings and fled. Eliza made a conciliatory gesture for her to stay, but she paid no heed.

"She's from the Burrow estate. She would not have wanted you to see her here," Cleo said, beginning to put small jars and herbs back in place.

"Why would that concern me?"

"Because she shouldn't be on your land. She should be working."

"I hardly feel that this is my land."

"Well, it is not mine."

"What are you doing?"

Cleo paused and then obliged her with an answer.

"You people call it Obeah. I call it healing. I call it what my mother, and her mother, and her mother before that taught us."

"Are all slaves of the same belief? Are you not Christian? I thought the chapel was frequented on Sunday."

"Are all white people of the same belief?"

Eliza smiled, but then the curve of her lips rapidly turned into open astonishment, and a look of relief crossed her features.

"You have an ability...a gift. I knew it! There is something different about you, something strange. You've always gazed at me like you knew me, like you understood me."

"You are young and do not know what you got yourself into. But you came into this world with knowledge, and it will see you through."

"I do not understand. Is Obeah a place? Is that where you are from?" she asked, sitting down on a straw-stuffed cushion.

"No. I am Igbo. They tricked my family. My own people, mind you. They said my father had stolen another man's horse. We were sent to a cave to see the oracle, and he decreed that my father's punishment was to lose his family. They made us walk further into the cave until we could see the light again. We left the cave and saw the water and a boat waiting for us. They took me first. I never saw them again. They put us on different ships, and I was carried off to Haiti. But I at once saw that place would never see peace, and so I made my way to this island. The old Lord Sharpe bought me. And I am still here."

Eliza did not know how to respond, so she remained silent.

"You say you left one island for this colony. Why do you remain here?"

"I am waiting on two things: a little one and my freedom. A baby boy," Cleo replied with a laugh. "Oh, I'll get my freedom. I did enough for this family. It's coming to me. And then I will be gone."

Eliza looked at her in confusion. Cleo appeared past the age of childbearing years, and she was unsure what she meant.

"I'm afraid that's not how it works. No matter how deserving or justified it might be. But, if you help me now, I swear on my very life I will help you become free."

"That is a grand gesture, Miss Ellie. But it does not mean I can help you in the way that you want."

Cleo began to tidy her surroundings. She straightened a white candle fixed into a coconut shell holder. She arranged a series of soursop fruit in a semi-circle. But Eliza did not want to leave. She wanted to continue the conversation. She felt comforted in Cleo's dwelling, modest and bare as it was.

"It's remarkable. There are no insects in here. If only my room could offer such solace!"

"Burn a husk from the coconut fruit. Keeps the biting ones away. Tobacco leaves work good too, but they are not grown in these parts. Coconuts, however, are plenty."

She pointed toward a small pan where a husk was lit and burning like incense. Eliza watched the ribbon of orange ember slowly consume it.

"What about treatment for the bites? The pain sunburn brings? I have been meaning to ask you such things for some time now."

"Fevergrass oil applied to your skin before you go outside. I can make some up for you, Miss Ellie. Your ankles already look like pin cushions. To block the sun, perhaps some coconut oil. But linen is better. Cover yourself in linen and stay out of the sun at midday. Do not go wandering when it's hot."

"But that is when I prefer to swim."

"Let's focus on the insects. Tomorrow we can walk around the property, and I can show you what all these plants can do. You like learning. I have seen you with that book, down by the shore, writing and writing."

"Thank you, Cleo. You are always so patient with me."

Cleo retrieved a small square of purple cloth, laying it on a low-hand-carved wooden table, and began to arrange a pile of dried herbs and what looked like dirt in the center.

"You know, I think I met an Obeah man once. The very first day I came here."

Cleo looked up at her and laughed.

"There is no Obeah man on this island. Maybe on Andros. But I know there's no men that do what I do for miles."

"But he reminded me of you. He was at the governor's house. He was so charming. He spoke to me in a riddle, and I've never made sense of it. It sounded so clever. *I know about you, but you don't know about me. I open the gate, and I hold the key. One will strike from the sky, his mother...the sea.*"

Cleo's demeanor suddenly shifted.

"I apologize. I must be bothering you. You are forced to deal with me every other day of the week; I should not make it a habit to intrude on a day like this."

"What did this man look like?" Cleo asked.

"He had a tall hat in the French style. And a silver cane. There was a yellow band on the hat, and his clothes were so refined it must surely mean he is a free man. His smile was captivating, but he did not give his name. He only spoke the riddle, and then he was gone. Perhaps he lives in New-Guinea town, past the hill."

Cleo stared at her, and Eliza feared she had accidentally delivered some insult in her description.

"There is no free man with clothes like that living behind the town, Miss Ellie."

"It was so very strange. I often think of it. And I confess I sometimes feel the house is likewise strange. Like it is watching me. I am not saying it is haunted, but it is such an uncanny feeling."

Eliza felt foolish at mentioning the strange woman she had seen in her bedroom. She knew Cleo would have a sympathetic ear, but something made her hold her tongue.

"Ghosts are everywhere. Old houses, new houses, land where no house was ever built. Some people talk about the *sperrids* in the trees. They claim they can only live in the tops of the silk cotton trees." Cleo clicked her tongue in disagreement.

"There are so many that line the path to Pleasant Hall," Eliza replied, her eyes growing larger.

"Spirits can walk everywhere man can and more. The ancestors are all around us. They try to keep them in check, but sometimes people like me need to maintain the balance. Some spirits did not come from people. Those are the ones you have to watch for," Cleo said ominously.

Eliza's questions multiplied in her mind.

"Do you think Pleasant Hall is haunted?" she asked.

"The whole island is haunted. It's all this water. As beautiful as it is, it is like a mirror to the other side. They can pass through as easily as the sun setting into the horizon when there's water around," Cleo explained.

"How fascinating. The sea in England is nothing like the water here. I knew this water was special. I never felt anything like it. I always feel better after I go in," Eliza said.

"That's the salt. It cleanses you."

"So, the ocean has its flaws, but it can be beneficial as well…"

"There are shipwrecks on the cays, but it also puts a meal on the plate. One day you'll learn to look at things in the world not as good or bad but understand that everything presented to you is complicated. Life is a game of balance," Cleo replied.

Cleo was simple in her manner of speaking, but Eliza could instinctively understand that she was much wiser than her. Eliza abruptly shifted the tone of their conversation with her following statement.

"Then you understand my situation. It is dire. You need to help me."

"Help you with what, Miss Ellie?"

"I came here hoping you could provide assistance, but now I know you can," Eliza said breathlessly, pointing to the dried herbs and bottles around them.

Cleo looked at her long and hard.

"Do other women come and seek assistance from you often?"

"Women and men," Cleo replied with a stiff lip.

"Then please, I beg of you…"

"Oh, Miss Ellie, I cannot give you what you want."

Eliza heard the other women grumbling outside, but she did not care.

"I cannot be married to this man any longer," Eliza said.

"You just got together."

"He is beyond what I can handle. He does not act as a husband should. I cannot bear it. Last night, the way he treated me...I am sure you or the others heard."

"You bring out the passion in him. It is true."

"Passion? He is a horrible, cruel man."

"I raised that boy. He is a good boy," Cleo said wryly, a deep smile growing on her face.

"I do not understand. Then how..."

"I never said he was without flaws."

"Please help me. Make him leave me alone."

"I cannot do that. I don't do love spells. I don't do spells to make you a fortune. I just do not do them."

"But you fail to say you cannot. If you can do such things, why not do them?"

"It is not natural, and it will only end bad. You cannot force someone to love you, and you cannot force someone to stop loving you. Just like you cannot make someone rich and keep them happy. Money and happiness are not the same matter."

"No, no, they certainly are not," Eliza replied, impressed with her reasoning. "What about protection? Surely, you can offer some kind of protection?"

Cleo shook her head.

"I just overheard you help the woman before me. Why do you refuse me?"

"You don't need it."

"How can you say that? I receive nothing but ill-usage from that man. Please, Cleo, please help me," Eliza cried, her voice quavering.

Cleo took a deep inhalation and sighed, looking off to the side. But she did not offer a reply. Eliza bit her lip and looked down, fixated on a pile of pale objects spilling from a silken pouch.

"What are those?"

"Pig knuckles. Bones," Cleo answered as she began to return them to the bag.

"Can you divine with them?" Eliza asked.

"Most white people think they're dice. Gambling folk. You seem to know a lot without quite knowing it, Miss Ellie."

Eliza's curiosity bordered on impatience.

"I saw you shake them for the other woman," she said.

"I get some messages from looking with my eyes, but I get more detail from talking to spirit. The bones help with that," Cleo said.

"What do they say about me? About my future? Please, Cleo, please. I am desperate," Eliza said. "I cannot tolerate that man."

"You are bound to him. In a union. Sealed with words."

"The vows are nothing more than a mere script we were called to repeat. I cannot fathom being wedded to him. I cannot tolerate such an existence."

"Oh, you will be just fine. In fact, you will flourish. Appearances can be unreliable. Spirit sometimes hides the most profound lessons in plain sight, Miss Ellie."

Cleo's words hardly satisfied her.

"Do not mistake me. I only criticize the man within. I mean to comment on his character. It is foul. Surely you can do something."

"I will not touch a hair on that man's head."

"He is a heartless brute. I desire nothing more than to be rid of him," Eliza said loudly.

It had her intended effect. She watched as Cleo grabbed the bones and shook them, releasing them back to the table, her impassivity nearly breaking. Eliza herself could not decipher any clear message from the pattern the bones had fallen into, but Cleo seemed focused on one piece with a small crack in it.

"You are sidled up to him for a long time. It cannot be broken," Cleo said flatly.

Eliza's heart plummeted.

"Sometimes another person hesitates with words because there is no good news to deliver, Miss Ellie. This is one of those circumstances."

"But what do you mean? Even if one of us dies? If I run away? Even if he does not return home?"

"Do not regret your words. Words are powerful."

"I need you to do something to him. I overheard you. You helped the woman before me with her overseer. Surely you can do something for me," she pleaded.

"I raised that boy, Miss Ellie. I know him. I cannot teach him any longer. That's your task now."

"I refuse to do anything of the sort. He is a grown man!" Eliza replied in disgust.

"He is grown, but he is not necessarily a *man* yet. You are right about that part," Cleo said, moving the bones slightly. "You help him to that. You are the only woman that can help him."

"He is many years older than me. He is responsible for his actions, and I will not tolerate it. I do not deserve such treatment."

"Age is only a number of the years you have been breathing. Wisdom is something else entirely. Some of the boys working in the fields, hauling water, are wiser than men double their age."

"This is unfair…"

"I do not envy you, Miss Ellie. But you are up to the task," Cleo said with a sigh.

"I refuse the task."

Cleo barked out a laugh.

"Of course you do. And that's why they picked you."

"Who?" Eliza exclaimed, flabbergasted.

"The *orisha*. The mighty emissaries of God who govern all aspects of heaven and earth. They know your agreement. We all come into this life with one. Do not ever underestimate your *ashe,* your power. You were put here to discover it."

"I never agreed to any of this. I only—"

"Agreed to marriage. To a union with him. We may not like what we're given, but we are given what we need."

"I am tired of riddles! I cannot comprehend this. What do the bones say?"

"Longevity, but there is a split, a fracture, the bones grow around it, grow stronger…"

"What can that possibly mean? A division? Do I leave him?"

"I cannot stop you. It just may take longer for you to accomplish what you are supposed to. Your place is here."

Eliza's heart flooded with despair and confusion.

"If I were you, I would ask for help."

"I am, Cleo. I am pleading!"

"Not from me. Call on Erzulie Dantor. But be careful when working with her."

"Where is she? Can I see her today?"

"She is all around us. She is a *lwa*, a spirit, from my land. She rules the heart. She offers protection to women."

"What do I have to do?"

"It would be best to make a space for her in your bedroom, but you must be secretive. Go somewhere. Somewhere you feel safe and pray to her. Ask for her intercession. Offer something beautiful, something valuable, and a bit of rum."

Eliza was quiet for some time as she stared at the bones, lost in her thoughts.

"Before I came here, I was going to refuse to return to the house. I considered running away. But I trust you, and I will try this, although I confess, I do not know what I am doing."

"Keep it simple and focus on the intention. They will take care of the rest."

Someone rushed into the small hut with angry and frustrated footsteps.

"What is she doing here?"

Eliza turned to find Celia behind her, the whites of her eyes glaring down at her.

"Consulting me as you wish to," Cleo said, her voice stoic.

"She has no right! This is our space! These are our dwellings. She should not journey past the banana trees if she knows what's good for her!"

Eliza tensed up. She had not encountered Celia since that terrible night. Now she worked in the fields, and their interactions were limited.

"I am sorry. I—" Eliza started.

"Watch your tongue before you make a mistake," Cleo said sternly to Celia.

"I cannot make a mistake when I am given no choice. She chose this. She *chose* this life, and still, she complains about it to you," Celia exclaimed and then, turning to Eliza, asked, "Must you people take everything from us?"

Eliza rushed to stand, her hands held high to diffuse the outburst.

"Wait outside, and I will call you when I am done," Cleo warned Eliza.

"I do not understand why she despises me so. I have not wronged her," she quietly replied to Cleo.

"But she is expecting you to, and for some people, that is all they need. The blame is not yours."

She thanked Cleo for her time and walked past a fuming Celia. More people had gathered outside the room, curiosity causing them to gawk at Eliza's departure. Cleo and Celia continued their strained discussion, and Eliza could hear their impassioned exchange. She stood outside the dwelling.

"You are willing to get flogged? For her?" Celia bellowed.

"She does not know that these ways are forbidden. She is innocent," Cleo responded.

"Oh, and do you not think she will reveal the work you do? Why would you share with the one who takes from you?"

"She hasn't taken anything. She has seen things."

"I see a lot of things when I drink too. And she drinks plenty of French wine every single night. Lucy has told me they empty at least two bottles at times."

"Perhaps she drinks to forget," Cleo said slowly.

"She is a foolish girl," Celia said.

"She has seen Legba. He has spoken with her."

This immediately silenced Celia, and Eliza took this as her cue to leave. The sun was beginning to descend, and she did not feel as welcome as she did when she had first arrived. These last few moments and her encounter with Celia had been jarring. Most of all, she did not understand the heated discussion she had just overheard. Who was the Legba man Cleo had referenced? Eliza had explored this part of the property as blithely as a schoolgirl, but after her talk with Cleo, she felt that matters had only grown more complicated and severe. And did Charles have any inkling of Cleo's abilities? Eliza had sworn to never disclose their discussion. It could only bring trouble.

She dreaded returning to the house. Dinner would be served soon. And she would have to face him. She truly felt as though she belonged nowhere. She could not honestly claim that her life at Bleinhill Manor had been a smoother arrangement. She had hoped the ship would carry her far from life's complications, but it seemed they had only doubled when she reached these shores. She had always faced problems in her life, but now she had enemies. One of whom she was wedded to. She sighed and walked along the shoreline, the crashing waves beating to the rhythm of her troubled thoughts.

The following day, Eliza looked around to ensure no one was observing her actions, and then she began to wade into the water. Once the warm current had surrounded her thighs, she spilled the contents of her cupped palms. Colorful flowers and small coins lay on the surface for the briefest moment, in a tangled clump bobbing up and down, until the coins slowly sank and the tide carried the flowers into scattered directions of white, red, and violet. Before the offering was completely lost, she hurriedly pulled out the tiny vial of rum she had procured, swirling it all around her. Eliza clasped her hands together. She had not prayed in a long time, but now, as she confronted nature and the boundless universe that hovered around and within her, she whispered urgently, asking for help from a faceless presence.

"Please accept this offering. Please hear me. Protect me. Deliver me from this hell," she whispered.

She felt like a fool, but she also knew she was desperate. And in her desperation, she was willing to try anything. Cleo had instructed her to make an offering to Erzulie Dantor, and she hoped it would produce results.

She could not abide by the sheer helplessness she felt. And she could not stand any more sleepless nights. She was exhausted from crying. Her eyelids were swollen, and the small red capillaries on her cheeks were broken and inflamed from her exertions. She prayed the only other prayer she knew, the Lord's Prayer, and then envisioned herself free and far from this island. She opened her eyes. The water sparkled in a thousand shimmering rainbows, dancing across the rippled, white-ridged sand.

Eliza sighed, not knowing if she had truly completed the task correctly. She was anxious to determine how she would ever understand any answer. If, indeed, some divine response would ever come. She had been so nervous to collect the flowers, the coins, and the rum without anyone's notice, but once she had released it all, it seemed so simple, so ordinary. The sea was calm today, and its surface was still. The warm water rose along her lower back as if it was goading her to walk further in.

She began to swim, diving beneath its surface. In the water, she was free to hear her own thoughts and propel herself in whichever direction she chose. All the restraints and pressures she felt on dry land, among other people in society, and the expectations she felt obligated to fulfill dissolved away with every pulse of the ocean.

Eliza floated over the plant-like mineral structures of coral gardens and observed the menagerie of colorful fish, whose names she was still trying to commit to memory. Two bluehead wrasse darted near her feet; their name was simple enough to recall. She could spot their blue heads from even above the surface. Small fish, striped in bands of yellow and black, followed her every move, along with one or two larger fish whose bodies were silver and flat like mirrors. A fish with salmon tones and a large red eye observed her as she passed by.

She mused that the hands of an omniscient artist stroking his brush over their scales could serve as the only explanation for the beauty of some fish; the colors were so arresting and bewildering. And no other fish stood out as the prime example of this other than the parrotfish with its comically large teeth and bright splatters of pinks and greens. Every time she spotted one, she noticed a new flash of color on its body: violet streaks on its lower fins, startlingly blue eyelids, and a burst of yellow on its tail. In the distance, she could see the ghostly eyes of a nurse shark as it rested on a wavering bed of seagrass. They seemed to be docile and listless creatures and nothing like their more predatory cousins.

Eliza made her way as far back as her limits would allow, past the white lines of sand and toward the patches of green where large starfish lay and turtles occasionally grazed. She usually paused in this spot to look for the pink conch shells she gathered here, but she did not stop today. She reached a shallower point as she passed over them, and her feet dropped into the sand as she paused and stood still. But something slipped and moved under her toes. Fearing she had stepped on some creature, perhaps a stingray with its barbed tail, she kicked up into a swim, looking downwards. Nothing stirred, and she could see what looked like a cord through her blurred vision. She took a breath and dived down, poking the strange object hesitantly. Perhaps a hermit crab had built a home under the sand, and she had disturbed it.

She pulled the cord, realizing it was connected to a pouch, and instantly felt a heavy weight. Then a single shining gold coin fell out. She grabbed it wildly, rushing up to the surface. Looking at it with incredulous eyes, the sunlight confirmed what she held in her fingers. It was a small coin. And it was solid gold, its edges perfectly round. With a small yelp of excitement, she swam back, using her hands to stir the grassy bed. There were several pouches, once tan, now bleached a creamy shade by the unrelenting sun. She clutched them all against her breast, her heart beating wildly when she realized they were too heavy to carry. Her chest contracted in pain, signaling a need for more air.

Above the water, she gasped, still clutching the solitary coin in her hand. She looked toward the house. There was no movement except for a single rider on horseback who slowly trotted eastward. His back faced her, and he posed no threat. Eliza returned to the sand and grabbed two bags, rushing out of the water as she made her way to the house. The first coin had looked unfamiliar to her, but there was no mistaking that it was indeed valuable. Her mind raced with a hundred thoughts—of sudden wealth and, more importantly, a sudden sense of liberation. She could leave Pleasant Hall. She could leave this island. She could be free of him.

Dripping wet, she ran into the house, rushing straight to her bedroom. She opened the two pouches with shaking hands, casting their contents onto her mantelpiece. They were filled with coins, at least twenty pieces in each bag. An image of a king had been hammered into them, with a coat of arms on the reverse. Some parts were blackened with verdigris, but it rubbed off easily with the pressure of her thumb.

She stared at her discovery, giddy with exhilaration. Her prayer had been answered. She gazed at the quiet surroundings of her room, with its ordinary bed and motionless curtains. Her life could change. She did not need to remain trapped here. A wavering sensation came underneath her eyes as she felt tears begin to appear. She had hoped and prayed that there was more to her life than being stranded in domestic misery. She could make her way to town, purchase passage on any ship, and leave. He would never know. No one would question these coins in a trading port like Nassau.

She could hear Lucy humming a song downstairs as she cleaned. She worried about the numerous puddles her footsteps had left behind on the stairs and in the entrance hall. And in a sudden flash of clarity, she began to wonder whose coins she had so excitedly gripped in her hands. How long had they been buried there? Would the owner come looking for them, or had they long since died? She considered whether Charles' father had planted them there or Charles himself. He did not want her to swim; perhaps there was a stronger edge to his words of warning. But she also did not care. He did not go in the water. He would not necessarily know that they were missing. Perhaps the spot had already been lost to memory.

She intrinsically felt like she would have time on her side. She could gather her few belongings and leave, and he would be none the wiser. She had prayed to an unseen deity, and she had been heard in some strange, seemingly miraculous way. She had a solution to her problems now.

There were more bags under the water. She pushed the spilled coins back into the pouches and ran outside to retrieve the rest.

Five glasses of wine mixed with exhaustion from swimming, and Eliza descended quickly into sleep. She had intended to read before going to bed, but the book lay untouched on the bed, her hand reposed in rest alongside it, and a different story played out beneath her closed eyes.

"She ran away, boy. You are a fool. She ran away because she didn't love this family," the father says.

The young boy wants to protest, but he cannot speak. He listens in solemn silence, understanding from that day on that his father is a liar.

A slave in a red headwrap takes the boy to his bedroom after dinner and ensures he is safe for the night. There is a thunderstorm, and the boy is scared. She offers what little comfort she can, and he is soon asleep.

She journeys to the cellar to fetch more liquor for the master. But she is really there to find her lady's body. She knows a shallow grave has been dug just outside the doorway. She is there but a few minutes when she is disturbed.

"Tabitha!" the master's voice growls.

She turns and sees him observing her. She is too many steps away from the liquor. The man at once suspects her intentions. He questions her, and she answers with an obvious truth. His whiskey bottle has sunk dangerously low. She is merely refilling it. He doesn't believe her, and she does not attempt to soothe away his doubts. She is full of righteous anger. Then she faces her fear and speaks the truth.

"You killed her. I saw it," she says, pointing to the earthen floor, recently disturbed.

Long lines, as if something heavy has been dragged across the ground, lead to the darkness outside. A man whose instincts are riddled with laziness does not care to sweep away his tracks. And now the dirt reveals his sins. In one move, the man walks up to her and grabs her throat, strangling and silencing her. She tries to fight him with every fiber of fury that has been stored in her bones since the days of her childhood. She puts up a struggle, but it is not enough. She grows weak, slips, and falls. He gains the upper hand, slamming her head against the damp stone wall. He takes her life too, and like his last victim, no measure of justice will be delivered.

He drags her limp body outside. He seeks the mangroves nearby, but they are too far for a man whose limbs are heavy with drink. The sea is closer, and with it comes the sharks. He throws her into the boat and ties a weight to her ankle. He rows out to the horizon, guided by slivers of moonlight. Darkened waves lap at the boat's sides, the only witness to his crime. He rolls her body into the depths. He can collect insurance on her corpse. She is a runaway now, and he only thinks about his greed. No one will find her. The whiskey burns the back of his throat, converting what he has done into nothing more than the soft renderings of a twisted dream. He will remember this night, but he will not regret it.

He struggles to return to shore, nearly tipping out of his boat. He does not bother to return it to its rightful place. He is a careless man. In the morning, they will ask about Tabitha's whereabouts. They will suspect, but no one will know except one. Tabitha's daughter knows her mother would never abandon her freely. The girl has yellow eyes and was carried into this world with more knowledge than most. And she knows one thing for certain. Cruel and unnatural death has visited this land more than once. And it resides in the cracks of her master's flawed and rough hands.

Eliza's eyes adjusted, focusing on the white cracked wall next to her, and she slowly came to. It was dark in her room now. The curtains billowed from a warm breeze, and she realized her light had succumbed to the draft. She looked toward her feet, fully expecting the visitor. And this time, she did not have fear. A heavy sadness descended upon her. And as she looked up at the woman she now understood as Tabitha, the image of her wavered and then disappeared like the smoke from a spent candle. But in a few moments of distinction, Eliza thought she saw a smile cross the woman's detached face. She had succeeded in sharing her story.

Eliza floated, weightless on the surface of the water, rippling with dappled light. The sun was bright, and she closed her eyes, extending her arms into a wide stretch. She inhaled, then sighed. She was aware that she was drifting too close to the limestone rocks that constituted a natural boundary between her familiar waters and the open sea. She turned, swimming back toward the shore when she saw a large milky shape under the water. The movement of its surface made it difficult to tell what she was seeing, but she grew excited at the thought of it being a large shell. The sea was constantly changing, and even as she bobbed above a surface she had investigated many times, the tides regularly brought in new shells and uncovered old ones. She had amassed a growing collection of seashells since her arrival. Her bedroom windowsills and mantle were lined with countless treasures.

She took a breath and dived, opening her eyes under the water. The salt stung her eyes for a few painful seconds, and then it ebbed away as she blinked into sharp focus. She recognized what she had seen from the surface and now noticed more than one of these objects, all cast around a piece of garbage. It had most likely been thrown overboard from a passing ship. The currents carried all sorts of things far and wide. She thought of the countless bottles, belt buckles, and bricks she had found on other swims. But she also recalled the discovery of the coins, and the intrigue she felt every time she spotted something curious in the water made her eager to find out what it was.

Eliza came up to the surface for air and then dived down again, the motion giving her the impression that her legs were long and full of grace, kicking furiously as she spiraled deeper so she could spend more time on the bottom.

She grasped it. It was no shell. It was hollow in her hand, and she watched in slow horror as it drifted back to the sand ridge from where it came. The middle was hollow, its core spongy and composed of marrow. It was a human vertebra. Eliza looked at the piece of debris she had so naively assumed was litter. It was actually a piece of fabric, and it billowed in the current. As she pushed her body away from it, the red material flowed in a new direction and revealed a line of bones, neatly arranged in a curved pattern, untouched after all these years. She did not wait to find the skull. It was too unbearable, and she desperately needed a breath of air.

She shot up to the surface, gasping, the full reality of her discovery only settling over her now. Eliza looked up at the charming white house above the sand dune, the horror of its history slowly erasing its innocuous presence and replacing it with a much darker one. She looked below her kicking feet, the red cloth appearing as only a wisp of color below the moving tide. She was frightened, afraid of what lay beneath the surface now and afraid of the accuracy of her dreams. It was too uncanny. What did it all mean?

She took a deep breath and returned to the sea floor, this time determined to hover over the same spot and not get swept away by the waves. She could not see all the skeleton fragments she assumed should be there. They must have laid further in the sand. But then, a shining object caught her eye. A single pewter hoop, half uncovered by the pulsating water, shifted an inch from its resting place. And with the earring in full view, Eliza knew without a doubt that she was gazing upon Tabitha's bones.

A sinking feeling twisted her gut, and the waves spun her legs one way and then another, the seawater seizing the opportunity to invade her ears. She kicked back to the surface madly, gulped more air, and then returned. She saw a withered green rope attached to a metal sinker from a new angle. The deliberateness of the cruel act chilled her, and she looked around despite knowing she was alone. Fish darted by, their substantial yellow eyes devoid of any emotion.

The scene before her was surreal and made her feel chillingly detached. She had uncovered something forbidden. She rushed out of the water, no longer wanting to be near the remains. She remembered the disturbingly solid silhouette of the figure by her bed and the sadness that emanated from her like a faint, eerie glow. They were not merely bones. They were the remains of a woman gravely wronged.

Her shaking legs stumbled up the porch. She was dripping far too much to go inside. She usually sat in the sun to dry her clothes quicker. She did not want to catch the servants' ire, but she needed to be far from the beach. Its soothing, repetitive waves concealed a dark secret. The shore that had once presented nothing but a calming sanctuary to her was now a looming horror. Giant droplets hit the walnut floorboards as she made her way inside. She retreated into the dim coolness of the house, only to stop midway in front of the stairs. She was not alone.

A thin, lanky man stood in the parlor, his hands prying open a gold-enameled snuffbox. His skin was tanned a deep brown, and his dark-blond hair was longer than any respectable gentleman would have kept it. He was dressed well but ostentatiously so. A long saber sat hilted at his hip, and a pistol was stashed in his waistband. She regretted her presence there but then remembered that he was the one intruding.

"May I help you with something?" she asked.

The man looked up with a critical look in his narrowed eyes.

"A mere girl is responsible for stealing from my men," he said, stepping forward.

He looked Eliza up and down and then sneered, shaking his head. He was conceited and bold: a dangerous combination.

"Who let you in?" she asked nervously.

She looked around her and then called for Lucy.

"I let myself in." He clasped his arms behind his back as he straightened his posture.

"May I help you with something?" she repeated more firmly.

"You have my *escudos*. I want them back."

He had a deep voice, but it sounded tight and strained.

"Forgive me, but I am unsure of your meaning, sir..."

"Hiram Bruin. And you are...Sharpe's sister? His woman—"

"His wife," Eliza promptly corrected.

"Ah, he did take a wife. I wouldn't have expected that. Then again, I wasn't expecting him to return to these shores. I would have calculated differently if I had that knowledge."

"You are an acquaintance of my husband?"

"You could say as much."

He inspected her with a scowl and then exhaled, running a hand through his messy hair. "Give me the *escudos*."

Even though he had said it a second time, his meaning was no clearer to her.

"Beg pardon, but what are *escudos*?"

"The coins, woman. Give me the coins you took." He laughed and looked off to the side.

Eliza stiffened up, unsure how to react. She had not anticipated something like this occurring. She had foolishly assumed the coins belonged to the Sharpe family. The sea was only yards from their property. She decided to admit to only half the truth and feign weakness. She did not recognize the man before her and could not make a sound decision about his trustworthiness.

"From my understanding, wracking is common practice on this island. I see no reason as to why you so confidently claim ownership of these coins you mention. Besides, I am a woman. I cannot swim."

"You can swim all right. Like a fish. You've been watched."

Eliza said nothing, clenching her jaw. Her annoyance grew at the idea that more than one man could make her feel trapped in her own home.

Mr. Bruin sharply inhaled. "Ah, and you have a pass from the governor, I take it?"

"I think we both understand that not everything is done the proper way here. I only recently arrived, and even I can see that," she said.

She felt momentarily comforted by the remembrance that she had finally buried them in the cellar only days before. She had stored another batch inside a queen conch shell on the side table in her room and a third lot underneath the back porch stairs.

"Pass or no pass, you of course, know you need to pay the fifth and tenth," he replied in a mocking tone.

"It's been handled accordingly," she lied, trying to mask her ignorance.

"Only I don't pay my fifth and tenth part of the find. Dunmore is not my governor. And George is not my king. So, if you did so, then you squandered my money, and you're in greater debt than before."

"Sir, I owe you nothing."

"Naivety does not suit you. My man Henry saw you diving in the area. He followed you back here. And the coins are missing. You were even foolish enough to drop some in the sand."

She had never seen any man watching her except the solitary horse rider on the day of her discovery. She inwardly cursed.

"Then you were fortunate. Perhaps more will be unexpectedly recovered," she countered.

"Are you attempting to negotiate with me? With my stolen property? I warn you, I am not a man of negotiation."

The elated happiness she had felt days earlier swiftly deflated in his presence. What if the discovery of the coins was not a blessing or an answer to her prayers? What if it only spelled more trouble? Had she been foolish to assume it was a fortuitous accident?

She refused to make this situation a problem. She would never tell this man where she had hidden them.

"Neither is my husband. It is not a new arena for me."

"I won't say it again. I will wait here until you fetch them."

If this captain was who she assumed he was, he had not attained those coins by any honorable means. And now he demanded his stolen goods back as if she was the criminal in the room. She could not believe his audacity.

"You speak as if you are a respectable merchant, but you profit off the misfortunes of others. My husband has indeed mentioned men like you, but never in a favorable light," she replied sharply.

Her tone was fiery, but she was still nervous. She desperately looked down the empty hallway but realized with the distant sound of Lucy humming upstairs that she was alone with him. The servant was most likely folding the laundered clothes and storing them in a chest upstairs. Eliza's isolation was inconvenient.

"I'm afraid that the morality of certain livelihoods leaves room for debate in this house," he said.

"That is my husband's affair, not mine," she snapped.

"But the *escudos* are indeed your responsibility."

"They are not here, sir. Please leave."

He strode forward and stopped inches away from her. He was nearly the same height as Charles but leaner and, from the lines on his face, decidedly a few years older.

"I will not leave until I have overturned every inch of this rotten house and recovered my loss."

"Then you might as well stay the night. I will tell the maid to prepare a room. I do not have them."

"You lie…" he growled.

She took a step back, but he still advanced.

"If you are an acquaintance of my husband, surely you recognize that he is a commissioned officer in His Majesty's army. I recall that his men have increased patrols on the coast looking for smugglers. Take that as a warning. You best depart before he arrives home."

This comment had little effect on the man. She was running out of options. He seemed prepared to follow her by the very heel like a stubborn dog. But then, by some miraculous cue, the bell rang in the yard, signaling Charles' arrival.

"And you heed this warning: watch yourself on these beaches. You never know who you will run into," Mr. Bruin said with a glare. "My men are everywhere."

He turned on his heel and stormed out of the room, not even closing the door. Moments later, the parlor was filled with a new dominating presence. She panicked for a moment, considering whether the two men had run into each other and what the subsequent reaction had been.

"Eliza?" Charles asked, wiping the sweat from his brow as he strode into the hallway. "Was that Captain Bruin I just saw departing? He seemed rather vexed. What on earth did he want?"

Eliza rushed to find an explanation that did not give her secret away.

"He came around to ask about an object one of his men had lost on the beach. He wanted to know if any of the slaves had seen it when they fished in the morning. I, of course, informed him that we only keep honest workers here and that if they ever found something, they would report it."

"Peculiar. Did he mention what it was?"

Charles studied her with the green eyes she knew could look straight through her. He was the only man who could make her feel as if she was naked, stripped bare of even the most basic clothing, and that he alone could read her very thoughts. And she hated him for it.

"He didn't say. No. I'm assuming it was something from his sloop."

"I don't trust that man. Men like him demean the title 'merchant'."

Charles walked to the hallway to remove his red jacket.

"Yes, he was quite rude."

He stopped, looking perturbed.

"What is your meaning, my dear?"

"Oh, nothing. His manner of addressing me, I suppose. It was rather rough. He seemed entirely unpleasant."

"The only time I've witnessed him act pleasantly is when he robs us at the card table. The man knows little else. Next time, tell him to return only when I am home. I know how to deal with his lot. The Dutch are easily misunderstood."

Eliza nodded and was about to dash up the stairs. She stopped halfway, unable to ignore the feeling of Charles watching her. She did not want to linger any longer, but he was already fixated on her.

"Eliza, were you dressed so when you spoke to him?"

She exhaled more forcefully than she intended.

"Eliza," he said sternly, stepping on the first stair.

"I was unaware that he was in our parlor."

"Must I endlessly repeat it? Perhaps he only ventured in here to catch a closer glimpse of you. How many times must I say it? Do not go swimming! You endanger yourself, and now you've put Captain Bruin in a compromising situation. You do no favors to anyone's honor!"

"I care little for that man's sense of honor. He is a ruffian at best. You, yourself, understand this."

"He only needs to say that my wife, the wife of a lieutenant colonel, prances around barely clothed. That you wear men's clothes! The talk that will ensue from that quarter! I do not need this, Eliza!"

"He hardly seemed interested in my person if that puts your mind at ease," she replied.

He moved closer to her.

"You understand nothing of men. I know how they think, and I do not need strangers to witness you like this day in and day out. I already had to stop the slaves from prattling on about witnessing a mermaid near the shoreline, but then I realized they had only seen my careless and insipid wife."

"I hardly believe the latter, and forgive me, but I sometimes fail to recall that there could be guests this far from Nassau. I sometimes find this place to be as still as the doldrums. Indeed, I even forget that we are part of a larger island and that it possesses a bustling town."

"Perhaps the error lies with you and your seeming reluctance to cultivate a friendship with ladies like Charlotte. Perhaps she would call here if you socialized with her more earnestly." Charles sounded enlivened by such a prospect. Then his voice softened. "Perhaps the governor himself would call here. I have social aspirations, Eliza, even though you may not."

"Why is it in my interest to cultivate a friendship with Charlotte? We are nothing alike, and you know it. Is it only because she is merely another man's wife?"

"She is not Lord Dunmore's wife. She is…" Charles began to say, stopping short.

Eliza looked at him questioningly. "You told me his wife was named Charlotte…"

"Yes, indeed she is," he said, sighing. "She is residing in Sicily for the season with their daughters. You are not naive; you must know by now that gentlemen often acquire a habit of keeping female acquaintances. It does not create a scandal in so much as such friendships are kept discreet at all times."

The realization of what Charles would not plainly say washed over her. Lord Dunmore's mistress shared the same name as his lawful wife. The irony of Charles' words and the governor's blatant carelessness was disturbing to her. She doubted his wife had been absent for only a few months. She wondered if she had ever stepped foot on this island at all. Eliza did not blame her for it.

"You mention discretion. I would posit he has absolutely failed in that endeavor. And you would urge me to keep company with people of such character?"

Charles looked down and said nothing.

"It is of no consequence. I daresay Lord Dunmore would not venture to any place where he cannot continually show his affluence off, and it appears that can only be accomplished within the walls of his own mansion. I also do not think that man would ever journey longer than a few minutes by carriage; the width of his frame would simply not tolerate it," she continued.

"You delight in insulting *my* superior, *your* superior, a man worthy of respect. He is the governor! He represents the king! I will not stand for this. You should wish to please me in all things!"

"Then you must excuse me, dear husband. For I have nothing pleasant to say about that man."

She turned to take another step upward, but he wrenched her arm down and nearly caused her to fall.

His green eyes narrowed.

"Be careful. There is a limit to my patience," he said.

She wrested herself out of his grip and headed to her room. She was in no mood for his unstable temper. Something altogether more disturbing consumed her thoughts now.

CHAPTER VII.

The livery-clad musicians raised their violins and started the upbeat, lilting music for dancing. A clash of perfumes and body odors mingled in the humid air. Hundreds of candles cast the mansion in shifting shadows, and even though every window and door were ajar, the rooms were still heavy with a balmy warmth. Every room and salon was even more crowded due to the number of footmen who stood watch and floated from reveler to reveler with silver trays of refreshments. So many people were present tonight that Eliza imagined the entire island was in attendance. There were scant opportunities for social occasions in the colony, and when Lord Dunmore arranged events, hardly anyone declined.

Despite being on the island for some time now, she still could not shake the uncomfortable irony of having slaves dressed in such garish clothes. There was a fetish toward orientalism in her time, and she could scarcely understand it. From the books she read, it made no sense to have slaves ripped from the coasts of Africa donned in the silk turbans of Bengal. There was a haunting element to such a visual. What made these slaves so different to be paraded around in such outlandish outfits while others toiled naked under the sun to be ravaged by insects and heat? This new world was stranger than the one she had left. And nowhere was this more apparent than in Lord Dunmore's mansion on the hill.

She swallowed the last of her punch and looked around for a second glass. In her lonely hours, she had realized a single fact. There were stages of defeat. In the beginning, she had scarcely let alcohol touch her lips. She blamed drink for her lack of inhibition that very first night. It had left her weakened and helpless. For the first week, she had staunchly refused wine with her meals. But then she grew desperate to erase the tension between her and Charles. Wine made his words less noisome, and the overwhelming silence that followed became tolerable.

And then, in the final stage, alcohol served as an escape from her monotonous days and even more dreadful nights. It soothed her pathos when the evening set in, and she could no longer roam the beach. Now, she leaned on its dulling effects like a cane, and the things she once anticipated with anxiety no longer caused her any alarm. Feminine chatter and stiff introductions rolled past her shoulders in a way they never had before in England. Alcohol delivered her from her torments, and plenty of it was in supply tonight.

Couples began to form on the dance floor, and others, more nervous about joining in, hesitated by the edge of the group. She took this as a cue to exit the room, but a hand stopped her.

"May I have this dance with my wife?" Charles asked.

She stared at her shoes as a drop of sweat left her face and darkened her skirt.

"I'm afraid I do not feel well," she deflected.

She passed her empty glass to a servant, eagerly looking for another tray with more drinks. When she spotted one, she was about to attempt her escape again when he grabbed her left hand.

"I insist."

They turned about the room in swooping circles, occasionally meeting again to touch extended hands. The walls, the windows, and the servants repeated endlessly. She was quickly losing interest in the dance, nearly forgetting which direction she was to turn, when she noticed a dark man wearing a strange hat. It was rather tall and made of a shiny material that caught the light as he turned. He was the man she had spoken with on the day of her arrival. She smiled, her interest piqued. As dancers moved around him, she could see contrasting black and white stripes underneath the tails of his coat. He maneuvered in and out of the crowd with ease. He was not dancing but had chosen to carve out a path in the middle of the ballroom.

Charles was staring at her, but she was mesmerized by this stranger. She watched him exit the room. The music reached a crescendo and then died down. As if on cue, three candles alongside the wall extinguished. Servants rushed to light the blackened wicks. Charles stood, trying to keep his composure, completely aware he had lost her attention once again. She slipped away from Charles and the other dancers and out a door into the hallway.

The man must have gone outside. He was nowhere else to be seen. A footman passed by her offering champagne, and she took one as her eyes scanned the darkness through the open doorway. A series of smashing glasses and gasps sounded next to her in another room. A servant had apparently dropped a glass of wine on the hardwood floor, but it had partially spilled on the shoe of an older man. The group in the room to her right stopped mid-motion as they awaited a reaction.

The footman apologized profusely, but it had little effect. The older man took his metal cane and battered the servant with a merciless blow as he cursed at him. The footman doubled over, losing his powdered wig and spilling two additional drinks. He still somehow managed to carry the silver tray aloft, but this did not catch anyone's notice. They only viewed him as a clumsy drudge, and this, in turn, made him a useless slave. Eliza watched in confusion and horror. She had witnessed plenty of guests spilling their drinks tonight, and the women around her seemed most susceptible to committing the crime. The mahogany floors were riddled with sticky puddles of sweet punch and trails of tiny ants. She bristled at the older man's overreaction.

"Are those tears I see? Please do not concern yourself with their breed."

Eliza turned to her left. Two middle-aged gentlemen were watching her response to the events with unabashed amusement. One had a reddish wig perched on his sweating head, and the other was wider in corpulence than any other guest she had seen that night. The most remarkable feature of his appearance was that he seemed to possess no neck and his bowl-shaped face merely rested on his pudgy shoulders. They did not even bother with introductions.

"I was not under the impression that we belonged to distinct breeds," she said curtly.

"And that, my dear Douglas, is why women are best left to discussions of lace and silk," the man with the red wig remarked.

Eliza recoiled from his words. He sipped his drink with arrogance.

"Do not mistake me. My sex does not hinder my mind. They are flesh and bone, no different than you and I."

"Have you ever seen a woman in command of anything besides the home and hearth?"

The thinner man turned to his friend as he awaited his answer.

"I have…last night at The Dolphin. Got my money's worth! And you did too, James, you devil!" Douglas rejoined.

The men broke out into bawdy laughter. But Eliza was determined to have the final say.

"Women do not command society, but it is not by choice. There are certain fleshy impediments standing in the way."

Eliza felt she had handled their ignorance as deftly as possible, and now she wanted to leave. She looked at the fat man and motioned that she intended to step forward, but he would not move aside.

"Where is Lord Sharpe?" Douglas asked James as if she was no longer within earshot.

"He should collect her," James said while he scanned the crowd.

"I do not need my husband to come and get me. I daresay, if you find my presence so odious, you are free to depart from my company," she said.

"It would be rather charitable of us to allow him an extra round of cards tonight. He clearly puts up with enough misfortune," Douglas chimed.

"He really should instruct her to be quiet with her Whig sympathies," James replied.

Douglas sipped his drink. "I am wholly surprised he allows such drivel."

"The only misfortune is that you are both entirely incapable of possessing an open mind with which to hear ideas that differ from your own," Eliza finally snapped.

"Good evening, Lady Sharpe. The other ladies are currently in the yellow parlor if you would be so inclined as to rejoin them," James said with an entirely different tone.

He leaned forward now, indicating the direction she should walk. His dismissal was blunt and final. She knew that if she lingered beyond this point, she would cause a scene. She curtsied out of politeness, but she was boiling with rage. She purposefully walked in the opposite direction toward the gardens. As she stepped out onto the veranda and the sultry breeze enveloped her, she caught a second glimpse of the mysterious man with the tall hat. From the open windows, she could hear fragments of socially polished conversation wafting in and out of the house. Someone was congratulating Charles on their marriage. She ridiculed the superficiality of it all.

She took a final swig of her champagne and threw her glass into the darkness. The crash was louder than expected, and she immediately heard hurried footsteps. The sound was undeniably headed in her direction, so she rushed down the wooden steps and into the humidity and sodden grass. The strange man ran into the hedgerow as she approached. In her haste, she failed to take into account exactly who else was strolling the manicured paths outside. Lifting her skirt up so as not to dampen the fabric while also watching where she stepped, she suddenly bumped into an implacable object.

"Lady Sharpe," a gruff voice responded.

She looked up and backed away.

"Governor," she said, managing a half-curtsy.

His double chin was covered in a pattern of sweat and stubble.

"Admiring the beauty of my gardens?" he asked, taking stock of her.

"Oh, yes, Lord Dunmore, they are quite stunning," she replied. "One wonders how you managed to conquer the tropical terrain and fashion such a continental design."

She looked over his shoulder, straining to follow the stranger's path.

"Yes, yes," he mumbled, taking a loud sip of his wine.

She was aware that he was staring quite boldly at her chest, and she endeavored to break away.

"Have you seen a man with a rather tall hat come walking this way?" she asked.

"A man with a hat? No…"

"He is a black man. A free man, I believe. Dressed very finely."

The governor barked out a laugh and took a step toward her.

"My dear, I can assure you I have invited no such characters into my home, and if you did see such a sight, I'm afraid one of my slaves has ransacked my wardrobe and taken off."

"Oh, no, I…I've seen him here before," she replied quickly.

"No," he said with an abruptness that signaled the end of his patience.

She looked back toward the mansion.

"I cannot tell you how much I appreciate a fine English import," the governor said.

The mosquitoes were ruthless on the lawn. She watched as one landed on the rolls of his neck and then another. She grew itchy watching the assault.

"The wine, sir? I thought it came from Loire."

He laughed again, his eyes narrowing down on her.

"No, my dear, *you*."

Eliza blushed. Now they were the only figures on the lawn, save one gentleman with dark hair standing idly on the veranda. The governor also seemed to take notice.

"Shall we discuss Lord Sharpe's promotion, perhaps?" he said, sniffing.

"Oh, no, I think that's a conversation better suited in his presence, my lord."

"Perhaps I am not being clear," he said, slightly annoyed.

She felt a grubby hand wrap around the small of her back. His breath reeked of alcohol and the sour smell of tooth decay.

"I have a quaint guest house near my Tuscan garden," he said, a smile revealing the source of the stench. "We can discuss his promotion to colonel. Alone. Away from the noise."

"With all due respect, sir, I do not find this a suitable time for such matters. I really must return to the house,"

She felt him hold her tighter.

"I know you have recently arrived in Nassau, and perhaps you do not quite understand the workings of this colony. I will not take slight at your refusal. So, I will try once again. I can make it worth your time, Lady Sharpe. Come, follow me."

Lord Dunmore began to steer her towards the darkened trees. She broke free from him and ran back to the house, her ears burning with shame. She almost collided with the man standing near the door. He had most likely witnessed the entire scene. Her heart was pounding. Who else had seen that?

She did not have to wait long to find out. Charles advanced on her as if she were a thief stealing silver. He was brazen to behave like this, especially in the public eye. Her misfortune was that nearly everyone was too impaired by drink to notice. He dragged her by the arm to the nook underneath the spiraling staircase. She almost tripped over her skirts, mumbling in quiet protest.

"I am not a gentle man," he said, turning his face to look at her.

"Neither are you a gentleman," she replied, her eyes full of anger.

She watched the open door with dread.

"Tell me what the governor said to you."

"He mentioned nothing of importance, husband."

Charles pushed himself away from the wall, surveying the room around them. A servant came bearing drinks which he silently declined with a harsh look.

"I do not think you understand your place in this society. You alone can help me with advancements."

"I am more than a mere ornament on your arm?"

"You are my wife," he seethed. "Wives look out for their husbands' benefit. The best imperial careers are born out of the mouths of women. You are not simply sipping tea and chatting about the sweltering climate. You are speaking with earpieces to the governor and to the magistrate. It is in our best interest for you to cultivate a friendship with Charlotte. And now you happened to stumble into Lord Dunmore himself. Do not take me for a fool. You surely did not discuss the weather with him."

With a hand on either side of her and their position behind the staircase, Eliza felt increasingly boxed in. So, it did not matter where they stood, she mused; a brute was still a brute regardless of his place in the home or with company. And yet, this latest demonstration actually revealed his insecurity. She smiled; she wanted Charles to embarrass himself tonight.

"No, husband, we discussed the layout of the garden," she replied pertly, enjoying his frustration.

He dropped his hands in anger and took a step back, only to return very close to her face.

"Our lives depend on the generosity of his patronage. You must treat every word spoken by that man with the utmost seriousness. Furthermore, you should seek him out at every opportunity. When he walks into the room, your first aim should be to engage him. Do you understand?" Charles asked, his green eyes searching hers. "A single word from Lord Dunmore can either elevate our fortunes or destroy any chance of happiness we may have."

"I believe it is too late for the latter, husband," Eliza said, spotting an opening to leave. "Someone else has already accomplished that deed."

Eliza curtsied and walked away from Charles and the shadows of the staircase. It was immediately put to much better use with a drunken couple seeking a corner of privacy. Only after she passed them did she recognize that the man was Reverend Samuel. She was disgusted for a moment, but then she cleared the image from her mind. She walked with her chin held high, not knowing where she was headed but elated all the same. She had no need to impress these people. She strolled through a pool of hypocrites, and Charles was no better in his quest for *their* approval. She had finally found an advantage over him: the nagging weakness that kept him awake at night.

Eliza wandered from room to room, rushing from one area to another until she was in a secluded parlor on the other side of the mansion that looked like a small library. She knew it was unseemly for her to parade around alone as if she was only there to explore the grand house. Ladies at balls would congregate with other members of their sex or be led coyly by an eligible gentleman to either the refreshment table or the dance floor. But her curiosity was stronger than her sense of etiquette. She did not need a man to conduct her from one humid room to another. Eliza had stopped caring for society's rules long before that night.

She threw herself down on a cushioned chair, whipping out her fan as her mind raced with thoughts. Her minor excitement was beginning to wear off, rapidly replaced by a sense of dread and panic. Had she just ruined her husband's entire career? Was this how things truly worked down here? Could men not be promoted from diligence and merit but only through blood and vulgar favors? Would he have wanted her to accept such a lewd proposition? Charles worked so hard at his post. Should she have accepted?

She saw Charles walking through a hallway with two ladies from a distance. No. Certainly not. Not for him. She tried to regain a steady breath and calm herself.

As her breathing steadied, she looked about the room. Several large maps hung on the walls. She studied the islands from a distance. She needed to leave this place. A new determination settled over her. She simply had to accept that this entire venture had been a failure. Surely, that was the first step in finding a solution. She would be ruined, of course, and could never marry again. She would probably die alone. But she would be free. She had the money. Her mind focused on the gold coins she had hidden throughout Pleasant Hall.

Eliza got up and walked toward a map. A yellow settee blocked the wall in front of it, so she kneeled on the seat to look closer. *The Bahama Islands*. She searched for the nearest neighboring island. Was it populated? Did it have a thriving port? Could she get there by boat from the cay near the house? Her fingers traced an invisible trail back to Nassau. The tide was too strong and the shoals too treacherous. Or could she get to town by horse and leave from the harbor? It would be risky. She would need to pass by the fort. Someone would surely notice her and set off the alarm.

She gazed northwards to the American colonies and its vast mass of unknown territory. The other ocean in the Pacific caught her attention next. Her fingers landed on Canton. Drawings of dragons swirled in the waves. She was mesmerized by how exotic it all seemed. She immediately thought of the coromandel screen in the upstairs parlor. Perhaps she could furtively make her way upstairs to take a longer glance at it in privacy.

"Oh…Canton. It's like a land from one's dreams," a voice punctuated the air next to her ears.

It sounded different than most voices she had heard, most notably for its lack of a pretentious drawl. It was light, full of energy, and faintly wrapped in a strange accent.

Eliza whipped around, nearly tumbling from the furniture. An impeccably dressed gentleman with a striking face stood in front of her. He appeared to be nearly the same age as Charles. His hair was a dark-brown shade, and he was shorter than her husband, but then again, most men were. Standing close to him now, she could see that his shoulders reached just a few inches above hers. His sapphire jacket complemented his large eyes, and its brass buttons shined in the golden light. In the shadows of the room, his pulled-back hair appeared nearly black. He flashed a charming smile, his hands clasped behind him.

This was the same gentleman she had almost run into on the veranda.

"I have been there myself. And to Batavia as well," he began to say, looking back at the map. "An arduous journey, to be sure, but I wish I could return." He sighed. "My apologies…I am Jean Charles de Longchamp."

She nearly forgot herself and rushed to extend her hand. He took it and gently pressed his lips to her skin.

Eliza was about to say her name, but drunken cheers rang out from the gentlemen's parlor. She realized his hold had lingered on her, and she hurriedly removed her hand.

"What is it like to travel so far?" she asked quietly, looking back at the map.

They surveyed it together, although she managed to steal another glance at him. He looked back at her with eyes that mimicked the blueness of the waters around the island. The wavering candlelight around them complemented his profile, and she was rapidly losing concentration on their discussion.

"It does not seem so far when it's part of a much longer journey. But once you make landfall and step on the ground, you truly realize how far away you are from home. It is a different land, with different peoples, different customs, strange legends, hills wrapped in mist and mystery…"

"Dragons?"

"Yes, in fact."

"Oh, nonsense. Truly?"

She laughed and looked down.

"Indeed, madame. I saw the bones myself. Never a live one, mind you, but I have seen the proof."

She studied his face trying to gauge how serious he was. He appeared fascinated with her reaction.

"Perhaps it doesn't matter as the Cantonese swear by their existence. You only need a solid belief in a thing to judge how real it truly is. Faith can be stronger than facts at times," he replied smoothly.

Eliza stepped away from the maps, smiled at him nervously, and started to leave the room. She was beginning to enjoy the conversation, but her small satisfaction after this miserable evening seemed to signal the very impossibility of innocent banter. Everyone on this island wanted to use people for their own gain. This man could surely be no different. It was brash enough of him to have wandered into the same empty room. He should have seen she was alone and kept walking. Besides, the man was talking about dragons, beings that had died long ago in the dust of medieval ignorance.

"*'There are more things on heaven and earth…than are dreamt of in your philosophy,'*" she heard him say.

She paused and turned around.

"Ah, Shakespeare!" she replied.

She felt herself drawn back into the room.

"Do not be mistaken. I am no Horatio. My curiosity seems to consume my very core at times," she said.

He laughed quietly.

"I find it strange to encounter a lady who doesn't fawn over the tragic romance of *Romeo and Juliet* or the fantasy of *A Midsummer Night's Dream*. No, *Hamlet* steals your fancy. Skulls, poison, murder, phantoms. You are making me nervous in your company, madame…"

His amusement seemed contagious.

"Eliza, Eliza Sharpe," she said, grinning.

She felt overwhelmingly intrigued by this man. For one, his head had remained perfectly straight and level. His blue eyes had never strayed from hers. Eliza knew that she should leave at once. There were rules of decorum that needed to be followed. And yet, she felt comfortable enough to join him on the settee. She wanted to hear more of what he had to say. Perhaps he could help her. She would gain no traction by following the rules everyone else seemed eager to break. She needed to be cunning on an island like this.

"Tell me more about the Orient. Are you a sailor?"

"My father owned a trading company. He worked for the old governor and, before that, for an earl. Much to my mother's dismay, he took me on a few journeys. Sometimes I wonder if I'm ever truly back, if I'm not stuck somewhere in Asia or Africa, and my time here isn't merely an illusion."

His bright eyes seemed to glow with intensity.

"Quite the poetic mind, sir. Africa, you say?"

She wandered back to the map, her fingers drifting over the continent.

"Yes, for the slave trade."

Her face paled. The fact that nearly everyone in this new world had some connection to the trade was disheartening. She looked back at its bulking mass on the map, its interior left completely blank. No rivers or mountains, or demarcations divided the negative space. Markings of trading ports dotted its coast up and down like dark stitches around its shape.

"Are there no rivers in the interior? It seems rather odd to me," Eliza said, indicating its place on the map.

"Yes, it is strange to be presented in such a way. I believe there are rivers. And mountain ranges as well. Men have not explored its depth and vastness at length. Or at least they haven't survived to tell the tale. They are unfortunately more occupied with its coasts. The trade in Africa is a lucrative business."

Eliza sighed with disdain and looked down.

"My father was involved in that, I cannot lie, but I was always more interested in the people and how they lived. Their culture is much older than ours, you know," he said.

This was the first person she had encountered to carry such an opinion. She thought of the book Mr. Wells had gifted her. She already had a list of queries she wanted to ask this man.

"And now we have them in chains like animals."

She made the statement comfortably, surmising that he was most likely of the same persuasion. He leaned in closer to her.

"I would watch your words, madame. Not for my sake but for the house you are standing in. It was built on their broken backs. This very island was. The better you know me, you will find you are not alone in that opinion, although it may be best not to discuss it here."

Eliza looked down at her hands, flushed at how accurately she had judged the stranger before her. She silently wondered what it could mean. A couple wandered into the room and quickly walked out, searching for better seclusion.

"They say women react with only their emotions and men with their logic, but I believe neither faculty is implemented in the enterprise of trading bodies. I think perhaps when dealing with slavery, it might be wise to see beyond mere profits," he continued.

"And is this why you are alone at the ball tonight, sir?" Eliza asked with a quick smile.

"Perhaps," he said, with mock dissatisfaction. "But I have noticed that I encountered you by yourself as well."

"I am not like most ladies," she said, examining her dirt-stained skirt. "Many would say it is a detriment."

"I see no detriment. Fine jewels stand apart from plain rocks, do they not? They are more noticeable. That is what they were meant to do, surely."

She felt her ears grow hot again but in an entirely different way this time. Eliza tried to maintain a polite distance and not stare at the man. She wondered who he was. He was not acting like the other men here. She truly enjoyed his company.

"Tell me more about trade in the Orient. Did you trade in *dragon* bones?" she asked.

"No, much too rare a commodity, I'm afraid. Tea leaves, spices, silks, pearls…"

"Pearls? Surely these islands have plenty."

"They do, to be sure. But pearls from the Orient are unlike ones found on these shores. They have such vivid colors and a largeness in size to be unmatched by what we have here," he explained.

"I have always loved pearls. Perhaps it is better that I do not journey there. I would save my husband's purse."

226

She deliberately said that word to test him. He did not seem to register her use of it. After what had happened with Charles, she knew better than to assume men were really interested in her words alone. Although, somehow, this one was proving to be different.

"Here," he said, producing a purple pearl tied on an elaborate red string. He placed the strange ornament in her hand. The pearl was the size of her thumbnail. She marveled at its size and color.

"It is a good fortune charm. The Cantonese believe that no harm will come to those who carry it. You can have it."

She tried to return it to him.

"Oh, no, sir. I am a stranger. I couldn't possibly accept this."

"No, no, I insist," he said, his hands raised. "I just saw that you do not have a drink. May I fetch one for you?"

She acquiesced, and he was gone from the room. The lack of his overwhelming presence made the room seem so quiet and dull without him in it. A clock chimed in the hallway. She studied the pearl some more and then tucked it into the folds of her stays. He returned a few moments later, and she felt herself smile in an unrefined manner. They clinked glasses and continued their conversation on travel.

Across the room, Eliza saw Charles stroll through the hallway again. He had a scowl on his face. She felt proud. She was finally navigating the twists and turns of this society. She secretly hoped he felt envy. He walked about with other ladies. Why should she not enjoy talking to a man? The words Charlotte had spoken to her during the early days of their ill-fated cordiality echoed throughout her mind.

Jean and Eliza sat silently for a moment, observing the frivolities of a drunken woman whose hair feather was tilted at an odd angle.

"I have a question, I must admit," Jean said.

Eliza perked up, sipping more of her drink.

"I have been saving this discussion for the presence of a stranger, and I think I've found the perfect one."

He looked at her and smiled. Her heart began to race. *Is this what affections are supposed to feel like?* she mused.

"I will tell you my thoughts, and I would like your perfectly honest and unbiased opinion. I cannot ask my acquaintances as they are too informed of the situation to best guide me."

"Yes, I understand," she replied, taking another sip. "Go on."

"It is a matter of friendship."

"A male companion or a female companion?" she asked breathlessly.

"In regard to a male companion."

Her thudding heart fell to a quiet toll. But she was still intrigued.

"I will listen and give you my exact thoughts on the matter."

"Good, good," Jean replied, clearing his throat. "I have had a friend for some years now. He's more like a brother to me, really. We grew up together on neighboring estates. Played in the woods as young boys are wont to do. We had a fort made of sticks, and we played soldiers. He always accepted me, which is a kindness I cannot easily forget."

"I am not sure of your meaning, sir?"

"My family is from France, and my parents had the foresight to flee from our lands before all the troubles began. I didn't understand at the time, but now I am most grateful. It is no simple feat to be employed in His Majesty's interests when you have the blood of the enemy coursing through your veins."

"Oh, nonsense! I can hardly detect any difference in you at all. Not even the slightest accent."

She felt her face burning. She was lying: the cadence in his voice made her cling to his every word.

"Yes, well, I was a young boy. But my superiors can still point out certain words I pronounce more like a Frenchman."

He looked down at the patterns on the rug.

"I quite enjoy your company, sir, if I may be so bold as to say. Perhaps I belong in France with like minds."

"Not these days, madame. It is no place for people like us." He sighed and continued. "Going back to my tale, this friend did not care where I came from. To him, I was just as good as any Englishman. We grew up side by side, joined the army, and moved through the ranks together. He, being a better soldier than I, was always a position above me, of course," he said, laughing. "But he always was more competitive in nature. He has ambition like a tiger. We fought alongside each other in the American colonies…"

"What was that like?" she asked, completely mesmerized.

"A story for another night and more drink, madame. But, of course, gossip and rumors abound in a group as tightly linked as a regiment. Some started to question my ancestry. They even went so far as to suggest I was perhaps working for both sides. You may deem such behavior limited to the ladies' parlor, but I assure you, it is not."

Eliza gasped.

"They said I was a spy. As you can see tonight, not too many people here want to engage in any sort of conversation with me. When I came to this island in June, and not as a soldier but as a bureaucrat...well, many familiar faces viewed me with distrust. They do not understand my profession. Misunderstanding belies truth and encourages loose lips. I have arrived on this island only recently, and matters have deteriorated since. What I once thought was ill-timing or the occasional accident of rudeness has proven to be deliberate malice. I am Lord Dunmore's secretary, but I wonder that I was even invited tonight."

"Are you dangerous, sir?"

She reached out, touched his arm, and then recoiled at how brazen her behavior was. She looked down at her half-empty glass; she internally reprimanded herself that she should take slower sips. Jean did not laugh with her. He seemed pained.

"I am sorry. I know you are trying to source my advice in earnest. This is not a laughing matter," she said softly.

"It causes me a great deal of stress from time to time. But I can sense you are not like the others."

"If it is any consolation, I, for one, have never fit in with my surroundings either."

"Yes, I can see that," he replied.

Eliza made a face as if insulted.

"You are too intelligent and beautiful for most people, man or woman, to abide."

She blushed deeply. The champagne disappeared. He left to retrieve new drinks. Her mind raced with thoughts she didn't usually have. She was a married woman. And he knew this. But did that matter? From the gaiety and laughter in the surrounding rooms, there did not seem to be a strict rule of propriety. Restrictions on this island only existed as platitudes, and not in deed, if they existed at all. This must have mirrored the debauchery of London salons. Still, she thought it better to act more demure. He was a stranger, after all. Jean returned and continued his story.

"Our friendship was stronger than ever, but then he returned home. I journeyed to work in Minorca, and then I was stationed here to work for the governor. Enforcing His Majesty's laws, collecting importation duties, fighting foreign privateers...Lord Dunmore was impressed with my acumen, and he promoted me to the position of secretary rather quickly. My enemies are green with envy," he said with a smirk. But it quickly vanished.

"I believe something happened to my friend in England. Someone must have poisoned his ear. He married and returned here, but he is a changed man. He will not speak with me or even acknowledge that he knows me. Worst of all, he has participated in these vile rumors floating around. He has tried to get me removed from my post. If I make any new acquaintances, I know they will not last long because of him. Even my business dealings have suffered. He is quite the dominating presence in any circle."

"That is terrible. I am sorry about your situation. From what I've heard, I can tell you this man's behavior is despicable. I can assure you that no one will be able to sway me."

"Yes, I wouldn't imagine so. You are quite independent. My question to you is…should I maintain my dignity and move from room to room as if I truly do not know him and return his boorish behavior? Or should I confront him? He is ruining my honor by the day. I do not want to have a heated spectacle. He does have quite the temper, and I would never engage in a duel with him. I am unsure how to proceed. I am like a stalemated chess piece."

"Hmm…" Eliza said, thinking aloud. "Is this fraternal bond you spoke of still alive in your heart?"

"Yes, very much so."

"Well then, based on the simple virtues of patience and goodwill, I should not see why such a matter would be constantly tossed about and not resolved. If you were as close as you mentioned, I think you should still be able to have a moment with him."

Jean seemed distracted and was gazing out toward the hallway.

"Is he here tonight?"

"Yes, I'm afraid so. I nearly didn't come tonight for fear of running into him."

"Then this is your moment. I do not think that you encountered me, and we are discussing this by chance. Tonight is the time. I would pull him aside and explain your feelings. You owe it to your old bond to reveal what is occurring, and if no civil recourse can be taken, then at least you may have said your piece. Then you can move forward. It will only make him look less the gentleman, and you will have retained some of your honor lest these vile people try to destroy it further."

He seemed impressed with her answer.

"I like the way you think, madame. I feel more consoled already. At least, I can say I have tried. This life is short and oftentimes cruel. And there is no space or time to feel tormented as if I were a schoolboy in a strange country once again."

"My thoughts precisely. He was there for you in the beginning. That should count for something. His heart may be darkened now, but you can at least express gratitude for days past."

Eliza studied his perfect form and felt sad that someone could direct such malice toward him. He was not obnoxious or obtrusive. He was unlike any of the men there tonight. But that was what caused such a problem in this group. He was simply too different to blend in on Lord Dunmore's island. Eliza decided that this was precisely what made him so charming. And she marveled at how this stranger seemed to trust her almost blindly.

He stood up and extended his arm.

"Let me bring you back to the party, and I will do as you suggested. Thank you for your ear and your words."

He acted like the perfect courtier as they walked through the bustling hallway. It upset her to think these miserable people rejected him so.

"Now that we are acquainted, may I ask who this person is?" she asked, with mischief in her dark eyes. "It will never leave my lips."

They stood in the hallway between rooms of laughter and music. He appeared to be amused by her request.

"Yes, I was afraid you would ask me. Very well."

"Yes?"

Her fascination was on full display. He took her hand and squeezed it.

"Your husband, Lord Sharpe. I will be sure to sing your praises to him if we reconcile. Consider the pearl a wedding gift. He could not have picked a more lovely bride."

Jean bowed and then he was off.

Eliza stood there alone, feeling the shock hit her in waves. They had an enemy in common. She backed away to a cool wall across from the sweeping staircase. What had she just done? Had she spoken too much? Her mind raced with paranoia and anxiety. She had allowed herself to become infatuated with her husband's childhood friend. The weight of her folly panicked her. It served as a chilling reminder that she walked among strangers in this house. The people of this colony had a history, and it was one she did not yet know. She needed to tread carefully.

Now Eliza wanted to leave. She had had enough festivities for one night. And enough petty conversations with the women of this colony. An hour passed, then another. She watched as the provost marshal, John Baker, a man whose face was pitted with smallpox scarring, held a conversation in the shadows with another man, and they exchanged a leather pouch of coins between them. A few minutes later, two women and a gentleman rushed upstairs, their arms interlinked and their fidelity left behind.

She did not feel comfortable in this crowd and had never felt more tired. Sleep was calling her. The drinks made her head feel heavy. She assumed that Jean had had enough time to talk to her husband, so she made her way to the gentlemen's parlor. She could tell its location by the volume of noise erupting from it. Charles was surrounded by several men at the far end of the smoky room flanked by French doors.

"Ah, my lovely bride has come to greet us!" he said, noticing her.

She felt herself cringe at the word 'bride'.

"Your husband has dealt quite the hand here tonight," said an older man, chuckling.

She smiled in acknowledgment and bent down to whisper her intentions to leave soon. Charles, in turn, grabbed her without warning and sat her on his lap. Eliza almost fell over from the force and clung to the table edge, her face red.

"This is my beautiful wife, Eliza," Charles declared boldly, the stink of liquor heavy on his breath.

She had trouble regaining her composure. She knew he would not let her free, and now she could feel him breathing on her neck and smelling the back of her hair. She sat there, frozen and rigid, her eyes locked on the green cloth of the gaming table. She leaned forward slightly to ease the cramping pressure of her stays.

The men began to introduce themselves.

"I am Mr. Egred. This is Reverend Samuel—" began the older man.

"He needs the funds to rebuild his church after that last storm. I heard it was brutal," Charles interjected, squeezing Eliza for emphasis.

She laughed nervously, attempting to gloss over the awkwardness of her situation. She looked at the reverend questioningly. She had never shared the company of a religious man so in need of what he preached.

"This is the town surgeon, Mr. Tallis, a fine trader from West Florida, and Captain Bruin."

The last man had his head lowered, and she could only see the brim of his weathered tricorn hat. He slowly raised his eyes to look at her.

"A pleasure to meet you," he said slowly, the sarcasm heavy in his voice.

They both stared at each other for a moment. Eliza hadn't thought of an encounter like this happening. She wondered why Charles had mentioned his name as if it was an introduction. She could not tell if it was formality or an excess of liquor that explained such a gaffe. She avoided glancing at that corner of the room and pretended to be oblivious that she had not yet responded.

"My dear, have you had too much drink?" barked Charles, slapping the table. "Forgive me. My wife forgets herself."

"I think it best to take her home now, Lord Sharpe," replied Mr. Egred. "You must strike whilst the night is young!"

A loud chorus of drunken cheers followed from the table. Eliza scrambled to get up.

"Yes, I couldn't agree more. Please fetch the carriage. I just need a moment of privacy," she said to Charles.

She didn't wait for him to answer. She dashed out of the room. From the corner of her eye, she could see Captain Bruin stand up and follow after her. Eliza was hurrying through the halls when she was pulled into a room by a dainty hand.

"Lady Sharpe, I must say you like to avoid the fairer sex at these functions! I haven't been able to steal you away for one moment! Ladies, here is the newly arrived Lady Eliza Sharpe. Welcome her to our small island," Charlotte said.

There was a chatter of feigned polite greetings. It was clear there was an invisible demarcation between Eliza and the women here tonight. These were the kind of women Eliza would typically avoid if at home. Their milky white bosoms were pushed upwards on display, and the ladies in this room were heavily powdered despite the humidity. They had barely left their cushioned seats all evening. They all exchanged nods in unison. An older lady sat her down and put a teacup in her hand.

"So, tell me about your night so far, Lady Sharpe," Charlotte said, studying her dress with an envious glare.

"I have quite enjoyed myself. Thank you for the kindness of your invitation."

"Well, we have to get you to leave Pleasant Hall one way or another. It must be dreadfully dull to be the only lady there."

"Oh, no, we have many women working there."

Charlotte almost spit out her tea.

"Quite the jester, I nearly forgot. Isn't she delightful? I told you," she said to the group of women. "I meant ladies of your station, dearest Eliza."

Eliza sat there trying to finish her tea and simultaneously come up with an excuse to leave.

"The evening has been quite entertaining, but I confess I must depart…"

"I'm afraid it hasn't had much to do with me or the festivities that *I* arranged," Charlotte said, demurely taking a sip.

The garish women all looked at each other, waiting for her to finish.

"You are quite the social creature," she said simply.

"I'm afraid I do not understand your meaning."

"Prattling up a storm with my husband, according to Caroline here, a few drinks taken with that fellow, Longchamp, quite a dashing man, I must say. Invading the men's quarters whilst they gamble. Tell me, how do you do it? Quite bold, if you ask me."

Eliza did not know how to respond, but she could hear the men exiting the next room.

"I really must prepare myself to leave now. Thank you again for this evening," she said as she stood up and curtsied.

"Excuse me, but I would like a moment with Lady Sharpe," a voice bordering on rudeness interrupted.

Hiram Bruin stood at the edge of the room like a threatening storm cloud. There was a ripple of girlish giggles.

"Here we go again, I see! Do they not understand that she is taken? My word!" Charlotte said in an exaggerated whisper.

Eliza stretched her neck to see if there was another exit, but a series of small tables displaying the tea service blocked the pocket door leading to the next room. She was trapped.

"Maybe another time, Captain Bruin. It is getting quite late, and I am fatigued. There are many other suitable ladies here that would love to converse with a gentleman such as yourself," Eliza said with a polished smile.

"No, no, the man has asked for you!" Charlotte insisted.

She gave her a nudge toward the doorway. As Eliza felt herself take a series of involuntary steps to her newest calamity, she heard Charlotte continue her blathering.

"At this rate, I wouldn't be surprised if she missed an entire season only to re-enter our society with a little one in her arms. Her poor husband. I doubt the child will share his looks. I wonder who it will resemble. I gave her a word or two of womanly advice, but mark me, I did not realize she would take it to heart!"

Catty laughter sounded behind Eliza.

"Charlotte, you are louder than you think with drink on your tongue!"

"Drink? It is only tea."

"Tilly-tally."

"Have you seen how dark she lets her skin get? How unrefined."

"I heard she goes swimming every day. Have you ever heard of such a thing?"

"That is most likely how she's cultivated this crop of admirers, Miss Shelley."

Eliza stood fixed by the edge of the room with nowhere to go. She couldn't return to that cluster of women, and she knew Captain Bruin's foreboding presence awaited her in the hall. Then she heard deep laughter from Charles and a series of footsteps. She waited a few more minutes and then flung herself into the hallway.

"Ah, tonight's victor!" she declared, reaching her arm up to him.

Charles looked wholly surprised. She tried to pull him to her to block the now glowering captain. Charles fell for her ruse and broke away from the rest of the men while safely shielding her from Bruin. Her strategy was to simply ignore him. Even if it meant embracing the man she detested.

"You…are…my good luck charm, my dear. I am going to buy you the most exquisite pair of earrings to grace that slender neck of yours," a drunken Charles said as he kissed her neck in front of the crowd.

She tensed up immediately. Perhaps this was a terrible alternative.

"Oh, please, Charles, not here. You must behave yourself!" she said in an attempt at playfulness.

But she couldn't hide the nervousness in her tone. As if to break the tension building in the hall, Bruin angrily strode past them and bumped into another man as he exited the house. He had clearly had enough of her tricks. Her present danger was over, but she feared the situation she found herself in.

"If not here," he said, leaning toward her, "then where?"

He stroked the side of her face. His eyes were dark. She didn't answer because she could not answer. She had wanted nothing more than to leave the ball, but now that she looked at the open door covered in darkness, she wanted to stay. Charles took her hand and began pulling her around to say their farewells. She knew the answer to his question, and it frightened her. She needed to get to her room and secure the door with a chair. Tonight would not be peaceful.

The night creatures around them blared with metallic clicks. As they walked along the dark sandy path to the carriages, her mind raced with troubling thoughts. It was all too much to comprehend. Her husband, who worked tirelessly for his military career, had, in fact, little to no control over his rank. The army did not automatically reward merit. It was up to a pig-like man who was enraptured by any woman who crossed his path. As they continued walking past gusty torches, Charles intermittently pressed her hand into his.

And what would she do about him? To have someone speak so darkly about a stranger only to reveal that she was married to the monster discussed was horrifying. Had the two men talked matters through? What kind of man asked for the opinion of his enemy's wife? Did Jean have any idea that she shared the same thoughts about this brute roughly pulling her to their carriage? Could they continue their friendship after this? Perhaps any notion of companionship had already been struck down. Jean had not seemed to mind that she was married. Maybe it did not matter. Perhaps such companionship had always been one-sided. It was entirely inappropriate either way. But Eliza did not know where matters stood if he and Charles had exchanged words. She only knew what she wanted. She turned back to see if she could catch a final glimpse of Jean, but she did not see him.

And the pirate. A rogue turned gentleman trader. A privateer in polite circles. Clean-shaven, sitting at the governor's ball with officers who wanted to capture the likes of men such as himself. She did not understand this world. A footman opened the door, and she climbed inside, followed by Charles. She was so consumed by the flurry of her thoughts that she did not notice how intensely Charles was fixated on her.

He was nearly on top of her as the carriage started to move. She threw herself into the back of her seat to get away from him, and he stopped mid-motion, looking at her petrified face. His mouth nearly touched hers. His finger brushed across her firmly sealed lips. She kept her eyes closed, barely breathing. He clicked his tongue in disgust. Charles turned his face to the side.

"You turn your emotions on and off. Like an actress in a theater," he said in a very low tone. "Like...A WHORE!"

His fist slammed into the cushioned wall next to her. Fear began to sober her up quicker than a cold bath. The drowsiness caused by her many drinks departed and was replaced with a heightened sense of alert and a sour stomach. She swallowed nervously. She felt very small across from him in the tiny, shadowed carriage.

"Please..." she began to say when he lunged at her again.

She flung her hands up in defense. Before she could think, she knocked three times on the frame of the coach door. The carriage rolled to a stop. Charles was confused, and she took advantage. Eliza flung the door open and jumped down.

"Eliza! Stop this! Eliza!" he shouted after her.

He tried to grab her, but the material of her dress slipped through his hands.

She ran into the night without looking back, straight into the pointed bushes that cut her dress and tore at her skin like a knife. She stumbled but followed the distant lights that marked the governor's mansion. Invisible branches and sharp edges scratched her with every step until she finally made it through a line of trees. She fell into another less busy roadway. Two soldiers idly walking down the dirt path stopped in their tracks. One was unusually short, and the other very tall and thin.

"Halt! Who goes there?" the taller one called.

Eliza raised her hands up, fixing a strand of hair that had fallen down on her face.

"I have lost my way and am trying to reach the governor's house," she lied through her panting breath.

She did not have a plan and refused to tell these strangers the truth.

"You're on his lands. How did someone like you end up back here in the dark?" the tall soldier asked with suspicion. He raised his lantern to look at her.

"There's been a misunderstanding. I was a guest at the ball. My...my carriage had an accident. The wheel is stuck in a rut. I'm afraid I..."

"Yer carriage is stuck in't road? Why 'ave ye left it? A lass can't go traipsin' off by 'erself at night...not wi' all t'darkies 'ere lurkin' abouts," the short one said, his Yorkshire accent thick.

"My slave was sent to get help but hasn't returned in quite some time, so I wandered off to seek assistance."

"We'll bring you directly to the governor. He'll get this sorted out. No fears, missus," the tall man said, extending a hand to direct her back to the house.

That was the last thing that Eliza wanted. She was about to protest when a rider came onto the path. Jean sat atop a slender white horse, and he slowly approached them.

"Gentlemen, what do we have here?" he asked, peering into the dark.

"We found a lass traipsin' in't woods by 'erself, sir," the short soldier reported.

Once he recognized her, Jean got down from his horse and strode over to them.

"You may continue your patrol, men. I will escort the lady," he said, motioning for them to depart.

Eliza let out a deep exhale.

"Lady Sharpe, are you all right? Have you fallen?" he said, staring at her appearance.

She latched onto his arm, oblivious to how unkempt she looked. She was entirely ignorant of the cuts across her cheek and her eyes.

"Please, you must help me," she pleaded with labored, panicked breaths. "I fear ill-usage tonight. Please, I beg you to help me!"

"What has happened? Where is Lord Sharpe?" he asked.

She didn't answer and looked at the ground, her chest still heaving.

"Have you been assaulted?" he asked in a firm tone.

"No, no. I ran through the bush here. I…"

"Whatever for? It is blackness out here."

"I do not love him!" Eliza exclaimed, breathless.

As he moved away from her, he looked taken aback by her outburst. Then he composed himself. She could see him thinking as if torn in two opposing directions. Then his gaze darted back up to her, calmness settling in his blue eyes.

"Please, Eliza, steady yourself. You can barely breathe."

She looked at him and began to pace with her hands on her hips.

"You have shared your feelings concerning him with me. Now let me share mine. Regardless of whatever you two discussed tonight…I refuse to go back to Pleasant Hall."

"Oh my," Jean said, realizing how serious she was.

A breeze rustled through the palms and pines.

"I must confess that I did not get very far in my endeavors either," he said quietly.

"Take me to the harbor. I am boarding a ship and returning home," Eliza said with determination as she walked toward his horse. "I do not have coins on my person, but I assure you that I will pay you for your efforts."

"Eliza, please, you must think this through."

"If you will not help me, then I will walk."

"Winter is approaching. The passage will be rough. You have no clothes. You've completely ruined your dress. You have no money," Jean replied. "Do you not think that he would find out and chase after you? Please, this needs to be planned."

Her fury began to settle down as she realized he was not entirely trying to stop her.

"I cannot go back to him," she said, tears beginning to fall from her eyes.

Her escape from the carriage had alerted her senses, and now she felt ravished by an onslaught of emotions.

"I'm afraid you must. For the moment," he said, with a measure of sympathy. "You've already run away. You need to wait for matters to settle."

More tears streamed down her cheeks as she realized he was right.

"Come, let me escort you back to the house."

Jean extended his hand. His face was downcast, his actions driven more by a sense of duty than willingness. He helped her atop his horse and then got on himself. They began to slowly trot down the road. She continued to cry, squeezing the back of his coat harder than she intended.

"I have never had a wife. I do not claim to understand the art of marriage. But I somehow do not think it should look like this," he said as they traveled through the dark.

The sound of waves crashing along the shore grew louder. A silent mist descended upon them as the moon's brightness was engulfed inside darker clouds. The wetness made her face burn, and she winced. Regret was starting to make an appearance: regret of the branches she had so carelessly disregarded earlier, regret that she had only inflamed the situation awaiting her at the house. The steady rhythmic walk of the horse began to soothe her. Eliza sighed. She knew she could only focus on the future; what had happened was already done.

"You will help me leave?" she asked him midway through the ride.

He was quiet for a moment. She prepared herself for disappointment, for a change of mind.

"Yes. You do realize the magnitude of what you desire?"

"Yes," she said sullenly. "I have failed my family miserably. I will not be able to return home."

"My sister lives near Le Havre, in Harfleur. I can write to her."

"You would do quite a lot for a stranger."

"I would say that we are no longer strangers after this."

They rode the rest of the way in silence until the lights from Pleasant Hall appeared along the horizon.

"You are afraid," Jean said.

Eliza began to disagree.

"You are holding on to me tighter," he countered.

Eliza eased her grip on him, heat flushing her face. She was thankful for the darkness. They passed the iron gates and went up along the path. The bell behind them tolled.

"Go straight to bed. I will vouch for you and give him a reasonable explanation. I will tell him you are too tired and need to rest. At least this way, he will have time to lose his anger."

"I cannot thank you enough," she said softly.

He helped her down from the horse. She stood transfixed near the steps of the porch.

"Would you like me to stay outside here tonight?" he asked.

"No, please, you have done quite enough," she said out of politeness.

Inwardly, she wished he would.

They ascended the steps together. Eliza heard Lucy call out their arrival. The door opened, revealing a haggard-looking Charles.

"Well, this is a sight to behold," he mocked.

"Charles, I found her stumbling through the woods. She is not hurt, thankfully, but she is quite frightened. I thought it best to deliver her back to you at once. She needs to rest," Jean said as he guided her through the doorway.

He and Charles began a banal conversation, but Jean intended to distract him. He stood between Charles and her, and then in one swift move, Jean ushered her toward the stairs where Lucy took her.

"Sometimes women cannot watch their drink. This is all very new to her," Jean continued in a quieter tone. "Added with this heat, it is an unfortunate combination. She has not been here very long."

Charles sighed and looked down at his boots.

"Yes, yes, so it is. Thank you, Jean," he said, running a hand through his hair. "Shall we have a glass of brandy before you go?"

CHAPTER VIII.

Eliza leaned against the porch railing as Lucy swept the deck beams to her left. She drew circles with her bare feet in the sand, lost in a reverie. A dark crab crawled onto the porch, its claws attempting to pick at the door. The sight was entertaining until Lucy shrieked and swept it back to the sand, and a new phase of boredom began.

She twirled a round seagrape leaf between her fingers. The plant was thick and solid, like translucent green paper, and she held it up to the light to observe the multitude of golden veins that ran through it. She put it down next to the collection of curiosities she had gathered that morning: a pair of small, speckled conch shells, a hard brown sea fern, and a pink magnolia cone, furry and velvety in texture. She looked at the yard before her, soothed by the ever-persistent beat of the waves scraping the shore. The more Eliza observed the palm trees surrounding the house, the more she began noticing distinguishing shapes within them. The one closest to her had a deep gash in its bark that nearly resembled the form of a crawling iguana, but it was only a trick of the heat and the sun.

Horse hooves approached, muffled by the sand. Looking to the side, she became alert, snapping her idle form upward. Jean Charles de Longchamp sat on his white mare, looking down at her.

"Lady Sharpe, my apologies for the intrusion. Has your husband returned from his duties?"

She shook her head, suddenly wanting Lucy to disappear from the scene.

"Not a day for swimming?" he asked, peering out at the shoreline.

His horse snorted and paced backward.

"The current is far too strong," Eliza replied.

She was anxious to say many things, but the desire to appear detached in front of him stopped her. She had already revealed too much during their last encounter.

"But you are a strong swimmer. I've seen you," he said with a smile.

Her heart thudded against her chest. She looked down and away. Her mind raced back to recent days and wondered when he had seen her and if she had looked as foolish as she feared.

"The water is rough, however, and then it is harder to look for things underneath the waves. Shells…specifically. They get tossed under the sand ridges if the tide is strong," she said.

"Yes, yes, naturally. Although these waters are uncannily beautiful. You'd have to travel far to see shades like this outside the West Indies. It's the whiteness of the sand as well. Other islands further south are more volcanic in nature and possess darker sand. Some bays I've dipped into are no different than the Thames, I swear it. The silt muddies up the current."

Her interest was piqued.

"You swim as well?"

"Occasionally. It is helpful in cooling off. But there is a whole other world down there, isn't there? And to think most people never see it, even if they spend their lives at sea. They still only dwell on the surface."

Eliza realized she was staring at him. His voice and blue eyes, not unlike the water they were discussing, and even his presence rapidly made her forget her place. His eyes were even more beautiful in the natural light.

"I'm sorry. I'm afraid I speak too much at times," he said.

He looked behind her toward Lucy.

"I could listen to you for hours, the places you must have seen…" she quickly remarked.

Then she realized the manner of his discretion. Lucy had slowed down her sweeping.

"May I invite you for a ride? Have you been on the trails on the other side of the island? I think you'd rather like them."

At first, their trip was silent, but without the usual awkwardness she felt around Charles. Jean rode in front of her as the bush path was too narrow to ride side by side, and she took the opportunity to observe him unguarded. The figure of his fitted navy jacket astride his horse was the most intriguing sight she had observed in days. The idea that an excursion like this, alone, was entirely improper only made such a venture more exciting.

"Have you explored the island at length, Eliza?" Jean called back, breaking her concentration.

He had used her first name. She wondered if it was deliberate or whether she was infusing extra meaning to an unintended slip of tongue.

"No, I haven't quite had the opportunity. Lord Sharpe would not be pleased."

"Ah, a sensible husband. But with a chaperone and a guide, the matter is entirely different. Besides, what else does he expect you to fill your time with?" he quipped.

Eliza ducked away from a low-hanging branch and steered her horse around a mud-filled hole.

"More lady-like pursuits, I would imagine. Embroidery. Needlework."

"And how are you in that skill set?"

"Dreadful. It's never occupied much of my time. There are scores of other habits I'd rather entertain."

"It can be no worse than what my hand does with a fine needle," Jean said, turning around with a smile.

The teetering squawk of green parrots high in the trees grew louder as they pushed further into the dense forest. Cicadas blared around them in noisy protest. She studied his back, watching his graceful movement on the horse. She remembered how it had felt to cling to his warm body that night the week before. She wanted to feel the sensation again.

"Is there much to see if you continue in this direction?" she asked as their horses walked at a comfortable pace.

Insects started to gather around her ankles, and she swatted them away with indifference. She would willingly follow this man anywhere. The fact that he was a stranger and a barely formed new acquaintance did little in the way of causing her any hesitation.

"If you take this trail for another three hours, you'll run into William Wylly's plantation. Two and a half if you use a fast horse. Although I don't know why anyone would be of a mind to rush in that direction."

"William Wylly? I've not heard of him."

"An American Loyalist. From Georgia, I believe. I hear he is of a mind to sell. The cotton production on this rocky soil leaves much to be desired."

"I can't imagine living any further from town. What a considerable amount of time it must take to get anything accomplished."

"Yes, even Pleasant Hall is over an hour's ride away from Nassau," Jean replied.

"Is it really? I've never noticed. The journeys at night by carriage do seem to take longer. I suppose the beauty of the sights along the ride eases the journey. I think Pleasant Hall is perfectly situated on the island."

He turned to look at her.

"Ah, so you now enjoy living there, Lady Sharpe?"

Eliza colored with embarrassment.

"Do not mistake my love for this island for any attachment to my situation. I am still set on what we discussed that night," she said bitterly.

"Have you written to your family? Do your parents know of your intentions in this matter?"

She sighed; the burden of the affair weighed heavily on her.

"I have sent three letters to my father. He was initially against my leaving for such a faraway place," she said quietly. "I presumed he would be most understanding of my problem, but I haven't received a single letter back."

"The delays in the post can be very irritating. Battles can be won or lost by the time crucial information is shared. It is an unpleasant fact of our age."

"Even if he did receive my letters, I do not think it matters much. I haven't received any mail from England except for one letter when I first arrived. The silence speaks enough for me. I can never return to my childhood home. I've disgraced my family name. I would not blame them for it. I have only caused dishonor."

He abruptly stopped his horse as hers drew up parallel to him.

"You must not say such things about yourself, Eliza," he said, a look of concern passing over his face.

"What is to become of me? I can abandon my responsibilities, but I cannot guarantee myself true freedom. A man can more easily break apart contracts and engage in new affairs, but a woman entering into a new relationship when the former has not been dissolved? Such a thing is unheard of."

Part of her was simply voicing her worries in front of him, but another part spoke of such things because she wildly wanted to reveal her willingness to find romance. She was desperate for human connection, and despite finding trivial pursuits to cope with the isolation of Pleasant Hall, nothing could dull the persistent ache she felt every day. Nothing except for his presence.

"He may yet grant you a divorce. Perhaps…"

"I have read that it can only be obtained through cases of infidelity."

"Do you have any knowledge of such behavior from him?"

"Unfortunately, no. He appears as principled in his morals as he is determined to act detrimental to mine," she said, looking forward. "No, he will not stand for it. Even if I possess the stomach for it."

She regretted her last words. She spoke too freely. But Jean did not react.

"Abandonment may be the most painless course."

"I fear he will chase after me. He can threaten me and any future happiness I may find. But I still choose to run. I fear it is terribly selfish. But I yearn for freedom above all else."

"It is not selfish to fight for survival. That is an instinct not easily ignored."

"And the money that will be squandered from my dowry. To think I could cost my family such a precious amount only to lose it."

She wondered if the value of the coins she had found could cover the loss.

"Your happiness and security are worth more than any amount of money," Jean countered, gently putting a hand over her arm.

She gawked at the sight of his hand touching her and feared that she appeared completely foolish. The horses began to quietly grumble due to the lack of space. Jean adjusted his reins and continued down the trail. A breeze began to pick up, and the insect attacks lessened. She could tell they were approaching the shore. The horses intensified their steps as they trod through the sand. The conversation had lulled, but her mind was racing with new concerns and worries. The pine trees began to separate, and they left the line of forest for a deserted beach. Infant palm trees grew out of the powdery sand like giant awkward sprouts. She sighed at the sight of the calming water and looked down the shoreline to see if she recognized any of its features.

Jean eventually stopped his mare and jumped down, securing his horse to a tropical almond tree. Eliza followed suit, stretching her limbs. They had ridden for quite a while.

"You have brought me to a beach?" she asked, with amusement, as he tended to her horse.

"I have brought you to a very secret place. That was no ordinary goat path. Come," he said with a mischievous air.

He began to walk down the beach, and she followed at a distance until he stopped in front of a limestone outcrop. A pile of dark and light rocks tumbled from a narrow stone slab covered in scrub. Scattered piles of decaying sea ferns and seaweed were strewn around, and a strong wind whipped past them.

"Are there tidal pools here?" she asked in confusion.

"There is a cave," he said proudly.

Eliza was perplexed until she watched him walk under the slab and vanish into shadow. From the viewpoint of the beach, it was hardly noticeable that there was indeed an opening amidst the rocks. She rushed to follow him until they stood in the darkness of the cave's mouth. She looked around in amazement. It was surreal to now stand inside the abject coolness of the space, having felt the baking heat on her sweat-covered skin only moments before. The breaking of close-by waves was still audible and echoed off the limestone walls. The azure water directly across from them seemed even more enhanced in its beauty as it contrasted with the natural vignette of the shadows around them.

"I did not know there were caves on this island! Do you think that pirates ever used this?" Eliza asked, stepping further and further inside.

"I know they used it."

Eliza walked in further and stopped as a giant cockroach scurried deeper into the cave. He laughed, his jovial voice booming throughout the cavern.

"I have never seen a woman have such courage around a roach," Jean said, catching up with her.

"I do not enjoy the sight of them inside the house, but I find that, as we are in a cave, perhaps this is their natural habitat, and now I am the guest."

In the darkness, his hand found hers, leading her further inside.

"Hold on to my hand. It is slightly difficult for the next few steps, then it is more level again," he said, pulling her forward.

His hand was warm, his grip solid and confident. Eliza was beginning to enjoy the sensation when he let go of her just as quickly. A prominent smell began to penetrate her nostrils. It smelled like stale urine, but she convinced herself it was some other acidic odor.

"The odor is from the bat droppings. Can you smell it? And the water that sits here, never moving," he said.

Now she began to notice a slight dripping sound that dominated the space as the noise of the waves crashing on the shore receded into the background. She began to ask him a copious number of questions before his lack of a response signaled her pause.

"I find myself like Odysseus being tormented by Kalypso," he said, with a smile as he sidestepped some shallow puddles.

She immediately recognized that he was comparing her to the famous Grecian nymph, but she failed to see that he intended it as a compliment.

"And what goal am I diverting you from?" Eliza asked, attempting to mask her disappointment.

She was worried she had annoyed him. More lonely afternoons on the porch loomed in her mind, and the image was terrifying.

"Was she not a distraction and a diversion? He squandered seven years in that cave with her," Jean countered.

Some low-hanging bats swooped into the darkness as they approached.

"Ah, but she helped build the boat that allowed Odysseus to finally continue his journey home," she replied.

"Indeed. You bring up an interesting counter. Was he really a prisoner, or did the comfort of love help lessen his torments? I meant no insult from the remark, Eliza. She was unworldly beautiful...yet plagued by relentless sadness."

She looked up momentarily to find he was staring at her. Eliza looked away just as quickly, pretending to focus more on where she was placing her feet. She was grateful for the shadows: they masked her searing blush. She had gravely misread him. Or perhaps it was her own nagging fear that so viciously distorted what was in front of her.

"I am more intrigued by Plato's allegory. At times, I find I am like the prisoner sitting in the cave, and I am able to question the shadows. Yet I still struggle to break free from my chains."

"And what are your chains?" he asked quietly. "What holds you back?"

She hadn't looked upwards for some time and didn't notice that Jean had stopped. She nearly collided with him, then slipped as she tried to back away. He grabbed her arm and steadied her.

"My sex," she answered, her voice blunt.

"I cannot confess to understanding your position. But surely, it cannot be all that bad? Beauty creates so much joy in this world, and men are clearly not responsible for the bulk of it. Women create life; they sustain it. To see one pained so, to think she only feels weighed down. Restricted…"

Eliza felt horror when he mentioned childbearing and failed to listen to the rest of his statement.

"It only creates problems for me. I find I am quite limited in my freedom at times, even though my only company are those without an ounce of freedom to their names. It is an enduring contradiction."

He seemed to be focusing on her words intensely.

"Forgive me, I am blathering," she said.

"Well, I hope my company is a refreshing change to your situation," Jean replied.

"I think you've strayed from your original course of action. What does any of this have to do with my husband or his duties?" she asked in a sly voice.

"You could argue that I am relieving him of them. A man must entertain his wife, and it is clear he does not have the time to do so. So, I can be of service in this regard."

Eliza was about to take a step when she felt no ground beneath her feet. His hands took her by the waist as he lowered her to the level where he stood. She let out a muted scream from the unexpectedness of it.

"Forgive me. I failed to alert you of the drop there," he said quietly.

They continued without speaking for some time, he out of concentration and she from embarrassment. Eliza decided to return to the previous subject of conversation.

"I admit I have spent far too little time reflecting on Kalypso. My tutor only ever mentioned that she was near like a monster. She tore Odysseus away from the world and away from his wife."

"Your tutor must have had quite the narrow read on Homer then. I think Odysseus longed to be removed from the world but lacked the strength to truly abandon it. How else could a man be restrained for so many years? She, on the other hand, truly loved him and, in the end, was able to let him go."

Eliza laughed as they continued forward at a painfully slow pace.

"Are you an apologist for a monster, sir?" she asked, readjusting her skirts.

"I would rather be an apologist for misunderstood women…"

"You do craft your words well. I will admit that, at least."

"And I find I have one right here, before my very eyes."

She paused at his forwardness but found a polite rebuttal.

"And I would counter that such a sighting is hardly rare, Mr. Longchamp."

"Jean, call me Jean. You do not like attention directed at you. Why is that?" he asked, studying her expression.

"It only creates problems for me," she replied with a smirk. "I confess I did not find compliment in your Kalypso comparison."

"I feared as much from your reaction. Kalypso was the daughter of Atlas, the god of magic. She took a piss-reeking cave and created a beautiful oasis where they both lived. I suppose you're not accustomed to someone who admires your talents."

"Talents? I have none," she scoffed. "A forward tongue and an insatiable mind. They are hardly the hallmark of a talented woman."

"I would rather a fiery curiosity and a gifted intellect."

"Perhaps I have deceived you with an enchantment. I am a nymph, after all."

"I live in absolute terror of it ever since the night we first met."

He had made the remark in jest, but she preferred to perceive it as truth. She enjoyed envisioning herself as a magical being. That she was powerful. They continued to walk, the cave silent and sacred like a chapel. There was only the faint whisper of wind and the constant, eerie drip of unseen water.

"It is many degrees cooler the further you go inside. Can you feel it now?" Jean asked, the shadows draping across his face. "Pirates and sailors like to store their goods in here. The cave keeps them from spoiling."

"How do you know about this place?"

"It is my job to know about places like this."

They stopped in front of a smooth section of limestone. The flatness of the rock was marred by deep engravings that resulted in a myriad of repeating circles and other nameless shapes. Eliza raised her hand to the wall and traced the outlines of the petroglyphs.

"Who left these here?" she asked in wonder.

"Indians left these carvings behind. Many years ago," he said. "The Lucayans, a branch of the Taino people, I believe."

The more she gazed at it, the more she could decipher objects like pipes and boat paddles among the petroglyphs. Some figures seemed to be a blend of both beast and man, and other faces were crowned with rays. Or perhaps they were grinning fish. She turned back to him.

"How old is this?"

"Many hundreds of years old. I do not think anyone is really sure. I also do not know if many people are aware this is even here. Columbus himself encountered the Lucayans when he landed on an island near this place. The Indians asked if the men had come from heaven, or so I am told."

"There is something horribly sad about it. I wonder how long they lived on this island. Whatever happened to them?"

"They perished from disease. Or enslavement. I know of other caves on these islands that are so deep an entire chaise may be driven inside it. You can find antiquities and utensils if you look hard enough."

Eliza studied the wall like she was reading a map.

"When I was in Alexandria, I found it absolutely fascinating to see the ancient Egyptian ruins covered in Roman graffiti and Greek writing before that. I myself carved my initials in a temple by the water. It's just the way of the world. One empire rises, and another falls," he said gravely. "I wonder who will belong to the empire of the coming century."

Eliza sighed, walking away from the wall.

"It is so—"

An eruption of clanging noise and the gruff voices of men interrupted her.

"Shhh!" Jean whispered.

They both stood, suspended in motion, waiting for more sounds. Eliza's heart beat with excitement as she wondered if she would finally encounter the terrible men she had read about so often in her books. It seemed only fitting for the environment they were in.

The talking grew louder, and the wavering glow of a torch began to dance on the walls around them. Jean took her hand and rushed to a large rock where they both crouched. It was clear from the shadows that three men were approaching. Their voices were difficult to distinguish, but then she realized they were speaking

French. She had studied the language and actually enjoyed it but had lacked the opportunity to ever use it. They did not sound like they spoke in the proper form. She struggled to interpret what they said.

"*Je ne veux pas rester ici,*" ("I do not want to remain here,") one man said clearly.

"*Et si les Espagnols étaient là?*" ("What if the Spaniards are here?") another added. "*Ce plan semble trop beau pour être vrai.*" ("This plan seems too good to be true.")

"*Il a dit qu'il y avait deux chevaux dehors,*" ("He said there were two horses outside,") the third man replied. "*Les hommes ne peuvent pas être loin.*" ("The men cannot be far.")

"They know we are here!" she uttered softly.

Jean looked around the corner of the rock and cursed under his breath.

"Stay here, no matter what happens," he said, pressing her hand firmly.

He disappeared before she could even protest.

"*Mes amies! Mes amies!*" ("My friends! My friends!") Jean exclaimed in a conciliatory tone, "*Je suis désolé de te déranger.*" ("I am sorry to disturb you.")

She could hear the cocking of multiple pistols and the shuffling of feet. The men continued the conversation in French.

"You see, I was studying the cave art. I heard voices, and so I hid. I was worried someone else was approaching. Frederic told me you would be here at this time," Jean lied flawlessly.

His voice sounded even more bold and confident in his native language. It sounded like a melody to her ears.

"You know Frederic?" the man with the deepest voice asked.

"He told you of our meeting today, no? He was drinking quite heavily last night when I saw him," Jean answered.

"He failed to mention it. And you are?" the second man demanded.

Eliza was desperate to see what was happening but dared not move.

"Philippe," Jean said. "I am looking for work."

"And you are...alone?" another asked.

"Yes, of course," Jean replied lightly.

"But we were told that two horses were spotted outside the entrance..."

"Yes, one is mine. The other I stole. I am an enterprising man. Are you still mainly doing business with John?"

The group of men seemed satisfied by his responses. She even heard a gun being holstered.

"Yes, the wine we just brought in will be delivered tonight. The gunpowder comes tomorrow. There are always more requests."

"And Frederic was not exaggerating the profits?"

The men laughed.

"No, it will be worth your while, believe me," the main speaker replied.

"A man can make money on these islands," another said.

"Thank God for good fortune," Jean responded. "I will see you soon."

There was more shuffling of feet, and the torchlight began to retreat from the walls. She waited until she could no longer hear them before standing upright from the rock. Jean did not meet her eyes, saying nothing until he led her to the exit. The walk back passed much more quickly than the journey inside. The glaring sun was beginning to descend, its blinding rays slanting in a downward arc.

"That was incredible! They completely believed every word you said. How did you ever..." she started to say excitedly as they walked out to the sand.

"Promise me you will not return to the cave alone," Jean said solemnly.

"Were they wreckers?"

"No."

"Were they smugglers? Pirates?"

"No," Jean said, his voice flat. "They were ordinary sailors. Merchants."

"Oh."

Eliza felt disappointed.

"Your French is good," he said, his blue eyes fixated on her.

"How thrilling. I thought we were almost in danger for a moment. Thank you for taking me there. I can scarcely believe the day we've had!"

"I did not realize," he muttered quietly, in an aside to himself.

"Perhaps you can take me somewhere else next time. Perhaps to the pond..."

He said nothing and walked back to the horses, swiftly untying them. She rushed to keep up with his pace.

"You even came up with names that they understood. How ever did you do it?"

"It is easy when you use a common name. Promise me you will not come back here," he said, handing her the reins.

"But I'd like to sketch the petroglyphs. I found them so fascinating. And maybe we can find some artifacts like you said. They meant us no harm. They were looking for the Spanish," she said, mounting her horse.

"Eliza, listen to me. They are mere sailors, but they can become dangerous men in an instant. You cannot go there alone."

The last sentence came out harshly. She felt a bit taken aback by it.

"I will take you back. Soon. One day. We can spend more time then," he offered as they trotted back toward the woods. "I have to return you to Pleasant Hall. I did not realize the time. I apologize for my terseness."

She nodded and followed him back into the trees as she attempted to distract herself from feeling disappointed that they would part soon.

The sun had grown brighter and brighter until it finally descended to the wavering horizon line of the sea, a bright orange ball cradled by a mass of yellow clouds streaking below it. The sequence of light set the ocean ablaze in a shimmering column of smoldering tangerine. Now that she lived closer to the equator, the light seemed to disappear much faster once the sun vanished, and darkness set in quickly over the settling land. No matter how many days had passed, the sunsets never failed to inspire her astonishment.

And now it distracted her from the conversation she held with Charles. He had been silent when he arrived at the table, and she asked him about his day. And then, when his mouth started moving, she became lost in the display outside the window. She heard the slightest mention of a name that caught her interest.

"Monticello?" she asked, interrupting him. "You were in Monticello during the war? The home of Mr. Jefferson…Thomas Jefferson? What was it like?"

"We were sent to capture him. He was the rebel-declared 'governor' of Virginia. He is nothing but an ungrateful criminal."

Charles' disdainful tone did not diminish her fascination.

"I do wonder what kind of books a man like that would keep in his library. From what I've read, he has quite a thinking mind…"

"It was not as impressive as one would assume. To reach it, our party had to ride up a steep and savage hill, only to find the house perched on top like Olympus itself, utterly abandoned except for one or two slaves. He had received warning of our approach. I saw but a few shelves of books in a single room. I suspect he had already carried off the more valuable items beforehand. He fled from us like a coward."

"Would you not do the same if the enemy approached? Can you blame the man?"

"No, my dear, I would stay and fight like a man. Like a soldier. That Jefferson is a fool. He is ruled by ideals and cannot commit a single one to action. I do not understand why the Americans revere him so."

"He authored the new country's declaration of their freedoms. He's written many works…"

Charles crudely ripped apart a piece of bread.

"And have you read a single tract? American opinions deserve little notice. I think they will soon discover that accomplishing their newly found independence is not quite as easy as declaring it on paper. It is an offense of justice. They had no prior peace among them but the peace of the king. Now they will see what mayhem their renunciation of allegiance will inevitably cause," he replied between bites.

Eliza looked downward, lost in thought, as she swirled her wine.

"Did you destroy the house?" she asked quietly.

Charles shook his head in ridicule.

"No. But we made ample use of the wine cellar. We did not set fire to everything. We rode further south and destroyed his other plantation, Elk Hill, I believe, instead. Now, as I was saying, the damage the goats are causing to the soil is monumental. Agriculture on this island is simply not the same as plantations further north. This island is overrun with goats. They are ceaselessly destroying the backfield."

Eliza wanted to appear interested in the conversation because she feared further reproach, so she spoke without much consideration.

"How terrible indeed. Although sometimes, a simple goat trail can lead to something very exciting. I stumbled across a cave today. I never thought I would see such markings on the wall like I did. It is so very old," she gushed.

He spluttered, choking on his wine.

"You found what?"

"The most wonderful cave. It…"

It was only then that she realized her mistake.

"I have sent scouts down there in the last two weeks looking for that blasted cave. You stumbled upon it yourself?"

He was eyeing her now in a manner she found most disconcerting. She hesitated, uncomfortable with his intensity.

"By fortuitous chance!"

She hoped her words would convince him. She personally thought she sounded stupid and prayed that he was not of the same mind.

"One report claimed there is no clear opening to the cave, yet you stumbled in. Tell me, how did you realize you could enter inside?"

Charles was unrelenting. She decided to prattle on in the futile hope she could disinterest him.

"You never told me anything about natives. To think this land was theirs. They used to call this beautiful island home…"

"What?"

"The people who lived here before we made the island a colony. There was a civilization here. They had a culture. There are even antiquities to be found. It's remarkable!"

"And now it is covered in bat feces," he scoffed. He appeared a shade less engrossed. "I am looking for a cave further west of here. But my men have not been able to find it. The sole survivor's report of its location is dubious at best. And smugglers make it a treacherous affair. I lost two men down there."

"How terrible. The cave I found is being used by sailors. It cannot possibly be the same."

Eliza took a full bite of her fish, confident she had lost his interest in the subject.

"So, you weren't alone?"

"At one point, there were French sailors, but they did not see me. I made sure of it."

She smiled with false confidence, but his features hardened

"Goddammit, Eliza!" He slammed a fist on the table. "Reckless! You are utterly reckless! You could be killed down there or worse. They could take your virtue!"

Eliza clanked her fork against the plate. She had distracted him on one topic only to infuriate him on another.

"They did not see me, I assure you," she said, attempting to allay his anger.

He glared at her briefly and ran a hand through his hair.

"I forbid you to go to that cave."

"I wasn't planning on returning," she said solemnly.

She wondered if he had figured out how to detect her lies yet.

"It sounds like you've found a lost Grecian city by the way you describe it. You cannot return there, Eliza."

His voice was commanding and loud and didn't require a response. Eliza looked down at her food, absentmindedly stabbing at her fish.

Charles sighed as if he regretted the conversation.

"I can take you to see things. I can take you to the pond inland or the reef," he offered in a much quieter tone. "One must be cautious on this island. There is a village of runaway slaves further west on the beach. It is dangerous for a young woman riding alone."

Eliza glanced at him, unimpressed. She downed her wine and motioned for Lucy to refill her cup.

"Yes, you've said so for many weeks," she said dryly.

"You know my duties are demanding, Eliza. I ask for patience."

As much as she found his earlier inquiries troubling, his attempts at wooing her were even more unbearable.

"Yes, husband," she said demurely. "I understand that the fort is a higher priority."

"I did not say that. Dammit, Eliza, must you twist my every word…"

She turned toward the window. A dark shelf cloud now loomed above the water. The fascinating display of light had entirely disappeared. It seemed to reflect her very mood. Every conversation between them, no matter how innocuous, eventually boiled into an argument.

"I mean no offense. It is enough to dine with you every night."

She hoped it didn't sound as caustic as she inwardly intended. She reminded herself to be more grateful that he had an occupation off the plantation and that their interactions were mostly limited to the evenings.

"Forgive my temper these last few days. You know I enjoy returning home to you," Charles said softly.

He took her hand and stroked it, his touch rough and hot. She counted to ten, then pulled away from him, reaching for her full glass of wine instead.

A sense of wonder had a peculiar way of dulling when one returned to a fantastic place for the second time. It was as if the heightened sense of unknowing had been dampened, and the movement from one spot to another quickened with a measure of expectation.

In Eliza's case, her curiosity had in no way lessened, but the lingering journey to the secret beach had seemed a mere minute's ride from Pleasant Hall when she returned by herself. She had tied her horse to the same tree as last time and waited by the edge of the cave to listen for any alarming noises. The task seemed entirely fruitless as the waves were much louder than any sound from the cave. But after she waited a decent length of time, she felt confident the cave was clear and stepped into the darkness.

Without Jean's assistance, the path to the wall art seemed much more treacherous, and she was a bit slower to reach the same spot that had captivated her. Once she was in front of it, she unpacked the small bag she had brought and lit a candle before taking out her sketchbook and stick of graphite. She felt completely free to study each carving at her leisure, yet due to her solitude, every single unknown noise she heard caused her to freeze and look behind her. The quiet cave now appeared to be louder than she recalled. She thought she heard a shuffle to her left, but when she looked, she saw the same wall of blackness as before. She realized her ears were playing tricks with her mind, so she continued sketching.

Eliza's eyes roved over the strange, ancient shapes, and she committed their likeness to paper, her fingers occasionally lingering on each curve and stroke. She was fascinated by one nameless symbol when she heard the familiar shuffling noise a second time. She was about to turn to check behind her when a heavy hand covered her face, stifling her mouth. Eliza instantly dropped her book and graphite, the materials clattering to the cave floor in a singular, thin echo.

"Someone could wring your neck down here, and your body would never be recovered! Are you a fool?" a familiar, deep voice growled in her ear.

Eliza's body had been tense before, but now it stiffened even more in recognition of her husband.

"There is a lookout point above us. They can see you come and go," Charles continued, his voice a sharp hiss.

She heard him withdraw his pistol and used the opportunity to slip out of his grasp. She scrambled to grab her belongings and then rushed back toward the cave's exit. The further away from him she was, the easier she could breathe.

"Stay here," he commanded. "Do not make a sound!"

It was only a whisper, but it was nonetheless ominous. Eliza watched his shadow loom monstrously large next to hers on the dripping cave wall, then grow ever smaller as he moved away. He continued into the cave, holding his firearm aloft in the air as he rounded a corner. All was silent for a few agonizing moments of stillness. She was afraid. She wanted to run and return to the house without him as if this would make some kind of difference to his angry reception. She used to dread his outbursts, but now she feared his silent steps.

As she hesitated whether to leave or stay, there was an explosion of yells and the metallic clang of swords unsheathed, followed by a booming gunshot. The blast erupted into the cave. Eliza ducked, covering her ears. A countless multitude of shrieking bats fled from the cavern, and she crouched even lower, regretting her visit with every passing whir of humid, stinking air. The fluttering beating of leathery wings against soft bodies created an eerie symphony, and she heard footsteps fleeing further inside.

The sound of a slow dragging motion clamored around her now until she saw Charles reappear, his movement staggered and struggling as he lugged a motionless figure alongside him. The unconscious man was one of the French sailors she had witnessed with Jean the week before. A prominent hole in his thigh was spilling blood into the murky cave puddles. She made an audible gasp as Charles moved past her and continued toward the light-filled exit. Eliza followed behind him unwillingly as if his hand forced her steps. Outside the cave, the scene appeared much as it did before, but the sight of Charles dragging the limp man through the sand clashed with the soothing presence of the lapping waves.

"I caught one of them. Scoundrels. They did not put up much of a fight. The other two ran. There must be a second exit. The French," he said with disdain.

She said nothing as she watched him drape the man over Alastor. The man's blood streaked Charles' breeches, but he did not seem to care or notice. His hands were likewise stained a brownish red.

"Lord Dunmore will be pleased with this. I shall ride straight to the fort," he said with no regard to her reaction. "Return home at once."

She could feel his anger even though he did not speak of it. It was as palpable as the salt air hovering around them. She rushed to her horse, her head cast down to avoid any further interaction with him. She climbed atop her mare and was about to trot into the bush when Charles galloped in front of her. Alastor snorted with the exertion.

"Eliza, mark me, if you dare disobey me again, there will be consequences."

She looked down at the unconscious man and at the size of the hole in his leg oozing blood. The more she looked at him, the more she prayed he was only reposed and not deceased. No movement from the horse's flank seemed to disturb him. As she watched in horror, it seemed that the man served as a physical warning. She swallowed her nerves and looked up at Charles.

"Yes, husband. Forgive me," she said quietly.

Her jaw was clenched so tightly it pained her. He glared at her a moment longer and then kicked at his horse and took off down the beach.

CHAPTER IX.

The heat from the sun felt intense on her skin. Eliza sat on the porch stairs, twirling a green leaf she had plucked from the bougainvillea bush next to her. Looking up, she thought she saw a familiar figure. A young woman with a proud arch in her back was carrying a basket.

"Celia!" Eliza called as she walked over to her.

Celia turned, and Eliza stepped back, startled by what she saw. She had lost weight, and her cheekbones were more prominent. A deep purple welt hung under her left eye, disfiguring her face.

"Yes, Lady Sharpe?"

Her tone was hardly reminiscent of a question and seemed more of a thoughtless remark.

"What happened?"

Celia exhaled in annoyance, putting her basket of produce on the ground.

"I work in the fields, Lady Sharpe. I ain't no domestic no more."

"Did the overseer do this? I will complain to Charles. Mr. Bailey is not allowed to strike you!"

"*Mr. Bailey* is allowed to manage the workers, and if we don't work as fast as he wants or we don't do what he wants, then Lady Sharpe, he can strike us. He's done more to my person than what your eyes can see."

Celia picked up the basket and started off again.

"No, no…wait!" Eliza called, following her. "Please, I know you do not wish to speak with me, but I cannot stand for this. I must help. Please tell me what I can do."

Celia looked up with her sharp eyes. Eliza always admired the contrast of her honey-yellow eyes against her dark skin. She was so beautiful, even with a bruised eye. Eliza wondered if she had been born in a different world, whether artists would clamor to render her likeness. Celia was not responsive, and her gaze was turning into a glare. Eliza had said too much. She looked down at her shoes in frustration.

"I know you despise me," Eliza finally said. "I am free, and you are not. I thought by showing you kindness, I could gain your trust. I understand now…"

"You think you are free?" Celia said with a sneer.

Eliza paused, disturbed by her question.

"Of course, I am free. I—"

"You are a woman. Like me."

The two women looked at each other for a moment, and Eliza suddenly yearned to confide in her. It was an uncanny sensation. Celia had never shown even temporary benevolence, but now, as she gazed upon her marked face, Eliza believed she understood the reason for her hardness.

"We are two sides of the same coin, and, believe me, I've seen enough to know that coin is worth less than a man's. Man is in control of the scales. He determines how much they weigh. And women weigh least of all," Celia said.

"I cannot imagine the difficulties you've endured."

"Slavery is when you don't know who you are. You don't know your age, don't know where or when you were born. You don't even have a name."

Celia's statement was a sort of low growl as if it emanated from deep inside her. As if every word she spoke caused her pain and was bursting to finally be released.

"I think your name is lovely. I…" Eliza quieted down, sensing irritation.

"You don't know nothing. I'm not talking about me. I speak for everyone else here, toiling in these fields. I know who my momma was. She gave me this name, and I carry it proudly."

"Heaven. It means 'heaven' in Latin. It's beautiful."

"She was intelligent. She could read. But it didn't help her."

Celia looked up at Pleasant Hall, the white panels of its exterior blinding in the heat of the midday sun.

"I have a rage to destroy all these great houses. I want to make all these people pay. Ain't nothing fair about this trade, about this *commerce*. Business. It ain't nothing but death, and nothing but death can stop it. I hear about what they doing in Grenada, on some other islands, and I feel joy at the destruction. I got this internal fire raging in my bones that raged in my momma's bones and her momma before her. It gets lit the minute a man puts his hand on you and says you ain't *nothing* but his property. It gets lit the minute you get punished for wanting what everybody else wants. What they take for granted. What they deny you."

Celia grabbed one of Eliza's tanned arms, studying the different tones and paleness of her skin, then released her. She stared out to the yard, watching the other slaves observe them in conversation.

"When you a slave, there ain't no difference between you and his cattle. You ain't no person. You ain't no one. You are nothing but dirt, and one fine day, you gonna return to it, and that's the only time your constant troubles are gonna come to an end. And when you die, ain't no one gonna know you walked this earth. That your tears and blood stained this ground. Won't be a trace of it left except some fine white house."

"I do not condone this. You must understand me. I offered you help in the past, but I was foolish. It was reckless. I can give you a greater amount. It should afford you better help. I gave you my word, and I must honor it."

"I know what I did wrong last time. I won't ever do that again."

Celia started walking away, her steps in time with a distant bell's toll.

"I released you, and you were ill-suited for the task. I can better prepare you," Eliza said, thinking of the gold coins.

"The only difference between you and me is that your name gonna be written down on some fine paper in some church or on some stone in its yard. Maybe someone will come one day and pray over your body while my bones lay under a road somewhere. Forgotten."

"Please, let me try one final time," Eliza said, blocking her path. "Meet me past midnight at the stable. Tell no one."

"I told you I know what I done wrong. And that was listen to you," she replied.

"I will keep trying, Celia. Please believe me."

Celia shook her head and continued walking down the row of trees until the searing heat blended her figure into a curve of bodies that moved and toiled against the glare of the sun, tilling and breaking the earth in repetitive motions. They moved mechanically among the dusty, dried-out, scratchy vegetation. It was a thankless and frustrating task to make an unfertile soil yield produce again and again. This thin, rocky earth was never created for bountiful farming; the salt water seeped under the ground and choked the crops while the merciless sun beat down any growth that managed to climb upward. The production of vegetables was an exercise in folly on soil like this.

The work was made even more distasteful because those who worked the land, who tended to it from sunrise until evening, could not claim any single part of it. They still plodded forward, each and every day, their actions like the machinations of a clock face, the fear of pain and punishment goading them into perpetual movement as the promise of freedom slipped further and further from their grasps, evading them with every single drop of sweat that fell from their brows down to the ground stamped with a hundred nameless footsteps.

The cistern closest to the house required repair, and nothing was left inside the pitcher in Eliza's room. She saw Lucy walk by the doorway, and she stopped her.

"Have my stays been washed? I will need them for tonight. And I will also need water in my basin, please," Eliza asked.

Lucy nodded and went to the side porch, commanding someone else to fetch the water. A few minutes passed by, and then Eliza inquired a second time.

"It'll be here in a moment, Lady Sharpe. Just a moment," she replied, polishing the dining table rapidly.

Lucy then ran out of the house without any explanation. Eliza's eyes fell on a copy of the *Gazette*. It was perhaps three weeks old, but her eyes nonetheless scanned the contents: *UNREST IN JAMAICA!*

The clock chimed in the hallway, and she knew it was exactly five in the afternoon with its resounding bell. She needed to prepare herself for dinner. Growing impatient, she walked to the porch. It appeared Lucy had left to tend to other duties in the kitchen. Two fieldworkers with vertical stripes of sweat on the backs of their shirts toiled in the guinea corn closest to the house. She saw no one else walking toward her. The person Lucy had asked had clearly forgotten. It became a frequent occurrence for her requests to linger unfulfilled now that Celia was no longer her personal attendant.

She started down the steps to head to the pump herself when she saw him. A small boy, no older than eight or so, was struggling to carry and lift the bucket of water. Its contents sloshed out and spilled, wetting the parched dust that caked his bare feet. A slave with a basket perched on her head made a snide comment as she passed him.

"You are not fit for housework, boy."

Eliza was startled by the sight before her, half in denial that the boy was completing her request. She shamefully regretted her prior irritation. She had grown annoyed at a child attempting to complete the tasks of an adult, someone twice his size and strength. She quickly stopped him when it became apparent that he was shuffling his way to her.

"Thank you, I can take that," she said, bending down toward him.

He barely came up to her waist. He was so small. His eyes were huge, like a startled rabbit.

"I supposed to fill that bowl with this water. I can't stop here, my lady," he said, looking down at his feet.

His face was full of guilt. He knew he had failed at his mission.

"That is perfectly fine. Here, it was for me. I can take it. Go run along now," Eliza said gently.

The boy reluctantly put the bucket down, and Eliza lifted it. It had to weigh over one stone. She froze. It shouldn't have surprised her. But in this instance, it did. She knew the wooden buckets on the property were heavy, even when devoid of their contents, but to see a young child struggling to lift it? She felt ashamed. Even at Bleinhill Manor, the servant girls didn't start to lift water until at least fifteen. The boy didn't move. He just stared at her, seemingly afraid of her impending disapproval. She smiled at him, and he ran off toward the slave quarters.

A deep hollow emptiness consumed her. What exactly did the children here do? How early did they begin their back-breaking work? How did that boy spend his days? The young servants she was used to in England were paid small amounts, but most of all, they acquired skills and could advance to higher positions. Only a few men served in a household here, if they did at all. He would be sentenced to the scorching heat and endless labor of the fields, and all he had concern for was whether or not he had brought the bucket to the right spot.

She felt sick to her stomach as she brought the cumbersome pail back to the house. But as she watched the water spill over the sides when she placed it down, she lost the will to use it. The young boy had disappeared from view, but she could not stop thinking about what had just occurred.

Charles was obsessed with breeding the slaves as if they were livestock. And what of these children's futures? Had that young boy any idea of what it held? Or was the undying optimism and spirit of youth still present in someone with skin as dark as his?

Eliza looked all around her. If she stood still at any point on this property, thirty or so slaves would pass by. They were in the fields as far back as the eye could see, tending to the crops, maintaining the trees and bushes, and carrying feed for the livestock. If one was blind, it almost resembled a community. But she knew better. Not one of these people was to be rewarded, or could look forward to the joys of life, or advance to a better position than was currently occupied. And one single thing struck at her core the deepest: not one of them was there of their own volition.

Eliza had found some contentedness in the last few weeks, despite the hardships of being Charles' wife. But the heavy sadness draped around the eaves of the stately white house had reared its ugly head once again. And the truth was bitter to swallow. The slaves around her were all there against their will, and yet they completed their duties with an efficiency of step and a carefully crafted vacancy of expression on their faces. Their brilliant smiles, set in contrast against the darkness of their skin, had never failed to put her mind at ease when she doubted their exchanges.

She thought of her requests for laundered sheets, for yet another glass of wine, for her bucket that stood on the porch that required endless refilling; so many frivolous and unnecessary demands from dawn to dusk, tasks added upon tasks that merited no reward, other than her verbal gratitude. She had convinced herself that it was acceptable, that it was fait accompli. That nothing more could be done to resolve the situation. Pleasant Hall was a plantation, a system of operations she had merely stepped into. But now she could not help but feel a fool. She had offered to help Celia but had not thought beyond that, and now the weight of helplessness threatened to overwhelm her. She could not possibly help them all.

It was delusion at best. The lull of ocean waves, the rustle of dry palms, and the noise of tiny frogs as evening approached did an impeccable job of masking Pleasant Hall's reality. A reality where no pleasantries existed of genuine accord. A place where no friendship naturally grew by its own merit. Instead, it was a place made rigid by fear and constraint, where every kind word, every polite gesture, and every hesitant smile was contrived. It was no wonder the air was taut despite the fluid humidity and breeze that rippled through the palm fronds. The natural beauty was distracting, but even the most dazzling waters and the greenest leaves could not mask the actions of men.

In seeking their freedom from the constraints of monarchy, men had left England and the American colonies and, in desperation, had clung to the rocky shores of New Providence despite its isolation and impoverished soil. Men, who had survived tempests and shipwrecks, near starvation, and the hellish climate, continued to prosper in the town of Nassau despite the odds. Men, who in securing their own independence, had bolstered it by robbing their fellow men of their freedoms, rending them from their homes in filthy chains and dragging them from one coastline to a foreign one, where neither the language nor compassion would ever become familiar to them.

Eliza sighed, looking at her surroundings. In a place such as this, was it even a wonder that the prospect of marital love could never flourish? That anything borne from goodwill and kindness would eventually be stifled under the unrelenting weight of misery and heat?

Eliza walked past the green rows in the fields to the back of the house. Cleo surely understood her intentions. Cleo knew that Eliza confided in her as an equal, yet not a breath of true equality lingered between them. If it were not for the situation at hand, would Cleo even want to be friends with her? How could one befriend a captor? She knew she could not draw up any amiable relations with Charles. Why had she expected the same from Cleo? She had always expected to be treated as she treated others, but surely this ideology could not apply when the scales were so off-kilter.

Celia's icy disposition seared through her memory. Most of these people assumed she was nothing but a horrible mistress, an accessory to Charles' rage, which they were so familiar with. How could they expect any different? They did not know her. They barely saw her unless they happened to pass by in the yard while she was out walking. Her mind raced to every moment she had been frustrated, impatient, and cross. Cold waves sank down her spine. She had focused for far too long on how unfortunate her circumstances were, how tragic her life had become. But what was her sadness compared to theirs?

She quickened her steps and found herself entering the small dilapidated chapel where some of the slaves came to worship on Sundays. It was empty, and she sank down into a crudely hewn pew. She leaned forward, burying her face in her hands. Her mind swirled with past events, violently reconfigured in a different light. A slave was sweeping the path outside with a bundle of dried leaves. Chickens clucked as they beat the dust for pellets of feed on the other side of the building. The way of life here at Pleasant Hall had existed in this way for years before she had ever taken her first breath, and it would continue to march on, repeating its endless cycle of sorrow and pain long after she had left this place.

Someone entered the church, and her despair increased as she realized she had sought solace in the one structure that was resoundingly theirs. She collected herself and was about to rush away, but she stopped when she saw him. It was Jean. He swiftly joined her in the pew and sat down a few feet away. He looked forward at first.

Eliza's heart fluttered, unsure of how to act or what to say. With his large eyes looking reverently up, he almost looked angelic. His physical beauty set him apart from everyone else she had ever seen. But the way he looked at his surroundings was always too pensive. He could have been an angel for the seeming perfection of his face. A troubled angel. The kind that artists depicted cast out of paradise, tumbling headlong down to a cold and cruel earth.

She sharply inhaled, increasingly jittery in his presence. As if anticipating her building anxiety, he turned to her with a smile and withdrew a worn leather journal, and started to scribble a message. Before reassuming a prayerful stance, he closed the book and handed it to her.

I am sorry that you haven't seen me more often, it read.

Her heart seized up. There was so much she wanted to ask him. To tell him. She had the uncanny desire to divulge her innermost thoughts, despite the relative newness of their acquaintance. The contents that tortured her mind screamed inside her louder than before, but she held back. All that came from her thoughts were two simple questions.

What do you do? Why are you here now? she wrote, passing the journal back.

It was strange to sit there, in the small sultry chapel, communicating in the manner they were. But it was thrilling. It was a game that he was playing, and he had invited her to join him. It was a distraction from the thoughts that troubled her. And it was an invitation to escape. Part of her wanted to hold on to that journal and read its contents as if it was a new tome from the bookseller's shop. But she desired, above all, to not show any sign of the wild and flaming intensity of feeling she felt towards Jean. After all, she did not know him. She knew he was the governor's secretary, but he still concealed something. The man was mystery personified. He had no family, no acquaintances, had traveled the world, and, most significantly, had no wife.

She could see why some in the town did not like him. But the very thing that repelled them only lured her to Jean like a moth to a candle flame. She watched him, staring at him openly without shame because they were alone, and she relished it. The woman outside hummed as she swept, her back turned to them.

Jean looked back at her, his blue eyes glowing in the heat of the fading sun. He glanced down, smiling once more, and closed the book, returning it to his pocket. He kneeled for a while longer, and then, in an instant, he was by her side.

"You will soon find out," he whispered in her ear, his voice coy. "This, I promise."

But he remained close to her. The moment seemed to drag on, and Eliza froze, not daring to move. He smelled good, like leather and the faintest hint of citrus. She could feel the heat radiating off his body, and then she suddenly regretted her present look. She was sweaty and damp-haired, and the salt of the sea clung to her dry skin. And then she felt his lips press against her cheek briefly, and he was gone.

Eliza knew she had acted honorably, keeping in perfect alignment with her virtues. Yet nothing about that chaste kiss was proper, and she knew it in her bones. She wanted to see him again. Alone. She needed to. Her mind flashed with other scenarios. What had he meant by this meeting? He had never answered her query. Her heart seized up, wondering if she had received a kiss on her cheek only as a last resort and if his sudden departure had served to mask his failing control. She pressed her back against the rigid wood and released a deep sigh.

Eliza's gaze drifted toward the ground, staring into the bone-colored dust below her feet. A dark shape lay just beyond her immediate field of vision. It was long and narrow, and resembled a spear. Only it did not look like it belonged here on this island in its design. It was from another ocean. As she turned to see the strange object more clearly, it sharpened into the shape of a broken palm leaf. Her eyes were playing tricks on her. The heat was young, but it was strong in the early morning. Her pulse thudded in her ears like an internal drumbeat. And as she listened to the rhythm grow louder, she heard gunshots explode near the tree line of the woods. Her heart throbbed against her chest with unsettling certainty. Celia.

She had last seen her two days ago, after nights of waiting in the stable. Eliza almost lost hope of Celia ever placing trust in her again, but then she appeared in the light of the waning moon. The words of their hasty exchange resurfaced in her mind.

"Here," Eliza had said. *"Take this and make your way to the harbor. Do not take anyone with you, and do not stop for any reason. I do not claim to know how you can escape, only that this amount of coins should secure passage on any ship away from this place."*

Celia's eyes had grown wide as she felt the weight of the pouch.

"If I get caught with this, I will die."

Celia had seemed to be on the verge of saying something else that night, but the coins disappeared into her dress, and in one quick step, she had vanished into the darkness and away from the stables.

Eliza recalled the apprehension that descended upon her since that night as if every step Celia took only compounded the error she had made. She feared the repercussions should this attempt fail, and she dreaded her husband's reaction. With an unsettling twist in her stomach, she knew the ramifications of that secret rendezvous were now hurtling toward the property in a rush of chaos.

Eliza chose to meet it. She took off running to the trees, her skirts in hand, her shoes kicking up clouds of dust. As she approached the forest, she heard a commotion emanating from within. She tensely stood on the edge, waiting for whatever would come from the source of the noise. This could not be good. Had Celia been caught? What was crashing back through the bush? Suddenly, Celia appeared between the dead trees, her face scratched and bloody. Shots followed after her as bullets ricocheted off branches. She made it to the edge of the bush and kept running. Eliza caught up with her, and they collided.

"They mean to kill me. He got away. I...I could, couldn't...keep up with him anymore," she said breathlessly.

"Who? Who? I said to go alone!"

"The man...he said...he would help...get me on a boat."

The effort to speak was too much for her, and she bowed her head as she gulped the hot air. Eliza looked in the direction Celia had come from, and she could see the outlines of figures racing toward them.

"This way," she said, grabbing Celia's arm as they ran in step.

Eliza directed her to the rows of guinea corn, and they rushed into the red-topped stalks. They ran so fast Eliza feared they would tumble headfirst to the ground. They stopped midway in the field and ducked. Celia collapsed, her chest heaving from racing back to the estate. Eliza quickly gave her a handful of her skirts to cover her mouth.

"Here," she said, her own voice short-winded, "cover your mouth to silence your breathing."

Celia listened, blocking her mouth and inhaling the fabric. Her eyes were wild. She furiously dug in her dress and produced the bag of coins, throwing them at Eliza as if they were tainted. Eliza took it back with shaking hands as if its presence alone made her realize how severe matters had become. The situation was unraveling out of control faster than she had anticipated. Despite worrying about this scenario for days, she could only cower between the stalks, wishing for invisibility or a retreat into time.

"If anyone asks, you were not running away," Eliza said in a hushed tone, well aware of the trouble they found themselves in. "You were simply collecting herbs for me since I feel unwell."

"But the soldiers…" Celia managed to utter. "I think they saw me talking to that man. I gave him a coin. They know. They will know."

"You were frightened and ran. You were not thinking clear—"

Eliza paused. She could not mistake the sound of the click of boots and weaponry she associated with the king's troops. She heard the noise nearly every day, and it did not fail to instill dread in her once again.

"Shhh…" Eliza raised her hand.

They both waited in silence, wishing to be safely hidden from the eyes of men. They hovered in stillness, with the sun beating down upon them as the smell of damp earth rose to meet them. Eliza caught a glimpse of a bayonet. Its metal shone in the light, and then it came closer, slicing through the stalks.

Their sanctuary was intruded upon, and two sets of arms reached for the women. The first she noticed was Mr. Bailey's large and hairy muscular arms. He swiftly grabbed Celia and pulled her away violently through the corn stalks. The second set of arms locked onto Eliza and pulled her upright but away from Celia. They both screamed, Celia in horror and Eliza in anger.

"Stop! Let me go at once!" Eliza shouted as she was dragged through the guinea corn back to the dirt path beyond the field.

Two soldiers were studying her. The one who was not holding her promptly announced their intentions.

"You have committed a crime against a personage of the Crown by enabling the slave to escape. You are, therefore, to be brought to the gaol to await trial. Any persons willfully partaking in the robbery of any of His Majesty's…" he recited from rote.

She tried to wrestle her arm away from the soldier holding her.

"This is a mistake. She was not running away! Let me—"

"…subjects are guilty of committing a crime and will stand trial…"

"I own her, you fool!" Eliza shouted.

It was strange to utter such words. The soldiers looked aghast at her outburst. Then the one who had spoken in such a perfunctory tone looked at her with confusion.

"Then you mean to commit insurance fraud. Do you deny it?"

"To heavens! I have committed no crime. She was not running!"

Celia's screams reached a fever pitch. Eliza whipped around to see where she was being taken. She knew with dread that it was to the post near the almond tree.

"Do you know who I am? Unhand me this instant!" she said, looking the silent soldier in the eye.

"Woman! You are unruly!" he shouted.

He wrenched her arm downward, tightening his restraint on her. Eliza began to strike his chest.

"Let me go, you fool! You are not listening—"

He struck her without hesitation. She was stunned at first. She had calculated such a reaction to be more likely from the first soldier, but either way, she was glad. He had unhanded her in the process. She was now free. She took off back to the house as fast as her legs could carry her. As she reached the main house, she saw Charles stepping away from the porch. The lane curved, and she caught a glimpse of Mr. Bailey and Celia. A small group of slaves had gathered to watch the spectacle. Celia was being dragged by her wrists along the ground as she wailed.

"Charles!" Eliza exclaimed, rushing up to him. "Please, you must stop this at once! There is a mistake! I sent Celia to fetch me some herbs in the bush, and you must help! These soldiers believe her to be a runaway, and I can vouch that she is no such thing. Please!"

Charles seemed to be intently listening, but then the next thing he said revealed that to not be the case.

"Eliza, did Barnett just strike you? Or am I mistaken?"

She looked back at the two soldiers. It was now abundantly clear why they had not pursued her flight.

"Yes, but that's of no importance. Please, tell Mr. Bailey to stop this at once! Please…"

Charles ignored her pleas and stormed down the steps to the two soldiers. The one who had captured Eliza turned pale as he realized his grave error. Charles began to yell at them. The soldier handed over his weapons. An instant later, he was cowering on the ground after Charles had punched him in the face. But Eliza was too preoccupied to follow those events. They were of no interest to her. She turned back to her left.

Mr. Bailey dragged Celia to the post and tied her wrists with some rope. Celia was still fighting him like Eliza had never seen before. She realized then she was about to witness what Celia had endured that night when she had failed to escape the first time. Eliza dashed toward them.

"Mr. Bailey, as mistress of this plantation, I ask you to stop this at once."

She had said it as firmly as she could, not even entirely confident that this attempt would gain any traction.

The other slaves stared at her with huge eyes. Cleo was watching from an upstairs window, her eyes downcast.

"I'm afraid I cannae help ye, Lady Sharpe. Celia belongs tae the Lord Sharpe, not ye. She's not yer property. She's his, and ye know it," he answered gruffly, spitting on the ground.

He continued to fuss with Celia's bound wrists, pressing against her backside with his corpulent abdomen. Eliza stepped in as close as she could manage.

"No! No, she is. She *is* my property."

The sentence was heavy on her tongue. He looked at Eliza, unimpressed. Tugging the rope, he hoisted Celia upwards to a stand. She wailed. He ripped open the back of her dress.

"But surely, there is no need for punishment when no wrong has been committed?" Eliza added, the urgency in her voice hardly masked.

She desperately looked around for Charles. He was still in a heated debate with the two soldiers. She inwardly cursed at his priorities.

"Aye, she was runnin' away. She's a sleekit chancer if ever I saw one. And all chancers need a good skelpin'. I worked this land long enough tae know when a Negro stayin' and a Negro runnin'. This one was runnin', I tell ye. And she got caught. Look how afeard she is," Angus said.

He slapped her back, and Celia cried out with a wince.

"Mr. Bailey, I order you to stop," Eliza said, stepping closer to him again.

He stank of old whiskey and hay.

"I cannae take nae orders from nae woman," he said, towering over her.

"Please inform me of what is going on here," Charles said. "I am in charge of the agricultural tasks."

Eliza turned with relief to hear his voice approaching. It was a strange sensation, but she did not have the time to process it further.

Angus assumed an air of professionalism at once and cleared his throat.

"Aye, my lord. This Negro was caught in the woods by two soldiers. She was attemptin' tae run away. But old Bailey apprehended her in time, I did," he replied proudly.

"How fortunate. Thank you very much for your service, Bailey," Charles said. "Eliza, I wish to speak with you in the parlor about what just occurred."

Angus nodded and then bent down to pick up his whip. Eliza felt her face pale in horror. As Charles made his way back to the porch, she chased after him.

"You must put a stop to this, Charles. She did no such thing. I can vouch for her, please!" she implored. "This is not right. You must stop this."

The width of her skirts hit against his leg, and the pouch of coins made the smallest jingle. He looked down at her with worn-out patience, then back to the scene in the yard.

"Excuse me, Bailey..." he called out.

The man sighed; his arm paused in the air, poised for destruction.

"Aye, my lord?"

"Is this truly the proper method to handle such matters these days?"

"Aye, 'tis. O' course, my lord. This is how yer late father, God rest his soul, would have handled such an occurrence," Angus said with a nod.

"Carry on," Charles replied with a false smile.

The whip cracked as loud as a gunshot, and Celia's scream tore through Eliza.

"No! No!" Eliza continued to beg.

But Charles was not interested. Then she thought of another way. She would use her limitations as an advantage. She refused to be defeated in this.

"She's with child! Please, dear husband! Please show her mercy!" she groveled.

This caught his attention. He stopped in the doorway.

"With child? Are you sure? My God. What precipitous news."

"Entirely..." Eliza lowered her head and took a deep inhalation. "She has been going off to the woods lately because she is sick. With morning sickness. From bearing her child," she lied.

"Bailey! Stop this at once!" Charles called down, raising his hand.

Celia strained to look at Charles, her tear-soaked face in shock. She dropped her head in sheer exhaustion, a thin diagonal line of red marking her heaving back.

"I dinnae understand, my lord," Angus said with irritation.

"We cannot have you damaging her. She's providing me with a child."

"But sir, she was runnin'—"

"I do not claim to understand the ways of women, my friend, but I assure you she was not attempting to escape. I have it on the word of my wife," Charles said.

Angus glowered at Eliza and dropped the whip. Eliza stood on the porch, wanting to remain there until she knew Celia was safe. She felt Charles beckon her to follow him inside.

"What a strange morning. If she has a healthy term, we will nearly make up for this season's shortcomings," he said, pleased with himself. "I truly had no inkling."

"Yes, dear husband. You handled that quite well," she replied, disgusted by the situation she found herself in.

"Now to more urgent matters. I do not wish to speak of my exchange with the soldiers. You have been subjected to enough, and I have reprimanded Barnett accordingly. I will let no man treat you in such a manner. You are my wife and worthy of the deepest respect."

Eliza's ears burned with the irony of his statement. He looked down at her, a hand lightly brushing her cheek, his green eyes examining her profile.

"I do not see any damage, thank God. Your beauty is still intact."

Eliza stepped back from him. She craved more reassurance about Celia's situation.

"Perhaps Celia can return to the house now that she is carrying a child. Fieldwork is surely not suitable for a woman in her condition. Not in this climate."

"Excellent point. You are learning the trade quite efficiently, Lady Sharpe," Charles said, amusement flickering in his eyes. "I knew you would make a good study, my dear."

He bent down and kissed her slowly, raising her chin ever so slightly. The breath left her chest as if his mouth were a void capable of extinguishing any solace she had gathered from her chaotic victory. She had never been in the company of a man whose every move, regardless of her endless stratagems and maneuvers, only made her feel constant defeat. He kissed her a second time, and her mind raced to find an excuse to leave his presence. Her hand grazed the fabric of her skirt, made taut with the weight of the coin purse concealed within, and the determination to quit this strange and cruel island returned stronger than before.

Charles called her name, so she went underneath the archway.

"Yes, husband?" she said, barely looking at him.

"Do you have a moment to speak with me?" he asked.

Her heart stopped. What was his intended meaning? His demeanor was grave. She briefly considered if this exchange was about the coins she had discovered. Had she said too much to Cleo? Had Celia told the others about the pouch she had handed her? But then she buried the worry away.

He does not know. How could he know? she thought.

She swallowed, determined to appear unaffected by his question. Charles put a finger to his mouth as he carefully contemplated his words.

"I am afraid it concerns a serious matter."

That caught her notice. Guilt started to flood her system. Her stomach felt like it had risen to her throat, buoyed only by her quaking nerves. What if it was not about the coins, but it concerned Jean? Had Charles noticed something between her and him? She knew with certainty he had not seen them together. Jean's visits always occurred when Charles was occupied at the fort. But did he have suspicions? She did not like feeling so vulnerable. She clenched her jaw, anxiously awaiting his next statement. She knew an explosive reaction would follow if he grew upset.

Charles walked over to the round table in the center of the parlor, his boots causing the floorboards to creak as he stepped closer to her. The edges of her hair grew damp with nervous sweat.

"This came for you today," Charles said, looking down at a letter. "I opened it by mistake. I thought it was mine."

He looked off to the side and then stepped back. As soon as he was at a comfortable distance, she walked to the table and began to read the letter.

She barely got past the first sentence when she felt the floor almost move beneath her. She reread it again.

Dearest Eliza,

It is with deepest remorse that I regret to inform you of the passing of your parents. As you know, my sister was not faring well these past months and ultimately succumbed to the pox. Not long after, your father, in his grief, was also not spared this fate. In my responsibilities, I have taken management of their estate and lands…

All of the determination and hope she had felt coursing through her lately left her like a flame crudely blown out. She lowered the letter with a quivering hand.

The date inscribed was at least three months old. She had spent every day obsessed with nothing but her own thoughts and loathing her current situation. She had wished for nothing more than to escape, but now regret consumed her. She really would never be able to return home now. The conversation she had had with Jean the first night they met had never weighed more on her consciousness than it did at that moment.

She felt Charles put his hand on hers, but the room spinning around her stole her attention. She felt lightheaded and unstable. Life had suddenly sped up; the walls and trappings of the house that usually made her feel dreary were now cast in motion, mobile and whirling, while only she remained still.

"These things are, unfortunately, a part of life," he clumsily said.

She heard his words but refused to listen to them. They floated past as her mind raced with a tumult of emotions. She had been angry with her parents. She had been furious with them for casting her into this situation thousands of miles away. Eliza had always trusted her mother and father and, in turn, had trusted Charles, who had irrevocably shattered that faith. She had only ever received one letter during her stay in the Bahamas. A shallow customary farewell letter; she had perceived it as nothing more than a fond send-off for a girl now officially molded into a woman. Its formality had stiffened any sentiment she could possibly derive from between the lines, and it read as nothing but coldness to a new bride desperate for escape.

She had sent dozens of letters, thereafter all unanswered. At first, she blamed the weather, the harsh seas, and the insurmountable distance between them. She even pinned the blame on Charles. He must have inspected her letters, read their contents, and tossed them into the fire. It was dramatic but satisfying. Only something so outrageous could sufficiently explain the lack of response. Then she finally came to the hollow, sinking realization that no answer would ever come.

She had not spoken of the beautiful crystalline waters surrounding the house, the wonder of the cave in the west, or even how she had finally become acclimated to her new society. Every letter was a desperate plea for help, to extricate her from her situation. To alert them of their terrible mistake in securing her hand to his. And in the manner of all business contracts that had already been fulfilled, she knew there was nothing more to be done and that, in all events, her mother and sisters probably sat in contempt and judgment of her situation. They only saw the sugar money, despite the fact that no sugarcane could ever prosper on this limestone island. They assumed the island she had been forsaken to was similar to all the other tiny jungle-covered dots on this side of the Atlantic. And they most likely believed her to be a foolish, immature child, her distressing letters a testament that all those years of training had never really stuck.

Charles had wounded her so deeply that it was impossible to view the rest of the world as a neutral bystander. She had sat with the idea that her parents had refused to hear her. But now the confirmation that disease had taken them burned her ears. She had been so quick to judge. One card of fate had fallen, its face bitter and harsh, and then another, and another in the past year. She had been only too happy to assume the very worst. It was easy to retain such a negative disposition.

But her mother and father had *not* abandoned her in the manner she presumed. How long had they been ill? Had the entire family been occupied with nursing them? It seemed incredibly cruel to bear witness to this news. Smallpox. An invisible killer, only revealing itself when it is too late. The money from their vast estate and their worldly riches weren't sufficient to spare her parents. Death came for all, and when was death ever truly welcome?

Lost in a swirl of grief, she returned to the dark wood-paneled room baking in the afternoon sun. She withdrew her hand from his as if it had scorched her skin.

"Do not touch me," she seethed.

She waited for his anger, but none came. He carried the same demeanor as before, quietly producing a second packet. It was a bundle of yellowed and bent envelopes.

"This…also came in the post. It appears that your letters were returned once they reached Plymouth. I am not entirely sure why they were never delivered."

He dropped them on the table, folding his hands behind his back. He bit his lip, awaiting her reaction.

"My letters."

"Yes, I'm afraid so. Eliza, I am so very sorry."

She could see the stamps on them, the markings, and other apparent signs they had been handled.

"To heavens…" she whispered, tears welling up in her eyes.

The source of so much pain could only be attributed to simple anonymous human error. This was the conclusion that had evaded her for months. There was no grandiose explanation, let alone a satisfying one. Her family had most likely assumed she had refused to write. Now *she* had never truly answered them. She looked up angrily at Charles. He was so cold, so unfeeling. And now he stood there, still as stone, without even realizing he had robbed her of the last vestige of her ignorance. That ignorance had been a small source of comfort, and she had not even realized it until now. The truth of the matter was much worse.

The letters had not been lost. They had not been stolen. Moreover, they had yet to be destroyed. In a moment of clarity, she now realized their presence could complicate her situation if Charles ever read the contents of the packet that had been in his hands and if he ever knew the extent of her hatred towards him; the thought made her shudder.

Eliza took the packet and tossed it angrily into the fire, much like she had pictured Charles doing again and again. Only, he had never done such a thing. She returned to the table, taking her uncle's letter in her shaking hands. A tortured sob escaped her.

"At least they were able to see our union before they were taken," he said softly. "Time will heal your sorrow like no other medicine can."

Her stomach roiled as he said that. His words were like grating poison to her ears.

"If you need to rest in your room, please do so. I know this can put you in a delicate state—"

"You are cruel," Eliza hissed.

Charles seemed taken aback. His eyes filled with confusion.

"This, this is how you inform me of my parents' deaths. As if this was any ordinary missive that you opened by mistake?"

She tossed the letter to the floor. Tears streamed down her face.

"You never receive letters here. I did not realize until I had opened it—"

"Thank you for reminding your grieving wife of her constant seclusion. How it gladdens my spirit."

She attempted to storm out of the room, but he blocked her path.

"Eliza, I am your husband. You have me. This should be a source of consolation…"

She stepped closer to him, scanning his eyes.

"It is nothing but a source of misery."

Through her watery view, she could see the hurt on his face. She knew she had cut him deeply, but she felt nothing but fury towards him. He was not her concern. Some part of her knew it was wrong, but it temporarily eased her suffering. And he had been such an overwhelming cause of it. She gathered her skirts and rushed up the stairs, leaving a shocked Charles in her wake.

CHAPTER X.

F eminine conversation was far more tedious than she recalled. Not five minutes had passed in Charlotte's company, and Eliza already felt tortured.

There was an uncanny sensation that occurred when a person in mourning attended social events. When one decided to participate, it was only because the pain of grief had seemingly ebbed away to nothing, but then in the company of those less aware of one's loss, among people even appearing indifferent at times, every glib comment or innocent question seemed to heighten the pain and return it to focus. Discussions surrounding Christmas left the realm of benign chatter and suddenly became treacherous, rendering her composed state tender once again. Her muddled and confused thoughts had not even considered that December would arrive the following week. She had not felt the approaching cold, watched the slow descent of papery leaves from the trees, or witnessed the servants decking garland and other greenery around the ground floor of Bleinhill Manor.

Instead, the change on the island was barely perceptible. The evenings were cooler, and the sea had grown less warm, but the idea of winter seemed a fantastic concept. The upcoming holiday had slipped entirely from her mind, and she found herself completely unprepared to sit among the women tonight. She was sure that Charles would have mentioned something to Lord Dunmore about her family's circumstances, and in turn, this would have reached Charlotte's ears, although there was no measure of sympathy on her face. Nevertheless, Eliza did not want to speak about something so dear to someone false like her. And so, she sat among the women, smiling when she assumed she should and appearing to listen intently during other phases of the conversation.

Charles had disappeared in the back of the house as soon as they had entered. A temporary gaming room had been set up again, and every green table was occupied with raucous gentlemen. There was dancing in one room, but Eliza feared Charles' hand more than she enjoyed the bouncing melodies of the quartet. She had excused herself to fetch another drink and then another, feeling that the glasses offered on the silver trays were too small to satisfy her.

In fairness, Charles had offered to let her remain home. But she wanted to come tonight. She wanted to see Jean, and her current wanderings were dedicated to satisfying that aim.

She walked past what appeared to be a study. The door stood ajar, with noise erupting from it.

"Bloody hell! Where are my letters?" a booming voice shouted.

A half-empty inkwell suddenly rolled across the floor and stopped by Eliza's shoes. She picked it up and walked into the room without a second thought.

Lord Dunmore stood by a massive kidney-shaped desk, his papers and folios scattered everywhere. His wig was tilted at an odd angle, and beads of sweat decked his thick brow. He snatched the ink from her, glaring first, and then he began to compose himself. The boorish attitude she always thought he concealed within his portly body was fully displayed. She needed no further demonstration to confirm she should depart from the room. She had begun to excuse herself when he raised a hand.

"No need. Stay. Are you enjoying the festivities, Lady Sharpe?" he asked, dabbing his face with a handkerchief.

"Yes, very much. Although the noise of it all can cause one's head to ache, I'm afraid. I do prefer the quiet."

Eliza regretted her words instantly. She had made a mistake coming in here. She wanted to leave the room.

"But surely you are excited to have reason to leave your side of the island?"

"On occasion."

"I do confess, I am not sure how you—a lively, young, spirited woman—can pass the time in such isolation."

"I prefer my solitude. It gives me freedom. I find I am quite partial to it."

Lord Dunmore sucked on his lip, then stared back at her. She recognized his leer. There was a time when such a glance would not have registered with her when she was more innocent, but that time had long since passed.

"I think I will return to the parlor and visit the ladies. We have much catching up to do, and I am in need of more wine."

She was distinctly aware of the half-filled glass she carried in her hand. She brought it to her lips, and it disappeared. Eliza curtsied and was about to turn out of the room. He watched her with greedy, impatient eyes.

"Tarry a moment, my dear! I have my liquor cabinet here. I have some fine Canary wine from my personal collection. Much better than the stuff the footmen are serving."

Eliza wanted to turn down the offer and even insult the man, but she felt fixed. He was the governor, after all. And so, she responded with politeness.

"Oh, that would be lovely. Thank you."

Lord Dunmore grinned with a crooked smile and hobbled over to a niche in the wall where a rosewood cabinet stood. The crystal glasses trembled as he stepped near, and he roughly pulled open the creaking door. He poured her a drink and handed it to her.

"I do hope you continue to enjoy this fine evening, Lady Sharpe."

She took the glass and rapidly backed away.

"I will, thank you."

She curtsied a second time and rushed out of the room, swallowing the wine faster than she could reach the parlor. The crystal was distinctive, and she did not need to bring attention to the preferential treatment she had been shown. She handed the glass to a servant and hastily grabbed a cup of black tea. She required a stimulant to endure the petty and superficial conversations that would soon ravage her ears again.

Her return to the women caused stifled conversations and a few scowls. It was clear that they had engaged in gossip during her absence. The ladies did not appear enthused by her presence in the slightest and carried on with a more neutral topic.

Eliza found herself staring at the molding in the ceiling, noticing the fine cracks and bubbling of paint delivered by the tropical humidity. The buzz of mosquitoes flitted about her head. But then, as if revived with a fresh burst of vivacity, the room around her became alive and vibrant. All seven nearby conversations throttled her ears at full volume, a plethora of female voices assaulting her mind.

The ceiling seemed to dip lower, then higher again, distorted and fluctuating above her. She studied her teacup, noticing for the first time new details previously undetected, like the mistakes the painter had left behind on the fine bone china. The swirls of ivy and arabesques that didn't quite align with one another left her feeling disappointed. It rivaled the superficiality of her current environment. And then a deep voice sounded in her ear.

A turquoise-clad servant stood behind the sofa. A few women turned, then resumed their talks when they realized the message was not meant for them.

"Lord Dunmore requests your presence in the garden at once, Lady Sharpe," he said, his eyes bloodshot and yellowed.

She turned away, confused by his meaning. Charlotte's razor-sharp attention focused on her, her eyes small and beady like daggers.

"Tell him I am otherwise engaged," Eliza hastily said.

The room started to pulse around her. She straightened her posture against a cushion and toyed with a stray curl near her ear. A second servant entered the parlor from the hall bearing a folded note. He dropped it on her lap and quickly left. Eliza felt more eyes on her. She opened the missive, accidentally ripping the envelope, and read its contents aloud without realizing it.

"*Butterflies...*"

She recognized Jean's handwriting. But she had not seen him tonight. Her heart pounded against the lining of her stays. He wanted to speak with her. His strange absence was partly why this ball seemed so miserable. Charles had begun gambling two hours ago, and she felt confident he would remain there for hours still.

"Butterflies? What do you mean, Lady Sharpe?" An older widow by the name of Lady Whitten looked at her.

Eliza felt startled, realizing she had spoken aloud to the audience before her.

"Forgive me. I am afraid my mind is wandering," she said quietly.

She herself had the same query. What could Jean possibly mean by this?

"A turn about the house would do you good, Lady Sharpe," one voice remarked.

Eliza nodded, still staring at the note. A red-haired woman rolled her eyes without attempting to conceal it.

"I heard word that you are quite the naturalist, Eliza. Is it true?" Lady Whitten asked.

"I am quite intrigued by nature, yes."

"Have you seen the collection of butterflies they have in this house? Many local varieties, but some are from further south. The colors they contain are something to behold."

Lady Whitten did not seem to carry the same malice as the younger members of the room. Eliza regretted not recognizing this feature before. What did she, as an older woman, have in common with Charlotte and her clique? It was more than entirely possible that she was also miserable tonight.

"Oh, I was not aware."

"Yes, why don't you take a look and see? Cassie can show you. It's right up the grand staircase."

Lady Whitten snapped her fingers, and a reluctant-looking housemaid appeared.

Eliza hesitated and then considered it was the only sensible meaning of the mysterious note. The two of them walked up the stairs. Eliza felt more worn out with every step.

"Are you well, ma'am?" Cassie asked out of obligation, her voice flat.

"Yes, I am fine, thank you. Feeling a bit weary, that is all."

Her body began to feel heavy, and every movement strangely required a great deal of physical effort. They turned after the stairs and proceeded down a long hallway.

"Here are the insects, ma'am. Many Lord Dunmore collected himself. It took many years to accomplish this.

315

The species to make a note of are the malachite and several swallowtail specimens. Also, please look at the atala, a small but beautiful creature found on this island. I will be serving downstairs if you need me." Cassie rattled it off as if she had said this many times.

She waited before leaving her, and Eliza realized Cassie expected a tip. She reached into her pocket and handed her a small coin. Within moments, Eliza was left alone in the empty hall. The energy felt so deserted and hollow up there compared to the crowded and dense loudness of the first floor. She looked at the framed insects, marveling at the colors, but then grew frustrated that none were named. She understood the malachite butterfly to be green but saw no green insects before her. It seemed quite predictable that Lord Dunmore had fumbled such an enterprise. He had surely killed these creatures for sport, not education.

She sighed and looked around her. She felt so very tired. And the note's meaning had not been made any more evident. All the doors on this floor were closed except one that was open and lit. It appeared to be a guestroom. She could see more framed specimens inside, so she entered.

"Jean! You startle me!" she exclaimed, stopping midway.

Jean stood inside, tensely leaning against the edge of the mantlepiece by the fire. He looked as if he had been waiting for her longer than he intended. He rushed up to her, grasping her arms.

"Eliza, listen to me carefully. Lord Dunmore gave you something. He put it in your wine. I saw him."

"How? I was alone with him."

"It appeared so, but I was in the office, looking for something. I heard him approaching, and I hid. But I could observe the both of you clearly."

"What were you doing in there?"

"I will explain it all one day soon, I promise you. Now hear me…he poured something into your wine, Eliza. How are you feeling?"

Jean's blue eyes looked large and pained. She had never seen him so uneasy.

"Quite strange, I must admit. What do you mean by all of this?" she asked, her head shaking slowly. "Poison?"

Her voice grew frantic with panic. She reached for her chest.

"No, no, not poison," he said, motioning for her to speak softly as he closed the heavy door behind her. His footsteps were quiet and calculated.

"I do not understand…"

"Laudanum."

"I am not familiar."

"It overthrows the balance of your faculties. The mixture of it and alcohol combined will leave you intoxicated beyond control."

"But I feel so very heightened now. I've experienced the strangest sensations. My mind seems to be racing."

"But your body is weak. Your mind is riddled with euphoria, but it is fleeting. You will fall asleep soon and remain inert for a long time."

She looked down at his hands holding her and then at his concerned face. She had yearned for a moment like this, but not for the current circumstances that brought them together.

"Why?"

Jean looked down at the floor.

"As a means of seducing you," he replied through gritted teeth.

She laughed, but he remained serious.

"But what use would he have of me if I am to fall into such a state?"

"If you are weakened, then you cannot resist his advances. He will attempt to gain intimate knowledge of you, and once he has succeeded, he will use it as a means to extort you."

"And what end could this possibly serve?"

"He will have power over you."

"But I do not understand—"

"He seeks to control Charles and reduce him to nothing. He knows he is powerful. You are the gateway. Charles represents the old families, the Conchs, as they are known. He has the militia at his beck and call. Once Charles realizes what Lord Dunmore has committed in recent days, he will try to stop him. And the governor wants the threat extinguished before it can become a threat."

Eliza's eyes grew huge and then watery. Before stepping foot on this island, she had never realized the full scale of politics or the deviousness of men. The repulsive man whose voice thundered below them downstairs had once seen fit to use her body as a form of bribery and now as a form of blackmail.

"But it will not happen. I will protect you," Jean said firmly.

She shook her head, wresting free from him.

"I must tell my husband. Yes, I should leave. I need to leave!"

Jean blocked the door.

"He will not understand. I have seen this happen before. They will only blame you and claim you drank too much. The game is only too easy for men in power."

"But this cannot be. Surely, people must know what he is doing...if he has done this before. There must be rumors!"

"He is the governor. He is an agent of the Crown. He is the most powerful man on this island. I had my suspicions, but I never saw it in its entirety until now. I am sorry, Eliza."

"I feel a fool. This is not right. How can this be?"

He looked at her and then away, sadness sharpening his clear eyes.

"Am I to needlessly suffer for a man I do not love?" she asked.

"Your breathing is growing shallow. This is what we will do. I will leave, and then I want you to lock yourself in this room and slide the key under the door to the hall. I will retrieve it and stand guard outside. Go to bed and when sleep comes to you, let it. Do not fight it. Do you understand?"

He motioned to open the door.

"Wait! You cannot leave me! Don't leave me here! I want to go home! Call for my carriage, and it can drop me at Pleasant Hall, and Julius can return for Charles."

"I don't think we will have time."

"How do you know of this? You speak with such certainty."

"Men at court in London are no different from the false kings that inhabit this island, Eliza."

"Stay with me," she implored.

"I cannot. I will not impugn your honor."

She looked toward the bed, knowing he was right.

"Damn my honor! I care not!"

She began to breathe louder, panic gripping her.

"You already have troubles, and I will not be the source of more."

Jean looked frustrated as he bit his lower lip and glanced away. He took a chair and dragged it to the door.

"Come, sit down. I will be just outside."

"Please, Jean! Do not leave!"

"Please, you must trust me. Take a seat and steady your breathing. You will fall asleep soon."

He handed her the key and stepped outside, closing the door behind him. Eliza locked it with shaking hands and reluctantly slid the key underneath the door. She pressed her face against the wooden divider separating her from him.

"Jean, my God…"

He didn't immediately respond.

"Jean? Jean, I cannot hear you. Where are you? Are you still there?"

"Yes, yes, I am here."

"How can I know if I cannot see you!" she said her voice breaking.

"I will not leave. I promise you."

His voice was soft and reassuring, but anger and fear took hold of her. She did not want to remain in this place, in this empty room, in Lord Dunmore's house. She looked around for other points of entry but thankfully saw none. Then a second fear took hold.

Her dark eyes flitted madly in terror as she spoke through the door. "My husband will be angry."

"No, I will explain it to him. Do not trouble yourself with that."

"He will find a way to blame me for this. I know it."

Now she could hear Jean's measured footsteps pacing back and forth in the hall.

"Do not leave me! It will be worse if I am alone!"

"I am here. I am right next to you."

She savored the sound of his voice. It helped her stay alert. She ran her fingers along the door as he spoke.

"It will be over soon, and you can go home. I will explain everything to Charles. Your character will not look worse for what has been done to you," he continued.

His voice sounded loud and clear, and she knew he was pressed against the door like her. She looked away, starting to feel weak. Her body felt like it was struggling with even the slightest movement. She did not know whether it was from the anticipation swirling within her mind or if it truly was the sedative. She reached for the chair and brought it to her, scratching it along the floor. She sat there quite still, her breathing still frantic. Her pulse seemed to echo within her, and her heart throbbed in slow, heavy beats. Shadows from the candelabras wavered in split images of three and four likenesses along the plastered walls. Eliza looked toward the door again, finding peace in its simple symmetry, when a sudden rush of panic gripped her. Her surroundings were too quiet.

"You've left! You've left me! It is too quiet here. Surely you have departed by now and left me!"

"Shhh...I am still with you."

"Thank you," she said softly.

A drunken howl resounded from the lower level, followed by the crash of breaking glass.

"Would you like me to tell you about India?" he asked.

"Yes," she whispered.

"I had never seen such a land of marked contrasts. Canton was like a dream; it lulled my senses. But India...India stirred me awake. The cacophony of sounds, the brilliant colors, the temples, and palaces. It overwhelms you."

She closed her eyes as she brushed her cheek against the cool door. The sound of his voice so close to her ears was enough to overpower her. She was lost in thoughts of the blue clarity of his eyes and how it complemented the dark, nearly black shade of his hair. She wondered if he realized he possessed such handsome features. Women did not gravitate toward him, at least not in this town. But that was precisely what she liked about him. His allure, endless charms, and constant attention on her all felt like a marvelous secret. Her breaths felt weighted now, and sleep inched its way closer. He continued to speak, the cadence of his voice pleasing to her senses.

"There is a river there called the Ganges, and it is holy, and the people believe merely bathing in it can forgive all transgressions and help you attain salvation..."

He continued, and although she hung upon his every word, she felt her eyelids close and open less and less until she succumbed to sleep.

Eliza awoke with a jolt, nearly falling out of the chair. Violent knocks sounded at the door. She moved for the first time in hours, the ache of bone upon bone hitting her. She could hear someone fidgeting with the key, and the door flew open.

Charles and a startled Cassie rushed into the room. Eliza stood up, looking around in confusion as she struggled to remember what had occurred. When she did recall it, her stomach felt sick. The hallway was empty. Jean had left. Daylight was creeping into the black sky beyond the windows.

"Lord Dunmore gave me something! He put it in my drink!" she said, not caring that Cassie was present.

The reaction she sought from him was not forthcoming. Charles appeared troubled but not overly so.

"Yes, Eliza. I already spoke to him. Jean alerted me of the situation. Lord Dunmore is at fault here, but I have assurance of his good intentions."

"What?"

"When you complained of a headache from the noise earlier, he gave you medicine but failed to tell you. You are feeling better now, I presume?"

What Charles implied was bewildering to her ears.

"I feel more myself, yes, but I didn't complain of a headache," she said, baffled.

"In his study. You two spoke, and he repeated the conversation verbatim to me. Did you not complain about the noise?"

"Yes, but I was making polite conversation. I never requested any medicine."

"You do not remember, my dear. You wanted relief."

"I never said any such thing," she replied, her temper rising.

"You drank too much wine, perhaps. Even the slaves noticed. You emptied many glasses, and Cassie reported you had difficulty ascending the stairs."

She glared at Cassie, who only offered a disinterested glance in return. She had never encountered a servant so undeserving of a tip. Then she turned her wrath onto Charles.

"From what he put in my wine! To help me was not his intention, I assure you."

Now the slave's eyes widened. Another servant hurriedly entered.

"Lord Dunmore regrets that he is retiring to bed and cannot say farewell, but wishes for your speedy recovery, Lady Sharpe," he said with a bow.

"And we most heartily thank him. Thank you," Charles rejoined with a nod.

Eliza could not tolerate his display of willful blindness a moment longer.

"I was not in need of recovery. He was trying to incapacitate me."

Charles grabbed her in a fury.

"You wish to assail the governor's honor when he has shown you nothing but the greatest welcome and hospitality time and again? I will not hear of this!"

His eyes were fixed on hers like piercing blades. She said nothing, breaking away from his gaze.

"Our carriage at the ready," he ordered Cassie.

She left, and Eliza felt fooled. Tears welled up in her eyes. Jean had been right. Charles did not understand. He did not want to hear what she had to say.

"Where is Jean? He said that—"

"I truly do not comprehend you, Eliza. Do you not understand what you claim? Incapacitate you? For what purpose? The damage you would cause to his reputation! He has given us everything, Eliza!"

"He has made advances on me tonight and in the past," she hissed.

This information seemed to startle him for a moment, but his features hardened again. He shook his head.

"You continue to tarnish his character," he said quietly. "Alcohol is not good for your weak constitution. You cannot perceive matters as they are. Even if he did what you so unabashedly claim, your job as a woman is to resist. Do you not think even a wretch like Cassie occasionally receives advances from men? And what can she do? Try with all her might to resist them. That is what honorable women do. We would not be in this situation if you had even an ounce of her character. A slave, Eliza. Think on it."

Eliza could not listen to another word. She stormed out of the room and down the stairs. The house had nearly emptied, with the exception of a few drunk stragglers. The mourning doves were cooing in the bushes around the veranda, and the heat was already rising.

"Eliza!" he called out after her.

Charles caught up with her on the lawn and wrenched her arm, pulling her to him.

"Do not embarrass me by causing a scene."

"Do not fret. I will never step foot here again," she spat.

"I daresay you'd be so fortunate to be invited to Lord Dunmore's functions after this charade."

Their carriage rolled up, and they climbed inside. The ride home was nearly suffocating with its stormy silence. She would not look at him. She did not know what she had expected from him. Any reaction other than what he offered would be preferable. He seemed so possessive, so desperate to control her in every other way. Why did he not care about the governor's advances? Why did he not seem distressed about the implications? Why did he not *believe* her? She could feel Charles' eyes burning in her direction.

The vivid bursts of orange from the sun relit the bright waters of the ocean as they passed the shore. She had always noticed how flat and dark the sea appeared until the sun was higher in the sky. Then it would return to its magnificent shades of dark and vivid cerulean. The beauty around her at least offered some distraction. She sighed. Charles had upset her once again. He was callous and unfeeling. But a different matter pressed her thoughts. Another ball had ended, and all Eliza could look forward to was the chance of seeing Jean again. Anxiety barraged her. She did not know when that would be, but she also knew she could not be patient. His presence was like a tonic, and the more she exposed herself to him, the more she yearned to never leave his side.

CHAPTER XI.

"You misunderstand, Lord Sharpe," the clerk said. "I was given explicit instructions from Lord Altringham. The interest on what you owe is also due in payment today."

Charles stroked his jaw, inquisitively looking around his yard as if he could spot a source of untapped wealth. He was in an impossible situation, and Eliza knew it. She felt a wave of perverse joy course through her. The crops failed miserably last season, and he had made no profit. He had been so consumed with tasks at the fort that the interest the clerk spoke of slipped his mind entirely. His hawkish green eyes scanned the property until he found a solution. It was standing next to him.

"Here," he said, grabbing Lucy by the arm, "You can take this Negro. She is young and of good stock. Nearly sixteen years of age, I believe. Trained for the house. She will bear Lord Altringham more slaves yet."

Eliza's mouth dropped open. Lucy looked petrified. Her eyes stared at Charles and then at her in panic. Eliza watched as the clerk ascended the porch stairs and proceeded to pat her body down in full sight of the others. There were no rules of propriety afforded to slaves, most especially concerning the men who bought and sold them.

"She comes from good stock, you say?" the man asked, brazenly eyeing her curves.

"Yes," Charles turned her slowly, continuing Lucy's humiliation. "Her mother cost us twice as much as the debt I owe. I assure you it is a most generous offer."

Eliza tried to catch Charles' gaze, but he deftly avoided it. She stepped toward him.

"Husband, may we discuss this transaction before it proceeds? I—"

With his other hand, he steered her behind him, back into the cooler darkness of the house.

"No, we may not," he said tersely.

"It is a deal, my lord. She will make an attractive addition to the estate," the clerk said, leading Lucy down the porch steps.

Lucy's face looked abjectly terrified. She looked around wildly for her mother.

"May I remind you that Cleo runs the management of this house and is the best domestic servant you have? They are family! You cannot separate them!" Eliza said, grabbing him by the arm.

Charles strode into his study, rifling through yellowed papers in his walnut secretary desk.

"Charles!" Eliza said, pulling at him.

He spun around, towering over her.

"May I remind you of your station, woman! Your voice does not matter here. You do not make decisions for this family. You do not run the books. You do not understand the precariousness of our situation. It is unstable at best. Now take leave of me!" he shouted, pushing her away.

"Please, please reconsider," she said. "I have offered wise advice before. You said so yourself. Please tarry a moment…"

"Yes, you mistakenly informed me that Celia was with child. And she is not."

"She is. She told me so!"

"Then she lied, and you foolishly believed her."

Eliza looked at him incredulously.

"I think I would recognize the signs of pregnancy, husband."

"Oh, yes? Why is that? You yourself have never carried a child."

His words were insulting, but she carried on.

"How do you know she is not?"

"I had her examined."

Eliza looked horrified as she imagined what that must have entailed. And now she knew the reason for his darkened mood the last few days. He had allowed Celia to remain in the house despite knowing her supposed pregnancy to be nothing but a ruse. Eliza felt herself blushing with embarrassment.

"There are taxes to be paid. Taxes that are owed in order to secure Pleasant Hall. Our expenses are daunting," Charles said without affording her a glance.

"But surely you can choose another…"

He stopped on a sheet of paper that wasn't as faded.

"They are all someone's daughter," he said bluntly, looking at her.

Eliza bit her lip, feeling the opportunity slip past her. He studied the sheet.

"What about Jacob? Jacob came from another island. He has no kin here; he is without ties. Sell him. You can sell—"

Charles slammed the paper down on the desk. Then he regained a level of composure.

"Women are more valuable. Lucy will cover the debt I owe," he said.

"But Jacob is more skilled. He tends to the horses. He can even improve on his smithing skills."

"Eliza, let me tend to the affairs of the house as you are not fit to do so. You know nothing. You understand *nothing*. You do not know what forces turn the world. Women are more valuable to sell because they breed, my dear. Your purchase of one nearly guarantees additional slaves for your land," Charles said as he surveyed her reaction. "Unlike a marriage contract, as I have unfortunately found out much too late."

He looked at her with a sneer and stepped out of the house. Charles handed the papers detailing ownership of Lucy to the clerk, and he beckoned her to climb into the back of his wagon. The man bound Lucy's shaking wrists with rope and clicked for the horse to move.

Eliza stood immobile, the immensity of human cruelty hitting her like a rogue wave. She understood the rules of plantation life but had found comfort in the assumption that some things were sacred. She had believed that family was something not to be touched. At least in Pleasant Hall. She had heard of other estates separating families but had never seen it. She had never felt it until now. Every time she was faced with the cruelty that abounded on this land, she thought it could grow no worse, and then, each time, the pendulum swung even further still.

The wagon began to roll, and Eliza watched as Lucy grew distant, her eyes watery as she moved away from the place she had been forced to accept as her home. They mirrored Eliza's eyes, and her world grew blurry as her first tears fell. She hated him. She hated the man she was wed to. He was a heartless creature.

A woman carrying a basket of browned leaves and twigs rushed to where the wagon had been, stopping by the tracks of Lucy's footprints. She bent down, scooped some sand into her hand, and let out a mournful noise. The sound was strange and loud, then unsettlingly soft as a whisper.

"*Oya! Rewoh Oya! Oya, rewoh Oya. Oya! Kamah go rewoh Oya, rewoh Oya...*" she sang.

Another woman carrying sticks passed by in answer to her song.

"*Oya! Rewoh Oya!*" she answered flatly.

Before Eliza knew it, several voices were repeating the same uncommon words. Then the woman started a new song. She cried out louder.

"*Eh eh eh eh eh...eh eh eh ah, awa ye awa, awa ye awa! Awa ye awa oba koso...*" she sang as she walked toward the slaves' quarters.

The second time she started the chant with a cry, more voices joined her. Some were close but hidden from view, working inside the kitchen; others called from the fields, their song a solid shout carried through the distance. Eliza followed them, spellbound, tears streaming down her face. She watched them join in solidarity, communicating in a language that was not her own. She could not interpret their meaning, but she understood the solemn cry of grief without a doubt. They all knew, no matter where they stood on the plantation, what had transpired. All but one. And they were making their way to her small hut now.

Their joined voices rang out, so powerful and clear; it was like what Eliza imagined the choruses of heaven to resemble. She had heard such stirrings before when the slaves praised God in their chapel. When they had danced before great fires in celebrations unknown to her. But in those times, joy and vitality had pulsed from their words. Now, an overwhelming note of loss resounded through the air.

More miraculously, without any cue, they all fell silent after three more rounds of the song. The first woman stopped by the entrance of Cleo's dwelling. Cleo came out, expressionless, holding a burgundy stitch of fabric. She opened the cloth, and the woman poured the sand she had carried into it. She left without another word.

"Cleo, they took Lucy," Eliza said stupidly.

Eliza could not control the urge to fill the deafening space between them with well-intentioned words. She knew it was foolish. For one, she had done nothing to stop it, and secondly, Cleo was already well aware.

"I'm so sorry, Cleo. I…" Eliza continued.

Cleo outstretched her weathered palm. She shook her head, eyes closed to the world, and hummed.

"Cleo!" Eliza said.

"Shhh…*Oya, rewoh Oya, Oya, rewoh Oya…*" Cleo mumbled, tying the burgundy cloth into a little sack.

Cleo beat the bag to her chest as the wind picked up, and the palm trees shook in a cacophonous trill.

"What should we do?" Eliza asked.

"What do you mean by '*we*' do? Oya will help."

"Oya? Who is that? You never told me about—"

"Oya! The Mother of Nine! *Iyansan*. She is not for you. She sees the dead like I do. She brings justice, like Shango, to women like me. She is the wind…" Cleo said, looking up at the bent palms above them. "Her winds from my land in Africa carry over the waters to become storms here on these islands."

The loud crash of rough surf breaking on the coral along the shore made them both turn.

"I will try to purchase her back. I have the money. I will—" Eliza started.

Cleo grasped both of her hands in her large steady grip. "Always tell the people you love that you love them. You and your people do not see what I can. The endings are always a surprise to you."

It was clear that Cleo was steadfastly focused on something other than the tragedy that consumed Eliza.

"You will not see Oya. She is not meant for you. But that does not mean she is not here."

"But Cleo, Charles…I cannot fathom how you believe he is in possession of a good heart. How can he blindly destroy what little family you have left? Why do you let me, of all people, take counsel from you? I cannot fathom it. I…"

"The fire you are born with is the color I can see. All people have their own color inside, and it hangs around their shoulders. I can read what every color is, and I know what each one stands for. What I mean to say is that you cannot change your soul. A man can sell his soul. He can give it to another. That is how a good man can lose his truth. But that is not the case here. A man born with a bad soul can only be bad. The same is true for a man with a good soul. The test of life is to live with your color. It is a constant trial, but no one is perfect. It is most trying for a man born with a good soul living in a world without mercy. That kind of world wants to put out his fire. But where it is hidden, inside, they can never reach it."

She pursed her lips and watched Eliza's confused reaction. Cleo began to hum.

"Many people want answers, but they do not want the truth. To them, the matter is two separate things. But you cannot hide the truth for long," Cleo said.

Eliza's mind was spinning in circles, but she could not help but detect that, no matter what transpired, Cleo would always defend the monster in both of their lives.

"How much longer must I wait? Should I stand idle until the day my life is forfeit?"

"A day is a breath to those above us. Your clocks do not mean anything to them," Cleo replied, lighting a candle in her cabin.

Eliza stepped into the doorway.

"I am leaving here, Cleo. I now have the means to do so, and I am quitting this place. I know what you have said, but I am choosing freedom. Perhaps you insist I stay because you must stay. You have no freedom. Your daughter has been carted off like a mule to pay my husband's debts. You sit here in the dark, put sand in a bag, and chant and expect something to happen!"

Cleo said nothing, her face like an indecipherable stone.

"If these orishas exist, if all these prayers work, why is there slavery? Why are you sitting here as a slave when you could control the island with your gift of sight? Isn't that why we condemn witchcraft? Because people like you are dangerous? You are powerful! Why did we burn witches at the stake? Why are *you* a slave?" Eliza said, breathless with frustration.

She was intrinsically aware that the weather had shifted outside. The sun had left, replaced by a dark gray sky. The candle's flame danced, bending thin like the edge of a razor's width.

"Perhaps I have the sight because the One knows I do not seek power. Their time is not our time, their language is not our words, and their agreements do not need to make sense to us. Part of our truth, the essence of the fire in us, is to understand and remember what we agreed to before we were born."

"You claim that thousands of slaves find themselves at our mercy because they agreed to it? No, never in my wildest—"

"No," Cleo said, shaking her head. "That is a story for another time. That is because the matriarchs of my people were betrayed. The men of that time were jealous. They beat and killed them to steal their power. And the matriarchs cursed them. Who is it, may I ask, that controls the world? Who is it, may I ask, that makes slaves of other men? This tale has continued for many, many centuries. It is only now that white men have joined the cycle. Do not be so presumptuous as to think your race created all things.

They did not create slavery. What I mean to say is, they only agreed to profit from it, like many, many before them."

The bulk of Cleo's words escaped Eliza's grasp.

"I did not agree to be wed to this man. I did not agree to be endlessly tortured by an arrogant brute who lacks any redeeming qualities. I did not agree to…" Eliza ranted.

Cleo smiled, admiring her boldness.

"No, no, you did not," she replied, shaking her head, "not to the man, no. But you did to his soul."

Cleo barked out a laugh, brushing her hands together. Then her mirth abruptly stopped. She raised a hand in dominance.

"Leave. I need to pray, child," she said.

"I enjoyed our walk, Eliza," Jean said as they stepped onto the back porch. "It certainly is helpful to escape one's duties from time to time."

"It is pleasant to be in the company of someone who knows how to take the liberty to do so," Eliza replied.

They hovered near the French doors for a moment. Neither of them had brought up the events of the last ball. A couple of weeks had passed since that night, and she still did not truly understand Jean or what he was doing on this island. She had waited in anticipation every time he spoke that afternoon, hoping he would finally reveal matters, but the moment she had longed for did not arrive. The more days that passed between them, the more the events of that night faded into obscurity. But she could not forget his promise. Now she desperately hoped he would speak, as he appeared to be departing imminently. And her impatience was unnerving.

Jean surveyed the area around them and stepped closer to her.

"I have arranged for your passage back to Europe. Once spring has passed, you will board *The Ferme*, headed to Le Havre. I have already written to my sister Anne concerning your journey."

Birds called out from the tall pines around them. Eliza's dark eyes grew huge. Freedom was within grasp.

"I cannot thank you enough for your kindness," she said, bewildered. "I can pay you for your efforts."

"No, no. It is not necessary. I have you traveling under the name François Brottier. I think it is prudent to have you disguised as a male passenger on the ship's register. You will receive word of when the journey will commence, so you will have ample time to prepare."

His voice seemed satisfied as he told her this, yet his face was pained. But she was not entirely content. She decided to coax the answers she sought out of him.

"Is something troubling you?" she asked.

He looked at her and then smiled.

"I may have to leave soon. There is a matter that has arisen recently…concerning my work. I may have to return to London."

"What is your *work*, Jean? You promised to tell me."

He was silent at first. A single invisible cicada's buzz rang through the air.

"I fear I cannot say, for I do not wish to entangle you in these affairs. For your personal security."

She was silent as she measured the weight of her next question. The thought had swirled in the recesses of her mind when dark worries overcame her. It marched in step alongside the idea that she couldn't possibly be in possession of this much joy from Jean's mere acquaintance alone. Their relationship was simply too flawless to be considered a natural occurrence.

"Tell me, are you in the employ of my husband?" she asked.

Her body tensed up as she waited for his answer.

"Beg pardon?"

"Are you in the employ of my husband? Has he sent you here to befriend me, to gain my confidence, in order to spy on me?"

A pair of parrots cawed out in the distance. Once. Twice. The silence between them was torturous. Jean's reaction was maddeningly indecipherable, and he was taking his time to respond. The heat in her face was nearly enough to cause her to flee the scene. He finally spoke.

"I am in the employ of Lord Grenville," he answered, looking away.

"The Foreign Secretary? What are you doing here then? Shouldn't you…"

He took her arm and pulled her closer.

"I beg you to tread carefully," he urged. "Most believe me to be Lord Dunmore's secretary. I arrived on this island as a commissioner of the customs. But the idea that I've left my post as a military officer is suspicious to many. And my sudden elevation in position proves even more questionable."

"What could possibly be of such importance on this island that your presence is necessary? Surely Jamaica or Barbados produces more wealth."

"Do not mistake this island for some low-lying rock cast out in the Atlantic. It's the very gateway to our first overseas empire. If the Bahama Islands were to fall into Spanish or French hands, it would cut off the lifeline of our economy. We've already lost America, Canada is a fledgling territory, and trouble is brewing on the Continent. These islands are obscure to most officials in London. Many do not even understand where these islands begin or end. Our possession here ranges over nearly five hundred miles of ocean. Think of it. The king needs eyes everywhere."

"You are a spy," she said breathlessly. "You were looking for something in the governor's study. That is the reason for your unexplained absence that night."

He did not confirm or deny it. The thrill of their clandestine exchange was intoxicating to her.

"Are you in some kind of danger?" she pressed.

His blue eyes seemed to shine as she asked this.

"Not if my strategy goes accordingly," he said, changing his stance. "I tell you this in the strictest confidence—"

"You have my word," she interjected.

Jean reached for her hand.

"I know, Eliza," he said as he held her fingers. "I do not wish to burden you in any way. But I can say this. An earl is a rare thing on this side of the Atlantic, and the son of a convicted traitor in possession of a governorship even more so. We both know that Lord Dunmore carries outsized ambitions, but now I have proof he has dangerous ones…" He paused when he saw the look of astonishment on her face. "I am afraid I have spoken too freely. The less you know, the better."

"Lord Dunmore? What folly could that cretin possibly commit?" she quipped.

"Do not mistake him for a fool, Eliza. The acquisition of money is his whole system. And he faces a mountain of debt. Lord Grenville had ordered a moratorium on the construction of the fort two years ago. There were concerns of fraudulent accounting practices, but what I've uncovered is astounding. Even to someone in my position."

Eliza stepped closer to him, squeezing his hand.

"You must tell me. Do not be cruel…"

"He seeks to reverse the outcome of the war in the American colonies. He means to seize Florida and the lower Mississippi Valley from the Spanish without the official backing of the Crown. The Bahama Islands are nothing but a staging ground to him. There are rumors he has already raised nearly eighteen thousand men. Attempts to secure his recall have been in vain, but I now carry information to ensure his undoing."

Eliza looked off to the side, her mind spinning from his words.

"I'm afraid I'll need to leave the island immediately. There are wicked people in powerful positions who will not want me to succeed."

"The very people who insult you and spread lies about your character," she said.

"Indeed. People are quick to advance such slander when it serves as a distraction from their own misdeeds. Whatever people accuse you of, I nearly always find that they are the guilty party. And it certainly holds true in this regard. I am protected by my employer and may even say protected by his benefactor, but unfortunately, even he cannot control events thousands of miles away."

He chuckled as he said this but stopped because she was gaping at him.

"I have said too much. I do not want to embroil you in this heated conflict. I love my country and my king, and I aim to uphold that institution. The state of affairs on the Continent threatens all that we hold dear, and we cannot afford a single loss in these waters."

"You are not what you seem," she stated, staring at his clothes.

It was all starting to fall into place now. His activities, the island's suspicion, the all-pervading atmosphere of secrecy around him.

"I am a soldier, but my life is not simple. I am waging war on a very different front."

He wore no uniform, yet he was risking his life for his country just the same.

"Does Charles know of this?"

"Not yet. But I mean to tell him soon. Now that we are reconciled. I am eager to resolve the fog of mystery between us."

"When will you leave?" Eliza asked, unable to mask the sadness in her voice.

"It is not so much the timing of my departure that I wish to inform you of, but rather the sudden unexpectedness it may possess. Whatever may happen in the next few months, please do not anguish over me."

"This all seems so formidable. I can scarcely believe what you have told me."

"You must not speak a word of this to anyone. There are few people here that can be trusted."

"You have my silence."

She looked down. He was still holding onto her hand. He seemed to realize this at the same precise moment. They stood closer to each other than she could ever recall. A breeze swept past them, enveloping them in a rush of warm air.

"I have toiled over these feelings, but I will not make you an indecent woman. Nor can I betray a friend. I am grateful we have met, although I do often desire that it had been under different circumstances," he said, his voice strained.

Jean leaned over and pressed his lips to her forehead. A rush of emotion seemed to overcome him, yet he still retained a thin veneer of control. He let go of her and stepped back as if forcing himself to remain in his role.

The act of him pulling away was too much for her to bear. She had craved a moment like this for so many weeks: the feeling of space between them disappearing, the heat and energy coming off his body. All she yearned for was meaningful connection. She wanted something to live for, a reason to rise from her bed in the mornings. Being in his presence was a source of newfound hope, a constant internal rush in her body that stirred every fiber inside her into vivid alertness. Eliza had never felt like this before. And she knew that only he could have such an effect on her.

Eliza hurtled into him and kissed him deeply. She could feel the sheer bewilderment on his lips. He stood there in shock as if afraid to touch her.

"And if I *choose* to be an indecent woman?" she said, breathless, her cheek touching his.

His eyes closed against the side of her face. She briefly felt his hands reach up her waist, and then he stepped away. Her heart raced against her chest with the realization of what she had just done. She had broken the invisible barrier between them. She had decided her own fate. And with her kiss, she had revealed the feelings mere words had failed to convey.

A jumble of footsteps sounded as Cleo threw open the door to shake out a rug. She stopped and looked at the lack of space between them.

"Excuse me, Lady Sharpe, sir…" she said, bowing slightly, as she rushed back inside.

"I am sorry, but I must go," Jean said, not meeting her eyes.

He darted around the corner, returning to his white horse, leaving Eliza alone. She paused there for a moment, a hand on her stays. She reveled in the thrill of what she had just done. The danger felt titillating. It ran through her bones at a fever pitch and made her feel alive. She could hear his horse galloping back toward town. Still floating in her reverie, she stepped inside the house. Alarm bells rang in the back of her mind, but her heart had silenced them for now. He had not quite reacted as she had envisioned in her many distractions. The element of surprise could have accounted for that. He was a gentleman at all times. She had probably shocked him. She sighed.

"You cannot be with that man," said Cleo, interrupting the flurry of thoughts within Eliza's head.

Cleo's eyes glowed large and solemn. A feather duster lay motionless in her hand.

Eliza tossed her linen kerchief on the newly polished table.

"I don't know what you're talking about," she said, slightly irritated.

"You heard me," Cleo said, placing her hands on her hips. "You cannot be with that man."

Eliza was about to turn around and walk away when she stopped herself.

"I assure you, he's nothing more than a companion."

"Do not lie to me, Miss Ellie. I saw you. He has the shadow behind him. I didn't see it the other times. But I saw it this time."

"The shadow?"

"You know…something is not right. With the path he is walking," Cleo said vaguely, pursing her lips.

"I've had enough of your hogwash for the moment," Eliza replied. "Are you finished?"

She was about to exit the room when Cleo spoke again.

"It is not you. It has nothing to do with you. It is something with him. Something is not right there. There is a dark shadow trailing behind him when that man walks. I would be careful if I were you."

STRANGE EDEN

"Thank you for your concern, Cleo," Eliza said with ice in her voice.

Eliza knew exactly what Cleo was seeing, but Cleo could never know the truth. Jean lived dangerously, and he survived in part due to skillful deception. She would need to meet Cleo's queries with scorn. She felt guilty because she had observed Cleo acting differently ever since Lucy had been sold. But she knew she had to protect Jean's secret. His very life was in danger.

"And I trust you won't speak of this to anyone. What you witnessed."

"And I trust that you will listen to me. If you know what is best, Miss Ellie."

Eliza stepped into the hallway with a view of a sullen Charles resting in his chair.

She had not realized he had returned. She worried if he had overheard anything for a moment, but then she reveled in her secret. Her mood was glorious. Nothing could unsettle her newfound joy. What had transpired felt more delicious and satisfying than a crisp sip of champagne. Her lips tingled with the excitement of a touch that was forbidden. A touch she had unexpectedly initiated.

She inwardly smiled. She was not an improper woman. She was a free woman. She was defiant. And she was rebelling against her restraints. Charles had not the slightest idea that she would soon leave this place. She was overjoyed at the thought of the ship, but she felt hesitation also. There was the uncertainty of the journey and what lay on the other side of the voyage. But there was also the thought that her freedom meant leaving the one person who had enabled such an occurrence, and the pain surrounding

345

this idea was unsettling despite the verve of excitement within her heart.

Every evening, Charles and Eliza came together to share a meal. This was generally the only time the two of them could be found occupying the same space. As was customary, it mostly took place in silence, with the occasional metallic clink of a utensil or the more delicate chime of crystal punctuating the stillness. The plates were cleared, new courses laid out, and the red wine refilled.

Tonight, when it was complete, she excused herself and was about to go to sleep when she first heard it. A slight but constant drumbeat sounded in the distance. It was a sudden reminder that a new year would arrive in a matter of hours. The governor had invited them to a ball tonight, but Charles had declined out of embarrassment. Eliza was glad to be relieved of the opportunity. She only regretted not seeing Jean. She had not seen him since her brazen show of affection, and even though only two weeks had passed, it nearly felt like two months to her impatient mind. She feared he was avoiding her at times, but then she would ease her mind with distraction. Like the strange drums she now heard.

When she opened her bedroom window, she heard them more clearly, accompanied by what sounded like the blaring of horns. The jumble seemed so disjointed yet rhythmic. And the beat only enticed her. She crept back down the stairs, the hallway shifting in shadows from a candle's flame, and saw Charles in the parlor studying the fire in front of him. Eliza made it out of the house, but instead of heading for the beach, she made her way toward the fields.

Tonight, the old white house was bathed in a blue hue from the steady moonlight, and the air was chilly. She encountered almost no slaves and knew intuitively that they must also be near the source of the noise. She walked past the kitchen attended by two servants, past the still and slumbering fields, quiet except for the chirping frogs and tiny insects, down the dusty lane. She ventured further than ever, even passing Cleo's hut and the row of abandoned slave quarters. A border of tall, rustling palms flanked the path on either side of her when she first smelled the earthy, reassuring smell of the bonfire. Then she saw its massive glow appear on the horizon.

Eliza quickened her pace when she saw Cleo clapping and dancing, and she hesitated in the shadows until heads began to turn and eyes saw her. The strange tunes of homemade drums and rattles pierced the air as the slaves clapped and danced to words she had never heard before. The women all appeared to be wearing white dresses and colorful headscarves. Their frenetic energy was all-consuming. They were happy and celebrating, and it mesmerized her.

Cleo turned and pulled her into the group and, with the same addictive sense of cheer, led her into clapping along with the beat as she called out, singing certain words louder than the rest. A shaking rattle came closer to Eliza as a woman she had never seen before shook it, lost in the tempo. She danced around her, looking up at her but once, as if Eliza belonged there with them, and continued in her frenzied circle around the fire. A medley of conch shell horns, cowbells, sweaty hands, and stamping feet formed the foundation of the organic music. Eliza bobbed her head, laughing and smiling as she raised her hands. She looked around them and only recognized a handful of their own workers, but Cleo seemed so relaxed.

"I don't know what I'm doing," Eliza said breathlessly as she followed Cleo's movements.

"You don't need to, child; it's inside you. It has been waiting there the whole time," she replied, her eyes closed.

A number of people began to change the words, and the tune began to rise and quicken. Men and women chatted and exchanged whoops and cries. Their liveliness only animated Eliza further. A group of women shouted louder than the rest and seemed to taunt the men, the men answering in grounded, deeper tones.

"*Ayibobo ayibobo eh! Baba wa...*"

A multitude of voices sounded at once, different chants and songs coexisting simultaneously, but the same steady beat of the drums continued. For a moment, it seemed like the disjointed voices would eventually break the continuous rhythm, but then the choir of voices began to agree on a single song again, and the rattles increased in frequency. Eliza's heart was beating madly as she danced to keep up with a surprisingly energetic Cleo. It seemed so simplistic yet sacred in its origin to be connected to the earthen ground beneath their feet, a religion composed of drums, dance, and song.

One main singer started a new chant, and they all repeated his lines word for word. The heat from the fire was intense, and the breeze traveled through it, leaving sparks in its wake. Someone passed her a sticky dark bottle of rum, and Eliza took a swig of it with their encouragement. At first, the burning liquid disgusted her, but as it flowed through her veins, she felt invigorated. She boldly took another sip as the woman next to her made an undulating cry.

Eliza's laughter was more frequent, and she lifted her skirts as she began to dance in swirling circles between the faces and the fire. A bewildering rush descended on her that made her ears ring and left her lightheaded. Dizziness invaded her senses, and she stood still to slow the spinning world down, only moving her head from side to side, her hands raised to the sky. The sensation consumed her as a pervasive heat approached her chest, and she opened her eyes, expecting to see someone in front of her. But it was only her and the wild fire.

She repeated the words obvious to her ears, not entirely sure if she was even correct in her pronunciation, but no one seemed to notice or care if she was out of place. The longer she stared at the flames, the more she began to see faint colors dancing within it and then small figures of people rolling up and down the tongues of fire, disappearing as soon as they had emerged. It was as if the bonfire itself had begun to sway to the music.

The bottle of rum came around again, and once more, she pressed her lips to it, despite the initial disgust she had felt from its formidable taste. She drank until all pretensions left her body, and she felt freer than she ever had as she left her inhibitions outside the moving circle. That was when she recognized an older, slender man with

349

a tall hat leaning against a tree, his smiling face glowing in the moving shadows. The mere sight of him instantly recalled fragments of a rhyme to her revolving mind.

"One will strike from the sky, his mother...the sea."

She had finally found him. She turned to Cleo, excited at her discovery, but Cleo was no longer near her. They all began to move clockwise around the circle, and she relished the feeling of her bare feet crushing the moist dirt beneath her. She had lost her shoes some time ago but did not care. Her surroundings started to blend in a whirl of colors, smiles, and darkness until she lost her balance, shifting her footing and weight too quickly. She laughed, dropping downwards until she recovered, and her gaze lay on the trembling flames again.

Eliza looked for the man, but the tree he had stood by a moment before was now abandoned. She raised her arms toward the sky, shouting the words she thought she heard alongside her, when a strong arm brutally grabbed her and pulled her aside.

The music and song continued. The drums rumbled around her but grew fainter as she was moved into the night to a dark horse.

"My God, Eliza!"

As her vision looped and spun, she knew she was on the horse, galloping headlong along a path. She recognized that voice. She hated that voice, but she heard another man as well. The roar of the ocean was perceptible again, and she knew she was near the house. The return journey seemed a brief, jolting blur compared to the time it had taken her to find the fire. A warm body behind her was like a wall she rested against until she was seized again and felt the levelness of solid ground. The other man was thanked for his assistance, and he departed, leaving her alone with the sound she despised. Confusion and blurriness subsided momentarily as her instinctive guard turned on.

"Eliza! What have they done to you?" Charles swung her around, looking her up and down once they were on the porch.

He was angry, but something else flooded his features. He was clearly inspecting her.

"Thank heavens for Julius. Your foot is bleeding!"

"I wasn't finished dancing!" Eliza protested.

"That was not dancing. That was some savage display of heathen revelry. Did you not see what they were doing?"

"Yes, I do have eyes, husband. It's called Obeah, something you wouldn't understand."

"It is nothing more than errant nonsense, and at its worst, it is cloaked insurrection."

"Did you not feel them? The ancestors? I cannot explain it, but there were a great many more people there than you or I could see."

Charles looked at her strangely, then leaned in to smell her breath.

"Are you drunk? My God, what did they give you?"

"A bit of rum. It is deliciously warming and heady, is it not?"

Eliza was swaying to the now distant drumbeats. She refused to make eye contact with him. The hardness of his eyes only confirmed his displeasure and her unfortunate reality. He represented reason right now when she only wanted to chase after her hazy surroundings, comfortable in wantonness, and her newfound freedom.

"I know men oftentimes enjoy the pleasures of rum…" she started to say, finally understanding why rum was their preferred drink of choice.

Charles didn't wait for her to finish her thought. He took her by the arm and led her up the stairs, pulling her when necessary.

"My God, they could have assaulted you, Eliza!" Charles said in horror.

Eliza stopped on the second floor, refusing to move. Her vision was becoming clearer as the situation grew ever more precarious. Standing in his presence was always a sobering experience. He tugged on her arm, but she would not budge.

"Much like you are doing now?" she said, her tone mocking.

The last drop of his patience seemingly vanished as he slammed her into the wall.

"Do not be mistaken, Eliza. These people are not your companions. They are my property. They are slaves! Do not assume for a moment that they enjoy your company," he sneered, examining her disheveled appearance. "They would like nothing better than to use you for their own ends."

"Use me for what purpose, husband?"

He exhaled sharply, looking for the right set of words. She slumped slightly, so he strengthened his grip on her arms.

"I wouldn't be surprised to see one of their women befriending you, taking advantage of your naivety, just so one dreadful day a fieldworker comes with the strength of a bull to assault you! They have lascivious appetites, Eliza. They prey on young white women."

Eliza burst out laughing.

"What utter nonsense! And you mock me for reading novels…"

Charles shook her.

"You don't think they would take you away without hesitation and ransom your pretty head for a fee? They'll drag you off to their miserable huts and demand I give them their freedom for yours. I have grown up around these people, and I understand them. You understand nothing but your own blindness concerning the subject."

The mirth disappeared from her face.

"Perhaps you have all these unfounded fears that creep into your heart because you, as cruel as you are, know in the depths of your soul that all of this is wrong. A man cannot and should not own another man," she said boldly, her stature straightened.

Charles looked down to the side, shaking his head.

"You sound like that damned fool Granville Sharp. You would be better off in England debating your weakly formed philosophies. But alas, you are a woman, Eliza, and you have no voice. The best you could do is paint your face and don a new gown and join those Negroes at one of their balls. I hear that in certain sectors of high society in London, they are all the rage."

"I imagine the women would look quite stunning, the contrast of rich colors…" she said lightly.

"You cannot debate a man, and your thoughts are as useless as a candle in a rainstorm. I admit I once questioned the restraints put upon your sex by our society, but after indulging what roams around your head, I have no doubt the world is better off without women like you speaking their minds."

"I suppose it is a natural occurrence for one to react in such a manner when one is confronted by such inconvenient truths."

His eyes narrowed.

"Your meaning, woman?" he asked, his voice full of disdain.

"I mean to say how very troubling it must be to know the depravity of everything you stand for. A soldier of the king, not defending the kingdom from imminent invasion but defending a small trading outpost, a dot in the vastness of the Atlantic. How all these islands would fall if it were not for their suffering. These colonies would be worthless. It is all so horribly wrong. To inherit a group of slaves from a man you consider less than a father. To know that the only woman you remember as a mother you now own like a sow. To have to follow duty blindly to receive simple praise from others. To receive even the slightest recognition as a man…"

He said nothing. She tried to walk away, but he stopped her, knocking down the light illuminating the hallway. It clattered to the floor and rolled away. The space was plunged into darkness.

"You know nothing of duty. You know nothing of honor. I have every right by law to strike you. I have every right to make you conform to my views. And instead of being grateful for the security I give you, for the small liberties I bestow upon you, you treat me so. Even I was whipped when I showed disrespect to my father, and I committed half the offenses you have. Yet I show you endless benevolence. It would seem I have chosen the wrong woman to wed. I know of no man who could tolerate the behavior you put forth day in and day out!" he seethed.

His spit sprayed her cheek. She did not immediately answer. His words had stirred some part of her memory, some forgotten fragment clipped from a dark dream.

"And I have accepted the wrong man."

Her hands grazed his back, and even through his shirt, she could feel the scars and lines that extended across his broad shoulders. Her thoughts raced to her first night at Pleasant Hall, how her hands had felt the same roughness while not fully understanding its source. She thought of the dream then and the first time she had seen Tabitha. She recalled the young man who had been scourged in the front yard.

"It was you," she said so quietly she assumed he could not hear.

"What?"

He pressed her harder into the wall, but then her resistance slacked. She was saddened by her thoughts, but it was quickly replaced by something more mischievous. Her legs opened slightly, and she curved her back, looking at him with a gleam in her eye.

"What are you doing?"

"I am trying to see if you are an honest man. To see if your hatred has obscured *all* of your faculties," she said as she sprawled against the wall.

Truthfully, she did not know why she presented herself in such a manner. The rum made her reckless and irrevocably so. She wanted to toy with him the way he had

355

done to her countless times before. She felt powerful in her delirium. The small measure of sympathy she felt for his past reduced the level of threat he now posed to her. Her pity made him appear nearly a different individual altogether.

Charles released her, stepping back. He seemed to hesitate at first, suspicious of her changed mood. Then he merged with her, his lips seeking hers. Their breaths collided for a moment, but then she evaded him. Eliza laughed and slipped away into her bedroom, slamming the door shut in his face.

"Eliza! Open this door at once!"

She moved to fix her chair against the door to keep him out as he pounded on it even harder.

He continued shouting. "Eliza! Open the door!"

Her game had been satisfying, but now the tone had shifted. She had miscalculated. He was the same brutish man. And she was too drunk to effectively keep the door closed. Her unsteady show of strength paled in comparison to his. He entered the room, freshly enraged with her behavior. Charles threw her onto the bed as she screamed. A crash sounded below them in his study, but neither of them seemed to care. He grabbed her silver pitcher and doused her with cold water. She blinked, confused, spitting some water out.

"You need to regain sobriety, and until you do, you will remain here," Charles said sternly.

He stormed out of the room, taking her dutiful chair with him. His angry footsteps receded to his chamber. She stood up, newly invigorated with adrenaline. Her hands were shaking, and her heart was pounding; she could not remain still. Eliza squeezed her damp hair out and smoothed her dress. She moved to the window, looking out at the glowing moon above the dark rolling waves. The beach seemed to call out to her with longing. The roof covering the porch was easy to reach from her window. Eliza slipped through the opening, but the drink clouded her judgment. She underestimated its distance and stumbled the rest of the way down, hitting the sand with a thud.

Eliza became acutely aware that a horse stood a few yards from her. She looked up to see her surroundings spinning, but she could clearly observe that the horse was white.

"Eliza? Did you just fall from that window? Are you injured?"

The voice was comforting to her ears.

She looked up, surprised to see Jean standing there. He looked alarmed.

"Whatever are you doing here?" she asked.

He quietly approached her, pausing before he answered.

A peal of bells sounded from the eastern part of the island, signaling that midnight had passed.

"I, I...was riding on the beach when I saw a fire and heard a great commotion come from inside the house," Jean said slowly.

"Perhaps you were looking for something here," she mumbled to herself.

Jean did not answer and kept his hands outstretched should she stumble again. She began to sway, humming a tune from before.

"Oh," she said, "the slaves are celebrating the end of the year. With great gaiety, I must admit. Would you like me to take you around to see them?"

She started to walk away.

"No, no, I'm afraid I must be on my way," he replied.

Eliza stopped, almost losing her balance when she realized he wasn't following her. She pouted, disregarding the usual pretense she carried around him. The liquor had erased all of her personal restraint.

"Why are you wet?" he asked.

She stopped moving for a moment, looking at him.

"Charles and I had a small disagreement. I am afraid we are unfortunately matched. But you already knew this."

She didn't wait for him to respond, remembering her first intention. She wanted to feel the tide at her feet. She began trekking through the sand toward the water.

"Wait, where are you going?"

"To the shore. I wish to gaze at the stars," she called over her shoulder.

Jean reluctantly began to follow her.

He watched her stride almost to the water's edge, her head tilted upwards. She moved as if she was slowly dancing, guided by unseen hands. Jean was afraid she would fall again. He knew he should leave. He wasn't even supposed to be there that night, but he needed the papers that had been distributed yesterday at the fort. True to his suspicions, Charles was in possession of the governor's latest request for additional troops—a much greater number of soldiers than the defense of this small island warranted.

Jean observed her movements and quickly removed his jacket, laying it on the damp sand. She plopped down on it in complete serenity. Eliza stretched in comfort, gazing heavenward. She was silent now and seemed intent on staying for a while. He sighed, joining her on the ground, lying an arm's length away from her.

"Have you ever seen such beauty? There are different stars here. Everything is different here. It's so wonderful," she said quietly.

"Yes, it is quite a beautiful island," he said, looking at her. "Are you not afraid to be here in the dark?"

"No, whatever for?"

"There might be ruffians, pirates, the sea might wash up…"

"Isn't it wondrous how the sea appears to be a black wall at night? It's only discernible by the white foam of the breaking waves. Otherwise, the line of division between the earth and ocean has all but disappeared. I so love to watch the sun slowly rise in the mornings. First, it is all shrouded by a wall of mist, of humidity, I suppose, which gradually breaks away to reveal shades of aquamarine and cobalt, and the colors only grow more intense as the sun rises. It is like watching a painting created by a divine hand…"

She seemed unaware that he had yet to look at the stars. Instead, he was focused squarely on her.

"May I be blunt, Eliza?" he asked directly.

"Yes."

"I do not like how he treats you."

The silence after he spoke was prolonged and painful. But the sound of surf bracing against sand lessened the awkwardness he felt. She turned to look at him.

"What of his treatment?" she asked, but the sadness in her tone revealed she knew the answer.

Jean grew nervous. He was crossing a line he had promised himself he would never cross. What was worse was that he remained there when he should have been back in town already. He was struck by the fact that only in her presence could he feel suddenly unsure of himself. She made him question everything he thought he knew.

"From what you have divulged on previous occasions, of course," he quickly covered.

He did not want to admit what he had seen. He did not want to draw more attention to the ways he secured information for his employer. She sighed, seemingly tired of the conversation.

"Well, then again, I am not an ideal wife."

"No," he said abruptly.

She looked at him as if offended.

"I think you are a perfect one."

Her insulted glance turned into a longing gaze. He recognized it immediately but couldn't will himself to look anywhere else. He was the first to finally break away, now turning his attention to the stars he had so artlessly neglected.

"My meaning is that it is not easy to have made the journey you did, and all matters considered, I feel you have adapted quite well to your surroundings."

Jean knew that he said quick and easy words to mask the feelings surging through him. But his distractions were not working on her.

"Why are you quite so far away, Jean?" she said mockingly. "I do not bite."

She drew herself closer to him as he completely tensed up. The alcohol was complicating matters. He desperately wanted to talk to her. He found this entire encounter rousing, but he knew he was being careless. At least one of them needed to maintain a handle on reason.

"I enjoy your company, Eliza, but I would not like to create a situation."

"What is your meaning?" she asked, propping herself up on one elbow.

"Concerning your honor. We are alone here on the beach. You are dressed in your shift," he began.

"I am usually dressed in this manner on the beach. My husband says it is improper."

"You have had drink. I have not."

"Which we must remedy immediately! Come! Cleo has the most intoxicating rum!"

Jean let out a laugh; he was susceptible to her charms. A rush of cold water hit their legs, startling them both. They stood up, retreating in laughter. He touched her arm.

"We cannot be so loud, Eliza," he cautioned, looking up at the white house.

Her dark eyes were dancing with mischief and the carelessness of youth.

"Then let us go to a place where we can celebrate. I enjoy the music they play on their drums. Don't you? Come, I want to take you there. Cleo has the rum!"

She began to sway back and forth again as the distant beat of drums grew more clear on the wind.

"I…" Jean began, watching her with a smile.

He tried to regain self-control. His face turned solemn.

"No, I must be off. I must go now. It is late," he said.

They walked back to the grove of palm trees on the side of the house where he had left his mare. He started to secure his pack on the saddle when he felt her press his hand. Jean turned to her. Eliza placed a hand on his shoulder, stepping closer. He looked down at her face, watching the space between them grow smaller.

"You make this impossible," he said, pained.

He searched her eyes, looking for anything that would alleviate the constant gnawing he felt inside of him. He was burning with impatience, but he, of all men, understood the importance of timing. Jean glanced up at the lights glowing from the house.

"What is the matter? You are free to leave," he heard her say.

Jean stroked the side of her face, smiling to himself. He understood that he was doing the right thing by leaving, but at the same time, it felt so incredibly injurious to her happiness. And devastating to him.

"Good evening, Jean Charles de Longchamp," she said, giving him a pitiful curtsy.

She was merely being playful, but then a dangerous thought occurred to him. As she rose to a stand, he grabbed her by the waist. She looked up in surprise.

"You make it impossible for me to resist you," he said.

He began to kiss her with wild intensity, pulling her body to his even more. She tasted like the rum she had been drinking. Eliza grabbed hold of his face with trembling fingers.

"You make it impossible for me to banish you from my mind," he continued, taking a breath.

His hands roamed across her body, her sweaty skin an uncharted and unfamiliar landscape.

"You make it impossible for me to control myself." He pressed her against him.

Eliza kissed the side of his neck, a feeling that beckoned him to forgo all reason. He felt her wet lips whisper into his ear.

"Lose your control."

He steered her toward a curved palm tree, and she leaned against it as he explored her body further, grabbing her breasts and sliding his hands down her curved torso. She wrapped her legs around him as he raised her skirt. He struggled to open his breeches and kiss her at the same time. But then he felt the sensation of victory. The intensity coursed through his body, and she lurched upwards and pressed her cheek against his, reveling in the pleasure. He felt her fingers dig through his hair, then up his back, urging him to push into her deeper. The rough bark of the tree rubbed against her skin. He feared it would leave marks, but the very thought also excited him.

"Your voice is too loud," he said.

He could feel her grinning against his face, her lips trailing his chin.

"Then you must do a better job at silencing me."

They locked mouths, tongues frenetically clashing against each other. Her thighs began to quiver, so he grasped them tighter and lifted her more. Her moans grew in volume again, signaling that his timing was flawless. He began to rock her in earnest, knowing he was on the brink of delivering her to an ecstasy he had always wanted to share with her.

He recalled the sight of her body as she had left the waves the first time he had ever seen her. How delightfully fitted her yellow dress had been at that first ball. And most of all, he marveled that a beauty such as her craved *his* touch. That her fairness did not simply comprise her outward appearance, but the enchantment she created ran deep alongside the inner workings of her mind and the troubles of her pure heart. How, on meeting her for the first time, his life had abruptly changed. That there was scarcely a night when his sleep was not interrupted by her appearance in a dream or his mind wasn't lost roving in the possibilities of future unsaid words. The thought of how forbidden their union was only goaded him headlong into abandon, and they peaked at nearly the same time.

She made no noise, but tensed up, her head back and mouth wide open in shock. He knew she was trying to process the sensations coursing through her body. He smiled, knowing he would never see such a vision like this again in his lifetime. She was so remarkably different. There were always pretty women, charming women, but never a woman like her. He made sure to kiss her again, softer and sweeter than he had before, as he slowly pulled away from her. Within moments they found themselves lying on their backs on the sand.

"You've rendered my limbs useless," she said breathlessly, clearly enjoying the feeling.

He had never felt such satisfaction in pleasing a woman before. Above them, the stars and angular palms spun in a dizzying turn as the flatness of the earth slowly brought him back to his senses. It all appeared surreal. His mind was racing with euphoria and possibility.

He pressed his lips to her forehead and held her hand. They lay in silence for a while. Then she turned to him, her eyes moist with tears.

"Is something wrong? Have I hurt you?" he asked with alarm.

She shook her head.

"Thank you for showing me such kindness, Jean."

She embraced him, her breasts bare, and at that moment, the gravity of his error lay upon him with full force. She was not his. She belonged to another man, a man he called his brother. He assumed the drink she had imbibed was responsible for her lack of awareness. But what of his excuse? Realizing he had none, his stomach sank.

He had taken advantage of the situation. His self-control had been impeccable all the other times, but tonight, when he had more reason to be sensible than she, he had failed. But the scent of her and the warmth of her arms around him nudged him into a realization of even darker dread.

He returned to the last thought he had before he took her. What had occurred was unmistakably wrong. In his mind, he could move past a mere physical act, but he knew he harbored an even deeper betrayal. Indeed, he was committing an even greater offense. Many other times when the potent thought had crossed his mind, he dismissed it without much difficulty, but there in her arms tonight, he knew it was indisputable. He loved another man's wife.

CHAPTER XII.

E liza walked back to the house as the sun hung at a low angle, suspended by the darkest lavender-hued clouds. It turned the water ablaze with ripples of fiery yellow. She was startled by a crash in the trees next to her. A large iguana jumped from one palm to another; it was surprisingly nimble despite its slow, laboring movements. She was so preoccupied with watching it travel through the trees and following its trail that she was initially oblivious of the strange stone markings before her. It was a grave. And not just any grave. A woman's name graced its front, barely legible underneath the ferns and vines that draped the tombstone's edges.

HERE lies the body of Jane Ada Sharpe, wife of Jeremiah Sharpe, who departed this life October the 12th 1762, in the 25th year of her age.

This seemed a strange place for a grave. Looking around her now, she noticed a very neglected path that had at one time led to the house. It seemed as if no one had come to this spot for quite a while. She brushed the foliage away and read the dates a second time. This had to be Charles' mother. She sighed, attempting to clear all the brush away from it. To think her uncaring husband barely paid even the most limited attention to his mother's resting place upset her.

"He does not come often," Cleo's voice sounded behind her.

"That does not surprise me. She was so young. She was the age I am now," Eliza said, reading the inscription.

"Jane was a good woman. A kind person."

"Why is she not buried in the churchyard? I don't understand."

"Lord Sharpe, Charles' father, did not want her in there. He said he wanted to keep her all to himself. But I knew he wanted to keep her away. Less questions. People forget about a person when they do not see a stone."

"But you come to visit her? Did you belong to her?"

Cleo laughed, her eyes reminiscent of a past played out long ago.

"No. I was in the fields then. I was not working inside the house. Another servant was in charge of that. She loved Miss Jane, too. They didn't leave this earth too far apart from one another. Sad business that was. And a sad childhood Charles had. He was only six when it happened. He barely had a childhood at all."

Eliza was intrigued. Cleo knew more, much more than she wanted to give air to.

"Was she not well-suited for motherhood?" she asked quietly.

"Jane? Let me tell you something. Oh, she was one of the most beautiful beings that ever walked this earth. She was nothing but goodness, grace, and light. I knew her best when I worked the gardens. She was always picking flowers. I was the outside help then. That was a long time ago. Bless her soul…"

Her broad hands clasped the top of the stone, brushing off the dried bits of plant debris that crowded it.

"I do not know why, but I wish I could have met her. She sounds like she was a charming person."

Cleo laughed to herself, looking at Eliza up and down.

"I do not doubt that you two would have gotten along. But that is not the way it was meant to work out. She was never meant to stay here long. No."

Eliza's face was troubled with different thoughts.

"You know things; you can judge someone instantly, and time will show it to be true. Yet you say that Charles is a good man. My mind cannot fathom it," Eliza replied.

In truth, she was really reflecting on the shadow around Jean that Cleo had seen.

"Everyone has a different color inside them. And sometimes, for good or for bad, that color will show up on the outside. I see all kinds of colors on people," Cleo said. "That is how I know what I know."

Eliza had heard this explanation before, and it was no less confusing the second time. Cleo's answer was frustratingly unsatisfactory, yet she still found it intriguing.

"What color am I?" Eliza asked, a smile on her lips.

The way she was staring at Eliza with her dark eyes, deep like tidal pools, made her shiver.

"The brightest yellow. A good yellow. Not too many people carry that color. Most people are a weak blue. The color hangs around their body tight. But your color is big. And it's bright. Like hers was."

Cleo sighed, gazing at the stone.

"I raised that boy since he was a child. I didn't help him into this world. Someone else did that much. But I came around when he was still a young one, and I raised him right. I know he is a good man. He was a good boy. A sweet boy."

Eliza grew disgusted by Cleo's routine disregard for her current situation. Reminiscing about a child one helped raise was very different from enduring a marriage with the man the child eventually became. She saw no traces of a childhood in Charles.

She sighed, wishing the stone was something more than a finely carved rock. She yearned to speak to his mother, to find the answers that evaded her. Waves crashed in the distance. She knew with a sullen finality that she would never find the solace she sought. She decided she would walk this path more often to visit his mother's forgotten resting place. Eliza slowly dragged her fingers across the stone, saying a silent goodbye to her newfound acquaintance.

A few hours later, she entered the house in a flurry. Eliza had heard the bell ring in the yard, and she wanted to avoid Charles at all costs. An argument would start the minute he saw her wet hair and damp stays. And then she saw something remarkable through the windows alongside the door. Lucy was in the yard, her hands covering her mouth in excitement.

"Did I just see Lucy? Could it be possible?" Eliza exclaimed.

She watched Cleo run to her daughter through the wavy glass. Celia walked by her, a tray in her hands.

"Just her luck. The man that bought her wanted a Creole domestic for his wife. She wants a certain household, they said. Not just any English-speaking slave. Lucy was too plain for them. Charles sold a field boy in her place. Says he's going to be a strong man one day, worth two boys. If he makes it that far. That man is a bastard."

Eliza was surprised to hear Celia utter such a word, but she agreed with the statement, and so she did not correct her. The joy she felt for Cleo superseded every other thought. Whatever magic Cleo had done had clearly worked. She had been proven right yet again. Eliza found herself recalling her warning about Jean. Surely, the misgiving Cleo felt was due to his secretive profession. Nothing more. Cleo could surely not condone her acting unfaithful to Charles. She was merely being a dutiful servant.

Celia watched her with a spiteful look as if she could judge her inner weaknesses with merely a glance. She exhaled sharply and began dusting the paintings that hung on the walls. Eliza continued to her room and then paused by the bottom of the stairs when she heard two sets of footsteps battering up the wooden porch. A pair of shadows further confirmed her observations, and Celia ran to open the front door.

"Ah, Eliza, just the person I wanted to see," Charles said as he entered the parlor.

That was when she saw a second remarkable thing. Jean was right behind him, his hat in his hand, smiling at a stony Celia. Time seemed to draw forth at a creeping pace. It moved slower than the barrage of thoughts that assaulted her mind as she looked at his face. The face she had yearned for over the course of one hundred and eighty-two days. She knew this precise number because she had counted them, despite her best efforts to distract and further occupy her mind. She had numbed herself to the idea that she could not see Jean every single day. But it had not prepared her for the pain of not seeing him at all.

She had willingly gone to one ball and then another, hoping against hope that she would run into him, just as they had managed to before. She had dressed in the finest dresses, with vivid memories of him, of him and her, weaving in and out of her mind as she gazed upon her reflection in the mirror. She had summoned hope and courage even the second time, but it was for naught. She had not seen him either night. Eliza feared he had been avoiding her, although she believed she had committed no wrong. Their last encounter seemed like the fragments of some half-remembered dream, and its greatness only served as the heaviest cruelty in the distance that followed.

She wanted to say a thousand things to him in the parlor. But she could not. It was nothing but a fantasy. Charles stood like a pillar next to him, his very presence capable of snuffing out the whimsies of her daydreams. They stood before each other as formal acquaintances, Jean as a guest of her husband and she as Charles' seemingly faithful wife.

But she was not faithful or devoted. She had wrapped her legs around Jean, and since that night, she could scarcely think of any other matter. Swimming and reading had served as necessary tools in the months that followed, diverting her mind from one man and driving her to completely avoid another. And now, it appeared to all collide in a single appealing yet regrettable instant.

She had missed Jean, fully knowing that it was improper to miss someone like him in that way. He was not her spouse. Eliza tried to convince herself that what had occurred that night was an ordinary event. Yet even the slightest reflection of him in her mind made her feel like she was on the edge of losing control. It served as a reminder that this was all very far from simple. Eliza instantly became flustered. Her hair was wet and unkempt, and she had not expected company that afternoon.

For months she had started at the sound of every horse entering the yard, waiting with bated breath to confirm if the horse was white. If its rider was indeed the man she was impatiently waiting for. Spring had come and gone, and she had not received even a single update from him about readying herself to depart from the island. *The Ferme*, her sole opportunity for escape, had yet to be sighted in the harbor. She only received information about the same set of ships laying anchor from Cleo whenever she went into town. Jean had not said a word to her. She wondered if the vessel even existed, and she could not help but compare the excitement and the possibility of quitting this place, at one time a tangible reality, to how her relationship with Jean had evolved. Both prospects had seemed to drift further from her longing fingers. But now, the man at the center of it all stood before her.

Eliza ran a nervous hand over her damp head, feeling the familiar scratchiness of sand upon her cheek. Maybe their separation was for the better. Her blood coursed through her now, feverishly hot and shameful, in front of Charles. But he clearly suspected nothing. And as this new idea took hold of her, her older unquenchable ruminations returned. She had pictured this moment in a thousand ways but had not expected to be caught so off guard.

She inwardly cursed at her poor timing. If only she had already been upstairs, she would have heard the commotion and been better prepared. Eliza wanted to appear at her very best in front of Jean. She wanted to remind him that he had desired her, and she wanted to feel that desire on full display again.

"I have invited Jean to stay the week with us, perhaps longer. Fever is raging in the barracks and in the town, and we must be prudent about these things. The air is spoiled in Nassau," Charles said as he removed his scarlet jacket.

She dared to look at Jean now as if her husband's mention of him had given her permission to do so. His face was the same as she remembered, the masculine beauty she had been captivated by still present within every inch of him. Her eyes roamed over his strong jaw, sweeping cheekbones, and dark brows that framed his enigmatic blue eyes. His eyes were mysterious as always, holding their communal liaison, their shared secret. She wondered what he thought as he stood before her, and she hoped he found her presence just as pleasing.

"Oh," Eliza said quietly, her heart pounding. "What an unexpected opportunity!"

Jean reached for her hand, and kissed it, looking up at her slowly. His eyes seemed to smolder as they looked upon her, and it triggered a palpable memory of his warm breath and the teasing words he had whispered into her ear that night so long ago. The image flashed boldly before her mind, retrieved from the drunken mist of her recollections, eager to be remembered. She savored his touch and hesitated to withdraw her hand, but she could not ignore the searing heat she felt around her ears as she considered that Charles was witness to everything that passed between them now. Her chest flushed red, and she looked away, fearful of a second encounter with Jean's direct gaze.

"It is a pleasure to make your acquaintance again, Lady Sharpe."

Her cheeks flushed with embarrassment at his feigned formality. She began to panic with thoughts of having to put on a performance for days on end. She feared she could not manage the discretion. But she also relished having Jean under the same roof. Such a rare opportunity was intoxicatingly sublime.

"Eliza will do. You are to be our guest. There is no need."

"Eliza."

He said it slowly and methodically as if the word was pleasing to his lips.

Charles' voice interrupted her reverie as she smiled at Jean.

"My dear, I understand this is all very unexpected, but please inform Cleo of the new arrangement and see to it that the entire household is aware of Jean's presence. I do not know what you intended for dinner tonight, but you'll want to inform the cook of the new situation."

A wave of dread washed over her. She had no actual experience of being the mistress of Pleasant Hall, let alone a hostess. She still delegated all these tasks to Cleo. Both men waited for her to act, and she felt the back of her neck burn.

"Yes...yes, of course. Please, wait here in the parlor while I see to the arrangements. Then you can freshen up before dinner," she said awkwardly.

She curtsied and then rushed down the hall to find Cleo. Cleo naturally found the situation amusing and was quick to admonish Eliza.

"I told you, Miss Ellie, I told you. One day I will not be here, and then who will you rely on? I have not done you any favors by not teaching you what you need to know. And now look at you. You are flustered for no reason. And do not get me started on that man. I will be watching," Cleo said to her as they walked along the outside path to the kitchen building.

Sleepy lizards flicked their eyes open and darted behind the shadows of swaying leaves.

"I hardly think it is appropriate to voice judgment on our guest. I think your only task is to serve him," Eliza quipped as they sped through a crowd of chickens.

One red-speckled hen refused to move to the side and pecked at her. Eliza attempted to shoo it away without success.

"Well, I think your task is to know what is expected of any wife, and it is clear you do not know how to plan a menu or entertain...a chicken, let alone a man," Cleo said with agitation.

"Please, Cleo, I beg of you. I need to make a good impression. It means a great deal to me!"

Cleo stopped outside the kitchen, her eyes full of scrutiny.

"I will help you, Miss Ellie. Mostly because I do not have a choice. What do you think that man likes to eat?"

"I'm not entirely sure."

Cleo rolled her eyes.

"Miss Ellie, are you telling me you are keen on this gentleman, but you do not know the first thing about him?" she asked.

"I know a great deal about him. I know his politics and where he's traveled and…" Eliza began to argue.

"Not a thing else. The way to fully knowing a man is understanding what he likes to eat. Men are simple creatures. Or at least they should be. You want him to enjoy himself, to remember his stay, to have his attention on you?"

"Yes, yes, all of those things!"

"Then you have to create meals he will remember. There are only two main ingredients. Good food and good conversation. Between the two of us, I think Mr. *Jean* will enjoy himself."

"Oh, I am indebted to you, Cleo. I truly am. I confess my heart nearly failed when I realized I didn't know a thing about these matters. Thank you, thank you a thousand times!" Eliza said, squeezing Cleo's hands in hers.

"Oh, and Miss Ellie… don't look too happy the next few days. It won't end well."

Eliza barely heard her warning. She had already turned down the path and ran back to the house. Her mind had switched to an equally daunting task: what to wear.

Nearly an hour later, Eliza made her way to the dining room, feeling more nervous than she could recall. It was ironic to feel such anxiety in the space she occupied every day, but that space had irrevocably changed with the presence of one man. Charles and Jean were already inside, and she could hear them having a pleasant conversation and laughing. The moment she entered the room, they ceased talking. She feared she had chosen the wrong dress. She wore a cornflower blue silk gown and had asked for stiffer baleen-lined stays. The effect on her figure was dramatic, and she arrested their attention entirely.

She had been delighted by her image in the mirror upstairs, emboldened by the contrast of light blue against her tanned skin and the contours of her collarbones and bust. This was in stark contrast to how she felt wearing that dress now, in front of others, in front of a masculine gaze, before her husband and her lover. It now seemed an outrageous idea, but even still, the thrill of it all goaded her onward.

The wooden chairs shifted against the floor as Charles and Jean stood to attention. She fluctuated between her apprehensive nerves and her desire to stand there, basking in the flickering candlelight. She knew the men were riveted by her. Eliza wanted to present herself as someone indifferent to their reaction, but she felt self-conscious just the same. Perhaps it was because she was the sole lady in the company of gentlemen.

She looked up and saw the servants around the room, their eyes downcast and their backs against the walls. She had always marveled at how they could observe a room without looking and stand present in company without really being there. With the dress she had on, she could afford no such escapism. Perhaps it was because of Charles' presence. She avoided dressing in such a way around him because she dreaded his attention. Somehow, tonight gave her an impression of protection—that Charles, ever mindful of appearances, could not and would not behave in an ill manner. Her femininity scared her, but she had never felt in control of a room before, and the novelty intrigued her.

Her thoughts returned to the days when she was presented before suitors. She had been a foolish girl then, blithely unaware of the world. But now she stood in the dining room, with all its glowing silver and crystal, and she knew the invisible rules that regulated affairs between men and women. Eliza at once understood her power, and she wanted to climb this new sensation to the very heights of her confidence.

Charles walked around to her, pulling out her chair, and the company was seated. Silence still reigned over the table, and she began to worry that she had unintentionally brought the dinner to a standstill.

"As I was saying, it is a blessing we can keep you here as our guest. The fever is taking down so many men in town and at the fort," Charles finally said.

"Yes, I am quite fortunate to stay here. With this company, who could say otherwise?" Jean replied.

He smiled at her, a more brazen move than she expected. It was clear they were engaged in a dangerous game.

"It is tragic what this climate can do to English blood. I am used to casualties on the field from enemy hands, not losses solely from rampant disease." Charles sighed.

"Yes, it is terrible, but it has brought us all together this night," Jean answered.

Charles raised his glass in a toast.

"To good company…that even during tragedy, we may face it together," he said.

"And be strengthened by the bonds of friendship," Jean added.

Eliza grinned as they all touched glasses, and the food service began. The men conversed on matters of local governance and events occurring back in England. After half an hour, they ventured onto topics of abolition and the trade. This caught Eliza's notice, and she impatiently waited for an entry point. She found it when Charles started a diatribe about how difficult it was to purchase good slaves.

"What I find remarkable is their unwaveringly calm demeanor. To find such composure when one is surrounded by brutality and violence is astounding," she said as Lucy removed her first course. "That any one of them should show me even the slightest bit of human kindness…" Eliza's voice broke with emotion.

The men stared at her. She looked at her freshly filled glass and wondered if it was her second or third glass of wine. She dared not drink this much alcohol on most ordinary evenings. She always wanted to be vigilant around Charles. But she was behaving quite differently tonight. She vowed to sip more slowly. She wanted to retain control of herself.

"That's because they're broken. Like a horse. That's when they're flaccid. Believe me, I have seen the opposite end of the spectrum, and it is a sight no man should behold," Charles said.

"Yes, yes…when they stormed Jamaica. That was a terrible affair," Jean added.

Charles shuddered with emphasis.

"If you speak of violence, perhaps it is because they are only met with violence. From the moment they are torn from their homelands to the first lash of a whip for some minor disobedience. It seems a natural result to me. I do not see why such enterprises are so unexpected," Eliza said.

Charles smirked wryly.

"Eliza, my dear, mark your words. You are speaking in front of a trader's son. I am sure he would not want to hear such sentiments."

"It is of no consequence to me, Charles. A more contrasting father and son you never did meet. Besides, I find Lady Sharpe's views most engrossing," Jean replied.

Charles seemed displeased by Jean's answer. He was determined to have the final word.

"Very well. The problem with women is that you are feeling creatures. Until you arrived on this island, you had never seen a dark face. And now, once on it, you are their steadfast friend and ally. Yet you never once looked at the sugar on your table or the cotton petticoat in your wardrobe and had such disquieting thoughts. That is the problem with your sex. You use the products of the trade but have nary a clue about how those products made their way to you. It's economics. It's rather simple," Charles said.

"Perhaps Eliza is merely commenting on the cruelty of the trade. Not its usefulness," Jean offered.

"There is no usefulness in making a slave out of a fellow man," she said somberly.

"I believe Pleasant Hall would beg to differ," Charles said, swirling his wine. "Look how you live, my dear."

"If I may embellish on a thought from Adam Smith: 'The *slave trade* has its origin in robbery. And the *plantation owners*, like all other men, love to reap where they never sowed and demand a rent for even the natural produce of the earth.' This, despite slavery's blatant inefficiencies, as he says," Eliza explained.

"Inefficiency? I have never seen more economic growth around me. Have you, Jean? In all your years?"

"Ah, yes. It is true. But from what I recall, I believe Smith was commenting on the idea that it would be a better enterprise for both slave *and* master. A free tenant completes his work with better spirit than the tortured slave. Profits would abound," Jean said.

"Smith also agreed that despite this supposed incompetence, slavery persists around the world, Eliza. Around the *world*..." Charles rejoined. "Why is that? Enlighten me. What have you discovered that all races and nations for centuries have been blind to see?"

"I believe that men enjoy dominating others. Whether it is women or their fellow man. There is no moral justification for the trade, and there never shall be."

"It is the natural order of things, my dear. You so enjoy observing nature. Do you not find that your observations in the natural world correspond with this one? Do not the strongest animals dominate the weaker ones?"

"No, I daresay I do not. I have yet to see crabs on the shoreline enslaving other crustaceans in chains and shackles," she replied as quickly as he asked it.

Jean laughed at her comment, then straightened his expression as he watched Charles' frustration grow.

"I meant the domination, my dear. Do you not see animals acting thus?"

"I believe we are called to act better. Otherwise, why would we possess such acumen and intelligence? Besides, we are made in the Lord's image. You've heard it a thousand times from Reverend Samuel."

"All this from the woman who lives in this house, on these estate grounds, with the many luxuries it affords you. Pray tell me, would you rather live in a hut with a dirt floor?"

"Europeans never needed the 'necessity' of the slave trade before. In medieval times, we—" Eliza began.

Charles laughed.

"Are you proposing we return to the Dark Ages? You preach romanticism of feudal days for its chivalry but forget the concept of serfs."

"You cannot *return* to an age when one has never left it."

There was a break in the tempo of conversation. Jean appeared to smile again. Charles seemed distraught.

"You are deluded, Eliza. Perhaps it is the wine," Charles said, seemingly short of temper.

"This fish is most delicious," Jean interjected.

Eliza sighed, releasing the tension she had carried throughout the conversation.

"Yes, it is quite good," she said quietly.

"The variety?"

"The local sea fare," Charles said indifferently.

"It is grouper," replied Eliza.

"Oh, you recognize the type?" Jean asked.

"That matters not," Charles cut in.

"Why? I daresay an Englishman would never call the fish 'local river fare' when he could simply call it pike," she said.

"We are not really from here, my dear."

"But we live here. Should you not know what's on your plate? Or that grouper, when ill-prepared, can be dangerous for your digestion?" Eliza said.

Charles laughed. "That is precisely why I have a cook," he replied, shaking his head.

"You would entrust your life to the very people you treat so cruelly. I think that is not the shrewdest decision."

The discussion had returned to slavery. Charles chugged his claret.

"The fish is very good indeed," Jean said.

The three of them descended into silence as they consumed their main course. The dishes were removed, and they awaited dessert.

"Jean, tell me, do you still carry that amulet on your person? I wager it saved our hides on more than one desperate occasion," Charles said as he drummed his fingers on the table.

"Oh, that? No, no, I lost it," he replied.

It took Eliza a moment to realize they were discussing the pearl tucked away in her stays. She smiled, completely incognizant of her hand grazing the neckline of her dress.

"Oh, shame!" Charles clicked his tongue.

"I lost it a long time ago. Perhaps it is in better hands," Jean said.

Eliza looked up and found him gazing at her. She nearly choked on her wine. She put her glass down without looking and made her fork clatter against it. He was unwaveringly staring at her now, his look inquisitive and appreciative. She looked down, blushing intensely.

"This meal has been most delicious. Please send my regards to the cook," Jean said as plates of sugared fruit arrived.

"Yes, I never realized my wife had such a domestic talent. You must feel free to experiment with the menu at your liberty, Eliza. I was pleasantly surprised by the pairings."

"And you must indulge me in tales of your war days. We have time enough for stories now. I do look forward to hearing what you two accomplished in America," she said, changing the subject.

"I fear it is not what you think, Eliza," Jean said.

"Oh, nonsense! She has the stomach for it. She's been begging me ever since we met," Charles said.

He leaned over and put his hand on hers. She wanted to reject his touch, but she kept still. When she looked up again, she recognized a familiar look in his darkened eyes.

"I am rather tired. All this political talk has quite worn me out. That and the sun, I'm afraid. I think I shall retire and leave you two in privacy," Eliza said quickly.

She had barely touched her dessert. She feared her motives were obvious, but she could read Charles' body and could no longer ignore her sense of foreboding. At least he would be occupied with Jean and their continued conversation tonight.

The air was thick with moisture, heavy, like a well-stirred broth. It was dense when drawn into the lungs, and no amount of sitting still could dissipate the heat. The world outside was alive with night creatures, the reverberations of nearly invisible frogs who started their songs the minute the shadow fell over them, and the more precise clicks of insects. The soothing lull of waves dragging back and forth on the sand quieted her mind, but her ears were focused on the low-grounded murmurs of the men deep in conversation. She had decided earlier that the sound of their laughter echoing throughout the downstairs hall was one of the most beautiful noises her ears had ever heard. It appeared they had lingered over a dram of whiskey. Now it seemed as though their voices would help her drift off to sleep.

But it was far too hot for sleeping. The breeze had long left the shore, and the insufferable heat lingered even though the sun had departed hours ago. She heard a laugh from Jean. His voice was distinguishable from any room. It wasn't as deep as Charles'. It had a wider range of cadence and a higher tone, yet it was still solid enough to penetrate the air. It was a sound that healed her, intoxicating, like wine to her lips, and one that she only craved more and more.

She dragged a finger across her perspiring chest, frustrated to know he could still be so far away despite hearing his voice below her room. Even if she hadn't intended to dodge Charles' advances, it would be unheard of for her to keep social hours this late. The freedom the other sex took for granted eluded her. Heat concentrated on her stomach, wrapping behind her ears and underneath her hair. It retained a steady temperature, warm enough to evade any comfort yet not hot enough to break a full sweat. It felt as though she was being baked from the inside, her darkened room a cruel, still oven.

Eliza moved her hair above her pillow, her dampened locks a sable fan. No doubt the men had removed their shirts by now. They were free to do so once she had retired. As always, silent and invisible laws of propriety guided their every move. And in this instance, it prevented her from joining them. In her mind, she only regretted this because of one guest.

No strange exception, no boundary-breaking climate made what she truly wanted acceptable. She had felt Jean undressing her with those deep blue eyes tonight. Doubt crawled through the recesses of her mind. He was here, in this house with her, and he would be for days. He had just arrived, but anxiety became caught in her throat. Would Jean make a single advance towards her? What kind of man would he be to do so under Pleasant Hall's roof, and what kind of woman was she to crave it? It made that night months ago feel like a drunken dream, fueled by a rum-soaked haze and her dark desires.

Now she relied on glances, a shift in tones, a hesitation, or at times, a rush of action to feed her hunger. She was hooked on his every word and move, not caring how naked her intentions were. Her behavior was audacious, and the feeling of shame had long left her. Charles was nothing more than her personal overseer, guarding her every move and inhibiting her very freedom.

The passing of time served only to seduce her further with their new arrangement. Every evening would now be marked with felicity, and she could not help but notice how dull her life had been before this strange new gathering.

It was a large house. It could easily host a family and multiple visitors in its prime, but it had been emptied these last few years, filled with only rage and hatred. Pleasant Hall finally hosted a guest once more, and now Eliza could see its charms on full display. There was warmth and joviality in its hallways again. She felt that even the very beams of wood in the floor and the verdigris walls benefited from the presence of their new guest.

These were unprecedented times; the ills of tropical life had returned to remind her naive mind that perhaps this was not a heavenly paradise. Yellow fever was ravaging the town, but she felt untouchable here on the beach. They heard the reverend had been busy blessing the graves of so many people that he had time for nothing else. But she had long ago lost respect for the clergy and their dull, meaningless sermons. Their endless push for obedience and conformity to a higher purpose seemed hypocritical to her now. Her time here had done nothing but open her eyes to the injustices of the world.

The cruelty of her age had not bothered her conscience before when she had lived at Bleinhill Manor. She had once valued her freedom as a girl. Now those days seemed nothing but a gilded cage, her eyes too young to truly see the reality of an empire.

Eliza mused that although she was a prisoner in an ill-matched marriage, perhaps she had never been freer. She could decide to do what she wanted during the day and sometimes felt she was the only inhabitant for miles. Charles came and went. And now Jean was providentially idle. She stretched her legs and curled onto her side. The image of her thighs wrapped around him teased her mind. While Charles might try with all of his brutal strength, he could not force her affection. Her body was his collateral, but her soul was hers.

She pictured the house empty without her presence. The days before her departure were dwindling fast. Although Jean had not spoken of their arrangement since his arrival, it was never far from her mind. She would leave Pleasant Hall and its misery behind. Eliza knew she would miss the natural beauty of these shores, but she also knew that new ones awaited her. The beaches of Africa and the East dallied with her mind, as intriguing as the words Jean would not say.

She had nearly toppled her water glass tonight. Such was the intensity of his gaze. Their connective energy was unspoken, but it did not mean it was not there. The intrigue of discovery and risk made her mind rush. His presence was addictive. And she prayed for the perfect opportunity of timing and privacy for the confirmation she so desperately craved. Tomorrow would be another day, another chance for affirmation.

The laughter receded as they settled into the stiff chairs of the parlor. The warmth was sweltering, the night pure heat. The sun had set that evening like a glowing red ball dangling between the frayed leaves of palms. But even as it descended past the horizon, the temperature did not lessen. The air was fragrant with notes of hibiscus and humidity. They faced each other, flushed and indolent. The heavy meal they had just consumed did not help matters.

Dinner had been unexpectedly pleasant once again. Jean's smiles and furtive glances, comprising an unspoken message, had the uncanny ability to reassure her. She still had questions for him. She was desperate to be alone with him. But she was grateful for even the shared time she experienced. Charles, seated at the end of the table, was simply an unfortunate obstacle in their way. In such a position, it was easy to ignore his presence. This was the case until the man spoke, of course.

"Tell me, Jean, why have you not found any lady on this island? No one catches your eye? I realize the selection is narrow, to be sure," Charles said.

"I'm not quite certain if this climate is tolerable to women of good breeding, although I have found that the odd few take to it like a fish to water," Jean replied, his eyes anchored on Eliza.

He was watching her gather glasses and pour the after-dinner drinks. She started with the glass for Charles, handing it to him with surprising merriment. Jean's eyes never left her; he was locked on her every movement. This had not failed Charles' notice. As soon as Jean discerned this, he hastily attempted to appear indifferent.

"I have pursued some in the past, but to no avail. I feel that my duty weighs heavily on my mind as of late. I do not think I can give a woman the attention she deserves. I choose instead to focus on other matters."

He smiled, taking a sip of his drink, but the expression on Charles' face did not alter.

"Well, you see, the problem with women is that they are never around when you want them. You have to catch them," Charles said, "like a fish, as you say."

As she walked to her seat, Charles grabbed her arm and stopped her. Her drink sloshed out of the glass, dampening the rug. An unspeakable tension between the party surfaced, creating a new heaviness in the air. Any pleasantries between them left like a flame extinguished. Jean's hand hovered by his holster momentarily. She looked at him frantically, but now Jean would not meet her gaze. She was desperate to pull away from Charles but dared not escalate the mood. Her hopes of resuming congenial remarks were rapidly sinking.

"Even this one, if you can believe it, is capable of avoiding the slightest tenderness. As charming and warm as she appears to be now, she is nothing but coldness in her element," Charles said, looking up at her with a misplaced benevolence. "I've missed your company these past few months…"

His tawny-colored hair was loose around his face, and he seemed drunk with fondness. But the tone of his voice bordered on a thinly veiled threat.

"You're, you're…spoiling the evening, my dear," she said with false gaiety.

When Charles did not immediately reply, Jean spoke next.

"Perhaps I should excuse myself," he said, though he stayed perfectly still.

Charles kept hold of her; the tension between them suspended longer another moment.

"Charles, I must say…" Jean began.

He finally released her arm, and she rushed to her seat, her body tense and her cheeks flushed with embarrassment.

"It doesn't stop me, as I find the chase and conquest just as thrilling, but it is tiring to be tormented so. If I knew such a change in temperament was a possibility, I would have dinner guests over more often. Then I would at least see my wife. I would at least see her acting in her true role. I've never seen her dress so finely. She's revealed quite the domestic hand. What a good performer she is."

Charles reached for his freshly poured whiskey, shot it down, and slammed the glass on the table.

"Tell me, Jean, what do you know of women?" he asked.

"I know of men and that true men do not act as you do."

Charles rushed at him and paused, pulling out his pistol and shoving it in his stomach with a fiendish laugh. Eliza shrieked.

"I am a monster. You've seen what I've done in the Carolinas."

He searched Jean's face.

"I am clearly not in a position to contest that," Jean replied solemnly.

Charles' mood lightened, and with a grin, he stepped back, holstering his pistol, and poured himself another drink. Eliza feared a second confrontation was imminent.

"You recall Colonel Agnew, don't you?" Charles started.

Jean's face remained unusually stoic, but then it shifted.

"That man is not someone I can easily forget," Jean's lip curled as he spoke.

It seemed to her that an opportunity for a lighter atmosphere had appeared. She was desperate for things to return to the way they had been the past few evenings.

"Are you finally going to regale me with tales from the American War?" Eliza asked brightly.

"Oh, yes, dear, I am. Colonel Agnew, where to begin…" Charles started.

"The man was a lunatic," Jean interrupted.

"Summer of 1780, if memory serves me correctly. We were based at the Stono River when we came across a plantation. Much larger than this one. Nearly twice the size. Grander. One cannot go wrong with planting rice. One day at luncheon, Colonel Agnew hears the owner's wife in the hallway. 'Mrs. Brice, would you care to grace us with your presence?' he asks. I remember the house was cool. Ample breezes wafted through. An ideal temperature. It was much better than what we were used to, isn't that so, Jean?"

"Perhaps you should begin with a different tale," Jean remarked.

"The woman doesn't answer. He asks again and observes that she's carrying an armful of candlesticks. 'Mrs. Brice, do you require any assistance?' he asks. The woman doesn't reply. The colonel shoots out of his chair and straight toward her. The next thing we see, candles are rolling all over the oak wood floors. And a slam!" Charles pounded the arm of his chair for emphasis.

Eliza leaned forward with anticipation. Charles took a slow sip of his drink, relishing her attention. Jean's eyes flitted from him to her.

"What happened?" she asked impatiently.

"There was a miserable cry, followed by some grunts...he ravished her in the hallway in front of the entire company!"

Raucous laughter bellowed out from him. It collided with a wall of icy silence. Eliza's face paled. Jean looked away into the darkened hallway. Charles sighed, disappointed by the lack of mutual amusement.

"What a character that man was. And what an education. No, Grand Tour for us, old Jean. We received consummate training under Colonel Agnew. Very *vigorous* indeed."

Jean fidgeted in his seat, but otherwise, he maintained his composure.

"I seem to recall that story differently," he replied slowly.

"Nonsense! You know he did it..."

"I seem to recall that an intrepid young captain was threatened with twenty-five lashes for his impudence toward the colonel," Jean said.

The clock in the hallway signaled a late hour. But the conversation continued.

"He always took what he wanted. Madeira, hogs, women. It didn't matter to him."

"I remember that I had to stop that same captain from interfering. It would be better to report such egregious conduct to the general I had warned—"

"*Egregious*?" Charles scoffed. "It was a bloody war!"

"You rushed over there regardless and started picking up the candles…"

Charles' green eyes flashed upwards in a wordless warning.

"Yes…" Then the gaiety of his tone resumed. "And what a look she gave me. Her pretty face was marred by a cut under her lip, and her fury was like a wild cat. 'Get out of my house!' she demanded. So, Colonel Agnew turns to her and says, 'Mrs. Brice, your husband is dead! Your house belongs to His Majesty and his troops now.' In that insufferable tone he always used. 'We are, however, gracious enough to let you stay here until affairs are settled.' What a figure. In her husband's own house…can you imagine?"

Eliza looked horrified, her gaze fixed on the intertwining spirals of the Turkish rug below her.

"Tell Eliza what you did. Tell her what you really did, Charles," Jean demanded.

Charles took another sip of his whiskey.

"That's of no interest to anyone."

"You confronted him outside at the water pump. You had the courage to do what we all wished we could."

"Stop glorifying the actions of a fool," Charles said with a sneer. His voice went quieter. "I went up to him and questioned what I had witnessed. He replied that it was necessary to help Mrs. Brice understand her place. I called it pure barbarism. He agreed…he said that is why women need husbands. For protection. And that if she were any wiser, she would use him for such a role. I threatened to report him to the general. He retaliated with threats. But then he told me, 'Do not get confused, boy. There is no honor in war.' Truer words were never spoken."

"Cease this saccharine portrayal of Agnew."

"Colonel, my dear Jean, colonel."

"There never was a man more undeserving of titled respect. There is no honor in war, Charles. It resides in the hearts of men. But not in men like Agnew or those who would idolize him."

Eliza looked up at them, surprised by Jean's words. Charles seemed non-phased by the challenge.

"Ah, *cher* Jean, winning hearts and minds. A poet never makes for a good soldier. No wonder it didn't suit you."

"You were a bold captain, Charles. A much better soldier than me. You put a stop to the whole affair the next day, and you were rewarded with a slew of fists. But that didn't matter to you. You knew right from wrong in those days."

Charles looked discontentedly at his now empty glass.

"That man isn't here anymore," he said bitterly.

"I think he is," Jean said.

"Perhaps you never really knew me."

He called for Lucy to bring more drink from the cellar. The potent amber liquid sloshed into their glasses.

"Then, one evening, I finally understood. I discovered why Colonel Agnew treated her the way he did. To have such power over something so beautiful. The thrill of it…of literally holding it in your arms," Charles continued.

He seemed incapable of reading the room. Eliza, for one, no longer wanted to hear war stories.

"That is not what happened. You never touched her." Jean countered.

"I am telling a story."

"No one needs to hear it. I hardly think it's necessary for your wife, of all people, to hear this. This perversion…"

A wicked smile flashed across Charles' face.

"Oh, yes. My wife. Strangely enough, she hardly acts like one unless she is in *your* company. Funny thing, that. I'll count myself amongst the fortunate tonight."

He tossed back the whiskey and poured himself another. His face was rapidly turning red and blotchy.

"I really think I've heard enough, Charles," Eliza said timidly.

He raised a hand to silence her and refilled Jean's glass.

"No, no, no. You cannot leave until your glass is empty. She constantly rallies to be treated without distinction, so tonight, we will have it. Now, let us discuss the matters that are normally much too delicate for feminine ears."

"War is never a suitable topic for any polite discussion."

"War is a necessary constant in life. Without war, there could be no empire."

"Ah, yes. To you, perhaps. But anyone would agree that the brutality of war fogs one's senses. Thus causing you to forget the beauty of the world around us."

Charles crossed one leg over the other and leaned back.

"Oh, I don't know. But I do confess, I do not regret killing. When I first killed a man, I felt alive. Isn't it uncanny?"

The tension heightened in the room like the high shrill of a buzzing mosquito.

"Indeed, the sky never seemed so blue, the autumn air so crisp. The whizzing thunder of iron, the spatter of blood on the leaves…" Charles said, the words slow and lazy on his tongue.

"Charles, I wouldn't speak like this in front of Eliza," Jean repeated, anger clear on his face.

"Oh, why not? She has a curious mind. She wonders about what we, I…did in the war. I'll tell her more than any old book ever could. She's asked me more times than I can count."

"I think I'll retire now. Good evening," Eliza said quickly, getting up from her chair to leave.

As she walked by him, Charles seized her and roughly sat her on his lap.

"You will do no such thing. You've neglected your ratafia. And I fear I have neglected *you* for far too long. Tonight is not a night for sleeping, my dear. All this talk has rather excited me."

She sat immobile, her cheeks colored by sheer discomfort. Her eyes sought the comforting pattern of the rug once more, and then she dared to look up at Jean's troubled eyes. She watched him grip the arm of his chair tighter.

"And so, you will sit. There…just…like…that," Charles said in a softer tone.

His finger toyed with a loose strand of her hair, curled by the ever-pervasive humidity. Jean fiddled with the dampened collar of his shirt.

"Now…for your education, my dear. Allow me to instruct you." Charles moved to the side to garner her reaction, but she would not turn. He took a deep breath and continued his tale regardless. "I remember the first time. I was scared. I had never seen death confront so many at the same moment before. The terror in the air. It hangs there like a heavy mantle. All I could think of was when a bullet rips through me, and such an occurrence is inevitable…how will it feel?" He traced an invisible line down the side of her neck. She balked at his touch.

"On the field, all men are reduced to the same draw. A farmer could fall just as easily as a duke. Neither wealth nor skill can save you. Only sheer luck. But then I had my opportunity. I shot a man. I watched him lie there on the ground in agony. I could scarcely move. I was transfixed…" Charles said softly, gazing at the way the flickering candlelight reflected in her dark hair. "And as the life seeped out of him, I could think of nothing but the rush, the exhilaration that seeped into me."

"Charles!" Jean snapped.

"You were no angel in the war, Jean. You were skilled with your pistol. I remember that the blood made your eyes even bluer." Charles readjusted himself and pulled her closer to his chest. "You see, Eliza, Jean and I have a bond you will never quite understand," he said, his mouth close to her ear. "A man will only ever truly know who he is and what he is capable of once he stands on a battlefield. Facing the fire of the enemy. Oh, we've fought together, killed together, whored together."

Charles laughed, his voice lighter and higher. "Do you remember Lieutenant Bowe's 'rose' in the bush, Jean? The boys had a good time with that. She had a pretty face, but toward the end, they marred it. War makes for savage men. We wear uniforms, but that's all that remains of common decency. It's a shell. A pretension."

"Charles, I urge you…"

"Well, that is war. And that was what was requested at our table tonight," Charles said.

"Eliza need not hear the vulgarities certain men committed. They were lower than beasts. It does not bear repeating." Jean glared at him with a closed fist pressed to his mouth.

"I hardly think so," Charles replied with a laugh.

"You knew it was wrong years ago, and you know it now."

"What do you think, Eliza? You're awfully quiet. What does our pupil have to say?" Charles asked.

Eliza swallowed a bout of nerves and then spoke.

"You have already afforded me ample instruction in the ways of men, thank you."

But neither man seemed to pay her much attention. Charles was irritated with Jean, and he refused to drop the subject.

"You seem to recollect that we terrorized the southern colonies during the war. It's such a shame that admiralty can be tainted by memory. I, for one, do not recall such events. I can't even recall one scream. Surely that is not ravishment. Truly, Jean."

Now Jean exhaled sharply and shifted his weight. "You would dare presume that it is only rape if a woman screams?" he asked with horror.

"Oh, come now! You know my intended meaning. You were always so preoccupied with words, Jean. There are exceptions to the rule. For instance…a husband cannot rape his wife."

Eliza could scarcely breathe. Jean's countenance did not alter. He glared at him with a steely look.

"Would you really posit that? Is a wife even in a position to decline?"

"It is a contractual obligation. A simple matter, really."

A moment of raw silence passed between them. Eliza's ears burned. She wanted this conversation to cease.

"I seem to remember another part of the marriage contract. To love, honor—" Jean began.

"And *obey*! Really, Jean, you need to find a wife. Then you'll understand."

"Curious that 'love' comes first in the line."

"And even more odd, that it usually arrives last to the union, if at all."

"There are those who wed for love."

"Damned fools the lot of them. Love cannot pay the tax collector. Love cannot keep the house warm in winter. Love cannot stave off hunger. The most successful marriages spring from the smartest matches. Blood and money speak louder than a gentle caress."

"Well, if you're speaking from experience, I'll comment no further."

Charles' smug expression faltered.

"Your meaning?"

"Forgive me, but perhaps you've drunk too much tonight. I meant no ill regard," Jean replied.

His tone was suffused with sudden capitulation as if he regretted his last words.

"For a man who lacks experience in this field, you are awfully ardent in your opinions."

"If Agnew had taken your wife in the hallway, perhaps you'd feel differently, Charles," Jean said.

"I would surely kill him. As I would kill any man who touched my wife."

Jean said nothing and smiled, a dark glimmer crossing his eyes. Charles' grip tightened on Eliza's waist. A glance shared between Jean and Eliza lingered from a brief encounter to something more, and Charles instinctively recognized that her attention had shifted.

He moved to get up, shoving her off him as he stood.

"I somehow think we are not discussing a war anymore but rather something entirely different," he said tensely as he glowered at them both. "I grow weary of this talk. Good evening."

He tossed back his remaining whiskey and left the room, the heavy thud of his boots moving up the stairs. Jean and Eliza remained perfectly still until they could no longer hear Charles making noise above them.

"Last year...what seems like such a long time ago, I asked you a question," she said quietly, her eyes full of sorrow. "I asked if you were spying on me for my husband's sake. But I perhaps failed to recognize that I could still be of use to you, despite the answer you gave. That you could indeed be spying on both of us. I could prove useful to you. And perhaps this is why no one trusts you."

Her voice was raw and full of hurt.

"How could you sit there and not say a word," she continued, shaking her head. "You did nothing…" Eliza said breathlessly, on the verge of tears.

"You saw what he did. What he said. And yet you remained planted in your chair," she stammered.

Jean crossed the room, placing his arms on hers. She withdrew from his touch. He had listened patiently but responded with anger.

"Am I supposed to be mortified by *this*? This was a display of kindness compared to what I've witnessed. Forgive me if I do not stir from my chair, but to cause a protest over such a trifle is sheer folly. I will not stand to risk losing everything over a momentary lapse of reason. I have watched and stood silent over far more severe abuses to your person."

She looked at him, confused.

"You ask if I am employing our friendship toward some underhanded device. Do you realize that anything I wish to obtain, I can easily retrieve on my own? That, in fact, I have snuck into this very house like a common thief, covered in darkness, looking for what I needed?" He took her by the wrist. "That I have been witness to the yelling and the fighting. To the marks he lays on you. I have seen you flee from this house both day and night. You do not merely wander the beach for diversion; you seek refuge.

And all of this time, I have patiently waited until I could stumble upon you at the ball. Our encounter was not by chance, Eliza. Do you realize how deeply the desire to make myself known to you has burned within me? I know he is not home during the course of the day. I know you are alone. But I will not spoil it. I will not falter from my objective."

"And what is your aim, Jean?" she asked dismally.

"The only thing I have ever wished to do with you was not to take something from you. Not to rob you. Or lie to or abuse you. But to give you something. Protection. *Freedom…*"

"Then why don't you?"

Jean approached her, speaking in a harsh whisper.

"If you recall, I have. I have secured your passage to Le Havre. What else do you want from me?"

Her dark eyes narrowed. She was desperate for him to confirm what they both knew. She wanted the words said aloud. His actions were not merely those of a compassionate onlooker.

"If it were not for this reminder, I would scarcely recall our original plan, so little do you speak of it. So little have you spoken to me. Why do you stay silent?"

Her statement was an internal question that raged through her thoughts repeatedly.

"The captain was waiting for fairer weather. That is the only reason for the delay. Make no mistake, this is no easy task, Eliza. I want nothing more than to…" his voice trailed off as he glanced at the walnut staircase. He took a slow breath. "What else can I offer you?" he asked with frustration.

She looked at him, her face pale in disbelief.

"I thought you held me in a different regard, but I have been a fool. Good night, Jean," she said with a brief curtsey.

"Eliza."

She paused, her back to him.

"You won't say it," she said in a trembling voice.

"Eliza, say what?"

She turned on her heel, a flash of outrage emanating from her.

"Say it. We are alone now," she said.

Jean remained silent, his eyes pleading with hers.

"You have been here for six nights and five days, and you refuse to even touch me. You would spark disagreement with my husband over the meaning of marital vows, yet you dare not approach me even as opportunity knocks. I confess our arrangement has been a happy one, yet I cannot fathom the wall you have so easily constructed between us. It renders me a fool since I am so clearly incapable of guarding my own heart's desires. The waiting...it has been unbearable, Jean. Where have you *been*?"

"I have been sorely preoccupied. I am not at liberty to explain."

His voice was impatient and defensive.

"Yet you say nothing of the time that has elapsed. Has it not been a strain for you as well? Or do I suffer in silence alone?"

Jean looked down, biting his lip.

"Jean...please..." she said softly. "You held me in the highest of confidences once. We engaged in the deepest of intimacies, and yet you now stand before me cold and unfeeling as if you were a stranger."

He still said nothing. It seemed as if no reassurance would come from him.

Eliza shook her head. She knew if she lingered, the words she so desperately wanted to hear might finally arrive on his lips. But his obstinacy to reveal even the slightest affection for her drove her beyond any measure of patience. This was not what she expected or wanted. She had waited for this moment for so long. The sting of disappointment reeled through her. She took a deep breath.

"Thank you for the confirmation. I apologize for my recent behavior," she said, her tone colored with a false courtesy, her voice cracking. "I bid you a pleasant sleep."

CHAPTER XIII.

A white flash stirred her from a turbulent dream. It had been long and drawn out, but she could only remember one scene. In it, she had sat across the table from Jean, and he would not look at her. No matter what words she spoke or how she acted, his eyes would not meet hers. Another flash burst into her room. She opened her eyes for that last one.

Lightning. Brilliant and blinding. A storm was on the horizon. But everything seemed so perfectly still in the stifling humidity. An earth-shaking rumble sounded above her, and the storm confirmed its appearance. Eliza should have known. These summer storms always came without warning, but with enough observation, there were occasional signs. The sky always seemed to turn much darker right before the thunder struck. It was not immediately noticeable, as there were hardly any lights near Pleasant Hall, but the dark sky transformed into a wall of black whenever a storm approached. She could always perceive it. There was a sense of electricity in the air, and the vibrancy only made her feel more alive.

Her past worries from the dream quickly left her. She could not lie to herself. Jean's recent actions were troubling. But the island itself offered a distraction now. Something more intriguing was stealing her attention. More thunder rumbled, and now she could feel its reverberations in her bones.

She jumped out of bed excitedly to get a clearer look from the window. The rain hit the roof with a force loud enough to stir anyone from sleep. She felt her anticipation grow. The nape of her neck was damp with sweat, but the descending sheet of rain looked refreshing. Orange and pink bolts appeared on the horizon line above the sea. The display was stunningly beautiful, and she watched it with huge eyes. Nature never disappointed on this island.

The wind came next, blowing out her bedside candle. The white transparent curtains billowed in her room. The palms and pines began to rustle and lash against one another, and she could feel the storm's energy crawl through her fingertips. She watched the trees as they rocked left and right with the hot violent gusts of air, and she secretly wanted one of the palms to be brought down to the earth. Eliza intrinsically knew the storm was powerful, and she wanted to see its consequences on full display.

Eliza crept downstairs and made her way to the door when a small voice interrupted her.

"Lady Sharpe, you can't go out there. If Lord Sharpe finds out…" Lucy whispered.

A round of lightning and thunder struck. Lucy jumped.

"Then you can tell him where I'll be."

"No! You can't go! It's not safe, Lady Sharpe!"

But Lucy's efforts were futile. Eliza passed through the doorway onto the slippery porch, where the lanterns had blown out from the force of the wind. She walked to the beach, stretching her arms wide as the rain pelted down on her. The smaller palms danced alongside her like people walking. The utter darkness of the black sky held her in a lucid trance, and the more she stared at it, the more she felt as though she could see birds flying above her, soaring with the wind. There were great black birds, like vultures, careening through the clouded dome.

Other strange, formless shapes appeared, but she struggled to see them clearly in the biting rain. As she stepped down the dune, she swore she saw men walking alongside her in the bush and became frightened. A flare of white light revealed the shape to be only a shrub, its spiny features distorted by wind and rain. But the illusion was not done toying with her yet. It evoked a memory, a recent memory. It was the peculiar feature of dreams that one could recall fragments of them without warning. It was the nature of such dreams to suddenly remember a narrative so vividly—an image which, only a moment before, one did not yet fully recall.

She sees a white light as she stands in a field of broken earth, strewn with the shattered bodies of fallen men. The world is full of tumult and violence. The air is filled with blood and cries for reprieve. She steps forward, confused by her surroundings. It is unfamiliar yet recognizable. She has seen it before. A white dress covers her body, the shift she wears to sleep, but neither the dirt nor the gore stain its hem. Soldiers are running past her, ahead of her, bayonets fixed. They all run further afield. A dead horse with lifeless eyes looks toward the gray smoke-filled sky; the blood pooling from its open mouth is old and clotting.

This fight has waged on for hours. She hears the roar of cannon. She sees the fiery explosions, but she steps forward. Nothing can touch her. The white light appears again, and she is drawn to it. It flickers once and fades and reveals a soldier. He is weary and startled. He is young, but what he has seen transpire around them has changed him. It has shifted his worldview in an indiscernible way. It cannot be measured in the present but only counted once years have passed, and the hardness that has grown inside him can no longer be ignored.

He will not speak about what he has done that day. Those words will not pass his lips but descend down into the well of his being, coiled, slumbering, forgotten. She doesn't recognize this man. But as she gazes further, she can tell she does know him. His eyes are green, like the trampled grass, assaulted by the strategies of war. It is her husband.

There it was. Vivid like the lightning. She had woken up with worries from the dream with Jean. But she had been so troubled. Her unease had stemmed from deeper within her mind. It had come from this image. The dream had not made much sense. But it had made her feel. She felt the fear, the panic, the pain. And what bothered her even more, was what she did *not* perceive. When she had seen Charles, she had not felt her usual measure of hatred. She had felt pity.

She turned to look back at the white house, glowing in the erratic light of the storm. His bedroom was blackened. She wondered if he still occupied that room or had chosen to sleep in the dark. Perhaps his candle had also been snuffed out. She was too far down the sand for him to do anything to stop her now. She shuddered, dismayed at the disconnect between how he appeared in her dream and how she knew him in her waking hours.

The wind was roaring now, like waves of the ocean. It was deafeningly loud. Whitecaps topped every invisible undulation of the dark water, and the shore was rough and frenzied. Blue fissures now appeared in the dark violet clouds. The squeak of an iron gate pierced through the night. The rain had eased, and only a few drops fell in scattered patterns around her. The lull of the storm was unexpected. She felt warm air but a chill down her back at the same time, and then the driving sheets of rain picked up again. The lightning pulsed faintly now, and the briefest appearance of stars sparkled between moving masses of clouds. She was alone, but she did not feel isolated. A kind of sacred communion between her and nature was unfolding, and she was the sole witness to its ancient performance.

The waves at the shoreline grew rougher again, but she remained where she was, not caring that they splashed her ankles. She was aware of a presence next to her. A man's presence. But she paid no attention. Josiah or Julius was likely coming to bring her back inside the house. Lucy had figured out a way to stop her after all. Another slow rumble passed over her, accompanied by a static flash. She did not want to go back inside yet. She closed her eyes, smiling as she looked up. She wanted to enjoy her final moments before he said something to her.

When she was ready, she turned, fully expecting to see a familiar face in front of her. But that was not what she saw. Towering over her stood a large black man, his face painted in shades of white and red. His eyes looked into hers and through hers, penetrating her very core. He did not seem angry but had a dominating presence that boasted his strength. He held a long spear in his hand, and he looked back at the water as a series of six lightning bolts descended to the horizon in an electric chorus. The sheer noise of it all echoed around them. She had never heard such a sound before.

A resounding explosion of thunder exploded throughout the air next, sounding above her head and seemingly bouncing off all parts of the earth before her, shaking the land beneath her very feet. She held her hands to her ears instinctively and cowered from its magnitude.

She blinked furiously as the pouring rain drenched her face, and when she opened her eyes a second time, the man was standing even closer to her. As more lightning flashed, she looked behind him and saw that he made no footprints in the damp sand. That was when the sound of drums began to beat wildly in her ears, louder than even the thunder.

She began to feel afraid. He was powerful, and he was like no one she had ever seen. He was different from Tabitha. He seemed fuller, more vibrant, threatening even. He reached a large hand toward her, and a corresponding flash of lightning made her lose her balance. The bolt had crashed perilously close to them. She felt her body descend to the ground, but the fall did not hurt her.

Disembodied voices seeped in and out of her mind endlessly, above her, in front of her, around her. Now the morning sun beamed down on her chest. The heat this early was warming and gentle, and it tingled across her skin.

"*The king does not hang, the king, the king...*" they said in different voices simultaneously. "*Oba koso, oba koso...*"

A melody of strange words accompanied their disembodied voices. An endlessly repeating barrage of drumbeats and claps reverberated in her ears.

And then it stopped. The silence was singularly loud and deafening. A wet nose with rapid, stinking breath descended on her cheek, and it urged her to consciousness. Eliza sat up on the beach to find a dog investigating her. A few slaves looked back at her with wide eyes. With disgust, she noticed a pile of stinking seaweed covered in flies flanking her. It was clear she had not intended to rest so close to it. Broken palm fronds littered the shoreline, but otherwise, the water had returned to small, calm ripples.

"Lady Sharpe, is you all right? How long you been down here?" Josiah asked, extending a nervous hand.

When she saw the person she had presumed had been at her side last night standing before her now, the memory of the strange experience shifted from a disturbed dream into a focused reality, hurtling before her, intense and loud like the storm had been. She did not know what to say. Eliza realized anything she could say would pale in comparison to what had just occurred. She wanted to rush to Cleo, but she also hesitated. She feared Cleo would disclose an unfavorable message about Jean. He had been there for almost two weeks now. Eliza knew Cleo had more than ample time to thoroughly survey him, and she feared another bad message.

The slaves around her waited for a response. The sun shifted behind a cloud, and a slight breeze came off the water.

"I came outside to watch the storm. It was so beautiful. Then I'm afraid I felt such exhaustion overcome me, and I fell asleep," she said, hoping beyond measure that they would accept her explanation.

One responded with a confused nod, and then three of them returned to their work. Josiah remained looking out at the startlingly blue water.

"I used to get scared when the storms passed through here, Lady Sharpe. But when I was young, Lord Sharpe would say, 'It's all right, you just frightened. It just happens.' And they always blow away," Josiah said, his eyes distant. "He told me that when I was real young."

Eliza brushed the white sand off her. The mere mention of Charles' name had made her lose interest. But Josiah was not done speaking.

"Before I came here, my people used to say things about storms like that. And that was some storm, Lady Sharpe. Before I knew better, I thought a man rode the clouds. A great warrior. That's what I remember my mama telling me."

Eliza's interest was piqued.

"You mean from where you came in Africa, Josiah? What do you remember?"

"I don't remember much about her. But I remember that. She told me a man would come down when the lightning struck, and he would come to take away those who weren't right. That was his job. He was a king from the old kingdom, and he'd come from the sky and carry out justice. That's why folks get scared when the storm comes. If you done wrong, you might see him."

Josiah's eyes grew huge in a display of feigned terror.

"But it wasn't only that, Lady Sharpe. Like I said, he was a great warrior. He protect the people too. And he come back to the earth to take soldiers. He come back to take them home. They called him Shango. He was a great king where I come from. But then Lord Sharpe explained the storms, and I wasn't so scared after that. Maybe it's because I still look for him in the clouds. It doesn't hurt no one to think about him. And it helps me remember her. My mama. And it keeps me going. Maybe he gonna come back one night."

Josiah retained a straight face and then broke out into laughter.

"Forgive me, Lady Sharpe. I talking too much. If you all right, I take my leave. I have to clear the east garden out before the day is done," he said, bowing his head.

"Thank you for sharing that with me, Josiah," Eliza said softly.

"Oh, it just a story, that's all. A man like me got plenty stories."

Josiah smiled, his teeth dazzling in the sun. And then he left her.

Eliza looked out as the waves gently came into shore. Shock coursed through her. Another story that was something more. These were not mere legends. They were not simply the lore of another place. Eliza could not explain her experiences. But she had seen enough to know one thing: it was true. She had wanted to tell Josiah what had happened and what she had seen, but she dared not complicate their relations. Even he might think she was mad. She, for one, was not entirely sure she didn't think the same. Eliza thought back to the night before. Had she had too much wine?

This king, Shango as Josiah had called him, had appeared before her. She intrinsically feared it was because she was guilty. She lusted after a man who was not her husband. She was a silent witness to slavery and did nothing. She could do more. She could always try harder. Yet, she didn't feel as scared as before. Daylight had softened the eerie strangeness of the experience.

Josiah had said that, in his capacity as a warrior, he sometimes came for soldiers. Was he coming for Jean? For Charles? She had been wronged. Greatly wronged. Perhaps justice would finally be delivered. Eliza turned back to the house. She knew what kind of justice she wanted. She wanted to be with Jean. She wanted to travel the world and be at his side. Her thoughts returned to her guilt. But why her? Why did she experience all of these encounters?

Fear returned as she thought of Cleo and her magic. None of these events had happened until she had befriended Cleo. Her magic was old, and while it was not dark magic, she inherently understood that it was indeed powerful. It retained a threatening aura. Eliza was playing with fire, and it was no ordinary flame. But something more unsettling stirred in her gut. It was simply not true. These otherworldly encounters on this strange island did not start after she had run to Cleo's dwelling. They had started her very first day on the island before she had ever known her. And what did the dream of the battlefield signify? She swallowed, her mind disquieted by it all.

The breeze began to pick up, gently stirring her skirt. The sky above her was a bright gray now, the kind of illusory state between rain and shine that tricked so many visitors of the island. She knew by now that it would come fast and hard when the rain did arrive, blurring the line between the horizon and the sea. As Eliza made her way toward the house, the sky finally broke, dumping a sheet of water on anyone exposed. The slaves tending the garden ran for cover under palm trees, knowing the rain would only last a few moments. The sun would return, and the puddles would evaporate in the searing West Indian heat. She was soaked through and through, but she laughed at this. It was a welcome distraction from her earlier thoughts. There was no sense in getting frustrated with events one could not control. She ascended the porch stairs and wrung her dark hair out. Standing outside the door, she noticed a figure inside the hall and recognized Jean.

She entered the house, breathless and still soaked, staring at him. She knew Charles was not around. She did not know how precisely she knew this, but she knew it just the same. She wanted to erase the troubling mood her dream had delivered. She wanted relief. Jean looked surprised, gawking at her wet appearance.

"Are you quite all right? Did you sleep well?" he asked with concern.

Eliza wanted to tell him. She wanted to speak of the glorious encounter she had just awoken from, but she dared not. Only Cleo would understand.

"Well, that is just it. I was not afforded much sleep at all, I'm afraid."

"We stayed up too long. The tricky thing is it appears one hour when you begin a good conversation and then many hours later in the blink of an eye."

"No, no, not that, I'm afraid," she said.

She wanted to tell him. It burned within her. She thought of their previous conversations. Perhaps there was a chance her experiences would not appear so outlandish to someone like him.

"I saw you. On the beach. In the thunderstorm. At first, I thought it was the whiskey, but there you were…"

Jean was studying her.

Eliza wavered in her deliberations. But there was one topic she did want to discuss with him.

"I am partial to storms. And I admit the lightning last night was so very striking," she said, staring at him.

"Yes, yes, it was. It was such a stunning orange hue."

Jean returned a smile, and they stood there unmoving.

Eliza still yearned for confirmation, despite her best efforts at self-control. She craved physical reassurance that Jean was more than a mere gentleman, more than an ordinary companion of her husband. That he stood seeped in righteous deception. Charles had made a grave error in letting his wife and her lover occupy the same space. Jean's presence in the house was a flagrant betrayal of Charles' trust.

Eliza understood at once that they were sinning. But she also believed their affair was a form of justice, even if the world they currently belonged to did not see it as such. Eliza was tired of the pain and the hurt. She knew that if she wanted a better life, she could not wait for it to be delivered. Images of a battle-scarred king descending from the clouds to rescue her from her situation seemed out of place now. She could make it happen herself.

She reached a hand to his chest, and on contact, she was brought back to the night they had lost control. Most of that evening appeared as a drunken haze to her, but the events with him were so clear in her mind. The drumbeats, the heat of the fire, and the fight with Charles were a rushed cacophony. But time had slowed down around Jean; it had become a blissful singularity the moment their eyes had met. The conversations she knew they could carry on for hours, the glances speaking of more forbidden desires, the separation and control, it had all slipped away breath by breath.

And then the boundary was gone. Their invisible barrier was broken when she allowed Jean to press her back against the coconut tree. Urging him to take her, press forward, and seize her whole being. How she had reveled in their connection, the realized satisfaction, their shared rhythm, his body and heat pushing against her, driving into her. How thrilling his breath on her neck had felt. The tree had scratched the skin of her back like coarse sandpaper, but she had let him move her, willing to go wherever he directed her. She wanted to be his, and she had waited for so very long. She had once feared she could never experience pleasure with a man, but in the grand paradox of emotions, she also knew such a feat could only be possible with him. She wanted Jean to touch her; she had ached under the expectancy of his body. Eliza inherently understood that every bold move of his had the power to undo the disgrace and humiliation she had felt from her husband's careless hands. Eliza had yearned for some measure of control, to experience the most sacred parts of herself with a lover of her choosing. And when the pleasure he directed into every aspect of her had reached unexpected heights, she had relished surrendering to him. It was wholly unanticipated, but at the same time, she had envisioned the way he would touch her. With unspeakable confidence, she had always known what he was capable of from the very first time she had met Jean. It had been her choice, and she would choose him again, consequences be damned.

Since then, he had presented himself so contrary to the way he had acted that night, and the more time passed, the more it all firmly slipped into the realm of myth. But here, now, touching him again, she could feel it all. Her breath was shaking, her fingers trembling with impatience. His blue eyes seemed enormous to her as the space between them dwindled. Eliza burned with the impulse to feel his lips on hers.

Jean looked at her longingly, and then his eyes went over her shoulder. She watched the light fade from them, and then he abruptly pushed her away, his movement unexpected and cold. He came at her again, this time shoving her into the study and slamming the door after her.

Eliza stood in shock, horrified and angry, and then scared as she realized the reason for Jean's actions. She heard her husband's voice. A cold drowning sensation flowed over her, and she stood breathless, her ear against the grain of the wooden door. Had he seen them?

The heavy, familiar boots thumped closer to the door.

"Jean? Is everything all right?"

A second set of footsteps sounded directly next to her.

"Perfectly fine. There is a terrible amount of heat coming from this room, so I thought I would close the door. Otherwise, it is stifling."

"Really? It is past midday. Have the servants shut the blinds? They should be closed."

Charles' steps became louder. Eliza looked fearfully at the French doors, wondering if she could slip outside without noise. She feared she would miss her only chance of escape.

"Yes, I'm afraid they are. It's no matter. This solves the issue."

She heard Charles sigh. "There are so many peculiar features to this house. It's a wonder I've lived here as long as I have. The servants complain of ghosts from time to time. Most of it is utter nonsense, of course. But there are the few moments even I cannot explain away."

They were quiet for a painfully long amount of time. She pressed her ear harder against the door, unsure if she had missed something.

"What are the latest reports from town?" Jean asked.

"Thirty more dead, twelve taken ill. Not very bright prospects. There is still hope, though, that the fever is winding down. And this letter came for you."

"Thank you. It is a shame. One can make so much progress on these islands just for nature and disease to tear it all down."

"Yes, yes. Whilst on the subject, I have some papers from the town clerk. He would like you to peruse them and advise him with your opinion. We can look over them…"

"I rather think I need to rest still. Between our late hours and that tumultuous storm last night, I still need to recuperate. Then I will be refreshed for tonight."

"Very well. I will go riding in that case. We can discuss it later. I admit the storms are quite disorderly on this side of the island. It is a miracle the house hasn't blown to pieces yet."

"Indeed. It is a pretty piece of land. The sunsets this house affords are remarkable."

A series of footsteps receded, but they were disjointed. Both men had stepped away. She heard Charles leave from the front door, and a single set of steps journeyed to the end of the hall where Jean's room stood. She took a deep breath and slowly opened the door, revealing an empty hallway. The edge of Celia's checkered skirt was visible near the corner of the parlor. She knew better than to sit down on any furniture, but that was precisely why she did it. At the very least, it assured that the space was clear.

Eliza walked and peered down the darkened end of the hall where Jean's room was. A part of her wanted to go that way, but another part was angry. She felt betrayed and confused. Jean had clearly acted so unexpectedly because of Charles. But what was the reason for him to retire to his chamber? They could be alone again. Charles had clearly stated that he would be occupied with his horses. That always consumed most of his attention. It seemed a more opportune moment than before for them to be alone together.

But he had chosen to leave. He did not want her. No sound stirred from that part of the house. Eliza knew that if he wanted to be with her, he would be in front of her again. But he was gone.

The wind was picking up as a dark shelf of clouds drew closer. It was still astonishing to see how quickly the weather could turn on the island. Nature had been so unpredictable of late. She mused that it was only mirroring her mood. She had avoided the house all day. She knew Jean was inside. And she did not wish to see him.

As she reached the side porch, she grabbed the shawl she had left and wrapped it around her. The water always seemed warmer than the temperature on land once you were wet. It was a curious feature of life in the tropics. Eliza entered through the study and stopped, water droplets dripping down to the rug. Jean was sitting at her husband's desk, looking at her as if he expected her. She looked away. Now his presence was nothing more than a slow torture. But what was worse was that he understood her longing. She had been very clear when he first arrived, perilously clear, and then there was how he had acted earlier that morning. Remembering his rejection stung her cheeks with embarrassment.

"I want to speak the truth," he said firmly, his emotive blue eyes staring at her.

"You've been very clear these last few days. I daresay I've never met a gentleman whose actions and words were so equally aligned as they are in you."

Beads of seawater ran down her chest as she clutched the shawl around her.

"Eliza, please, I must make a confession."

"You are a master of noble virtue. A true man of honor. Even the best of us fall from time to time, but none recover so remarkably as you do. When you make a dreadful error, it would appear that you only commit such a mistake once. Bravo, Jean."

"My life is a delicate balance of complications. If I make one false step, I could be ruined. But what is more, those I care for would fall with me."

"You are afraid," she said sharply. "You are afraid to take what you want."

Eliza turned on her heel and made for the doors where she had regretfully entered. He stopped her.

"It is not so simple. You know this."

"Heaven forbid you kiss my lips again when you've already had me. All of me."

Her eyes narrowed as she looked at him, and her fingers reached for the door handle. But his hand clamped down on hers.

"I owe you nothing, and I expect exactly the same from you," she said painfully. "Now, please move out of my way. We made a poor decision that night, which will not be repeated. I was a fool to think it was anything more."

"Eliza, I have been dishonest."

She stopped, surprised by his words. She looked at him incredulously. She had tried not to do this. Connecting with his eyes felt like falling into a pool of water, and she was sinking rapidly. She allowed him to move closer to her once more until they nearly touched. She stood transfixed, wanting him to kiss her while also yearning to leave the room.

"I am incredibly dishonest. I can think of nothing but your face from the minute I open my eyes in the morning until I fall asleep. And even then, I cannot gain reprieve. I see you in my dreams and wake up with the cruel reality that I cannot have you. I want to be with you. It burns inside me like the sun on my back when I am riding. I lose my concentration the moment I can think of a reason to stop by Pleasant Hall, and like someone possessed, I can do nothing until I have you in front of me." Jean's eyes were intense and unflinching, his voice trembling to a near whisper. "And even though it gives me joy, it is a slow torture because our time is so fleeting. For the minute I cannot remain here, I focus on nothing else until I have you in front of me again. I do not touch you because it would not be enough. I dared not approach you for so long precisely because I would not let you go again. I want you all the time. I *ache* for you."

Eliza was breathless and could look nowhere else but his eyes. At that moment, she felt herself drop to the bottom. And just like the vastness of the ocean, she could hear nothing but an incredible stillness. She could feel the force of a tide she could not control raging around her with every sentence he uttered.

Jean's hands grasped her face and pulled her to him.

"Eliza, please hear me. I love you," he finally said.

His voice shook as if the fear of saying the words aloud made them too heavy to bear. She, still swimming in the pull of her emotions, sank further into the depths by the revelation of his. Her stony stance softened under his touch. Her mind raced to process what he had said, but it was too astounding. His eyes were so close, they were all she could see, and his mouth was poised just above hers. She didn't know how to respond.

Weakness began to sweep through her, and Jean kissed her with such intensity he pushed her back into the glass door. She gasped for air; she had finally broken through the choppy surface. She had what she desired. Eliza had wanted confirmation that he longed for her, but the proclamation of love overwhelmed her. No man had ever expressed such feelings to her. She pressed herself against him, running her hands through his dark, wavy hair, inhaling the very closeness between them.

Giddiness flowed through her, a lightheaded feeling that was intoxicatingly welcome after so much tension and pain. A warmth sat over her chest, boring down on her like the setting sun over the water, enveloping her and opening her up. They nearly stumbled for lack of balance but he steadied her, his hands cradling her ribs. They said nothing; the language of their bodies, borne by their rhythm, conveyed unspoken words with desperate and longing mouths. The forbidden nature of their actions seemed misleading: she had never felt sensations so natural. A whisper of fear, of rationality, when her body and heart had overpowered her, arose last in her mind.

"Where is he?" she managed to say between kisses.

His lips pulled on hers as if he urged her to think of nothing else.

"He is far from here. I've locked the doors."

She turned her face to the side, exposing her neck. His mouth traveled there next as his hands worked to unlace her stays.

"But the…" she said, arching her body into his.

"All of them. I've locked all of them."

He had planned this. The thought thrilled her. Their actions were frenzied now. Her stays came off, and she raised her arms as he pulled her wet shift off her.

A few moments later, their clothes lay in heaps on the floor, and they paused to make the moment linger just a while longer. She stepped forward and entangled herself with him as he moved her toward the desk. He reached behind her and cleared the papers and objects off to the side. A few well-studied maps and construction plans for the fort hit the rug. The inkwell toppled off the desk, blackening out a portion of the scribbling on the yellowed papers. The mess stayed there, entirely forgotten.

"Do not make me wait any longer," she murmured in his ear.

She could feel him smiling against her cheek. She opened her body up to him, lying down against the cool hardness of the wood. He eagerly accepted her demand.

"If I have you in front of me, I should not wait another second."

His lips trailed from her hardened nipples down her waist to a place she had never expected to feel a man's mouth. His hands held her legs apart, and she forgot about the stiff desk beneath her back. She cried out, clutching his head, cursing. She felt helpless as the heat building between her thighs grew with every wet stroke. His hot breath and swirling tongue were about to push her over the edge when she stopped him. She rose up, searching for what she had craved since he had arrived. She wanted more precise, full satisfaction.

Eliza adjusted herself and guided him inside, watching his body move into hers. He moved slowly at first, reveling in their motions. She goaded him to move faster and deeper as she grabbed his face, sealing his mouth with hers. A synchronicity of kisses and thrusts began to form, and the pleasure she felt brought tremors to her legs. She wondered how long they could possibly continue like this as the feeling of danger crept into the back of her mind. But it also made their union exhilarating in a way she had never felt before.

That familiar wave he had caused that night months ago began to ebb through her again, but she could already tell it was much stronger than the last time. She felt confident it would crest soon; she was only too ready for such sensations. His skin touching hers, brushing against her, the smell of his hair, the power of his muscles, the familiarity of his tongue: she lost herself within him.

He unleashed all the feelings he had left unexpressed, and her movements in response underscored the glances they had shared across the table. For too many nights, over countless conversations, they had controlled themselves. But now, that wall of restraint had been broken. It had been too long since the time before. She never wanted to let him go. He said her name in her ear, and as if it was something uncommon to her, she went over the edge, sinking hopelessly under the waves, her body left to float in layers of bliss and mingled sweat. She had been loud, and the thought made her heart race even more.

Time seemed to slow. He took a few moments longer to join her. A dull pulse ran in electric lines from her fingertips to her feet, a kind of energy only he could deliver, and he kissed her forehead slowly as she collapsed beneath him. The intensity had made her eyes water, and she still held him inside her, between her, with closed eyes drifting through dull heartbeats and heated darkness. She did not want to move an inch but knew with a nagging awareness that they had to.

They began to slowly dress, the secretive nature of their intimacy leaving her even more heady. Her world, her being, and her existence in the white house by the water resembled more of a dream in that instant. She felt intoxicated with delight, a kind of rapture she had assumed she would never feel. The words he had spoken to her softly settled over her like an effusive glow. For now, she did not care to think of details or the future, bleak and distant as it might seem. She wanted to bask in their present. She was with him. And she accepted how precarious this made her position. She was willing to deal with whatever trouble threatened her.

He *loved* her. This singular fact was the only thing of importance to her now.

"My dear, you are awfully quiet this evening. Do our conversations not interest you in the slightest?" Charles asked Eliza.

His words starkly brought her back to the dining table. She had been preoccupied with what she had let Jean do to her in the study earlier. She had let her mind rove over treacherous thoughts. Thoughts of Jean becoming her actual husband, of him owning Pleasant Hall instead of Charles. That she carried his name. That Charles' presence did not matter at all. But she was mistaken. It did.

"I am afraid I am rather tired. That is all," she said, smiling and looking down.

"I do wonder what has stolen your stamina. I thought my day was trying," Charles replied.

"I swam too much today. The tide was quite…strong," she said slowly, feeling her ears and chest flush.

To compound her lack of shame, she looked directly at Jean as she said this, gazing at his face between wavering sets of candlelight.

"I warn her not to swim as she does, and she frequently disobeys me," Charles said to him.

"Perhaps you are looking at it all wrong. When one feels such a passion for a diversion, it would be remiss to overlook it. And if she enjoys it, all the more reason. There is something thrilling about letting the waves carry you," Jean replied with an upturned lip.

Now her face truly burned. The way Jean toyed with her husband with such boldness made her desire him even more. Her mind raced to find a way to be alone with him again.

"Yes, I suppose it is natural to seek satisfaction in one's life," Charles said.

"I couldn't agree more," Eliza added, holding Jean's stare.

Heat began to prickle down her back as they looked at one another unabashedly, daring to go beyond the boundaries of polite conversation. Charles scraped at his empty plate with a fork, and she assumed he was distracted enough not to see. She also recognized that she was starting to make light of the entire affair. There, in the dancing glow of the room, she felt as though she could rewrite the rules of the game. She felt her goals drawing toward her, alluringly close and nearly obtainable. Another day had drawn to a close, and another step toward the future had advanced.

The men picked up the conversation again, and she let her mind wander in her indolence. She wanted to observe the room and the people she shared it with. She wondered how she could retain such opposing feelings for Jean and Charles, who, by all appearances, seemed to get along so well with one another. Studying the men in such proximity, she noticed Charles' features were incredibly well-balanced on his face, but he lacked a certain kind of vivacity. His eyes were not small, but the way he looked at the world was, as if he was busy surveying it, studying it, and accounting for what he saw. Those same eyes instantly weighed risk and reward, downfall and profit, and were lined with caution. Jean had wide, large eyes that glowed with mirth when he spoke, eyes that seemed to drink in the very world he looked upon, taking in every experience as if it was more wine that filled his cup.

These men had very different eyes. Deep blue tenacious eyes, sparkling with mischief and a dash of risk

GINA GIORDANO

that pulsed with unspoken dreams, challenged cold green eyes that were unfeeling, retracted, made smaller by endless calculation, weary with the burden of stratagems. One sought joy in life and knew nothing could threaten him because of his innate lack of fear. He had honed his ability to play any card the hand of fate dealt, while the other had inexplicably seemed to have lost the same game more than once and was bitter and joyless because of it.

Charles excused himself from the table, and without hesitation, Jean reached over and grasped her hand.

"They can see…" she whispered, her eyes looking toward the back of the room where the servants waited.

She was particularly focused on Celia's notice. She stood unmoving as if she had not seen, but Eliza knew she was observant. Jean smiled, his thumb grazing the top of her knuckles.

"The moon is full tonight. Bright enough for a walk," he said.

"Is that an invitation?"

A delayed exhalation left her lips. This kind of talk was what she had longed for since his arrival.

"Perhaps. It is whatever you choose to make of it."

"I do enjoy walking on the beach when I cannot sleep."

"I know you do," he said, squeezing her hand. He leaned forward. "I received a new dispatch. The source of all our problems, the very tyrant on the hill himself, is soon to be recalled."

Her eyes grew wide.

"To heavens…are you entirely positive?"

"Yes. I received notice this morning. I did not want to spoil our exchange earlier, so I waited to relay the news."

Her mind was racing so fast that she could not find the will to speak. He released her the minute Charles could be heard returning to the hall. Eliza took a deep breath and sat upright, adjusting her skirts.

"What is this, I hear? Silence? My word, Eliza, you are awfully weary tonight," Charles said as he pulled his chair out and sat.

"Yes, I will retire early tonight. I promise I will be more spirited tomorrow," Eliza said.

They all stood as she walked from the room. She realized only too late she had not said good evening to Jean. This was no parting for them, and the need for discretion had not occurred to her. She smiled and ascended the stairs.

"Well, that leaves us free to discuss some business," she heard Charles say to Jean.

"I'm afraid I'm also quite fatigued. I've never eaten such good food in my life. Thank you. Thank you for such limitless hospitality, my brother."

For a moment, she paused at the top of the stairs, suspended by a sudden flurry of nerves. Could their newfound arrangement really be so uncomplicated? Could it truly be this simple? A flash of shame flickered within her heart, but it faded as she continued walking. She left the stairs she had climbed on other evenings with tears in her eyes, past the walls where he had held her by her wrists, stepping through the door she had so desperately tried to barricade him from entering. A hundred sleepless nights and the terror she had experienced living with him as his wife flooded her memory. And the presence of shame left her body entirely.

Charles did not deserve anything from her, not even the slightest regret.

The morning was already sizzling, and it had not even reached midday. Jean hovered around the writing desk, surveying what papers held Charles' interest so steadily.

"I have something I would like to discuss. A rather delicate matter," he said, hands clasped behind his back.

His vivid blue eyes surveyed his companion, sizing him up. Every bit of hardened muscle could prove a threat, and he knew it. Charles glanced up, appearing impatient to return to the tract he was holding.

"Can it wait? I'm rather preoccupied."

"I'm afraid it cannot any longer."

This caught Charles' notice. "Oh?"

"I have been keeping something from you. And I think it is time you should know."

Jean paused, taking a hard swallow.

"Continue."

Charles was terse, already expecting the worst.

"For the past four years, I have been engaged in specific work for someone. It has led me to uncover several grave matters concerning gentlemen around us. At first, I did not want to believe my findings, but the proof is insurmountable."

A thin veil of tension coiled in the air like invisible smoke. Charles' eyes moved from dull indifference to a slow smolder.

"Speak plainly, Jean," he said tensely. "You have been shrouded in mystery and ill-conceived rumors, which I have tried in all my virtue to ignore. What is it?"

"You are working for a very dangerous tyrant. You are risking everything you hold dear for a prominent military post. And you need to tread carefully."

Jean exhaled slightly now that the core of his message had been released. Charles' hand coiled into a fist.

"You dare to speak of Lord Dunmore in this way?"

Jean nodded, unyielding.

"I know you found a cave with smugglers storing their wares in it. You saw some of the things I speak of with your own eyes. That was no mere accident. Those merchants were invited to do so. By Lord Dunmore himself."

"Nonsense! The man would never invite smugglers ashore…"

Jean continued speaking over him, his tone loud and solid.

"The governor will be the destruction of this island and more if he achieves the post he is truly seeking. He sees his governorship as nothing more than a mechanism to deal in criminal enterprises and enrich himself on the suffering of others. The sphere of the empire is changing, Charles. You are nothing more than a pawn in his game. Times are ever more unstable. Imperial order is little more than a precarious illusion. We have already lost the

American colonies, but Lord Dunmore seeks to reverse the outcome of the war."

"Don't we all, dear Jean?" Charles quipped.

"If our island colonies continue to suffer under the hands of such incompetence, we could easily lose our entire position in the Atlantic to the French. A war is coming to France, and if certain tides prove strong enough, waves of anarchy will sweep the whole of Europe."

Charles was silent for a moment. The mirth drained from his face as he took a few strides to meet him on the other side of the room.

"Yes, yes…you know an awful lot about your people, the French," Charles rejoined.

"My people are here with you, and I live to serve my king," Jean said thickly.

"But to die for your king is another matter entirely. What happened to you, brother, after the war in America?"

"I can ask the same of you. I enjoyed the past few days, truly. Yet I cannot ignore that you have changed. The man standing before me is hardly distinguishable from a stranger. Nevertheless, I have tried to make you understand, and I am trying for one final time now."

"You cannot convince me of a single utterance if you cannot answer my queries."

"As you wish, Charles."

Charles smirked, walking back and forth.

"Who is the man I have opened my home up to for the past two weeks?"

"The man you have always known. A man who fights for king and country and all it stands for."

He stood still as Charles paced, the frenetic movement exposing Jean's vulnerability. Charles stopped on his heel and rushed up to him. He towered over him and looked down as he spoke.

"Do not speak to me of king and country. Your heart knows no allegiance, only greed. I have heard all the salacious rumors about you between my men, and I believe every one of them. Not because I desire to but because I have seen the man I once knew change incontrovertibly. And yet you claim that *I* have changed. You mock me, sir. You claim to be fighting for His Majesty, yet you wear no uniform. You wear no colors. You fight no battles. You do not sleep in the garrison. You do not bleed and sweat and toil like the men I command, who die every day from this miserable heat and sickness."

"Not all soldiers appear as soldiers thus."

Jean's answer was simple and infuriatingly plain. Charles had stormed to the fireplace but stopped, turning slightly.

"Be careful, Longchamp. You know of my position, and you know what my duties are. I will not hesitate to fulfill them. A friendship means nothing when it is not built on trust."

Jean paused, carefully considering his next words.

"It saddens me to hear your position. But it will not stop me."

He saw no point in relaying all the information he held. He knew his words would be met with further disbelief. And so, he chose to get to the heart of the matter.

"You are in danger," he said.

Charles said nothing and studied him with unblinking eyes.

"I am privy to knowledge that will make some very powerful people seek my death. They will stop at nothing. They will spread false rumors, throw my character into the dirt, and produce fabrications beyond belief to end my mission. And if they cannot get me, they will tear down everything around me to make me suffer."

Charles took a slow breath. "Continue."

"I am afraid that your association with me has now endangered you as well. Your kindness and hospitality these past few days have put you in the line of fire. And your ties with the old Conch families on this island and your position as a lieutenant colonel further complicate matters. They will first try to come for me and then for you. I finally have the proof I need to secure the recall of Lord Dunmore. I am leaving for England tomorrow. I must again warn you of the precariousness of your position, Charles. It is not safe here," Jean pleaded.

Charles stepped closer. He looked up at him in disbelief, then down to the floorboards.

"So, it is true. You…are a spy," he finally said.

Jean's face was implacable.

"I am employed in gathering intelligence wherever enemies of the Crown are concerned."

"Where is the honor in spying? You take money from military expenditures to do what exactly? Sneak and lie and do your master's bidding? Are these enemies of the Crown or political enemies? No English gentleman of honor would ever be employed in such a manner! The deception is too great!"

"I have no master. Unlike you."

"You are the dangerous snake Lord Dunmore has cautioned us about. You claim to work for the Crown while you are in league with the French. You commit nothing but treason, sir."

"You are wrong, Charles."

Charles lunged at him, knocking over a chair. Jean rushed backward, into the hallway, with his hands in reconciliation. He made no attempt to stop him, not yet reaching for his pistol.

"I am working for the Foreign Office. What I do serves the national interest," Jean said, stepping away.

This stopped Charles' offensive for a moment.

"My employer is Lord Grenville," he continued.

Charles' face seemed surprised. Jean moved into the parlor.

"The Secretary of State? You are a liar!" Charles said in bewilderment.

He stalked him like a predator.

"Please understand I am risking my life by telling—"

Charles lunged for him again, and the two men met in a collision of force. Charles was infused with brute strength and rage. But Jean's skills were observation and strategy. He had known this man for years and had watched his weaknesses. Charles would throw his punches in an obvious pattern, acting first and thinking only later. Jean hit his stomach, causing him to back away, and then used the advantage of space between them to dodge his subsequent attacks. Charles' fist was unsurprisingly directed at his face, and he ducked and bowed out of the way.

"Charles, you must believe me," he said as he watched a pistol be drawn.

Now a line had been crossed. Jean threw himself forward, lunging for the pistol, and twisted it downwards as a shot went off into the floor. They wrestled for a few more moments until Jean maneuvered the gun away and out of his grasp, throwing it across the room.

He had focused too much on removing the weapon at hand and became momentarily distracted. An infuriated Charles struck Jean squarely in the jaw with a succession of hits. Jean careened backward, knocking over a glass decanter on the side table. He scrambled back up quickly, wincing in pain. Wiping away blood from the corner of his mouth, he stumbled to the porch, but Charles was relentless. They struggled at each other's throats as they bounded out the door. A few kicks of the knee did not do any noticeable damage to Charles until Jean's knee landed between his legs.

Charles cursed, bowing over as Jean paced in front of him. His shirt was ripped, and his mouth was bleeding.

"There is no point, Charles. We are wasting time," he said breathlessly, blood coloring his teeth. "You are interfering with the duties of an agent of the Crown, despite being told—"

Charles stood up, grabbed him by the shirt, and plowed him into the wall of the house. Eliza could be heard screaming as she made her way from the beach.

"How could you do this? How could you betray your king? Me, after all I have done for you?" Charles seethed in his face.

"We are fighting for the same cause, brother," he managed to say, his bright teeth stained.

He choked as Charles strangled him, but a third voice interrupted.

"Stop! Stop this at once! Oh my God..." Eliza shrieked.

She futilely grabbed at Charles' arms.

"Get back!" he roared as he shoved her away.

She hit the porch, crawling to a shaking stand. It was too rough for Jean's taste, and seeing his once friend's cruelty on full display, he could no longer stand silent. He had already confessed one secret, and now he had nothing to lose. He used the moment of freedom to reach for his dagger and pressed the blade's tip against Charles' neck. Charles knew he had lost. He eased up, taking a slight step backward.

"You are a waste of a soldier and an even worse husband. I pity her. Not because she is a woman but because she must live with you," Jean said with venom, twisting the blade even tighter.

A hairline more, and it would break into his flesh. Charles' green eyes bored into him with a kind of rage that blinded him to all rationality. The eyes that looked back at Jean were cold, brutal, and without feeling.

"You cannot possibly love her like..." Jean started.

He stopped, realizing that letting his emotions take rein would help no one. He was completely losing his facade and risking his life. But more worrisome was what it would mean for *her* life. She would not be safe the minute he walked away. He needed to ensure her security while she still lived in this house. What he wanted to do at that moment would not be fair to her.

"...like a man should love his wife," he bitterly concluded.

Jean could detect sadness on her face as she heard him. Perhaps she had wanted him to say more, to even make a second confession. But that was one secret he refused to reveal. He had gambled his life away. He had made his choices. He could feel the walls begin to close around him, and time never seemed in such desperate, short supply. But she still had a chance at a peaceful life. Her well-being was all that mattered to him. He pushed a defeated Charles away and stormed off the porch.

"Thank you for your hospitality, Lady Sharpe. And when your husband returns to his senses, please give him my gratitude as well," Jean said in a weary tone.

His demeanor was hardened in a way she had not witnessed before, but for a single moment, he still managed to show her a look of promise. Jean didn't seem to care if Charles saw it as well. Eliza knew he was past the point of civility. He turned and spat blood into the dusty sand.

Lucy came out to the porch, bearing the pistol tossed under the settee. Charles looked at her, displeased with the sight of her holding his weapon, and snatched it away from her hands. He straightened it, aiming at the small of Jean's back as he walked away, his rage making his grip quiver.

"No! No!" Eliza snarled, her arms outstretched toward the gun.

Charles lowered it with hesitation. He looked at her with the slightest trace of disgust. But she failed to care.

Eliza watched Jean gallop down the road into safety, kicking up a cloud of unsettled dirt in his wake.

"That man is an extraordinary liar. And because of this, he is a dangerous man. You are not to speak to him in any manner, and he is not allowed to step foot on this property hereafter," Charles said as he descended the porch steps and headed to the stables. "Go inside!"

Her sense of impending doom began to ebb away as she stood there alone, but her stomach still felt unsettled. She had no idea what Jean had tried to discuss with Charles. She could guess the subject's content but hoped the most dangerous confession had remained a secret.

For a moment, when Jean had defeated him, it had seemed so obvious, so self-evident, that the only remaining thing left to do was pronounce their affair into the air. Eliza had felt it simmering between them, unspoken. But he had not. And because of that, she remained on the porch, untouched and secure. She clutched at her breast, subconsciously fondling the pearl tucked away in her stays.

All she knew with certainty was that the collective, if illusory and fleeting, paradise they had experienced these last few days was forever shattered. Like the glass decanter Celia and Lucy were attempting to clean up through the doorway, the chimera she had sought so hard to attain was crushed into a thousand tiny fragments, dashed to the ground, leaving only the cold, hardness of reality to consume her as she sank further into despair.

Eliza shot up, her arms clutching the sheets. The dream's message unraveled slowly into oblivion from her waking memory, like the edges of burning paper curling underneath the weight of a flame. But while she soon forgot the core of what she had just seen, she could still recall the terrible yelling. The shouts of Jean and Charles echoed in the back of her mind. And when she heard the slightest creak issue from a floorboard, she understood that she was not alone in the room. For a moment, she feared that Charles had found a way to get through the door. Had the dream been a warning?

But the shadows that usually hung in her dark room carried a different shape that night. A feminine silhouette, with a headwrap crowning her brow, drifted into view. The familiar ringing sounded in her ears, and Eliza groaned and buried her face underneath the sheet. She wondered what Tabitha wanted. She had not seen her for months.

Although Eliza had not willed sleep to return, she began to drift and descend into its murky depths. One part of her mind feared being in the same room as Tabitha, but the other half craved the softness of slumber. A second dream came, deep and realistic in its detail.

Youth and elegance transformed the house, radiating it with a light that makes Pleasant Hall look nearly unrecognizable. The woman picks flowers and laughs with the other women gardening around the porch. They are different from her, but she does not live by these distinctions. The papery bougainvillea petals fall to the ground; a new season approaches. Her stomach is curved, bearing the weight of new life. One small boy already clutches her skirts. She tends to him and takes long walks to the back of the property along the wide-rutted road lined with banana trees.

In a dark hut, she meets with a slave, a secret encounter. He is a young man, and she knows what he needs. The small boy is there, but he will not talk. He will not speak of his mother's crime. Books and primers illuminated by candle flame share the power of knowledge, a lesson in discernment. But the woman glows and cannot hide her footsteps. She cannot mask her constant disappearances. The man with white hair bursts in and catches the three of them inside the dark hut. But his feet do not see the books he has trampled. He only sees his wife in the presence of his slave. The secret has been uncovered.

The palms bend and blow in the wind. An oncoming storm lands on the island. The woman is sick in bed, a fever dewing her fair brows. Next to her awaits the boy who is afraid of her coughs. He has not heard her sing for many days now. A tiny baby coos in his crib, newly delivered with the aid of her trusted companion. Now the servant dabs at her forehead, whispering encouragement to her. Sickness came to claim her as if to threaten death to someone who has just delivered life, but her companion knows which plants will heal her. It is a friendship formed in trust but weighed down by the shackles of a cruel world. But in her company, the amber-skinned woman cannot remember her restraints. She worries for her. This is the effect her mistress has on those fortunate enough to share her company.

The man storms into the room, throwing the servant outside to the hall. The boy who clings to her skirts knows he has not been seen, so he cowers beneath a nightstand, grasping the humid and sticky wall. Words are exchanged, but the man is loud and unknowing. All he understands is rage. He shouts and yells, a fist slams down on the bed, and the boy sees what causes his mother grief. He now knows why, despite his mother's smile, there is sadness in her green eyes. The man she is bound to does not love her. The man does not believe that she is good. And he grasps a pillow and covers her face, his hold on her unflinching.

She wants to fight him, but he chose the opportunity wisely. She is too weak this time. The air is smothered from her screaming lips, and the man bends down, pressing harder and harder. He has come to punish the sins he believes she has committed. He cannot understand that he is the only wrongdoer. The boy screams and reveals himself, his green eyes wavering with sorrow, and leaves his hidden spot. His mother's hand moves for the final time, the muscles falling into limpness.

The father turns to the boy next and explains his justification. His mother is a whore. There was a reason for it all. The boy stands in the room, unwilling to flee, unable to move. He waits for his mother to stir through tearful eyes that look onto a brutal life. He will never hear his mother sing again. And from this day forward, he will no longer see the purple flowers that grow around the porch. The man curses and departs. He seeks the company of liquor in the study.

But the boy is not the only witness. The slave has watched it all through the narrow crack in the door. With trembling hands, she goes to the woman, lifeless and cold. She cries for her and cries for the extinguishment of the small measure of hope she still possesses. The frightened boy is there, but he will not talk. He will not speak of his father's crime. He will use force and strength to bury what he cannot speak of, to forever silence the sobbing child inside. Youth and elegance once transformed this place, and when it left, the house was no longer a home.

Eliza awoke while the words she heard within her mind still rang out, the voice slow and melodious and clear in her head. The figure on her bed had not moved. But Eliza now looked upon her and recognized her role in the dream. Tabitha was the woman who had held the mother's hand. Her eyes were shut now as if they were closed to this world, yet Eliza wondered what events and stories she could see in the next life. She wondered what other secrets she kept, what other events she held in her arms, unknown to the living.

But the more aware of her surroundings she became, Eliza recognized the room and the very same bed from the dream. She now lay in it, alive and only recently oblivious to the torment someone else in her exact position had suffered. The many glasses of wine she had consumed that night roiled her stomach, and the image of murder threw her over the edge. Eliza leaned over and retched into the chamber pot next to her bed. She heaved, unsure if the wave of nausea had stopped, and then she turned to look at the end of the bed. The spirit had vanished.

Eliza took a shaking hand and wiped her mouth. She lay back down, her uneasy head reluctant to relax against her pillow. The one space where she had felt genuinely secure was no longer safe. She pondered its meaning, and she considered whether it was a warning. Was she also in danger? The disquiet from these dreams was much darker than what she faced in her waking day.

She questioned what she had seen. How a nightmare had seemingly bled into a message with more substance. The little boy. The slave tending to the beautiful woman. The mistress of Pleasant Hall. This time, however, a new detail had emerged. What disturbed her beyond measure was that she recognized the boy. She could identify those green eyes at any age. It was Charles.

The nightly dreams that had assaulted Eliza were disturbing and violent, but nothing was in greater violation of the laws of nature than what she had just witnessed. Charles' father had been a monster. She now understood her husband's coldness. His brisk attitude. And with a disheartening effect, she slowly felt herself sympathize with the one man she had sworn to hate until the end of her days.

But the longer she remained awake and listened to the night creatures preening outside her window, the less she felt it. She was glad of it. The feeling the dream had left her with was like a bad taste in her mouth. She reassured herself that the pity she felt upon waking could only extend to his childhood, a phase that had come and gone many years before. He was a different man now, an entirely different person. And like the translucent crabs she often watched on the shoreline, she quickly buried the thought away in the sands of her mind. She was alone again in her room; the space was ordinary in its emptiness and innocent shadows. It was a dream and nothing more. She heard a strange bird call out into the night, breaking the troubled silence, and she sighed, settling back into the cushion of her pillow. It was her only comfort in a waking nightmare.

CHAPTER XIV.

A week, prolonged and slow with idleness, had passed since Jean left in the heat of the argument. But she had received written word from him. *The Ferme* was finally bound to set sail. Her feelings hovered between a sense of destiny and the aloofness of foreboding. Great changes in life always brought conflicting emotions, and this was no different. In two days' time, she would board a ship to France, and Charles had nary a suspicion.

There was one thing she would desperately miss: these waters. She lay in the ocean, rocked by gilded waves, as the blazing sun began to dip toward the horizon. Charles and Eliza had not exchanged a word or a glance. He had been so busy with his official duties that they had not even eaten together. It was a small benefit of her current situation.

A loud commotion in the bush sounded to her right. The noise came and went, and it was hard to discern with the sound of water surrounding her. Then he appeared. Jean charged down the lane into the plantation, urging his horse into a full gallop. A plume of dust swirled in his wake. He was so fast that if she blinked, she would not have noticed his arrival. He pulled around to the back of the house and dismounted. She started to wade out of the water, confusion slowing her down. He disappeared into the house. The meaning of his return was unclear. Had he come to see her or Charles? What was this pressing matter?

As she climbed up the sand dune, a cacophony of hooves and metal erupted from the grove of silk cotton trees. In the distance, she could make out a group of soldiers headed toward the white house. She picked up her pace and made her way to the back porch. As she entered, she could hear shouting. Celia and Lucy were pressed against the study door listening to the men argue in the parlor. When they realized she had joined them, they went outside, flushed by the revelation of their eavesdropping. Eliza did not rebuke them. She was too focused on what Jean and Charles were saying.

"Please, listen to me. You must go! There is no time!"

Jean's voice was pleading, desperate even.

"Give me one reason why I should trust a word that leaves your mouth."

"You must believe me. You must leave the island. Take her with you and leave now, before it is too late! It is—"

Violent knocking boomed on the main door, and both men ceased talking. Eliza made her presence known after Jean's last statement. The idea of Charles taking her anywhere was inherently abhorrent. That was not the plan she and Jean had agreed on. But the room was deserted now. A crowd gathered on the front porch; without thinking, she rushed outside to join the men.

"What is the meaning of this?" she asked.

Then she realized the soldiers had already reached the house and were ogling at her appearance. For the first time, she finally saw the results of what had occupied Charles' days. All present were cast in an orange glow from the setting sun. Most of the soldiers were black, and they looked stately and imposing in their red regimentals. She would have marveled at the sight of them for longer if it were not for the uncomfortable fact that she was now apparently the object of their attention. She had not thought of taking her shawl. Jean also watched her, but his face was pained. Charles looked downwards, his jaw tense and stiffened. Embarrassment flooded his face.

John Baker, a man introduced to her as the provost marshal many months ago, stepped forward. He was short, but his presence was as domineering as that of her husband. With the sun's direct light, the ways in which smallpox had ravaged his skin were far more distinguishable. He had always acted unpleasant, and today his mood seemed to have soured even more.

This, of course, had no immediate effect on her. She briefly wondered if she could make him go away with a strategic offering of coins like she had seen him accept in the governor's mansion. She had no respect for this man's authority. The hypocrisy on display enraged her. And so, she asked her question a second time.

"Lieutenant Colonel, do keep your household in order," the provost marshal barked.

"Get inside," Charles said to her. "At once."

The fury was palpable in his low tone.

She did not move.

"Jean Charles de Longchamp, you are hereby arrested for crimes of extortion and malpractice, the following of which you have committed in your office as secretary of these islands," John Baker said. "Do not make me arrest you by force. You have already caused a scene with your flight."

"This is a mistake. I wish to speak to Lord Dunmore," Jean replied, standing tall.

All the men watched him except for Charles. He would not look at him.

"You can have an audience with the governor, if he permits it, once you have been brought to the gaol. You must come with us."

"You have no right to arrest me, sir."

"Secretary, I have every right. And if you are a gentleman, you will not hesitate a moment longer."

"The lieutenant colonel will speak on my behalf, surely..." Jean said.

"Very well. This man claims you can vouch for his innocence. Can you?"

Charles remained motionless, his face downturned, his hands clenched into fists. He looked up briefly and only at the provost marshal.

"I cannot, sir."

Eliza's face dropped. The betrayal was swift and merciless.

"How dare you..." Eliza exclaimed, stepping out further.

"Woman, get inside!" Charles barked, pushing her back into the doorway. He reached for the handle and slammed it shut, closing her in.

With trembling hands, she touched the door. It was an unyielding barrier, separating her from Jean when she yearned to be at his side the most. It seemed as if the door, an inanimate object on any other day, had now personified Charles' anger. It stood in stark refusal, blocking her from joining Jean. She couldn't go back. It would be the height of absurdity. These were military officials, and she had already spoken out of turn. Eliza pressed her ear against the wood to listen better, trying to glance through the wavy panes of glass at the window.

"I trust you will serve your king and act as a witness to the secretary's criminal acts, Lieutenant Colonel?" John Baker asked in a drawling tone.

Charles hesitated for an uncomfortably long moment.

"Yes, sir. I will act accordingly," he said stiffly.

Baker ordered two soldiers to come and take Jean. Boots clambered up and then down the stairs.

"Have the prisoner's personal effects delivered to the fort shortly. Leave no papers or articles behind. Is that clear?" she heard the provost marshal ask.

"Consider it done," Charles answered.

It was then quiet for a while. Eliza crept toward the window and looked at an angle to see. They were gone. The door flung back open. She rushed at him.

"To your room," he shouted, not looking at her.

He stormed off to the back of the house and went outside. She chased after him.

"How can you do that? How can you let them take him?" she cried.

He ignored her and went to Jean's horse, digging furiously in his saddlebag. The white mare seemed oblivious that her owner had departed without her. Charles pulled the contents out of the pouch and returned to the house. He dumped the papers and books on the table in his study, rifling through pages and documents. He was in a frenzy, his temper barely concealed. Two sheets wafted down from the table and landed under a cabinet. Charles paid no heed and kept rustling through the pile in front of him.

"You must stop them. Surely you have the power to do something?"

"You are testing my patience, Eliza," he said sharply.

"This is ludicrous. This is—"

He slammed both hands on the table. The glass ink jars shook violently.

"God...*damn* you, woman!" he yelled, filling the room with rage.

She stood in front of the table, biting her lip, her hands clutching her damp skirt.

"Is it not enough that you have disrespected me in front of the regiment? That you are so emboldened as to not listen to a single thing I say?"

She did not answer.

"You are to stay in this house. If I so much hear a single mention of you going into town or even to the shore, there will be consequences. I have let you indulge in freedom for far too long. It is time to rein it in. If you will not act as a lady, then I will have to bend your resolve. You are too willful."

"I cannot believe my eyes. You have betrayed your friend. After all your years together, is your heart truly so blackened against him?"

He looked at her, his eyes revealing no softness. Sentimentality would not alter him.

"These are not matters made for a woman's sensibilities. This is a military affair. I do not expect you to understand any of it. Now leave me to it."

Charles gathered the papers and then made his way toward the door. Eliza followed after him.

"I understand. I understand more than you know. It is betrayal, and it is unjust. It is rather simple, and it is simple because it is the truth."

"Do not force me to be uncivil. Do not test me," he said, turning.

"I cannot force you to become something you naturally are. You are a disgrace. I am ashamed of you."

"You know nothing."

Charles put on his scarlet jacket and left the house, slamming the door behind him.

She remained where she was in the parlor, and the house was suddenly still once more. Celia returned and quietly made her way into the study to clean. Anger fumed inside Eliza. She could attempt to sneak out at night once Charles was asleep or had his fill of brandy. She would need to wait for the cover of darkness.

Or she could be bold. She could see Jean while Charles was away at the fort during the day.

Eliza looked upwards at the fort. Although incomplete, it was already an imposing structure. It sat on a raised hill, and its limestone facade seemed to absorb the light from the sun. It made the sight of it appear nearly blinding. Her eyes monitored the black men that toiled in the heat, moving limestone blocks with ropes and scraping mortar into joints. Sweating horses and donkeys pulling carts passed her. The town was busy at midday.

Julius had tried to stop her before she departed. He was only following her husband's orders. And she suspected those of Cleo. But she did not care. She only wanted to see Jean. But she had no inkling as to where the town gaol was. The sun was glaring down on the inhabitants now, and she peered down a narrow street, her hand shielding her face from the brightness.

"Excuse me, miss, would you happen to be Lord Sharpe's wife? Lady Sharpe?" a gruff voice asked.

She turned and saw three men standing close to her, their skin tanned like leather. They wore loose trousers and wide belts at their hips. The taller man among them was gaunt but had gold-colored rings on every finger. They appeared to be of the middling sort. They could have been fishermen or remnants of a crew that was in port. Perhaps they were aiding the construction and delivering materials further up the hill.

"Yes, I am Lady Sharpe," she replied.

She looked past them and back up at the workers moving on the hill. She had never really interacted with the men of the fort before. Perhaps this was why Charles never wanted to bring her around. She had always assumed he would want to show her the progress, but he had mocked the idea. One of the men glanced at Eliza and then looked away. He seemed nervous.

"You need to come with us, my lady," the thin one with the jewelry said.

"Forgive me, but what is this in regard to?"

"Your husband will inform you of that. For now, you will need to come with us."

He watched the passersby around them and then waited for her response.

"Are you soldiers?" she asked, distracted by their attire.

"You could say that. Call me Captain Alston, my lady," he said.

Her interest perked. This was a complication, to be sure, but there was a chance she could deduce the gaol's location along the way. And once she did, she would manage to sneak away. Charles could not learn that she had disobeyed him. The man's companions smiled. The one in the back coughed and spat on the ground.

"Come, follow me," Captain Alston said with an outstretched hand.

Eliza looked back to the fort, still unclear what was going on. A grunting mule bearing a cart of wood was heading directly at them, so she stepped out of the way, and the captain took off to the harbor. The other two men remained silent and walked behind her. She followed Captain Alston for a block and a half and stopped when he went toward the docks and boarded a schooner. The two men who had followed behind her now collided with her, and when she began to move, she realized they were pushing her.

"No protesting, woman," the man with the gruff voice said.

"Watch her. I hear she can swim faster than a fish," Captain Alston said.

Events unfolded quickly. Unable to move her arms or turn, she watched the ramp pass under her feet and found herself on the boat before she could even object. She tried to get back on the ramp, but the men blocked it. The captain had disappeared, but a group of even less presentable men stood gawking at her.

"What is the meaning of this?" she asked angrily.

"Wait there for further instructions," one said as he pointed to the other side of the ship.

She slowly followed his command and stood there, not knowing where to look. The men were staring at her. She saw no uniforms on board. Only sailors. Unkempt, unshaven, physically repulsive men. In the pit of her stomach, she felt uneasiness but stood there waiting for the captain to return. No one was explaining anything to her, and she felt increasingly uncomfortable. There was the awkwardness of assumptions, of following unclear instructions, of intrinsically knowing something was awry. Eliza turned, preferring to look down at the water rather than feel them watching her.

Movement transpired behind her, and she could hear ropes and a sail unfurling. An unfamiliar man approached her without her notice.

"Looks like they were able to accommodate our request, Rufus. It's our lucky day. God Bless Nassau, eh?" he called out. "And what a one I've got!"

Eliza turned, startled. He was tall and muscular, his head shaved nearly bald. A long scar ran from behind his ear to the front of his cheek. His eyes were yellowed and lacked focus.

"Excuse me, I am waiting to speak to the captain. I was told to wait here," she said.

"Of course you were. Only he's busy at the moment. Allow me to introduce myself. My name is Hawkins. Peter Hawkins. And this is my associate, Rufus. Now, the captain of this here ship is not aboard at the moment. But not to worry, lovey. I can find you another diversion while you wait. This way…" he said, as he grinned, revealing missing teeth.

Hawkins took Eliza by the arm and began to drag her to the far side of the ship. His grip was weak despite his size, and she wrested away from him. His breath stunk of liquor.

"Unhand me! There's been a misunderstanding!" she cried, keeping her eyes on the group of men.

The masts of the neighboring ships began to move around them, and she realized with horror that *their* ship was leaving the port. Captain Alston returned to the deck with a piece of paper in his hand as he walked over to some idle men.

"Him. That man. I need to speak to him at once," Eliza said.

She headed toward him, realizing that the drunken sailor was pursuing her. An argument erupted between the captain and another proud-sounding man.

"Damn it all! No, not under any circumstances. I won't do it. Turn this around!"

"You're not hearing me. She doesn't even know my name. She doesn't know anything, Duff!" the captain urged.

"And how did you convince her to come aboard? Do you realize how many laws you just broke? Or do you simply not care?" Duff replied.

"It's all in good fun. I'm telling you, look how many sailors are in town. She won't even remember our faces. And without any names...who would believe her?"

"Captain Alston, thank heavens. I need to speak with you at once. Can you please explain what is going on? What is this business of my husband that concerns me? Why am I here?" she asked forcefully.

The fury on the man named Duff magnified tenfold.

"*Captain*...Alston. You've gone too far now, you bloody prick!" Duff growled.

"Oh, did I say that, my lady? No, it's not any business with your husband. You see, he's up there, in the fort."

Alston laughed, revealing a score of missing molars, and then turned back to Duff, who was presently causing him more trouble. They bickered back and forth, the swearing growing more vulgar and louder by the second.

The nagging feeling that she had been fooled was glaringly obvious now. She looked at the two men and back at the other men watching the scene unfold. The bluntness of her new reality unfurled in a slowly paced blur. She stepped backward with an uneasy stride, away from the quarreling men and the crowd with curious faces.

The tall, bald man named Peter Hawkins returned to view, only too eager to see her walk away from Alston.

"Come away, now. Let me take you somewhere quiet, and I'll show—"

"I am not a whore," she said plainly.

The man raised his eyebrows in question.

"Aye, but you are, my lovey. Saw you entertaining a whole regiment this time last week I did. I'd remember those eyes at any port. I have coin enough. Let Hawkins make it worth your while."

He had her cornered again, but his presence wasn't menacing enough to force her entire submission. She blustered past him, only for him to take her by the arm once more.

"Do not touch me!" she said, edging away from him.

He shook his head, digging for something in his pocket. The metallic jingle she heard only infuriated her further.

"I am not a harlot. I am a—" she spat.

"And I'm the speaker of the house, my lovey. Are we going to play a game? I have ideas. I do. Hawkins has a mind for stories."

"I won't hang for this. I won't!" Duff yelled, raising the tempo of the disagreement.

The miscreant in front of her was counting coins in his hand. Eliza stiffened up, not knowing which man to watch.

"We simply need to convince her, is all. We can have a conversation, a friendly conversation, nothing more," Alston was saying. "How else are we going to do it? He already tried. I had her agreeable in town. We need that money back. It's striking two birds with the same stone. She has no choice!"

Eliza was so fixated on listening to them that she hadn't realized that the space between her and Hawkins had nearly disappeared. His hands were on her hips, but his balance was unstable. He was far from sober.

"I'm gentle with the flowers I pick. I don't want them wilting. That part, my lovey, comes later…" he started to say.

A breeze stirred her hair as the moving water slapped against the sides of the ship. One man whistled an unfamiliar tune that drifted to her ears between the heated shouts further down the deck. She looked from the bald man's dazed leer to something dark that caught her attention behind him. It was a black canvas, and as she continued to study it, she realized it was a sailcloth, blackened with tar and painted with whitewash. She recognized the flag; she had seen it depicted in gazettes and in her books. Men like this were known as privateers in these waters. But she only understood them as pirates.

To see a notorious flag lying there with such negligence, like any other object strewn on a ship, chilled her blood. Now she began to panic. She stood there, moving the man's arms away with fumbling hands.

"I'm not touching her. For fuck's sake, Alston! She's a bloody lieutenant colonel's wife!" Duff shouted, his voice loud and pitched.

"No one told me that. They said she was a lord's wife! But it doesn't matter, Duff. None of that matters! The governor promised us no trouble! We won't hang for it!"

Eliza's eyes grew huge at the mention of Lord Dunmore. Words Jean had spoken to her last year drifted back into her memory.

"You are the gateway. Charles represents the old families, the Conchs, as they are known. He has the militia at his beck and call. Once Charles realizes what Lord Dunmore has committed in recent days, he will try to stop him. And the governor wants the threat extinguished before it can become a threat."

Now the bumbling man in front of her only posed a mere annoyance. She brushed his advances away as she desperately tried to hear what they were saying.

"And what do you propose we do with her now? Take the ship back to port! If Captain Bruin finds out, you're dead! You're a fool!"

On hearing the sound of that name, her breath stopped. Now she fully appreciated the danger she was in. This was Bruin's ship. His crew. And they believed she had stolen from them. Did all of these men know Bruin's accusation towards her?

But there was a darker revelation of truth present. Captain Bruin was in league with the governor. That was the reason for his bravado at every social event. Not only did Bruin understand that he would never be prosecuted, the governor treated him like a respectable citizen. It was all a cover; the governor was using Bruin's services for personal gain.

The militia had come to arrest Jean, but even a pompous man like Lord Dunmore understood that the same soldiers would hesitate to replicate such an act with their commander. Charles could never be removed in such a public way. Jean had possessed damning knowledge about the royal governor. He carried permission from Whitehall to recall him from his seat. Lord Dunmore had removed the threat he posed by arresting him, and now he sought to do the same with her husband. Jean had understood this all along.

Eliza looked at the slowly moving water. They were at least a mile from the shore now, and the distance was only increasing. Any hope of escape was dwindling, and the men continued to argue about whether to keep her on board or let her go. Regardless of their decision or unruly tempers, she understood she possessed the deadly knowledge of knowing their names, their faces, their ship. She had heard the fragments of a plan that intended to use her as an expendable pawn. She was a witness to it and the fact that they dared to lay anchor in the town harbor. She was a knowing bystander to it all.

Eliza understood that her position in society, that her name alone, would make a pretty fee if the pirates decided to sue for ransom, and by the sound of it, that is precisely what they now intended. They would use her as a hostage to get to Charles. She felt bewildered by all these schemes and devices to trap the man she hated. She recalled pieces of conversation between Jean and Charles the day he was arrested. Jean had begged Charles to take her away, to leave with her. Jean had tried to warn him. But Charles had stubbornly refused to heed his pleas.

The island of New Providence was rapidly growing smaller as they sailed further out. Fear and disgust rippled through her, and it was not because of the drunken Peter Hawkins. She had ceased viewing him as a threat. The real danger lived in the mansion on the hill above the bustling town. She could see it even now; it was a charming structure and a prominent feature of Nassau. Every person on the island yearned to be invited inside its mahogany halls. Admittedly, she had once felt the same way. The governor's house had served as a convenient meeting ground for her and Jean.

But it had long lost its charm with her. Now the mansion only disgusted her. The governor wanted to destroy everything she cherished in her life. And she refused to take part in this game.

Eliza looked at the ship's railing once, twice, and then with a simplicity that surprised her, she pulled herself over the side. She feared the bald man's hands would grab her and catch some part of her dress, but she fell unhindered. The water's surface met her skin with the harshness of a slap, but she had left the ship, and that was all she cared about.

The water was cold, its chill all-consuming. She had never swum in waters this deep before. The sun above the waves appeared as a ball of rippling light on top. She felt suspended and realized how heavy her dress was from the saturation. She was not rising as she had anticipated. Then she saw a long, narrow shape appear in the distance. It slowly angled back and forth into focus.

A curious shark moved closer to her, a yellow sheen illuminating its silver body. She strangely felt no fear, as if she was merely watching the animal that brought terror into all men's hearts from behind a pane of glass. It was an uncanny sensation. She was captivated by it. It circled and swam closer and closer until she could see its eyes. She admired how easily it moved through the vast blue space around them.

Then the burning in her chest reminded her that she didn't belong in its aquatic world. She needed air. She swam upwards, and the shark backed away, disappearing into nothingness. But Eliza could not swim any higher, no matter how hard she kicked. She knew it was her dress. She struggled madly to get it off. After a dangerously long fight, she succeeded, and its dark form drifted sadly below to the curved bottom of the ocean floor.

Eliza kicked and kicked, moving a few feet more when she realized she would not make it. The distance to the surface and the wavering light above her were far too great. Time seemed to slow down. Her new companion appeared again from behind and darted closer to her. She still did not fear its presence, but she was afraid she would drown. She had treated the sea without any measure of serious caution for far too long. Now it would come to haunt her.

Shimmers of rainbow colors flashed with vivid intensity around the shark. Her vision grew narrow, and an encroaching blackness closed in, but she still stared at the gleaming reflections. Her brain felt muddled, and instead of kicking upwards, she felt the water embrace her, whirling around her until her senses could no longer fathom what was occurring. She was spinning, and she closed her eyes, surrendering.

Almost immediately, she saw the water again. But it was a different kind. She was in the shallows and couldn't figure out exactly how she had reached there. A sharp pain sat in her lungs, and she knew she still needed air. With only a minor push, she was able to arrive at the surface this time. She gasped and then went back down again as a wave rushed over her head. Her throat burned as she mistakenly gulped the salt water. It assaulted her, traveling down her nose and reaching the back of her neck. The burning sensation was relentless, and the water entered her ears next, deafening and disorientating her.

She let the next wave propel her forward and found herself on the shoreline, completely confused by the constantly changing depths. Eliza struggled to escape the crashing tide and pulled herself along on her stomach in the sand. She was coughing and trying to release the water she had swallowed when she heard him.

"Eliza? Eliza!" a voice called out. "Dear God…"

She looked up in confusion to see Charles standing on the beach, a golden spyglass in his hand. She was stunned, then disappointed.

"I thought you knew how to swim!" he continued to shout. "You told me you could swim!"

"I can swim. Better than most men," she managed to utter between coughs.

"You are mistaken, my dear."

Once the shock of his company wore off, Eliza paid him little attention and continued to gasp for air. She could feel his displeasure but had little concern for that. She was far from eager to see him. Her all-pervasive hatred had returned in full force. Sand and tiny fragments of broken shells covered her arms and chest. She still hadn't completely freed herself from the waves. Charles bent down and roughly pulled her to her feet as the water crashed against his polished boots.

Eliza looked back out to the horizon. The schooner was at such a great distance now. Her perplexed face inwardly calculated the distance from the ship to the shore where she now stood. Everything that had just occurred seemed so surreal, as if her abrupt departure from the water had been nothing more than an awakening from a curious dream.

"You're not even close to the house! You did not tell me you swim near the town. I've only tolerated this nonsense for so long because you assured me you knew how to swim!"

She doubled over, still trying to gain control of her breathing. She felt lightheaded, and her legs were shaking and wobbly. Charles did not care. She felt his pincer-like grip on her forearm as he began to drag her back toward his horse.

"We are going home now. I forbid you to go into the ocean. I already deal with enough troubles in my household, and I will not have a drowned wife to add to it. Not on my account."

She stood next to Alastor, unwilling to get on him in her shift. Charles let out an exasperated sigh and hoisted her up onto the saddle.

"What would you have done if I had not saved you?"

Anger flashed through her as she considered that he was the very cause of her ordeal. But she did not want to speak of it yet. She would wait until they were safely lodged in Pleasant Hall, and she ignored his diatribe to the best of her abilities. Then Eliza felt shame rush over her as she realized she would be riding all the way to the house in nothing but her shift. This was not quite the same as the secluded beach that bordered the plantation. They would surely pass people. Charles kicked the horse, and they were on their way.

"May I have your jacket, Charles?" she asked through gritted teeth.

She hated asking him, and it appeared dubious that a man so concerned with her propriety on every other occasion would overlook this.

"Mine?" he replied, scoffing. "Certainly not. You'll make it all wet. You stink of sea."

It was clear that he wanted to embarrass her. Already, some slaves working alongside the fields next to the path were staring.

"You do realize the danger you put yourself in? There was a ship in the distance flying a black flag only a few miles out. *Pirates*, Eliza. I had stopped my horse on the side of the road to observe their movements when you washed up. It appears they had the audacity to lay berth in the harbor, nearly undetected. And there you are, a foolish girl frolicking with death. I will not have it."

Eliza was grateful he couldn't see how disinterested she was in his conversation. A dark gray line stood as a demarcation in the sky, and it began to rain, only chilling Eliza further. Alastor trotted through white mud, the same color as the sky above them, and the raindrops turned into a series of pelting blows. The soil of the disturbed earth around them gave off the slightest smell of fish as they passed by the mangroves.

Her gaze became lost in the bluish-gray puddles that formed on the ground, a strange mixture of chalky white, reddish undertones, and dark-brown streaks of mud. The trail was littered with broken leaves and hoof marks scattered in all directions. At one point, they passed by a crudely constructed shack made of various-sized branches, under which a free black man stood peddling fish he had recently caught. He waved to attract Charles' notice, but he did not acknowledge him. It seemed as if he was deliberately urging Alastor on a more difficult path, and the horse had to jump several times to reach a clearing.

Eliza clung to Charles' jacket, reluctant to hold on tighter, watching flecks of gray mud splatter all over her shift and calves. The air was made colder with a relentless breeze, and the only thing that comforted her was the warmth from Alastor.

The dreadful ride lasted a quarter of an hour more, and they finally reached the house. Eliza envisioned tea, a warm fire in her room, and, most of all, solitude. She wanted to be far away from Charles after their journey. She was just considering how she would dismount without scratching or bruising her bare skin when she felt him pull her down. The pommel and stirrup caught her thigh. She knew it would leave a bruise.

But Charles wasn't done with her yet. She was pushed up the stairs to the porch, where they walked to the beachfront side. Eliza tried to go to her room, but he stopped her, holding up a hand with an impatient glare. He disappeared into the house.

She stood there uncomfortably. She had worn just as little on other occasions, but she mused that, in this instance, it was not by choice. The sun had completely disappeared behind huge gray clouds over the water. It would set soon. The wind was picking up around the house. The sudden change in temperature left her feeling even more vulnerable.

Eliza waited, wet and dripping, until he came outside once more, his agitated footsteps thundering against the battered wooden boards. Charles stood behind her, closer than she preferred, and wrapped her in a blanket. He began to press her dry. His arms were around her body in a half embrace as he crudely squeezed her from her feet upwards. She couldn't tell if he was still angry or if this was an attempt at kindness. She almost lost her balance from his roughness.

Charles paused once he reached her shoulders. He pulled her to him even more. She kept her eyes cast down, her body still shivering from the cold. She felt his breath as he leaned in closer to her face. She instinctively pulled away, but he held her in place. Charles was no longer trying to dry her. He remained still for a moment, then with a gentleness unlike his recent actions, he moved her wet hair to the side and began to kiss her neck, his lips slowly trailing down. He stopped by a laceration on her chest, holding a clump of her curled hair away from it. She had scratched herself in her frenzy to remove the dress, and now the blood was beginning to show.

"What do you do when I am not by your side?" he asked quietly.

His tone was one of fascination. Eliza felt his lips lightly brush against it, and then his hands were at her stiff breasts. His hair brushed against her neck. The blanket fell to the deck. She trembled with a forceful hatred. She wanted to be free of his advances. She at once rid herself of the notion of disclosing what had truly occurred. Why should she explain anything to a man like him? Jean had clearly attempted to do so, and the gesture had done him no favors. She had escaped from the ship. With a new gratitude for her freedom, it seemed sheer folly to complicate matters by embroiling Charles in it. He didn't deserve the warning Jean had tried to give him. And he likewise did not deserve her confirmation.

Charles moved her back a few steps toward the door. She limply followed his direction, weakened from her ordeal in the water. Her energy had already been spent with the events of the past few hours. But her mind was raging and hovered between disgust of him and thoughts of a second escape. He clutched her in such a way that she could feel the stiffness of every muscle beneath his breeches. A wave of nausea rose within her. His grip on her slackened momentarily, and then she realized he had spotted something else on her person.

"And here? Are you cut here as well?" he asked, staring at her chest, his hand reaching down to the center of her stays.

She immediately tensed up. He pulled out the red amulet Jean had given her at the first ball. She was relieved to see that it had not been lost. She had not even considered it in her haste to remove the dress. But then she panicked and turned with desperation to take the trinket back. The night she had met Jean felt like an eternity ago, but a conversation they had all just engaged in at the dinner table was much more recent.

Charles examined it in the palm of his hand without any emotion. But then his green eyes met hers, and she saw his fury burning behind them. He went to speak, but no words came out. He tried again, the rage within him making his words quiver.

"If you are going to spread your legs for another man, can you at least have the decency to avoid choosing one that I consider a friend?" he said slowly.

It had finally happened. The moment she had dreaded for so long dangled before her. He had accused her, and now he was waiting for a response, but all the words she had carefully armed herself with had dissolved. But then anger returned, taking the place of her fear. Eliza transformed from a docile victim to a feral cat disturbed. He closed his fist around the amulet. She stepped forward.

"Your friend? Your friend?" she shouted. "It would appear that you treat your friends not much better than you do your enemies!"

Charles stormed inside the dark house with repulsion.

"What are you doing? Give it back to me!" she cried, chasing after him.

He strode to the end of the hall to a side table with a lamp. His anger made his figure appear large and looming in the hallway. He suspended the amulet over the flame, but as she approached him, she read his intentions. She smacked the lamp off the table with a cry. It flew and smashed against the doorframe of the study. Fire crawled up the wood, fueled by oil and old timber.

"Are you mad? Have you completely lost your senses?" he barked.

Charles took her, pushing her to the opposite side of the hall, and searched for something to douse the flames. A shrieking Lucy and another house slave appeared and started to work on the fire, dumping buckets of sand over it. Eliza saw an opportunity and rushed at him again, reaching for the amulet. He tried to fight off her hands.

"You have taken everything from me! *Everything!*" she yelled, her voice raw and guttural.

They collided into each other, and in one movement, he had her pinned to the wall.

"Where have you been letting him have you?" Charles spat, his eyes smoldering. "Your bed? Perhaps mine? So you can pretend you're with him instead of me? Maybe you met him in that squalid inn where he lives. How convenient it must have been for you when I brought him here."

Eliza made no response, her energy directed on reclaiming her talisman. It was the sole physical object she owned that was proof of her newfound happiness. That someone in this harsh world loved her.

In her wrath, she charged at him again. He caught her and pushed her into a doorframe with extra intensity. She struggled to free herself despite the pain that ran along her spine. The fire was now extinguished, and she started to cough from the smoke. The servants disappeared outside to get more assistance.

"Look at me! Do you enjoy it?" he shouted, his voice a mix of unleashed emotions. A whirlwind of rage, desperation, and agony drove him. He shook her. "Do you? Do you enjoy giving him your body? Lying on your back for him?"

She turned her face to the side, waiting for his tirade to end.

"You are a whore. Do you deny it? Do you deny it?" he shouted.

She looked at him, unflinching.

"You are *his* whore…"

"I am his," she said finally.

Charles' eyes flared, but he stood still, holding her in the corner using his forearm as a brace. It was silent except for their exasperated breaths. Her back ached, but she did not care. Charles' face was inches from hers. His green eyes were darkened, bulging outward with fury. Eliza felt exposed. She was vulnerable now that she had confessed. She waited for his next move, dread seeping into her. He held her so tightly it seemed as if he had no intention of ever letting go. The strain of inaction began to bear on her. She wanted something to happen. She wanted to be free of his grasp.

"I will not deny the truth. You can darken my character all you want, but only do not utter a single word against Jean. He sits in a filthy cell because of you. He wasted his breath trying to warn you. Now he languishes in uncertainty because of your refusal to help him. What a true and loyal *friend* you are."

"Do not make this about his fate. That man made his decisions, and he chose gravely. This is about you. And your betrayal of this marriage," he fumed.

When she did not reply, he sighed with frustration. His temper appeared to subside.

"Why, why have you done this?"

His voice was breaking, and she thought she saw tears in his eyes.

"He is kind, Charles. He has shown me kindness."

"What you call kindness is nothing but weakness and a lack of discipline."

"We can disagree on his qualities, but one fact is irrefutable. He is not you."

"You cannot retreat from your position now," he said.

"You are mistaken. I do not mean to retreat. I will never surrender to you."

"I will kill him," Charles said, his voice trembling.

She did not respond and glared at him.

"You gave him your virtue. Do you understand what you have done?" he asked.

"Yes. And I would do so again. I do not beg forgiveness. I owe you nothing."

His anger returned, more forceful than before.

"You owe me everything. And you are an insipid fool to throw it all away!" he said, raising his arm to her throat.

"What will you do now? Strike me? I daresay it is the only thing you have not subjected me to."

"If I have not impressed this upon your mind, I am exceedingly tolerant. I am exceedingly patient. I am—"

"You are exceedingly cruel."

"I know men that would disfigure your face. They would not hesitate to beat you with a stick because it is their right to do so and because you need to be broken."

"I will never bend my will to that of a man. Not to you. And not to any man."

"Marriage is nothing but a business proposal, and if you've forgotten, let me make it abundantly clear. You have broken that contract. You have disgraced this house. You are not fit to be my wife. To carry my name!"

"That name means nothing to me. I want freedom, Charles…freedom…"

"You were your father's charge, and he signed your life unto me. A task I take on with great responsibility and duty, even if, at times, it only causes ever-increasing frustration and madness. I—"

"Madness? Madness is having to bear the thought that I am sidled to you for eternity! I am not living when I am with you. I exist in name only. This is not living; this is not marriage. This, this existence is torture…"

"How clearly you speak my miseries."

She saw an opportunity then, an overlooked possibility.

"End it. End this all," she said in a low tone. "Do not let one more day pass."

Charles looked down, frustration consuming him. He said nothing, and then he grabbed her by the chin.

"I will never let you go. You belong to me."

"I belong to no one," she hissed.

And then a dark smile crossed his face.

"We'll see."

With a good deal of restraint, he released her, walking to the other side of the hall to study the damage from the fire. She waited for some kind of outburst, but none came. He turned around and looked at her, a different atmosphere in the air around them now. Her core reeled from the intensity and force of her words. She could scarcely believe she had said them. Months of despair and contempt had led up to this point. And now they could never return to where they had once stood. Charles briefly looked at her again and then at the amulet he still gripped in his palm.

The sight enraged her. She was sick of men like him and how they tried to control her life. Eliza stepped forward and unsheathed his saber without thinking. She dropped it slightly and readjusted her grip as she pulled it out.

"If you refuse to return what is mine, then I will destroy something you cherish."

She dashed to the door. He shouted after her, his voice thundering against the walls.

Eliza turned around to face him, taking full satisfaction in her ruse.

"I am throwing it into the sea!"

He appeared more distraught than she had expected. She had never felt more revulsion.

"Drop the sword," he urged. "Drop the sword, Eliza."

She stood firm, holding it out to the side. He suddenly whipped out his pistol and pointed it at her. She was violently rushed back to reality, time slowing down to a soundless trickle. This was not some childish game. She had enraged a man. And a soldier. Someone who killed for a living. She felt her eyes well up as she fully realized her stupidity. She had built quite the trap for herself. Her mind ran over how she should have used different words and perhaps said no words at all. What *had* she said to him? It all seemed obscure now. Was it worth her very life?

With a loud clang, she dropped the sword. He fired, the blast piercing her ears. Eliza screamed and ducked into the wall, her hands covering her face. There was no noise for a few moments, and then she looked up. Charles stood there, his arm still outstretched, his smoking pistol fixed. The smell of gunpowder was pungent in the sticky air. He looked shocked. Then she realized that his focus was not on her. She whipped around. The overseer lay on the porch outside, a rifle in his grip and a massive hole in his gut. Blood pooled on the porch. Eliza put her hands to her mouth and let out a scream.

Charles walked to the door, stepping on the hemline of her shift. The overseer had proved to be a faithful servant, ready to defend his master to the very end. He was coughing and choking on blood. Charles fired a second round into him. He never looked toward Eliza. He stormed off the porch into the approaching darkness and tossed the amulet into the sand. With a sinking heart, she realized she would never find it. The sky outside was a weak color now. The sun's covered glow had faded, distorting the light between heavy clouds.

Then she realized, with an awful twist in her stomach, that Charles had actually saved her life. He could have killed her, and he would have been aided in taking her down. From his rage, she could only assume that he would have desired it. But he had not. This reversal sickened and frightened her. Nothing had been settled. The next trial between them poised in front of her, looming with unspoken threats, adamant in its refusal to ever be resolved. And now he possessed damning knowledge of her. In short, he had a defense for his ruthless behavior and no longer had any reason to show her mercy.

She had not denied the intimate relations between her and Jean and had instead conceded to the accusations. She had rashly declared her refusal to surrender. But she was engaged in an unequal match. He was stronger and more powerful than her. A man like Charles would never relent. That much was clear to her. Her passionate outburst had done her no favors. Instead, she had given him the key to her weakness and there was no remedy.

Another terrible thought crossed her mind. The promise of a new life offered by the ship to the Continent would evade her. She simply could not leave the island while Jean was imprisoned. Not after what had just occurred. She had taken a stand, and she would hold the line. *The Ferme* would have to set sail tomorrow without her. Jean was all that mattered; she could not possibly leave him. But worse still, the promise of a future together flickered dimmer among her prospects now that Charles was privy to their affair. She had foolishly risked it all in the heat of passion. Now Eliza would be fated to a life of misery and suffering. She slumped against the wall and began to sob.

CHAPTER XV.

"**G**ood evening, Charles," Eliza said, bowing her head slightly.

He was already dressed, his scarlet uniform exact and precise as always, like the hawkish gaze, he now placed on her. Several days had passed since their last argument, and they had exchanged very few words. Now, tonight at the ball, she would need to act presentable to polite society and find some sudden possession of happiness at his side. It was a daunting prospect. Only one person occupied her innermost thoughts, and it was not the man in front of her now. She saw a flash of Celia's checkered skirt near the stairs on the second floor and knew she was most likely listening to the conversation. Eliza did not care; she had nothing of importance to say.

"I will be ready in an hour."

Her tone was indifferent. There was no point in socializing if Jean would not be present. But she refused to remain idle while he sat in prison. Maybe she could figure out a way to help him tonight. Perhaps she could find a sympathetic ear.

Eliza stepped into the darkened foyer. As her eyes adjusted, she noticed a strange shape draped through the dowel rods of the walnut staircase. A rope was tied to it. Just as she realized what it was, Charles pounced on her, dragging her toward it. He pushed her backward on the side table, keeping both of her arms raised above her head. The other hand worked furiously to tie a painful knot. There was a quick scuffle, but he had pinned her down and completed the task so flawlessly that it was over in a moment. He adjusted his posture from the awkward stance he had held and removed himself from her with a deep exhalation. Charles now seemed relieved.

Eliza was in shock, lowering her bound wrists with what little freedom the bit of rope allowed her. The cord was rough and bristled against her sunburnt skin. Charles took a step back, surveying his work. He pushed the table away and dragged a chair to the spot.

"What is the meaning of…" she started quietly.

Her heart was already sinking.

"It's for your own safety, Eliza. I'm afraid you will not be attending the ball tonight."

She said nothing. She wondered if this had anything to do with Lord Dunmore's designs, but something about Charles' behavior seemed extreme. These were the actions of a desperate man. Apprehension washed over her as angry tears brimmed in her eyes. Charles wasn't telling the whole truth, and she knew it. He sighed.

"Jean is to be executed tomorrow at dawn."

His words hit the pit of her stomach like a heavy chain.

"His trial isn't until next week. I thought—" she said incredulously.

Charles held up his hand. He expected such a response.

"These are sensitive matters, military matters. The governor has seen fit to expedite the case and suspend a public hearing."

"He can't do that. He needs permission. He can't—"

"Eliza!" he thundered. "Lord Dunmore is the governor of this island, lest you need a reminder!"

Eliza felt the floor drop from beneath her feet. Not only did Charles not believe Jean, but he was also willing to stand by and let him die.

"This isn't right. And you know it. This isn't—"

"You have left me with no choice. I can no longer trust you. I cannot have you causing a scene tonight. Or tomorrow, for that matter. I had no choice," he said slowly. "If I locked you in your room, you would only flee from the window. Perhaps you can use this time to contemplate your recent behavior and role as a wife."

Sheer desperation urged her to reveal what she had yet to tell him. She was willing to try anything if it meant saving Jean.

"Cause a scene? Cause a scene! I am the only voice of reason! When will it be enough? Why can you not treat the words Jean has told you with even an ounce of gravity? When will you heed any of these warnings? I have only ever told the truth! Dunmore has tried to seduce me on multiple evenings. The man is in league with pirates! They attempted to hold me hostage just last week! That is what you witnessed when you found me, Charles. You know very well that I am a capable swimmer."

Charles paused, surveying her with a perplexed expression.

"You mean to tell me that a gang of thieving pirates took hold of your person, and you somehow escaped unscathed?"

"Yes!" she said breathlessly. "Captain Bruin is not a good man. Lord Dunmore is pursuing any means to try and stop you."

"Stop me from doing what precisely? You are speaking nonsense. How did you get from the ship to the shore?"

"I jumped."

"Eliza, that water is too deep. The currents are too strong. You couldn't have possibly swum that distance."

Her ears colored. She carried the same question herself.

"I cannot explain it."

Charles scoffed.

"I cannot explain many things, but I assure you that Jean does know. Dunmore is the son of a traitor. Jean must have tried to explain it to you, surely. I am not privy to the details, but Jean knows," she continued.

"You can be assured that whatever filth that man has filled your head with is simply that. Filth. There is not an ounce of truth to any of his accusations. I will not hear of it!"

"And what of the events *I* have witnessed? The words I have heard? The governor could barely restrain himself before he offered to promote your position on the condition that I share his bed. The very same man attempted to forcefully seduce me the next opportunity I found myself in his presence. Do you not see what he is trying to do? He is willing to use any means to get to *you*. You are in danger!"

Charles said nothing for a few moments, taking a slow pace back and forth as he considered his next words.

"The man is already in possession of a mistress. He does not want you, Eliza. You have been reduced to madness. I should never have brought you to this island. I pity you."

Tears streamed down her face. She saw then that Charles would never see the truth.

"You are wrong," she said quietly.

Charles strode forward, stopping inches from her face.

"You are a woman, Eliza. And these are powerful men! Very powerful. They can destroy you. And I will not have it. As your husband, I need to protect you. And I will do so for the rest of my life, God willing."

If the words had come from any other man, they might have warmed her heart, but since they fell from his lips, they only made her sink further into despair.

"Your words mean nothing to me. I don't need someone like *you* to protect me," she sneered. "Look how well you defend an innocent friend…"

Charles grabbed her by the chin.

"How must it feel to be a woman like you? How must all of this feel? To be so powerless despite the fury contained inside?"

Eliza felt her eyes grow watery again. Her mind raced but kept stopping with obstacles. The biggest impediment stood in front of her now. And what an arrogant and damnable opponent he was.

"Matters might have been different had I been able to trust you. As a husband should with a devoted wife. But to this day, I have never seen devotion. No…" Charles said slowly. "Instead, I've been met with only treachery and betrayal."

"Please…" she said in a low voice, casting her eyes down to the floor. "You know this is wrong. I know you do. You know this is all wrong."

"Perhaps you are not the one to lecture me on matters of morality, my dear," he said thickly.

Charles clasped his hands behind his back.

"I intend to enjoy myself tonight. It has been quite some time since I've attended society as a single man. I am sure there are members of the fairer sex willing to accommodate a man's needs. And when I am there, I know I will still have you. Remaining here. And I imagine you will be desperate to free yourself after all of those hours. Very desperate indeed." Charles moved closer to her face until his cheek nearly touched hers. "It is difficult to offer resistance when one is weakened and immovable as you will be. Don't think I haven't fully realized the advantages of your precarious position. I tried to present myself as a gentleman, but you are right. There is no need for pretense any longer. You have revealed your hand, and you have so miserably fallen. You need to be sorely reminded of your place, Lady Sharpe. And that is underneath me. I will have no difficulty reminding you of this. Over...and over...again," he whispered in her ear, his tone sickening.

Eliza stared ahead, trying her best to keep her face stoic, even as tears ran down her cheeks. Anger was beginning to make her body quake. But in her gut, she undeniably knew that she was also terrified. Charles walked a few paces away.

"Don't bother calling for help. The doors have all been locked. The slaves have been told to tend to the far field. Cleo is indisposed and sent away to the harbor. She will return tomorrow afternoon. Perhaps you can use the time to reflect on your recent conduct. Goodnight," he said with a nod.

"No! Wait!" she cried, pulling on the rope. "Please!"

He didn't even hesitate and continued walking to the door, leaving her alone in the creaking, stifling house. The clock struck eight. And with that came the realization of her fate. And that of Jean. The sinking feeling of failure hit her with a swift blow. Eliza released an otherworldly wail that racked her throat. Crumbling to her knees on the hardwood floor, her pretense of resolve and determination finally left her.

She cried and cried, her tears a torrent of all the pain she had felt since she had first stepped off that boat, fueled by the thoughts of the indescribable pain to come. She cared not for her future. There would be no future without Jean. He was the one person in her life who had taken away the pain and the fear, the one person who had inspired her to dream again. He had reminded her of the pulse of life, the fire of desire, and the warmth of the only love she had ever known. She could not return to the depths she had drifted to before ever hearing his voice.

She felt herself breaking down with each heaving sob, losing track of time and space. Kneeling as low as the rope would allow, her hands raised above her, she cried endlessly, slumped against the humid wall. The house was quiet, save for the wooden beams creaking as the moisture rose and the heat of the day finally receded. Outside, the tiny frogs began croaking their noises as if tonight was any other evening. A small reddish ant crawled in circles ceaselessly along the wall.

Her cries continued until, with a choking swallow, her heartbeat's pace overtook her and began a maddening short rhythm that made it difficult to breathe. Eliza gasped for breath, lightheadedness overcoming her. She knew that panic had taken over. She was no longer in control of these circumstances, not even in control of her own body.

Eliza pulled and pulled on the rope, the roughness turning her flesh raw to the point that it carved an uncomfortable sticky pink hue into her skin, eventually drawing drops of blood. At first, it beaded on her raw flesh, then as time passed, it transformed into dried brown strokes.

The clock chimed twice more. She hungered for a physical presence, any presence to break her from this twisted reverie. She had no thoughts of either food or drink or even relieving herself. It was as if she existed for one purpose and one reason only, and she knew she had failed to that end. Thinking of Jean's face and his eyes, the color of water at dawn, the same water that had comforted her during the first days here, started the flood of tears once more.

Her muscles ached with the strain of her cramped position. She thought of Jean sitting in his gaol cell. She had only tried to visit him once, and she had failed. She had never come. He would never know why.

Eliza slipped into a tepid slumber when she became acutely aware of a presence by her side. She at first feared Tabitha had returned. She opened her eyes to see Celia standing there with a rusted machete. Eliza jolted and screamed, but before she could recoil, the blade swung down. She felt a force descend on her wrists and shouted once more before realizing that Celia was hacking at the rope. Three cuts, and it was done.

Celia grabbed her up to a stand, Eliza's hands shaking as Celia worked on the remaining cord. Within moments, she was freed, and Eliza stared up at her in bewilderment.

"Go. Go to him," Celia said, madness in her honey-colored eyes.

"I…" Eliza started, trying to recover from her stupor. Her legs were weak and useless.

Celia passed her a canteen and shoved some papers at her.

"I found these in the study when I was cleaning the other day. He must have dropped them. I should have placed them on Lord Sharpe's desk, but I kept them. I planned on making you pay to have them returned…I'm sorry."

In a flash of clarity, Eliza recalled that two papers had fallen to the floor the day of Jean's arrest. With trembling hands, Eliza unfurled them, scanning their contents in utter disbelief. One sheet was a short and hardly legible inventory list. But the other letter caught her attention immediately.

To Mr. Jean Charles de Longchamp

Sir,

   The advantage of obtaining the earliest and best intelligence of the designs of the enemy and the good character given of you by Votre Pere, added to your capacity for an undertaking of this kind, have induced me to entrust the management of this business to your care until further orders are received on this head. For your care and trouble in this business, I agree on behalf of the public to allow you a hundred pounds per calendar month and herewith give you a warrant on the Paymaster of the Forces for the sum of five hundred pounds to pay those whom you may find necessary to employ in the transaction of this business, an account of the disbursements of which you are to render to me. I urge you to carry yourself with the greatest caution, as any indiscretion may lead to detection. Should your manifest efforts be foiled and after every zealous attempt, flight be at length necessary, the cause in which you suffer will hold itself bound to indemnify you for your losses and receive you with the honor your conduct deserves for such service to the Crown.

Given under my hand in tandem with the Foreign Office, this 6th day of April 1791

Lord Grenville

She read the letter twice, her eyes focused on Lord Grenville's signature. The weight of the wax seal and the complexity of its design reassured her of its authenticity. This letter was the key to Jean's exoneration or at least a delay in his execution. Lord Dunmore was a thief and a tyrant, but he couldn't possibly ignore orders from his superiors in London. Eliza nodded excitedly, scanning it over a third time. She had looked for the papers the night of Jean's arrest and had found the space beneath the cabinet empty. Now she understood why. Then an unrelated thought came to her mind.

"You can read, Celia. Just like your mother. I remember what you told me..." she said in amazement.

"And nobody except you needs to know it. Understand that."

A smile crossed Eliza's lips for the first time in hours. Celia remained humorless.

"My God, Celia, bless you! Bless you!"

She reached to embrace her, but Celia maintained her distance. Eliza rushed upstairs to retrieve a pouch of gold coins and returned to the hallway.

"But my husband took the carriage. How can I possibly get to town so late?"

"I have Julius bringing up Lord Sharpe's horse right now. Should be here any minute. That horse is mad, but he's the fastest I seen on this island. Now he'll be fast for you," Celia said, bringing her toward the porch.

They stood outside in the dark, fresh air near the steps. A light mist was settling in.

"Why are you doing this for me?" Eliza asked as Julius hoisted her onto the horse.

"I don't want to owe you nothing," she replied, her familiar attitude finally resurfacing as she spoke.

Alastor was a formidable animal, and Eliza was quickly reminded of that fact when she looked at him. Like his owner, he too seemed to have a temper and would occasionally snap at younger fillies. The horse's back was so broad it strained her legs, and the ground seemed a terrifying way down should she lose her grip. Yet the horse so far offered no protestations. She had once been afraid to ride him in the day, and the darkness of night only made such a venture even more daunting.

"What if he throws me off him?" Eliza asked Julius nervously as Celia stuffed the letter into Eliza's pocket.

"He won't. I trained him. He is a good boy. He's smart, that's all. Don't change your mind on him too much. He knows the way to town. Just give him a kick. He'll get going," Julius said.

Eliza looked down, trying to grasp the reins tightly in her already aching hands. She looked at Celia and Julius with confusion, dumbfounded in silent gratitude. Eliza flung her legs out, but the girth of the stallion made it awkward to kick. Julius returned to her side.

"Here, I'll get him moving."

And with that, he slapped the horse, and it bolted, galloping down the tree-lined path. Eliza screamed, leaning forward so as not to fall.

She stood before Lord Dunmore's door, breathless. She had never been to this wing of the house before. She was certain the servant had indicated that it was this door. She had paid her a generous tip to gain access. She questioned if she had bribed the right person, but she was fortunate not to have spotted Cassie's presence tonight. The upstairs was quiet, with the occasional feminine shriek of laughter and lower rumblings of male company.

A quarter of an hour ago, she had stormed the door of the magistrate, nearly bruising her hand in the process. His home was a modest wooden dwelling, and she knew he was home because of the shifting candlelight from the windows. He was an elderly man, so she assumed she could make headway with him, owing to either his respect for the law or his latent sympathies.

"Judge Collins, it is most urgent. I beg of you! I seek a pardon on behalf of a prisoner!"

She had called until her voice was raw, but it had been to no avail.

At one point, she had sworn she had seen a woman's face hovering near an upstairs window. And then the candles darkened. She knew she had reached an impasse, so she mounted the dark stallion and changed direction to the governor's mansion. She could feel tears rising within her, but she forced them back. This was undoubtedly her most crucial attempt tonight. And now she would try for the second time that evening to save a man's life.

Eliza took a slow inhalation and knocked on the bedroom door madly, her heart hammering. There was a new lapse of silence, and then she knocked again. She was convinced she had just heard a woman's voice speak in a whisper, and then the heavy footsteps of Lord Dunmore approached the door, and it opened.

He was dressed in his night robe, the material barely enough to cover his sweaty corpulence. She kept her chin upright, her jaw firm and her stance resolved.

"Who let you up here? I don't recall seeing you earlier tonight. Why are you standing before me? What is the meaning of this?" he asked, irritation rising.

She knew he was really expressing his surprise to see that another one of his ruses had been foiled. But a confrontation over what Bruin and his crew had almost accomplished was not her object tonight.

"I beg of you, put an end to what will occur tomorrow, Lord Dunmore…" she began to say.

"Why? What on earth is occurring tomorrow that would give you reason to disturb me tonight?"

"The prisoner you are holding, Jean Charles de Longchamp. He is an innocent man. I beg of you, grant him a pardon. I beseech you," she said emphatically.

On the mention of Jean's name, his meager lips curled upward. He shifted his weight, allowing her to see inside his bedchamber. A naked woman was lying on her stomach, dawdling with a blue ribbon between her fingers. She looked at Eliza with disinterest and then rolled to her side on the disheveled sheets.

"We can discuss this in the morning, Lady Sharpe. I am preoccupied," he said with impatience.

He moved to close the heavy door, but she stepped halfway inside.

"No!" she said in a low tone.

Lord Dunmore sighed. He allowed her to step further into the room. She was aware of the redness on her face and chest. She had never been more uncomfortable in his presence, and necessity had never dictated it as much as in this moment. What she said next could either save Jean's life or damn him.

"Reason will move you, surely," she began, with shaking hands. "I have a letter from the Foreign Secretary in his own hand. In it, he clearly states that Longchamp is rendering services to the Crown. That his work is indeed honorable. He has committed no malpractice! This guarantees his freedom. You cannot ignore the wishes of Lord Grenville. He is the Secretary of State!"

He was quiet for a moment as he considered her words. The other woman was inebriated; it was easy to forget her slow-breathing figure on the bed. Lord Dunmore's pudgy hands grabbed the piece of paper from Eliza, and he squinted as he read its contents.

"According to the law, you cannot execute him without a court martial. You cannot suspend the trial—"

"He's a criminal, not a soldier," he interrupted.

"He is supplied funds by the Paymaster of the Forces; he is clearly a member of the British Army. He is—"

"An inconvenience if I ever saw one," he spat.

And then Lord Dunmore threw it to the floor. He leaned closer to her, the stench of seasoned meat and red wine heavy on his breath.

"You're viewing this all wrong, my dear. I never gave a damn about his freedom. I do not care about his record. He is simply in my way, and there is no room for men who displease me on this island. Now, you are also encroaching on my space, and if you value your life, you will shut your mouth and close your eyes like any useful woman should. *You* have been merely lucky, you stupid woman. Nothing more," Lord Dunmore growled.

Eliza became aware of a presence behind her, and she turned to see one of his female domestics gawking at them.

"Ah…Abbey, burn this," he ordered.

Eliza rushed to retrieve it from the floor, but his fat hand clenched her wrist, wringing her arm as he began to push her back toward the hall. She watched with horror as the servant nimbly picked up the parchment and started walking to the fireplace.

"Please, my lord, is there anything I can do? He can leave. He can leave from here and never return. Commute his sentence to transportation. I can pay you in gold. What is your price? Surely, we can agree on something," she urged desperately. "Here, name your price..."

Eliza reached for the pouch of gold coins with her other hand. He took it, weighing it in his palm. He sneered.

"What do I look like? Does this house speak of material need? Have you seen the mahogany paneling of my chambers? Have you seen how many slaves I keep? Or are you blind?"

She ignored his insults.

"I know what you do with the privateers. I know you are a man that makes many deals. The pirates can seek refuge on Hog Island if they meet your terms. Your dealings are no secret. Let me make a deal with you, my lord. I beg you."

"You know nothing. You are a woman," he said.

She watched the servant stab at the fire as Jean's only validation burned to ashes. Her last resolve, her moral dignity, likewise burned. Her one opportunity was slipping through her fingers. Lord Dunmore exhaled sharply.

"My lord, what if it is not coin you seek but something else, something only I can offer you?"

Eliza's eyes watered, her red cheeks completely engulfed in silent mortification. By now, she understood he was only ever interested in her virtue as a means of collateral, and she felt likewise foolish for offering something he clearly had already possessed that night, but it was her last endeavor. She lowered her dress, allowing him to look at the swell of her breasts. His beady eyes looked down at her and then to the bed where his whore hardly stirred. Eliza feared her ruse would not work, but she remained there displaying her cleavage.

"What are your terms?"

Her response came out as a forced whisper.

"If you release Longchamp, you may have me for the night to do as you wish, my lord."

"Just for a single night?"

She had piqued his interest. The burning in her face became nearly unbearable. She swallowed.

"What is your pleasure?" she asked with a clenched jaw.

She was painfully aware that she was not hiding her disgust.

"You know…it is no wonder you never join your husband at the card table," he said with an inspecting glance. "You reveal your cards too easily."

Eliza's heart sank. His attention was dwindling. She was running out of time. A door creaked down the hall. She turned to see Charlotte observing the entire scene. Lord Dunmore looked behind her and laughed as he pushed Eliza further into the hallway. She hastily fixed the neckline of her dress.

"I am not a man who gives up things for what I want. I *take* what I want. If I wanted this, I would have had you in my bed already."

Lord Dunmore was cold and brimming with conceit. Humiliation coursed through her. He seemed to take equal pleasure in Eliza's torment and Charlotte's distress. He began to close the door.

"Wait! No, please! Governor! I will do anything, anything! Pray, hear me! I beg of you, my lord!" Eliza screamed.

Charlotte dropped her head and started walking to them. The door opened one final time.

"If you are not careful, Lady Sharpe, then you will find that your husband may not hold onto the position he so dearly clings to. I hear that even the best officers lose favor once they commit extortion and bribery. Especially if they engage in illegal trade with pirates. I can see rumors of him and the Spanish brewing already. A king's officer may even lose their life if they are not careful," he said. "You, my dear, are not helping anyone. Leave. At once."

It seemed as if Lord Dunmore's strategy included blaming others for the actions he himself committed time and again. The irony was not lost on Eliza.

"You cannot do this. You are corrupt beyond all measure, you—" she cried.

"I rule this tiny island, and it would serve you to remember your place on it," he roared.

Spittle flew from his rotting teeth as his fury bubbled to the surface. He slammed the door closed just as Charlotte threw herself on Eliza.

"You whore! I knew you had designs on his lordship! You conniving…" Charlotte seethed, her arms flailing at her.

Eliza blocked her weak advances with ease, pushing her away.

"On the contrary, I am the only one here who is not a paid whore, Mistress Charlotte. You can find one in his bed right now, and the other I am presently speaking to," Eliza said. "You may share a name with his wife, but you will never attain her status, no matter how wide you open your legs."

Charlotte's cat-like eyes narrowed in hatred.

"Get out. Get out of this house! I am calling the guards!"

Eliza turned on her heel and descended the servant's stairway, the rush of what had just occurred only rousing her ire further. She could hear the floor exploding into chaos as Charlotte flew into hysterics. She had no concern for what occurred in this house next. She would surely be banished from their company. It was no great loss. They were hypocrites through and through. She would head to the gaol next. She did not have another plan, but she could not stand idly by.

"Ma'am, ma'am! Wait!" a shrill voice called out as Eliza crossed the dark expanse of lawn.

The slave named Abbey from upstairs ran to her, clutching her chest.

"Here, ma'am! I gonna get in trouble for this, but I just couldn't burn it. I don't know nothing you talking about with the governor, but I know him and what kind of man he ain't, and I heard you say it's someone's freedom. I can't destroy another person's freedom when that's all I want myself."

Abbey held the now crumpled letter upright as if it were cast in gold, her eyes moistened with the audacity of what she had just committed. Eliza could not speak and took the letter from her. Her heart sank. It was only paper and worth nothing more in this corrupt colony.

A steady and solemn drum beat rang out in the courtyard, its noise chilling despite the morning heat. As she watched Jean leave the prison gates with a guard behind him, her heart seized up in a painful contraction. Their steps were painfully slow. His skin was pale, his face impassive. He did not look around him and kept his gaze straight.

She had waited all night for this moment. Seeking respite near a sea almond tree, Eliza had finally stopped her pursuit as the darkness of the sky had receded. Sheer exhaustion had overpowered her and made her drift into a disturbed sleep, only to be woken by the sunlight filtering through the leaves. She had got up and rushed to the gaol as its exterior gates were finally drawn open. And as she took her place at the back of the crowd, barely able to see in front of her, a cold sweat descended on her neck.

But she saw Jean now. Every fiber of her being wanted to run to him, to shout, to scream, to do something. She knew it would have no effect. She knew she had irrevocably failed. Waiting there, immobile and powerless, her situation wracked her insides as she stood alongside a group of strangers whose morbid curiosity had brought them there that morning.

The guard walked Jean toward the scaffold, where the executioner took over with an air of indifference. Straining her neck, she could see army officers and other island officials. She recognized Reverend Samuel and a few other men. The governor was nowhere to be seen. And then she saw Charles. He stood with the others, his face cast downwards. Charles would not move, even as Jean walked past him. He was rigid and unyielding.

Jean ascended the cart and faced the crowd. His eyes looked at the sky, the morning light transforming the blue hue within to an almost translucent shade. His eyes seized upon the clouds and the sky above them in wonder as if it were the first time he had truly seen them.

The beauty of his face and the vitality brimming from his figure had the distinct effect of reminding the crowd that his life would be cruelly extinguished in a matter of moments. These people did not know him. They had no grudges or grievances towards him. And now, the silence of so many people in the crowded courtyard, waiting with bated breath for the inevitable end, was suffocating. This was not the crude and rowdy diversion public executions generally promised. This crowd would not be pleased with this man's imminent death.

The executioner bound Jean's arms in front of his body and draped the hemp rope over his head. Jean took a slow and deep inhalation and then looked directly in front of him.

"The accused...Jean Charles de Longchamp...having been found guilty of the crimes of larceny, offenses against the public revenue, and forgery in his capacity as a civil servant to the Crown, shall hereby be executed. If the condemned has any last words, let him speak them now," the provost marshal called out in the still air.

Jean stood straight as he addressed the people before him.

"Whatever may be the opinion of my accusers, may it be known that I only ever acted in the interest of my king. And if you have love for your country, as I have, guard your freedom with every breath. For it is so difficult to attain and so very easy to lose," Jean said, his voice slow and deliberate.

He seemed as if he might say something else when she felt his gaze fixate on her. Her face brimmed with tears as she waited for the words she knew would never be spoken now. She wanted to hear him continue, to say something more, desperate to listen to any utterance because she did not want him to stop talking. She felt a searing pain behind her eyes, and her ears began to ring. Their shared gaze was too intense, and she looked away as her tears dropped to the parched ground. She could not stand there a moment longer; the surge of panic felt as though it would overwhelm her again.

She squeezed her eyes shut and clutched her heaving chest. When she looked up again, his face had been covered by a white cloth. With a creak, the cart was pulled away, and he was suspended. His body jolted from the motion, his legs and arms seized by tremors. He continued to jerk with painful movements, but still, he would not die. Jean hung there, dangling in the throes of death, waiting for a release that would not come.

Time crawled at an agonizing pace, and still, he flailed. Something was not right, and an air of grave miscalculation floated among the spectators. Whispered words of 'reprieve' filtered through them, growing loud with the voice of a single man near the front. The crowd was displeased. A parrot cawed out shrilly, oblivious to the manmade tragedy unfolding below. There was agitation in the group. And then a sudden unstoppable commotion.

"Damn you, you fool!" Charles barked at the executioner.

He broke rank with the other officers and grabbed Jean's struggling legs, yanking them downwards. Charles closed his eyes, pulling Jean down as forcefully as he could. In those exact moments, as she watched the life finally slip away from his struggling form, the rhythm of the earth around her seemed to slow down, to gel into a softer version of the brutal reality she had been forced to accept. And with debilitating timing, she realized a single, unalterable fact.

She loved Jean in return. She finally understood this because she was now enduring its loss. She was watching it slip away from her, like invisible ether into the air. *This* is what love felt like. Miraculous and devastating, filling her with hope and stealing her very breath at the same time. It had once supplied insurmountable happiness, and now it would only cause unrelenting agony. Eliza had never known pain like this before. She could not face the idea of life without him in it.

The crowd waited, tormented with anxiety for it to end. And then the rope became taut as it swung back and forth, creaking audibly, and Jean's body was still with the permanence of finality. There was peace in the gaol yard, but it was unnatural and disturbed.

A half-composed sob escaped from Charles' lips. He released his grip on Jean, stepping from his swinging body in a barely disguised state of horror. The shock was palpable. He took a step back, his hands stretched out, shaking as if trying to process what he had just done. This was not what the crowd had come to see. Surely there was no entertainment in a slow hanging. People who had never witnessed such a terrifying scene naively thought it would be a thrilling spectacle. It was only after the event had transpired that they realized how mistaken they had been. The regret of being present at such a scene now set among the crowd like a fine mist. And then a woman screamed.

An arm gripped Eliza's, and she turned to the burly man closest to her. It was unclear why he had touched her until she realized that the ear-piercing scream she had heard had actually issued from her own body. No one turned to see who had screamed like that except for Charles, whose hawkish eyes were, in this instant, scanning the back of the crowd where she stood.

Their eyes met, and his glare seared through her like a hot blade. Had he truly not seen her until now? She wasn't supposed to be there. Fear began to set in around her. She took one last bitter look at Jean, knowing that his beautiful eyes would no longer look at the same world as hers. He was forsaken and lost to the callous hands of fate. And so, she fled, unable to bear the weight of her new future.

The town bustled like any other day outside the prison's stone walls. The sun was out, the clouds a bright puffy white, and a gentle breeze enveloped her dress. With wicked irony, it seemed as though the world was just as vibrant, if not more so, without one particular life breathing its air. She strode past the other people, tears streaming down her face uncontrollably. Somehow, she got on Alastor, who she had left tied to a palm tree near the beach. She moved without thinking, her body guided by some unseen force. She only knew she needed to leave this place, to run. She urged the horse into a wild gallop, watching the dizzying rush of the ground below her feet with a morbid detachment.

Before today, the horse had scared her. Now, she no longer feared her old hesitations. After what she had witnessed, there seemed to be no point. She rode and rode, going past all the landmarks she was familiar with. The wind rushing past her and the jolts of the horse's dark limbs pounding the damp sand eased her mind into monotony. Time was lost to her now, as she kept being drawn back to an exact series of minutes: his body struggling, his prolonged suffering, fighting his fate until the inevitable end. It played on a horrendous loop in her mind, along with the events of last night, heavy and unbearable like a weight on her chest.

And then the horse stopped. In a mechanical way, her body seemed to anticipate the animal needing a break. She moved to slide off its heaving back and ended up falling in front of the horse. Now her torrent of grief unleashed as she lay there miserable in the sand. Her cries startled Alastor, and he slowly edged away from her, snorting excessively from the run. Feeling even the horse's presence abandon her, the sobs increased.

She had seen it. She had watched him die and the cruel way he had died, but it seemed unbelievable still. The devious whispers of grief urged her to think of theater trickery, biblical miracles, and Cleo's ancient magic. It could not have been the end. That was not the ending that Jean deserved. But in her gut, she understood. She would never see him again. They could never be together. He had been torn from her.

A future she had scarcely begun to envision had suddenly become so paramount to her existence.

She could *not* continue without him. How could she only realize now that the wild emotions and yearning she had so strongly felt for him subsisted of love? She had never spoken such words to him, and it was so utterly painful to realize it all meant nothing now. She was now one-half of a whole, a union that could never be fulfilled.

A dam had been broken, and her unbreakable resolve sieged. She cried for Jean and for the electrifying presence forever robbed from her. But the more she focused on this, other thoughts emerged from the recesses of her mind. Thoughts she had buried many months ago. She thought of how beautiful Bleinhill Manor had looked as the carriage had pulled away, how green the great lawn had appeared as it was enveloped in a soft, chilly fog. She had viewed the house as a prison, keeping her shut away from the wonders of the world. Now she realized it was the only safe refuge she had ever known.

She saw them as well. The smiling, waving figures of her parents and sisters as they stood outside her childhood home, wishing her farewell as her new life began. She wept for her father and her mother. She cried for her old life and her old self. She sobbed for losses, both material and even those less visible to the naked eye.

The pain from her first night with Charles returned with a vengeance. She recalled the anguish of the days spent with him and how alone and betrayed she had felt. Her misery seemed to wrap tendrils around her very throat as each cry made it more difficult to breathe. She tried to stop, to regain control of herself, but she only felt more and more suffocated. Her ribs heaved, and she gasped for air. And then she retched in the sand.

Charles had killed her one salvation. Throughout all her unhappiness, Jean had been her enduring grace. Touching his face, meeting his lips, feeling him inside of her, had been more than a physical sensation. When she touched him, she had touched some part of the divine. She had embraced some part of a higher mystery when he had held her in his arms. She had tapped into something eternal by sharing his presence.

And now Charles had taken that away. He had destroyed everything she held sacred. Her mind could not even comprehend what she had seen. She rushed back to thoughts of the evenings they had spent together, drinking and laughing openly. Their unending conversations. How precious those few evenings were to her. The seemingly false harmony she had felt around the old friends. The illusion that they could indeed be together, even in front of Charles. How had it come to this?

She dimly wondered if she was next, but she did not care about her own safety. Nothing mattered to her except that the world was missing the one person who had irrevocably changed her life. The one person she loved more intensely than she had ever felt before. He would never know of her feelings. And now she was truly alone.

A shifting sound grew louder next to her. She slowly rose to her knees and looked up, acutely aware of a stranger disturbing her. Anger at this intrusion surfaced first, then fear. Her face was covered in fluids; she did not want anyone to see her like this. She looked up with red, swollen eyes and saw an old man standing before her. His skin was dark, marked with scarification, and on his ankle was a solitary iron shackle.

"You hurt?" he asked, his hand outstretched.

His brown eyes were clouded with age, but she could see concern in them.

She was warmed by his gesture, but then sickening guilt crept in her as she looked at his shackled foot. Eliza had ridden far, miles past Pleasant Hall. This must have been the runaway slave village Charles had spoken of. She knew no fugitive with means would have left any mark of their former life on them. It made them more susceptible to recapture. Rumors spread around the island that the runway village was filled with wild men and women. After all, many freed black people lived in town, directly behind the governor's mansion. It was not uncommon to see them walking about on the streets. But the people that lived in the village on the outskirts of the island were desperate and poor. Some were even rumored to be vengeful.

But fear of danger was not what made Eliza shrink away from him. It was the sudden epiphany that washed over her as she looked into his eyes. Surely there were those with worse lots than what she had to deal with. Her mind was not equipped to think of philosophy or platitudes at that moment, and she could not begin to sit and make rational comparisons. But she knew one thing. Despite her pain, she endured it all, and she was free. Some people living around her did not even have that. Liberty.

She thought vaguely of her promises to Celia and their conversations. Celia had always remarked that her position as a woman, Charles' woman, was not a much better fate than hers. At the time, this shared understanding was pleasing to Eliza's ears. But now, kneeling there in the sand, in front of this stranger who offered nothing of earthly value but kindness, made her view her encounters with Celia in a different light. A woman's place in the world truly came with limitations, but she possessed freedom and her mind. She could work her way around every obstacle that confronted her, much like she had done in days past. And even if Celia's jaded view of society marked them in the same way, surely an ounce more of an advantage was an advantage still. Eliza knew she could not fix the world. But she could help the slaves she knew. What would they think if they saw her like this? Broken, covered in sand, and drowning in self-pity?

Eliza shook her head, her face cast down in shame, and she slowly stood. Standing upright, her ears began to ring, her eyes playing tricks on her in the brightness of the day. It reminded her of the need for sleep. She walked backward, searching for the horse who was nibbling a bush in the undergrowth near a series of seagrape trees. She mounted Alastor and began to trot away, back to the house and the fresh turmoil that awaited her there.

The ride to Pleasant Hall reminded her that time had passed. The sun was high now, and the midday heat was sweltering. She watched the world around her but felt severed from it. From this day forward, she could no longer be the same woman. A sliver of determination rested in her chest. Tears crept back into her eyes, spilling onto her hands. They came and went now, depending on what subjects her mind wandered over. She encountered no one else on the journey. Most people knew not to ride on the beach in the blazing sun. An invisible fire seemed to shroud her thighs, and sweat glistened on the back of the horse. Grimy moisture mixed with grief left a salty impression on the edges of her chapped lips.

Alastor needed water. She realized she should have been kinder to the animal. After all, he had been her sole companion these last few hours. She remotely thought of food and the last meal she had eaten. It all seemed so far away now. She was not hungry and wondered when she would feel those familiar pangs again. The only sensation she felt was nausea that came and rose in uncomfortable waves.

The steady trot of the horse felt soothing; its redundancy helped steady her thoughts. She reached to pat his neck in silent gratitude. She greedily pictured returning to Pleasant Hall with her stolen horse and cleaning up the destruction Charles had made and his father before him. It was a future without her husband, and this gave her the illusion of hope. But as they rounded the corner and the white house slowly loomed before her, she knew she was sorely deluded. Charles would be there. And she would have to confront him. The thought was terrifying.

Her stomach rose into her throat again, a painful squeeze of tension and nerves that had been overworked. She left the sand and moved past the towering rubber tree and the delicate magnolia, flowerless in the summer heat, and closed in on the house. The doors of Pleasant Hall had been left open to let the heat escape. But when she actually saw the outline of his figure leaning against the railing of the porch, an explosion of fury ignited within her. The discomfort seemed mutual as he momentarily looked up at her and ducked inside.

Eliza started toward the house, the ripples of rage and disgust she felt inflamed by the sight of Charles standing in the shadows of the hall. He had retreated from her. He had stood there on the porch as if this was an ordinary afternoon. And he had left at the sight of her. He was the last person she wanted to encounter, but now she dared him to come back outside. She reached the porch, yelling his name, and he marched toward her.

"I forbade you to go!" he shouted. "I ordered you to stay in the house!"

The next moments were a blur of angry tears and heat as she rushed at him and struck him repeatedly in the chest. Charles spun her around and moved her with his knee to the wooden railing, pressing her into it. She continued to flail until she felt a blade pressing into her neck. This finally made her stop.

"You are in hysterics," he hissed, his face against hers. "You will hurt yourself."

Charles was out of breath, his chest moving rapidly against her back. She felt a small sense of satisfaction. He hadn't expected this. She tried to move slightly, but he redoubled his position. The predicted contact with a sharp blade failed to materialize. It became apparent that the knife's edge was not against her neck, and only the handle was pressed against her skin. The pressure was still uncomfortable enough to want to move away from him. She tried in vain; her efforts were futile.

"If you have failed to notice, you are in a precarious situation. I wouldn't move an inch," he whispered loudly into her ear.

His other hand kept her firmly pinned against him. She struggled to overcome him, surrounded by his face on one side and his weapon on the other. A sniveling whimper of air escaped her lungs. The tenser she became, the harder he held on to her.

"Breathe, Eliza," he commanded.

His words brought attention to the reality of their newfound proximity. The warmth of his body emanating and mingling with hers was a disturbing comfort. But the feeling of their bodies breathing in rhythm repulsed her. Eliza's worldview lost clarity as frustrated tears muddled it.

"There we go. Now, listen to me. You were not meant to see that today. Despite what you may perceive as abject barbarity, I had to do that. I had to do all of those things. I am only trying to protect you, Eliza."

She felt the pressure leave her neck and heard metal shifting back into its hard case. But Eliza was still stuck there. He pressed her against the railing, her body shaking with resentment.

"That should have never happened. I had no choice but to end his suffering as quickly as I could," he continued.

She felt her resistance against him soften as grief ebbed out of her. The memory of Jean's face haunted her. She realized that his last moments would invade her mind when it was quiet, and her world was still. Jean had looked at her in the back of the crowd, and she had looked away.

She hated that her natural response to all of this was weakness. And she did not want to reveal her tears in front of this man. The hand that had once held the blade was now stroking her cheek with a strange softness. She instinctively felt disgust.

"You could have helped him. You could have lifted him upwards, not hastened his death," Eliza sobbed, her jaw shaking.

The back of her neck and jawline was overwrought with tension and ached. She knew it was from crying for hours.

"That was the only way I could help Jean," he said, the steadiness of his voice cracking.

The audacity of his words filled her with new anger. Or perhaps it was the sound of that name on his lips.

"You could have stopped it. You could have stopped all of it," she seethed.

Charles released her, stepping back. She turned to face him. He seemed taken aback, but she could tell he was still determined to defend himself.

"There was far too much damage done. The rope was too thick. I've seen botched executions, Eliza. A man can only last for so long at the end of a rope. The pain I've heard is unbearable. Death is a relief…"

She was trembling again, her hands clenched into fists.

"Eliza, there was nothing I could have done to save him," he said quietly.

She knew that he was talking about the larger forces at play this time. The elements outside of his control. The very elements that thwarted his own decisions. He was speaking of the indomitable corruption festering in the white mansion on top of the hill that directed this entire island.

"No, I suppose not," she began to say. "Your solution to every problem is violence. You killed your only friend. A brother. Out of mercy. You hold a knife to my throat. A weak, grieving woman. Out of compassion."

He said nothing, the veins in his temples bulging. The waves behind them crashed through the quiet.

"I needed to calm you."

"It would seem as if your sense of duty and honor is severely misplaced."

She stormed up to him and slapped him with as much strength as she could muster.

"I have never felt hatred for another soul as I do for you. You mean nothing to me. And you never will," she said with finality.

She waited for retaliation, but after a few moments, it was clear that there would be none. She turned to step into the house when he finally grabbed her arm.

"If you ever act like this again…" he threatened.

Eliza looked at him with narrowed eyes as she waited for the end of his ultimatum. No words came. He cast his face down. She pulled out the wrinkled letter from her dress and tossed it at his feet.

"How very wrong you are," she said quietly as she freed herself from his grip.

TO BE CONTINUED…

Bibliography

Adkins, Lesley, and Roy Adkins. *Jane Austen's England: Daily Life in the Georgian and Regency Periods.* New York: Penguin Books, 2013.

Aron, Paul. *Founding Feuds: The Rivalries, Clashes, and Conflicts That Forged a Nation.* Naperville: Sourcebooks, Inc., 2016.

Benezet, Anthony. *Some Historical Account of Guinea, Its Situation, Produce, and the General Disposition of Its Inhabitants with an Inquiry into the Rise and Progress of the Slave Trade, Its Nature, and Lamentable Effects.* Project Gutenberg eBook, 2004. https://www.gutenberg.org/files/11489/11489-h/11489-h.htm

Block, Sharon. *Rape and Sexual Power in Early America.* Chapel Hill: The University of North Carolina Press, 2006.

Byrne, Paula. *Belle: The Slave Daughter and the Lord Chief Justice*. New York: Harper Perennial, 2014.

Carpentier, Alejo. *The Kingdom of This World: A Novel*. 1949. Reprint. New York: Farrar, Straus and Giroux, 2006.

Cavendish, Georgiana. *The Sylph*. Edited by Jonathan Gross. Evanston, Illinois: Northwestern University Press, 2007.

Chambers, Douglas B. "Runaway Slaves in the Bahama Islands, 1784-1819," February 2014, 1–97.

Davis, Graeme, ed. *Colonial Horrors: Sleepy Hollow and Beyond*. New York: Pegasus Books Ltd, 2017.

Deren, Maya. *Divine Horsemen: The Living Gods of Haiti*. New York: McPherson & Company, 1953.

Equiano, Olaudah. *The Interesting Narrative and Other Writings*. 1789. Reprint. New York: Penguin Books, 2003.

Handley, Sasha. *Visions of an Unseen World: Ghost Beliefs and Ghost Stories in Eighteenth-Century England*. New York: Routledge, 2015.

Heyer, Georgette. *April Lady*. 1957. Reprint. Naperville: Sourcebooks Casablanca, 2011.

Hochschild, Adam. *Bury the Chains: Prophets and Rebels in the Fight to Free an Empire's Slaves*. Boston: Mariner Books, 2006.

Hoock, Holger. *Scars of Independence: America's Violent Birth*. New York: Crown, 2017.

Howard, Martin R. *Death before Glory! The British Soldier in the West Indies in the French Revolutionary and Napoleonic Wars 1793–1815*. Barnsley: Pen and Sword Military, 2015.

Jackson, Christopher C. "Preservation and the Future of the Bahamian Past: A Case Study of San Salvador Island's Historic Resources" (master's thesis, University of Georgia, 2018).

James, Erica Moriah. *The Awakening Landscape: The Nassau Watercolours of Gaspard Le Marchant Tupper*. National Art Gallery of the Bahamas, 2004.

Jasanoff, Maya. *Liberty's Exiles: American Loyalists in the Revolutionary War*. New York: Vintage Books, 2012.

Kemble, Frances Anne. *Journal of a Residence on a Georgian Plantation in 1838-1839*. Edited by John A. Scott. Athens: University of Georgia Press, 1984.

Knight, John. *War at Saber Point: Banastre Tarleton and the British Legion*. Yardley: Westholme Publishing, 2020.

Levy, Andrew. *The First Emancipator: Slavery, Religion, and the Quiet Revolution of Robert Carter*. New York: Random House, 2005.

Mackenzie, Henry. *The Man of Feeling*. Oxford: Oxford University Press, 2009.

Nedervelt, Ross Michael. "A Tumultuous Upheaval and Transformation: The Impact of the American Revolution on the Bahama Islands" (master's thesis, University of New Hampshire, 2012).

O'Shaughnessy, Andrew Jackson. *The Men Who Lost America: British Leadership, the American Revolution, and the Fate of the Empire*. New Haven: Yale University Press, 2013.

Peakman, Julie. *Lascivious Bodies: A Sexual History of the Eighteenth Century*. London: Atlantic Books, 2004.

Peters, Thelma. "The American Loyalists in the Bahama Islands: Who They Were," *Florida Historical Society* 40, no. 3 (January 1962): 226–40. https://doi.org/https://www.jstor.org/stable/30139824.

Reddie, Richard S. *Abolition! The Struggle to Abolish Slavery in the British Colonies*. Oxford, England: Lion, 2007.

Richardson, Samuel. *Pamela*. Oxford: Oxford University Press, 2008.

Ronald, D.A.B. *The Life of John André*. Havertown: Casemate Publishers, 2019.

Saunders, Gail. *Slavery in the Bahamas:1648-1838*. Nassau, Bahamas: Media Enterprises Ltd, 2015.

Schoepf, Johann David. *Travels in the Confederation [1783-1784]*. Translated by Alfred J. Morrison. Baltimore: The Lord Baltimore Press, 1911.

Schwartz, Marie Jenkins. *Ties That Bound: Founding First Ladies and Slaves*. Chicago: The University of Chicago Press, 2017.

Shirley, Paul Daniel. "Migration, Freedom and Enslavement in the Revolutionary Atlantic: The Bahamas, 1783–c. 1800" (PhD thesis, UCL, 2011).

Tanner, Lynette Ater, ed. *Chained to the Land: Voices from Cotton & Cane Plantations*. Winston-Salem: John F. Blair, 2014.

Vanhorn, Kellie Michelle. "Eighteenth-Century Colonial American Merchant Ship Construction" (master's thesis, Texas A&M University, 2004).

Washington, George. *George Washington's Barbados Diary: 1751-52*. Edited by Alicia K. Anderson and Lynn A. Price. Charlottesville: University of Virginia Press, 2018.

Weingast, Barry R. "Adam Smith's Theory of the Persistence of Slavery and Its Abolition in Western Europe," (Stanford University, July 2015): 1–28. https://doi.org/10.13140/RG.2.1.1354.9924.

Winters, Lisa Ze. *The Mulatta Concubine: Terror, Intimacy, Freedom, and Desire in the Black Transatlantic*. Athens: The University of Georgia Press, 2018.

Wolfram, Sybil. "Divorce in England 1700-1857," *Oxford Journal of Legal Studies* 5, no. 2 (1985): 155–86. https://doi.org/https://www.jstor.org/stable/76419 0.

Worsley, Lucy. *If Walls Could Talk: An Intimate History of the Home*. New York: Bloomsbury USA, 2011.

ACKNOWLEDGMENTS

I would first like to thank my mother for a lifetime of support and for anxiously awaiting this day. Thanks for saving all the cardboard books I made as a child. I am proud to present a sturdier bound version. Thank you for always recognizing my creativity and for endlessly nurturing it. It was really hard to keep this project a surprise from you!

Thank you to Michael, my husband and twin flame, for every little thing you do. You were the first to read this book, and thank you for the encouragement, buttercream cakes, and roses. I cannot wait to continue this adventure with you.

I have overwhelming gratitude for God, my Circle, and all of my ancestors. Thank you to Kay Lawson for sharing your wisdom with me, and to Lynn Austin, as well as to Amalia Camateros for guiding me. Thank you to Kari Field for enabling me to have a eureka moment when hope seemed lost. Thank you to Norimasa Suzuki; writing is a labor of love and also a pain in the back, so I am indebted to your expertise. Thank you to Kevin Chapman for years of laughter, friendship, and support. I am grateful to Frank Venezio for his enduring enthusiasm and encouragement. And finally, thank you to Nancy Barth Heller for your joy and for teaching me how to be organized in all areas of my life.

This book would not have seen the light of day without Lois Hoffman and her team. Lois literally rescued this project at the very last hour, and I am eternally grateful for all of her knowledge, expertise, patience, and support. You ensured this novel became a reality, and I am beyond grateful. I would like to also thank my amazing editor Cath Lauria for her tireless dedication, time, and brilliant insight. And thank you to Kim Flodin for all the tips and digital help. Finally, I am incredibly grateful to William Thomas for his artistic collaboration and for creating such beautiful photos for my marketing campaign. Thank you, thank you, thank you.

I believe that learning never truly ends, and, in this spirit, I would like to thank some of the most phenomenal teachers I have had the privilege of working with: Ann Auer – the notorious 'Project Queen', thank you for reading some of my earliest novel drafts in eighth grade and for always encouraging hard work, excellence, and above all, imagination. Thank you to Patricia Rohling and Joseph Grasso for further instilling my passion for all things historical. I would like to thank Charlie Weidig for his patience and teaching me perseverance. Dr. Miriam Nyhan Grey, thank you for being an early supporter of my novels and recording every class for me all those years ago. A special thanks to Dr. Bryan Brazeau, a brilliant linguist and professor. You are an amazing human, both inside and outside the classroom.

Thank you to the Bahamian people for their generous hospitality and beautiful, vibrant culture. Thank you to Perry Claire for countless rides to forts and museums for my research and to biologist Scott Johnson for providing the answers to all of my questions. I am also grateful to the Bahamas National Trust, stewards of both the land and sea, for their dedication to keeping the islands of the Bahamas pristine and beautiful for years to come.

Finally, I would be remiss if I did not thank my assistants, Tippy Bouvier, and Goonie, for their dedicated project oversight and ceaselessly amusing antics.

ABOUT THE AUTHOR

Gina Giordano always had an insatiable curiosity and a penchant for history. Born in New York City, she is a writer, artist, and a conjurer of the past. She holds a BA in history and a master's degree in historical fiction from New York University, and has traveled to over fifty countries across the globe. When she is not climbing ancient ruins or exploring forgotten palaces, she enjoys swimming with sharks in remote pristine waters. *Strange Eden* is her debut novel.

To sign up for exciting news and to find out more
about the author, visit her website at
www.ginagiordanobooks.net.

I'd love your feedback!
Please visit:
www.amazon.com/dp/B0BPVLPGNB
to leave a review.

THANK YOU!